BLUE POINTED STAR

LAUREN PARKER RHODES

DRIARN DUOLOGY

WILDFUL WRITINGS

NSW, Australia

This is a work of fiction. Its characters, places and incidents are a product of the author's imagination and any resemblance to actual persons, living or dead, or real events or locales, is entirely coincidental.

www.laurenparkerrhodes.com; Instagram: @laurenparkerrhodes

Paperback ISBN: 978-1-7637346-5-4

eBook ISBN: 978-1-7637346-6-1

ALSO BY LAUREN PARKER RHODES

Access Lauren's other books here, or at:
www.laurenparkerrhodes.com/books

DRIARN DUOLOGY
The Wife (short story prequel)
Amber Wolf
Blue Pointed Star

WHEN SECRETS BECKON

TRAITORS DUOLOGY
Traitors' Creed
Traitors' Promise

Author's note: Each of these books, with the exception of Traitors' Promise, were previously published by Lauren Searson-Patrick and have been republished, with permission, by Lauren Parker Rhodes. Traitors' Promise has only been published by Lauren Parker Rhodes.

Content Warnings

Blue Pointed Star is intended for adult audiences and contains mature themes. It also contains mention of historical, off-page, pregnancy loss.

For my husband, Jason
You'll always be my favourite x

PROLOGUE: THEN

The details of that day have never been lost to me. Even as the days that came after were an unknowable amount of darkness, that day still burns bright in my memory.

The pups were playful, their sharp teeth nipping at my fingers as they rolled in the grass. The creek I'd created to skirt the edge of their meadow bubbled softly around the rocks in its bend. Amber eyes watched quietly from the edge as the large male's young ones leapt and snapped at the butterflies. I'd seen many of his pups grow and change over our time together, but he, and the three others the Mother connected me with, always remained.

The trees behind me sighed contentedly and my stomach fluttered with the anticipation of Arlo's arrival.

I knew what we had was rare even before the wolves gifted him with their magic, bolstering his own beyond that of other Calahi, bringing him into the fold of protecting the Mother – and me – alongside my wolves and Sentinels. His commitment to the wolves I loved resonated deep in my bones. Commitment to protect them, nurture them, and ensure the rhythm of the world, a world they were but one part of, kept beating. Arlo Wolverton – the first of his line.

We both promised that sacred vow: the gifts given to us by the Mother would be used to nourish the world around us and thus ourselves. That the gifts given by the majestic wolves would be used to protect the ones from the Mother.

We both failed.

It was not a purposeful failure, but the outcome was the same.

I should have anticipated that the actions of a few could be so damaging, but I was too enraptured by the happiness in my own life to see the struggles of others. Arlo and me, and our respective young, were gladly, but blindly, occupied with the joys of our blended family. And wishes for young ones of our own making. I had the gift of creation, the only one with such a skill, and I ruled a world where incredible things were possible. And I did so with a loyal, enchanting, and loving partner at my side. One who would protect my dreams at all costs. And yet, I didn't see.

On that day, another perfect day, when the wildflowers bloomed with the life I'd given them and the fat clouds danced overhead, they came.

A pair I'd never given much thought to.

I'd sent my Sentinels away while I entertained Arlo in the meadow.

But he was late. And the sisters came instead.

They were powerful in their own right – we all were then – but they were stronger together.

I remember all the details of that day, many I do not care to relive.

My gifts from the Mother were coveted among my kind, and the sisters succumbed to their greed, their ambition, draining my gift as if it was theirs for the taking. Despite all the fight I could muster, I hollowed out as they laughed and the power rushed through their limbs. Through them instead of the world. Through them instead of in the creek, in the meadow, and the Realm. Butterflies burst forth from the green of the grass as the life, and love, in my magic flared, flooding the sky with colour.

The wolves howled in the distance as I fell to the ground, but they were too far to be of aid. We hadn't expected a threat from among our own. So I watched the butterflies and the wildflowers around me wither and die.

The butterflies fall, soft as snow.

The rainbow of colours simply washing away.

Then it was too late. Too late to recall what I should have remembered – not everyone will have pure intentions. Not everyone will see the beauty in small things. Not everyone will realise that, no matter how small, we all have a role.

My sapphire, a prized possession and a gift from the Mother herself, was held aloft and shattered. The pieces pocketed for other means. They didn't know then that this would incur her wrath, too.

But even then, shadow as I was, I felt it. As I was bound and entombed, I knew.

She would make them pay.

For a while, I watched from afar – even as it tore at my heart. Arlo almost came undone with grief. Though he alone rejected the belief I was no longer living, the difference between life and death was so slight. It was a gap I could not bridge, still cannot bridge, and so it made no difference. I was dead to him and dead to the world. I watched him do his best to protect what we worked for, the world we created and the young we'd brought together, as he tried to honour me through our blended family. I watched his vision narrow to only our world and forget about those outside our borders. My magic in the sisters' veins turned to poison as the Mother cursed them for their role in our destruction. But even she could not erase what they had done.

Then it became too painful to see – I couldn't watch him age and die. Our young ones, and more he eventually made, carrying on his legacy as the Wolvertons of the Realm, but not fully grasping what mine should have been. That I was supposed to give and receive in equal share, to support the Mother in her care for those that inhabit her. That I was not supposed to be bound. My power flooded back to me when the sisters were cursed but they left me unable to access it – the bind they jointly hold over my gift making it impossible to give it away. I couldn't watch, powerless, as the flowers I'd once loved disappeared into the soil, never to bloom again. Nor the wings of my people grow smaller with each generation until they grew no more.

But even as I turned my gaze from the pain, I could sense the wolves with me. Waiting. Could feel the butterflies try, and try again, for a longer stay.

Now, I simply wait. For time is a construct I no longer understand. So I become waiting and waiting becomes me. And I hold to the knowledge that, despite the lies that have become truth, the sapphire did not corrupt the Star. I wait for the wolves to tell me when it's time. Because, while stars do die, the Blue Pointed Star will burn again.

CHAPTER ONE

LISH

This Giving is harder than the last.

The cost of the magic being Given is like a dull fog that hangs over the city of Elenlea. Now knowing, with unwavering clarity, that it's my role to change it – fix it – only adds to the density of that fog. By claiming my rightful place as Queen of the Court of Airlie, I intend to do just that: stop the Givings that are draining my ... subjects, and find a way to stop the Mother from crumbling under the unyielding abuse of her inhabitants. A way that doesn't involve such extensive removal of their magic, that they, too, will die.

Even on our walk through the city, the cobbled sidewalks filled with Calahi of all ages, I'd noticed the change in the flowers on the balconies and in the gardens of the houses we passed. A slight drooping of their petals that would have once gone unnoticed. Until I realised I knew how to make them bloom brighter, stronger. Now the sight of them causes a constriction in my chest I can no longer ignore. A calling on my gold flame to give them something more.

I hover in the waiting area for Lochlain and Ciara, Will next to me soaking in every possible detail. His shoulders are tense under the thick, pale caramel cloak he wears that complements the darker tones in his skin. The Whispers may no longer be a threat now Lochlain leads them instead of Siosal but, being in this city, means I am almost completely exposed to the Custodian. His voice is a constant echo in my mind.

You're right on one point at least, he'd said. *You're not going back.*

I shiver as I push the memory away – the one of him cracking my mother's skull – and reach for Will's fingers. He squeezes mine in return, not even having to look at me to know I still sometimes need to draw on the comfort of his strength. His presence. One Siosal tried to take from me.

Drawing a breath deep into my lungs, I try to appreciate the order of the Giving, the way the forest green uniforms of the collectors make six long, straight lines along the room in front of me. How their brass trolleys glint in the light that streams in from the open doors and the windows that line the other walls. I search the faces of the Calahi around me for anything that might be out of place, but most wear a weary sort of pride. A hope, perhaps, that this sacrifice is for the greater good. Although it's hard not to remember the group of humans brought here for sacrificing at the first Giving I'd attended; even as the lack of the same brutality this time eases a knot of tension at the base of my neck – clear evidence Siosal's methods died with him.

But there's something else about the faces around me too. A dejectedness. Perhaps at the cost that's paid here under the banner of sacrificing for ultimate gain. And I can't help but wonder whose gain it's all for.

'How long are we going to let this go on?' a bitter voice says behind me in a low tone.

I don't turn around but I can feel the slight squaring of Will's shoulders against mine and know he's picked up on it too. That shift in the air.

'He assured us this was the only way,' another voice says quietly.

A harsh laugh cracks in the air. 'To what?' the first asks. 'Kill us most slowly?'

'Come now,' the second, female, voice says. 'The Mother will protect us. Our new General too, he'd never let anything go too far.'

My heart thumps readily in my chest because I know just how right she is.

'I found this on my way here,' the first person says. 'It wasn't the only one.' There's a long pause and I hold my breath as I strain to hear them. 'I've never seen so many like this before.'

The second person is silent so long I chance a glance over my shoulder. Two Calahi have their heads bent together, looking at something the male holds in his open palm. A dead butterfly, its vibrant orange wings almost taking up his whole hand.

They move away as I look back to the rows of Calahi having their magic drawn, the gently growing tension at my back slowly dissipating. It's not only a sense of disappointment in the room I can feel even without my gift, but an undercurrent of betrayal, simmering gently below the surface.

Lochlain and Ciara each straighten their spines as they sit in their black, metal chairs, waiting for the uniformed collectors. As Lochlain's presses the thick needle into his arm, I take an involuntary step forward, Will's grip on my elbow holding me in place. He nods subtly in the direction of a group of four Royal Watchmen, and I force myself to step back.

Their magic whirls into the vials that clink gently together as they're wheeled away to some unknown destination. Each a variant of the copper and gold that rings their eyes.

The Calahi next to me presses their arm into mine gently, but purposefully enough for me to glance at them.

'Your majesty,' a young-looking female whispers, averting her gaze to the floor.

I glance back to the Watchmen unsure what to make of what she's called me, but they remain distant.

'The Custodian returns in three days,' she says, still not looking at me, 'when he'll have an open Palace for petitioning.' She lifts her head as if she's also waiting for someone at the tables and I follow her gaze. 'We have arranged for you to meet with the Prominent Families tonight.'

My heart beats a little faster as I squeeze a fist, hard. Three days until I stop this. The rows and rows of uniformed Calahi that begin lining up to Give themselves, will no longer fill this large room for this purpose. We can redirect their energy to helping find another solution instead. But there is no question that this practice has to stop. To the citizens of Airlie, the increased Givings are to replenish the power of the Realm as the

Custodian continues the search for the rightful heir. But now, knowing he was personally responsible for the death of my mother, I also know he never truly intended to give up his Custodianship of Airlie. Which means he either genuinely believes these Givings are doing as he claims – saving the Mother – or there's another reason for them.

'Thank you,' I say quietly to the Royalist, but she's already gone.

Just three more days until the Custodian returns from his visit to the Court of Rothani and Queen Nakiasha, and I will present myself to him. In full view of the Court of Airlie – the same Calahi who supported Lochlain as I stood at his side – as the daughter of Queen Catriona, a claim supported by Siosal's magic before he died. And one the Custodian will not be able to refute in the eyes of the Court.

And then, as Queen, I will determine his punishment for killing my mother.

Will helps me guide Lochlain and Ciara to their respective beds, Lochlain holding my hand briefly and murmuring something I can't make out. I stroke a dark curl off his forehead before placing a kiss on his soft lips and heading downstairs to Will.

I sag into the couch, worry for Ciara and Lochlain beating in my chest, pounding out a rhythm that does nothing to minimise the tasks at hand. I look at Will warming his back at the fireplace as thoughts tumble around my head. I know I am *supposed* to be Queen, because my mother was, but—

'What if I'm not enough to stop this?' I ask quietly, tipping my head back on the couch and taking in the pale ceiling. 'Save the Calahi from the Givings, find out what the Commissioner of the Guard is up to ... I don't even know where to begin to find the pieces of the Blue Pointed Star.' I stroke the pendant at my chest and correct myself. 'The other pieces, anyway. And that's not even mentioning the fact I'm not yet Queen.'

He doesn't answer and I block out his emotions, something that's still much easier to do with my human friends than with Lochlain – I have resigned myself to never feeling anything from the other Calahi. But Will's face tells me everything anyway. There's too much confidence there.

'Shit, Will, what if there's someone better for this than me?' A headache throbs at my temples, and I press my fingers into either side of my head. 'I'm literally no one. An orphaned girl with nothing.' I sneak a glance at him. 'A woman with revenge in her heart and on her mind.'

The couch depresses where Will comes to sit next to me.

'That doesn't mean you are nothing, Lish – not to us, and not to them. Not when you will be able to stop this Giving madness.'

'What if Giving like this is the only solution?' The question is one I haven't yet been brave enough to voice to the Calahi.

'Then we'll work out why it hasn't made a difference yet, and correct it,' he says. 'We know nothing about how the Custodian is actually returning their magic to the Realm or the Mother. There might be something in the process we can amend. Maybe we bring together the magic of the Realm and the science in Driarn and have them work together?' He exhales heavily. 'It will be a big ask.'

I make a small sound of agreement as I mull over his words. I know he's right, but part of me yearns to know it will all be worth it. My mother left her people, and any opportunity to help them, for me. The question of whether I was worth her monumental sacrifice, one that ended with her death, weighs on me. But less so than the understanding that I am now the only one left to pick up what she would have done had the Custodian not killed her - return to Airlie, take the Throne and find the Star.

Will looks at me, showing no hint of judgement. 'And having revenge in your heart seems reasonable from where I'm sitting.'

I think of Lochlain upstairs, his body fighting to restore what's been lost – taken – and of Ciara in the bedroom down the hall. I haven't seen Rory and Aeyva but they will be the same. Powerful, mysterious, magical Calahi brought to their knees by something I could change. Something I must change – without exposing the Realm to the environmental extremes of Driarn. But, weather aside, there is more to Rhyton's involvement in Airlie than meets the eye; the Commissioner's presence at the Challenge made that very clear. The lack of understanding and desperate need for that knowledge presses further into my headache.

I lie back against the couch and look again at Will. 'Becoming Queen won't tie up all the loose ends,' I say.

Will makes a soft sound of agreement. 'No.' He turns his bronze-brown gaze on me. 'But it will put us in the best position to try.'

I let the comfortable quiet between us settle for a moment.

'I won't be able to do it without you.' It's more question than statement, even though he said 'us'.

He leans into me slightly, the warm pressure of his shoulder against mine easing some of the tension I hold in my joints.

'You won't have to, Lish. We're a team. Always.'

Lochlain and Ciara sleep while Will and I visit the market. It's become a routine of sorts that I get them home from the Giving and then stock up on fresh fruit and vegetables and cut flowers. The choice of food still makes my mouth water. But the mood is sombre today and there are fewer stalls than normal.

When I first arrived, there were acts of magic everywhere. They were incredible to me, even as Ciara described them as everyday tasks. Now, I don't see any. Even the fruit that used to twirl above its stall is still, the vendor gone. A lone, woven, basket sits next to his produce. I guess the hope of an honesty system is better than making no income today at all.

The food is good, though, and my basket is full when I return to Ciara's. Neither she nor Lochlain have risen yet, so I join Blaire on the deck while Will and Riley prepare dinner.

'You know one of the theories is that it corrupted Roisin somehow?' I ask, voicing another question today that I haven't broached with any of the Calahi.

A blue light sparkles furiously in the night sky as the words leave me.

'The sapphire?' Blaire asks in return.

I take a sip of my deep scarlet wine, the glass almost empty, and nod. 'The same one we're supposed to find – the Blue Pointed Star.'

'And yet, she's revered,' she says.

I frown at the undercurrent in her tone.

'Just,' she continues, 'the *corruption* isn't really talked about, not even in the essays the librarian gave you.' She takes her own sip of her wine. 'I've been thinking of the Custodian and how he literally manipulated a whole Realm – a world – into believing his lie about your mother's death. Who's to say this is any different?' She peers into her now empty glass and leans back in her deck chair, her blonde hair catching between the back and her shoulders. 'And the missing women in Rhyton too. It just – I don't know – it makes me wonder how much of what we believe is actually true?'

Nico's squeal from inside draws a smile to her face.

'You have to take it first!' he shouts as he leaps over Will's legs and crash tackles Phoenix. 'Then I'll save you, I'll—'

I look over Blaire's shoulder, back into Ciara's living room where Nico has descended into a fit of hopeless giggles as Will tickles him.

We keep the conversation light as we eat, an unspoken agreement not to add to Nico's nightmares. He already spends most nights wedged between Will and Sofia, terrified she will disappear again while he sleeps. I understand that fear all too well. Only my nightmare was one I never woke from – the person I lost never came back for the little girl she left under the kitchen floor.

Leaving the others downstairs, I creep across the room that was once only mine at Ciara's, and now has a slumbering Lochlain in it. Nestling myself into the armchair where I can watch him, I open the box of my mother's things. For the umpteenth time, I take out the librarian's letter and his journal, buried underneath the medallions my team wore at the Challenge. Since Lochlain's appointment to General, they haven't been necessary for them to wear. But I haven't been able to let the discs go just yet. The fact there is now one more of them than there is of us ...

My chest tightens as I think of Hayes and I let my fingers move off the cool metal, the feel of the engraving leaving the sensation on my skin lingering a fraction longer.

Benny's letter shakes slightly in my hands as I unfold it.

Your mother will have told you about the Blue Pointed Star. You need to find it.

If all has gone to plan, you will have part of this already – the Wolverton Pendant. Your task is a difficult one and I will be as clear as I can: claim your Throne and find the pieces of the Blue Pointed Star.

It's not the first time I have mulled this over. She did tell me about the Star, but it's only the story I remember, not the reasons why I need to find it. I flick through the journal. While there is a lot of talk of the Whispers, there are other snippets about the Realm. Roisin in particular, a giveaway of the librarian's interest in all things historical about the Realm he so loved.

We haven't pinned down his death to a particular individual, and it's unlikely we will. But there is no doubt General Siosal was the one issuing the command. Benny risked Siosal's position of being the first to attain me, so he was murdered. But not before he managed to get me some of his notes, and nowhere in here does he talk about Roisin's corruption, either. Perhaps there is hope for me that finding the sapphire doesn't equate to losing myself completely.

I think over what I've been told of the Star so far, which isn't actually that much. It supposedly sent Roisin mad and was broken into four pieces that were then scattered through the Realm. I know I already wear one around my neck and that there is another piece in my crown.

Claim your Throne.

One step at a time. Tonight, I will meet with the Prominent Families and gain their trust and support to face the Custodian. The Star, and the questions its story brings, will come after.

Claim your Throne.

Stop the Givings, I add to myself.

I close the journal and crawl into bed with Lochlain, curling myself around him. Resting my cheek on his back, I let the rise and fall of his breathing lull me to sleep.

Three days.

I have three days before the Custodian returns from his travels, and I will make my claim. Three days until I am ruler of this Court. Then, with my crown, I will not only stop the Givings, but I will be halfway to having all four pieces of the Blue Pointed Star.

CHAPTER TWO

LISH

What feels like only minutes later, Lochlain stirs behind me and I squint into the night. The moonlight through the window is silver and I fight the urge to pull the covers over my head and let sleep take me again. But today – tonight – is important. He pulls me back against him and I don't resist, his bare arms caging me in his warmth, dragging a sense of home along my skin. I wonder suddenly if this is how my mother felt with my father, a man she wasn't supposed to love. If it was this feeling that she fought for. One that bubbles through my centre, thickens my throat, and lines my eyes with grateful tears.

The arm that pulls me against him travels along my side, over the crest of my hip. Lochlain's breath is hot on my neck and all my nerve endings blink into awareness. His hand grips the fabric he finds in his way, his old t-shirt, and I feel his wicked grin against my ear.

'I'll never get tired of finding you in this.' His voice is like gravel, and those hot bubbles that were encasing my heart suddenly fire in the other direction. He lets the shirt fall away again and slips a hand underneath, against my bare skin, his fingers seeming to chase the sparks of sensation that skitter away at his touch. He inhales deeply and I close my eyes, arching my back and willing his hand higher. Or lower. Somewhere other than my waist.

'You up?' Ciara calls sleepily from the hallway and I choke on a laugh.

Lochlain groans and drops his head onto the back of mine, his breath blowing into my hair. I twist and give him a chaste kiss.

'If I didn't think you were safer here, with more of us around,' he all but growls, 'I'd move us into my loft.'

'Ah, but duty calls,' I say, unable to keep the smile from my face.

He nods solemnly in the soft light of the moon, his dark hair spread on the pillow underneath him and I can't stop the slip in my smile. I understand duty, and responsibility. I don't think I would have stepped into this role if I didn't. But I do it because I know it's the right thing to do; the knowledge that Lochlain's sense of duty is so tightly woven into who he is sits a little uncomfortably. Not because I don't agree, but because Aeyva told him once that he couldn't be both, and now I wonder what that meant. Because I don't think I'd be selfish enough to ask him to give up his duty to Airlie.

No matter the cost.

Something about Elenlea at night makes my gold flame sigh contentedly, deep in my chest, like the Realm itself is staking its claim. The houses we pass appear as sleepy as I felt before we left Ciara's and the thought of their inhabitants – both big and small, old and young – brings an urgency to my steps. The adults all Gave yesterday, the same as Lochlain and Ciara, and, as far as we know, that process is having no impact on bettering the state of the Mother. The thought of the young Calahi lining up to Give when they are old enough, turns my stomach. Exactly how the Custodian thinks it would help isn't clear and it's impossible to keep my mind from rolling around this question, even as I know I need to focus on getting on the Throne – at least there I will be able to make changes.

Because it's clear this is a question that the Calahi of Airlie are asking as well.

I drag my mind back to the Calahi we are on our way to meet. With Lochlain now firmly in position as General, and Siosal dead, the Prominent Families who have quietly supported the more ethical hunt for me – the rightful heir – have agreed to meet.

Tonight is the first time they will meet their true Queen. I swallow. The Calahi I have met so far haven't shown any particular reverence for me, but I wonder how much of that is due to meeting before any of us really knew who I am. From what I know of the Realm so far – the management of Lochlain's Challenge, the Givings, the firm belief in the Wolverton family and the almost worship-like respect of Lochlain – means I know this won't be like meeting more of his friends.

'Here we are,' Lochlain says quietly as we near a quaint white fence that almost glows in the dark of the night.

Ciara walks in ahead of us, holding the gate open behind her as we pass through. Little balls of light flicker into view along the path that leads to the front door as the gate closes quietly behind us. I suck in a breath filled with the scent of flowers. The illuminated sides of the path reveal petals in some of the most vibrant colours I've ever seen, even in paintings and photographs. It has been so long since my continent of Driarn has seen such lush colours in nature that even our art is changing. The sweetness in my nose takes a moment to adjust to and I take another heady breath, a slow smile pulling at my cheeks.

'This is ...' I search for the right word.

'The Mother,' Lochlain finishes for me, giving my hand a squeeze before letting it go. 'Without her, we're all nothing.'

My chest deflates with my exhale, remembering the gaunt, desperate people that line the gates of Rhyton. The hungry children that beg on the streets and the way my employment was partially decided by the access it gave me to reliable food and money.

'They're all here,' Aeyva says by way of greeting when we meet her outside the pale green front door, Rory and Will flanking the other side.

It's Will's face that sends nerves through my limbs. The boy who has seen me through just about everything – the one who knows who I am and where I've come from. Which was most definitely not a Palace. The lights of Nuala's porch bob gently in the breeze and catch the faith in his dark eyes. He steps forward and grips my shoulder, dropping his chin to look me square in the face.

'You've got this,' Will says. Just like he did the day I got the promotion to Team Leader in the Guard.

I force a smile up at him and nod, steeling myself with a deep breath as I reach for the worn, copper door handle.

The room immediately falls quiet as we enter and I take a moment to let my gaze take in everyone here, but it's not long enough to absorb their features. There's a tension in the air as all eyes land on me.

'Ha!' A loud, laugh-like sound bursts from one of the corners as a tall, blonde Calahi strides towards me – one whose shape is vaguely familiar. He eagerly takes my hand and I try not to start at this particularly warm, and exuberant, welcome. Lochlain is immediately at my side, close enough for me to feel that he's completely at ease with this Calahi but not close enough for me to reach out and slip my fingers into his for support in this sea of expectation.

'Your Majesty,' Lochlain says, and I feel my eyes go wide at the title as I hold the honey, jade-ringed gaze of the Calahi still holding my hand. 'Allow me to formally introduce you to Haryk Elmwood.'

I blink at him.

Haryk. The Calahi who stayed behind in General Siosal's compound while Lochlain got me out.

A warmth floods my chest at the same time an echo of the burns Siosal seared into my skin makes my small smile falter. He squeezes my hand harder and winks at me, pulling me back to the moment. With it comes an awareness of the critical gaze of the others in the room – about seven of them, excluding those I arrived with. And I realise this isn't totally unlike my trials for the Team Leader role. I am here to prove myself as their Queen.

'Haryk,' I breathe, letting my smile return.

He yanks my hand and pulls me into a hard hug that I don't hesitate to return. A gasp sounds in the room and someone else clears their throat but I hold him for a moment, collecting myself, before I press back and search his face. He's as handsome as the rest of the Calahi I've met, with a youthful confidence I'm unused to seeing. It's quite a comparison to the hard-won version of those behind me, Aeyva particularly.

Haryk's gaze slides between Lochlain and me as if measuring the distance between us.

'Good thing we don't leave anyone behind, right?' he says, the corners of his mouth quirking upwards.

Lochlain cocks a brow at him and Haryk swallows his cheeky smile before turning away and rejoining the rest of the group.

Lochlain steps forward as I look awkwardly around us. There are four female Calahi and three male, including Haryk, that stare back. Will, Rory, Ciara, and Aeyva remain behind me and I don't look at them, something telling me not to show any uncertainty to this group. Despite what Haryk already knows about me from that compound. I drag in a deep breath to try and clear the memories of the dark and the dirt. Of Will's face when Siosal drove the blade in—

'Prominent Families of Airlie,' Lochlain begins, cutting across my memories. 'For long, long years, I have rehearsed what I would say when I finally presented you with our Queen. But in the face of the actual event, no words are adequate. So, I will simply introduce you to Adelais Taylor, daughter of Catriona and rightful Queen of Airlie.'

As one, the Calahi around me drop to their knees or fold in half, faces dipped away from me. I whip around to find only Will still standing. The room spins slightly as I grapple for my next move.

'Thank you, General Wolverton,' I say quietly, and they all return to their original positions like puppets. One woman rearranges her coral-coloured skirts around her legs as she retakes her seat.

'Welcome, Your Majesty,' an older female Calahi with dark hair says as she walks towards me, a steaming mug floating just above the hand she holds palm up towards the ceiling. Her gaze flicks to Aeyva for a moment and she nods at her in acknowledgment before handing me the warm, brown mug. 'Please,' she says gesturing to an empty, upholstered chair with genuine affection in her tone, 'my home is yours.'

Nuala, I think as I lower myself into the plush cushions.

'Thank you all for joining us at this hour of the night,' she says, addressing the group from where she stands. 'I thought it best to keep our meeting from as many eyes as possible. For now.'

I glance to the large windows that look out onto the front garden we'd walked through and note how dark the sky still is. Yet no one here seems tired. There's a current running through the room, a tense sort of excitement. But it's hard for me to tell how much of that is real, or just me, given I can't actually feel their emotions, and the lack of information makes me a little off balance. When I'd faced challenges in the Guard, I was always able to relax into them or adjust my approach based on the reactions of those around me. But here, I have nothing to guide me. Nothing but the steadfast belief they have in the Queen of Airlie, even if they don't know the individual behind the title.

The thought makes me realise most, if not all, of the Calahi in the room would have known my mother and it brings a sense of injustice with it. The day he took her from me, the Custodian said something about her being selfish – about having poor judgement. I have no way of knowing what he was referring to when he made those claims, but the fact there is a room full of Calahi seemingly believing in me because of her, is more comforting than I knew I needed.

'We have much to discuss,' Nuala continues, and I attempt to ignore the gazes that keep finding their way back to me and focus on the Manorynx – a 'knowledge keeper' Ciara had called her once – her hands emphasising her points as she speaks. 'And not a huge amount of time to do it in. So, tonight, we will focus on the next, immediate steps and making sure the basics are in place. When the Queen is crowned, we will talk again. Tonight, we confirm how to get you your crown.'

CHAPTER THREE

LISH

A soft murmur of agreeance ripples around me. One male Calahi, who reminds me a little of Benny, smiles gently. Haryk openly grins as he crosses one leg over the other, his long, pale brown boots showing little sign of wear, and I happily return it. Taking a sip of the bracing hot drink Nuala handed me, I sigh into the sensation it curls into the corners of my insides.

'General Wolverton,' Nuala says and Lochlain steps forward again, my gaze automatically trailing to him and up his strong legs, across his broad shoulders and to his face. As I look back to the group, I catch the eye of an auburn-haired woman. Her gaze narrows as she looks between Lochlain and me, similarly to Haryk, but there's far less kindness in hers.

'Are you able to advise on the Sentinels for the Queen as yet?' Nuala asks.

Lochlain looks down at me, a flicker of pride running over my skin as he does. He gestures behind me, and I glance back to see Aeyva and Ciara taking positions on my left and right. There's a silence in the room that makes my heart beat a little faster. Aeyva subtly raises her chin as she meets the eye of everyone in the room. Nuala takes a long time to look away, but she eventually turns back to me.

'And you are comfortable with these two as your Sentinels, Your Majesty?' she asks. 'You trust them to guard and protect you against all threats, no matter the cost?' The echo in Nuala's words of my own thoughts earlier tonight, about what I wouldn't ask Lochlain to give up, sends a shiver down my spine. But I nod. There is no doubt in my mind that Ciara and Aeyva will do everything to protect Airlie and her Calahi. And now that includes me.

The room seems to pulse with something for a moment – a sort of awe – and I realise all faces in the room look between Lochlain and Ciara. The brother and sister, the Wolvertons, in their rightful positions, supporting mine. A flutter gently takes root in my stomach.

'Now that we see your face, we also know you stood by General Wolverton as he made his claim for the position against Siosal. So I trust you are confident he will discharge his duties honourably?' Nuala asks.

'I am,' I say, wondering what she sees as honourable for Lochlain, and if it's the same definition as his.

Lochlain's emotions gently prickle against my skin, and I find the conflict in them hard to discern. Nuala nods, looking at Aeyva once more before she returns her attention to the group. 'That is all the positions we need filled to solidify the Queen's presentation to the Custodian.Your Majesty,' she says, turning her shining eyes to me – I can't tell their colour from here, 'these are representatives of six of the nine Prominent Families of Airlie.'

I keep my gaze on her even as my mind snags on the 'six' she mentioned, not the seven in the room. She moves around the semi-circle of Calahi from left to right, each of them seated on a chair of some description. They're all different, like a finer version of the haphazard furniture that adorned the common room in the orphanage.

'Mulriarty,' Nuala says, indicating a male who looks to be the oldest in the room. 'Ahren, Kenne, Boydon and Pendita.' She finishes at the auburn-haired woman who is the only one that doesn't smile when she's introduced. 'I believe you already know Haryk.' As she rattles off their names, they slip through the spaces in my mind, but I relax a little in the knowledge I have the rest of my team to help me fill in the gaps when we leave.

'You're not one of the Prominent Families?' I ask her.

'No,' her gaze leaves me and lands to my right, on Aeyva, before it comes back to me. 'I am the last remaining Manorynx of Airlie – an integral part of your Court but not part of the Prominent Families. Where General Wolverton holds the figurative sword of Airlie, I hold its mind.' I search her face for any sense that her statement isn't as heavy as it feels. 'Between us, with the support of the Families and our forces, we protect and guide what's most important to Airlie and the Realm. Its heart. You.'

'Protect without claim,' the representatives say as one around me and I start at the sudden sound.

Nuala's gaze holds mine intently, as if she's trying to share a message only for me as the sharpness of Lochlain's ... I don't know what it is – regret maybe – runs along my forearms and across the backs of my hands.

'You said there are nine families?' I ask.

The Calahi around me shift a little, Ahren sniffing slightly. 'There are nine, Your Majesty,' she says, her voice almost silky. 'We are just the ones who could be here tonight. But we have no reason to believe the others won't support you as well.'

I look to Lochlain who stands on the other side of Ciara to my left and he nods without looking back, as if he knew I would need his confirmation.

The older male, Mulriarty, clears his throat. 'With all due respect, Nuala,' he says. 'How can we be sure the Custodian will know she is who we claim?'

I notice he doesn't talk of any doubt on his part, and I give him another smile, bolstered by the lack of hesitation of the Calahi at my back to step up into these required roles.

'We know Siosal traced her blood,' she says. I don't miss the bite in her words. 'Given he can no longer verify that tracing, Adelais will need to state it when she appears before the Custodian and the Calahi of Airlie. Voicing it, along with Siosal's name, in a public forum will be enough for the Custodian to need to confirm it.'

An unpleasant tightening sits low in my gut at the thought of facing him again.

'So, the immediate steps,' the auburn-haired one, Pendita, who'd been watching Lochlain and me, says, 'when the Custodian returns, we'—she gestures around the room—'will be ready in the throne room for your petition. General, you'—she nods her head at Lochlain—'will bring her to the Palace along with the Sentinels and make the claim.'

'We will meet the Queen and General at the Palace,' Ciara says.

'Is that wise?' asks a male in a dark grey vest. Kenne, I think.

'The less attention we draw to her before the claim is actually made, the better,' Haryk says, watching Lochlain. 'She and the General work well together, she'll be fiercely protected with him by her side.'

More than one of the Prominent Families turns to me and I feel a heat rushing across my chest, coupled with an uncomfortable sense of worry from Lochlain. But Haryk's not wrong. Lochlain's electric presence against mine has become my anchor. A cold shiver runs over my skin, and I find myself suddenly hoping the sensation never changes.

'When you reach the Custodian,' Nuala says, now turned to me, her chin length, dark hair swaying with the movement. 'You will simply need to tell him who you are and that General Siosal verified your bloodline. I'm sure he will be ... overjoyed to meet you.'

Her words ring so clearly false in my head I wonder if anyone else can hear it. Is it just because I have played that day over and over in my mind since he made the announcement of Lochlain's appointment? Do they genuinely not know what sort of person he is, and what I will actually be facing?

Nuala gives me a long look as I weigh up how much to tell them now.

'Word has reached us of the Custodian's true nature,' she says quietly and the Calahi around me press their palms to their chests. 'But, for this, you will have to put it from your mind. The Custodian does not know that we are now far more informed than he would like. But, until you are on that Throne and have taken control of Airlie, there is nought we can do against him.'

'So ...' I say, 'you're all expecting him to just roll over when I make myself known?'

'Yes, Your Majesty,' Mulriarty says, 'but not happily.'

Pendita's stare is the most critical of the group, as if she can see my every weakness and I try not to think how accurate she might be. At least when it comes to my abilities as a queen. Thinking about facing the Custodian only re-enforces how strongly I feel about bringing him to justice. But the Calahi in this room put him where he is. Have lived under his custodianship for almost as long as I have been alive.

'Why are you invested in removing him?' I ask and surprise lights Haryk's face. Beside me, Lochlain is still but there's a ghost of a smile in his features. 'You know he killed my mother, your Queen, but you've also lived ... well enough, I suppose – apart from the Givings – with him for a long time. Why upset that balance?'

I think of the Premier in Rhyton and his predecessors, who served far longer than they should have because the population was too scared to vote for change. Now they also know the Custodian is a murderer but is that enough for them to force change?

'Because,' Pendita responds, her eyes widening, 'we are a Court of honour. Airlie is the heartland of Roisin's reign, splintered as her Realm is now, we still hold the places closest to her heart. Now, however ... muddied,' she says, the side of her lip rising as she speaks, 'you are what remains of her bloodline. No matter the experience Zadicus has over you—'

'Zadicus?'

She interlaces her fingers in her lap.

'Zadicus Clay – the Custodian – experienced in running the Court or not, is not of her line. The best chance Airlie, the Realm, your world, have for a future, is for the line that started it all to return.' She lifts her chin so she looks down her nose at me. 'Do not think us so uncivilised we would abide by the murderer of our Queen sitting on her Throne.'

My brows lift. Uncivilised is probably the last way I would describe the Calahi. When it's clear she will say no more, Mulriarty breaks the silence.

'When you present in the presence of the Calahi of Airlie,' he says, 'he will have no choice but to take you seriously. He will be required to have Nuala re-verify your claims, in front of the Court, and then it will be settled. If he refuses, he faces a very real threat that the Calahi of Airlie will rally against him – and unrest in a Court is never a good thing for a leader. Particularly one who has seen how readily we will stand for the rights of our home and knows the desperation of Airlie for some sort of ... salvation.' His gaze flicks to Lochlain and I wonder how vocal he was at the Challenge when they demanded Lochlain be appointed to the role.

'Where did it go wrong for him?' I ask, the words out of my mouth before I've quite formed the thought. 'You all supported his installment as

Custodian?' I let the rest of my question go unasked – what possible good did they see in that Calahi?

A thick silence fills the room.

'Zadicus ...' Mulriarty begins, 'has always been an excellent strategist. He seems to see the opportunities and risks for our Court with greater speed and clarity than many of us have experienced before. At first, this skill was used to bolster Catriona's rule – to assist in trade negotiations, assess our healing systems and make our education settings unrivalled across the Realm.' He clears his throat a little. 'Catriona and he had been friends for a long time, so his critical thinking, along with her own intelligence and compassion, made for quite a formidable team. I think ... over time, and so many good decisions, we started to stop questioning his advice.'

'But my mother didn't?' I guess.

Mulriarty smiles grimly. 'Their arguments started to become legendary. The last one we heard was her wanting to change the structure of her advisers – broaden from just Zadicus.'

'Things moved quickly after that,' Haryk says. 'It wasn't long before your mother fled and, at the time, we had no reason to believe there was anything fundamentally ... wrong ... in appointing Zadicus to the role of Custodian.'

I nod slowly, soaking in the explanations. The new name that now rolls around in my head.

Zadicus Clay.

'And what if he refuses to let Nuala confirm who I am with witnesses?' The memory of the sound of his staff shudders through me and I think perhaps that wouldn't be so bad. I'm not sure I'd want witnesses for what I'd like to do to him either.

The man holds his hands out either side. 'Then we will stand and insist on it. He will not be able to back down in the face of the Prominent Families who put him where he is. Inside the Palace, he is trying hard to lock us out of his decisions but, in view of the whole Court, this will be virtually impossible without completely undermining his rule.'

As I look around the room I wonder, again, if holding the Throne was the Custodian's sole motive to kill my mother. And, if so, how far will he go to keep me from it now?

The meeting continues until the night turns from the deepest black to the first hint of morning, even though that's still hours away. Nuala stands from her cushioned chair in front of the window and the rest of us do the same. Aeyva and Ciara have remained standing and silent for most of the session, barely even shifting on their feet. I haven't once laid eyes on Will and Rory, somewhere behind me.

The different guests curtsy or bow as they take their leave and I incline my head and smile at each of them as they do, the faith in their eyes sparking more life into the flame in my chest. But at the same time, each one makes me feel more and more like an imposter. This was my mother's role, not mine.

I exhale as Haryk, the last one to do so, bows and leaves the room, clasping Lochlain's shoulder as he goes.

'I'm already forgetting their names,' I say as Nuala approaches.

'There'll be time for all that, my dear. You'll have barely brushed that Throne with your behind before they'll have you whisked away to work out the new order of things.' Her eyes crinkle at the sides with her gentle smile. 'Every one of them will be very interested in ensuring you are across their points of view.'

A faint throbbing starts at the back of my head.

'Before the Prominent Families though, is Kailoh.'

Kailoh, King of Mercasia. I know from Lochlain and Ciara that he supported the search for me from the beginning.

'It is critical that you, as Queen, form an alliance with him,' Nuala continues.

Aeyva stands a little taller.

'How do I do that?' I ask, frowning.

'That's what you have all of us here to help with,' she says. 'Let's get you crowned first, and we can face what comes after together.'

I reach out on impulse and take her hand. 'Thank you.'

'Lish,' she says, my heart warming further at her use of the name Will gave me, as she watches Lochlain and the others heading for the door. 'I also know you are eager to stop the Givings.' I nod my affirmation. 'But know this,' she says, dragging her gaze back to me. 'It will be complicated. There are systems, processes, Calahi whose livelihoods are made by collecting the Givings, that will all need to be wound back and replaced with something else. But, at the same time, you will need to avoid destroying Airlie's faith that you will find a better solution, and that the Mother won't continue to fall around us.'

My ribs press together and the throb in my head starts to pound.

'Do you know what the solution is?' I ask, even as I know how unlikely that is – if she did, they'd already be working on implementing it.

'No. But I know the Blue Pointed Star will lead you in the right direction. There are myths – legends – about the first of your line but the Star is the key to it all. You must find it. Once you're crowned and have that piece of sapphire, I will show you all I know about the Blue Pointed Star – fill in any gaps Benny wasn't able to share. Kailoh and Aeyva will be able to help, too,' she says, looking pointedly at her. 'Stopping the Givings will mean nothing if you can't find the Star.'

Become Queen, form an alliance with Kailoh, King of the Court of Mercasia, and seek his help to find the other two pieces of the Star ...

It's a lot to process and my headache speaks for itself. The tension of being Queen and finding the Star winds through my body. But now I know how to put one foot in front of the other. I know who is supporting me and I know how our roles fit together. And I know the Custodian does not fit where he is. Not only will I be able to oust him from his role, I'll be able to fulfil my mother's as Queen and my own as the vengeful daughter. All while I find the Star and save the Mother.

My gold flame flickers in response and my headache recedes, just a little.

CHAPTER FOUR

AEYVA

The kill was bloody. I'd taken him down outside the inn I'd found him in – sleeping in a dingy upstairs room – where the dirt would absorb most of the blood. But it still soaked the toes of my leather boots and parts of my shirt.

My mark had fought harder than I'd expected, but they never fight as hard as me. The gift in my veins is a counter to every magic I've come across. How effectively, or violently, it nullifies the gifts of others depends much on their power and particular skills. But I didn't need much for this assignment and, magic aside, I have become particularly practiced in death.

I used to do my own background on every assignment I received, to be absolutely sure I knew who I was ending and why. Now that I have served so long in the Society, I've earned the right to choose the assignments I take on. So I mostly work for one Calahi – one I trust to be as judicious as possible in the marks he chooses to meet this end. One I know has the best interests of the Realm firmly centred in his decision making.

And the male he'd requested my skills for was actively engaged in a circle of the Realm's worst. Those that lure the youngest humans they can find to the Realm to use as they see fit. Not only is the behaviour something I could never stand by, it potentially exposes the Realm to the attention of the humans as they search for their missing. Or if some of their young manage to escape back to the continent, like Lish did, and someone believes their stories of another, brutal, place ... the humans might come looking anyway.

While the humans are mostly occupied with their own world, never considering how closely it might align to another, there has always been some blurring of the lines between us. It only takes one to look too closely, one without an inherent interest like Lish and her team, and our very existence is at threat. I have watched humans enough to know that the Realm would never survive an onslaught from them, there are simply too many compared to the Calahi. Nor would we survive the intensity of human curiosity. Because curiosity from humans usually means the object on the other end is dissected in one way or another.

The stench of smoke from burning my work clothes clings to my hair as I step into the steaming shower of my private villa. It's a transition place. One I come to when I need to leave my life behind and become someone else. Where I come to wash away the darkness before I return to who I try to be. I might believe the kills I undertake are necessary, but the Society's purpose isn't always pure. When I committed my servitude, to be used as a weapon as any buyer saw fit, I didn't care – I just needed a channel for the shards of ice my insides had become, a way to stop those shards tearing me apart and to take someone else out instead. But now, in the dark of the villa I haven't bothered lighting, with the water pounding over my head, I allow myself a moment to wish I'd had someone to steer me away from this path. To make me understand it would only add more sharp edges to my insides, not less.

I close my eyes as the reality that I did have such a Calahi – do have such a Calahi – and I ignored her, settles in my chest.

I wash the blood from between my toes, the deep red clashing with the pink polish on my toenails. The paint from my cheeks stains my fingers temporarily as I scrub my face and soap my hair before rinsing away all traces of the night. As the water stops, the only regret I allow myself as I leave the shower is putting my clothes from the day back on – the ones I was wearing before I put on my now incinerated assignment clothes. My skin craves clean clothes, and I feel cheated not to wear them now. But I must look the same as I left.

'Done, I take it?' a familiar voice says as I emerge from the bathroom.

'What are you doing here?' I bristle a little, but I'm not surprised he's here. There are very few things that escape his attention, and it's normal for him to keep track of when the assignments he initiates are completed.

'Checking on an old friend,' he says, one leg crossed over the other as he lounges in the corner chair, top foot bouncing. 'How is said friend?' he asks.

I sigh. I never tell him all my secrets, but he's the only one I can talk to about this, the only one who knows of my involvement in the Society and what that costs me. He shifts forward and places his elbows on his knees. He's without much of his finery but still impeccably dressed.

'You're drawn, Aeyva. Tired.'

I almost laugh. 'We're getting close,' I say. 'She will present to the Custodian when he returns to Elenlea and then we'll—'

'You need to get out,' he says, sitting back again as he changes the subject.

'Harder to do than say.'

'True. But you will not be able to be a Sentinel of Airlie without getting out. You cannot be both.'

'I don't want to be both ... and I've already been confirmed as a Sentinel.'

He watches me for a moment, he knows he doesn't have to ask which I want to be – a Sentinel or part of the Society. Together, we have spent endless time discussing the First Queen's Sentinels. What they might have been like to know, why they are not talked about more in our histories, and the honour of that position – instead of my Societal role in the shadows. Doing what those in respectable positions can't, or won't, do.

'That's quite the honour, Aeyva. Are you sure it's the one you want?'

My lungs expand with the acknowledgment, one I will never say out loud, but it's a complicated statement and he knows it. It also brings a sharpness to the knowledge I will never be free of the Society. Never really able to step into being Sentinel. But, even if I was completely my own person, the sins of my work in the Society mean I could never allow myself to take the other role he's hinting at. The one Nuala thinks I'm destined for – her replacement. What is destiny if not something we only receive when it's deserved? No. I fight my battles with my hands and my blades, and being Sentinel is the place I want to be. I'll tear down anyone who shows a threat to my Court and the Calahi that live here – even if it's only as a weapon of the Society.

'Ciara is the other Sentinel I assume? Does she know about this?' he waves his hand to capture the villa, me, and himself.

I laugh. 'She's a Wolverton, she is literally hardwired to protect the Realm from those like me.'

'That's a 'no' then?'

I ignore him and sink into the dark couch, its fabric cool against my bare arms. Not like the warmth the one in Ciara's house exudes.

He drains the last of his drink, his cheeks puffing out slightly as he rolls the liquid on his tongue. 'Whatever you do, you need to make sure the Royalists, and your Watch, are ready.'

I cock my head. They are ready. At least, ready for Lish to present to the Custodian tomorrow and show their support. Then I will work on graduating them from our clandestine operation and into the Royal Watch proper, bolstering our numbers like the Custodian should have been doing for some time. The threat of Siosal is gone but, in addition to the Custodian being the worst kind of traitor, there have been rumours about the other Courts marching on Airlie to claim her for their own. My heart slows.

'I didn't think you had plans—'

'I don't. Not outside what we've already talked about – what we're seeing through with the alliance. But ... something's afoot,' he says. 'I just don't know what yet.'

It's his admission of not yet knowing the full picture that unsettles me the most. This is a King who prides himself on his understanding of not only the history of the Realm, but all its current moving parts. A Calahi I either get information from or share it with. But either way, he has the information.

'Nakiasha?' I ask, the pale face of the Queen of Rothani flashing behind my eyes.

'She wouldn't move on Airlie on her own, I don't think, not yet. Rumours of the true Queen will have found her Court as they have mine. But your Custodian has been spending quite a lot of time with her – they may try and form an alliance to move against Mercasia.'

I let him see the confusion on my face, I have little need to hide things from him.

'But, if Lish is Queen, I can talk to her about Airlie not supporting Rothani in a war against you,' I say.

'Assuming your Custodian follows the process when she presents. But what if Nakiasha moves on Mercasia anyway? Would Airlie come in aid?'

A whoosh of air leaves my chest. Fuck. A war in the Realm is one of the things we've been trying to make sure Airlie doesn't see – having a queen in place was supposed to avoid that.

'Do you really think that's what we're looking at?' I ask.

'The lack of a queen in Airlie has made things unstable for a long while, you know that. Now, with rumours of her return circulating, the Courts are shuffling to prepare for a new world order. I would suggest that's quite normal. Even with your new Queen in place, I would not say war is off the cards.' He presses his hands onto his legs as he prepares to stand. 'Whatever the case, your Royalists need to be prepared for anything.'

He's graceful as he stands, the motion more of an uncurling as he reaches up to tighten his red hair that's tied off his neck.

'I wouldn't be so sure you're as bad as you think, Aeyva.'

He looks down at me, a softness in his features I have long since become accustomed to – even if it never made sense to me how it could reside there after some of the decisions he's made. Or knowing I have carried out many of them.

'Having access to your talents,' he says, 'in neutralising threats to the Realm helps me keep a lot of Calahi alive – including in Airlie. But you do need to get out of the Society.'

'If only neutralising genuine threats was all I've done,' I say, noticing the lack of intonation in my voice, but he doesn't judge. He never does. 'I'll never be released. I'm too ... good ... at what I do.' I suppress a shudder. 'I committed all my functional years to the Society, and they're not over yet.'

'No.' His eyes find mine across the dimly lit room. I didn't bother with light, the small orb that hangs between us is his. 'And everyone has a past they're not entirely proud of. So not released, but what if I had a way to make you so unappealing to her she'd never want to see your face again?'

I don't have to ask which 'her' he's referring to. The leader of the Society doesn't need any introduction.

'I'd say that sounds like she'd kill me.'

'I didn't say it would be without risk. But you'd be significantly reducing her power over you. Over all the Society.'

'Then I'd say that's a risk in itself. Most of the Society are not individuals we want untethered in the Realm. Or out of it.'

'And if I had a solution for that too?' he asks.

I take a deep breath, pushing aside the tiny, foreign emotion his question calls forth – one that feels a lot like hope – my head still spinning with the possibilities of the risks he thinks we're facing. But being a legitimate Sentinel is the best way I can protect Airlie, and that means I need to be free of the Society.

'Then I'd say you better tell me of your plan to get me killed.'

CHAPTER FIVE

AEYVA

The Royalists have begun their training for the day, under my command. I watch them from my vantage point on the gentle rise that hides us from view of Elenlea. None of them wear uniforms – I'm not ready to draw that much attention to us – and we train in the early hours of the morning, just before the colours of the sky begin to shift. But many of them wear at least one item of blue – the colour of Airlie's royal bloodline and a recognition that, while they honour the forest green of Airlie itself, it's missing the rightful Queen. The colour of Roisin's bloodline. The most important Prominent Families have accepted Lish, in person, which is the first huge step in the right direction. But Kailoh's words from his recent visit keep haunting me - the fact that he thinks something is brewing.

As I watch the Calahi who prepare to support Lish in whatever way necessary, and their varying degrees of skill, a coldness settles at the back of my neck at what that threat might be and how I can make sure we're ready to face it.

'Hey,' Ciara's scent accompanies her voice and I turn to where she's gathered with the rest of my somewhat expanded team. Lish and Lochlain stand close together between the two halves, as if they're a bridge between our kinds. Bookending the group are Rory and Riley, and the others fall in between. I watch Ciara take the last steps towards me through the grass, her glossy dark hair over one shoulder.

'Hey,' I echo, and let my smile come.

On the surface we've had an easy relationship for a long, long time. One that covers what really burns underneath, at least for me. But there has been a shift since I released Lochlain from our bond and asked her to dance at his swearing in ceremony. The unsettled sensation that brings to my limbs isn't entirely unpleasant. I allow myself precisely two beats to recall the feel of her before I push it aside.

She hasn't touched me since and I don't expect her to again. I was bolstered by some unknown force the night of the ceremony but, in the clear light of day, I can see the hesitation in her face, and I know it's right to be there.

'Do you have a preference for today?' It's not a concession I give the others.

'Go steady with the humans.' Her gold and black eyes flick to mine, serious.

'No guarantees,' I say as I mentally divvy them up for the too-short hours we have. There's never enough time here, but I will take whatever I can get to prepare our Royalists for their entry into the Royal Watch.

'They're better than you give them credit for, Aeyva.'

'Right,' Lochlain cuts in as the others join us on the rise. 'What's it to be?'

I direct my answer at the whole group and send them to their various tasks. The humans don't complain. They're not total novices, but they are nothing compared to what I can do, and what I need to teach them if they are to join with us. I could throw everything I have at them, and we still wouldn't have time to prepare properly. Until I met with Kailoh I'd been confident we were close enough. Lochlain now leads the Whispers, Lish is about to take over the Royal Watch under the command of her Sentinels, and our Royalists are going to swell the numbers in both groups. But there was something in his warning ... it might not be just brute force that we need.

I watch the group of Calahi to my right start their blade practice under Lochlain's gaze and squeeze my hands together. The dark-haired one is skilled. The one he is partnered with has further to go before he can officially 'graduate' to the Royal Watch.

'They're doing well, Loch,' I tell him when he returns to me in his oversight of the training. 'But not all of them will be ready for the Watch or the Whispers.'

'Their training will continue after she's got the crown.'

'Is she ready?'

'To be Queen of a place she never knew existed?' he asks as he looks out over the Royalists. 'No. But she's ready to do the right thing. I think she was born wanting to do the right thing; she just didn't always know what that was for her.'

Loch looks to Lish where she's working on her healing gift with Rory. A small red river of blood drips down his arm and over his hand where he's sliced his skin, mixing with the dried blood from the numerous attempts they've made. We need to know if she can access it when she's not under duress. And if she can access it when someone other than Loch is in danger. I can tell just by the look on her face it's not going well. But there's a nagging in my mind that says there's more to it than only her skill in accessing it. That there's something underneath that I need to unearth.

'It's a big ask,' I say, coming back to the conversation with Lochlain. 'But the time for patience and not knowing is behind us. She needs to be strong. She needs to hold Airlie together once she's there, or it will fall apart beneath her, and we will never be able to hold off any other threats.'

'She has us,' he says softly.

'She needs more than us, Loch. She needs the forces loyal to Airlie – the Royal Watch and the alliance with the Court of Mercasia.'

'You know something.' He pins me with an all too knowing look.

'Kailoh ... thinks there's something coming.'

Some of the colour drains from Loch's face, but he knows we need to help stabilise Airlie with Mercasia's strength as much as I do. Not to mention we have a debt to their King for supporting us in our search for Lish; his support – Calahi, resources, and, of course, information sharing – were invaluable in getting us this far.

'Like what, exactly?' he grinds out.

'He doesn't know yet, but I believe him.'

'When?'

'We don't know,' I say. 'But with the increased Givings, the Custodian risks making us too weak to defend ourselves'—I pause—'or Mercasia, if it comes to that.'

He runs his hand through his hair, he knows I'm not wrong. The Custodian hasn't been totally inactive, but all his efforts have been centred around strengthening his relationship with Rothani and ordering as many Givings as possible – a decision that proved impossible for the Prominent Families to turn back. Not after they agreed to them in the first place. It hasn't included making any preparations for the citizens of Airlie who reside outside the Palace gates. And his work certainly doesn't seem to include measuring the effectiveness of whatever he is doing with our magic to heal the Mother.

'I assume Kailoh isn't double-crossing us,' Loch says. 'So he thinks Nakiasha is making a move?'

'Kailoh is as supportive of us, and getting Lish on the throne, as he was the day he became our silent patron.' Lochlain nods slowly. 'But you also know he won't let Nakiasha take Airlie instead of him. So if he has any hint she is moving, he does too ...' I let my voice trail off and his gaze slides to me even as his posture remains turned towards the training Royalists, their grunts of exertion puncturing the quiet morning.

'But?' he prompts.

'Kailoh agrees Nakiasha can't be ruled out of offensive action against either Airlie or Mercasia at some stage, but he doesn't think she has any current plans—'

'Which means he's worried the Custodian is planning a direct takeover himself, or there's an external threat. And that would mean the whole Realm is in danger, not just Airlie.'

We both fall silent, my mind wandering back to Lochlain's Challenge. This time, it's not Lish's magic that occupies me, but the uniformed human that sat on the dais with the Custodian. Having an ally of some description to erase knowledge of the Realm from the human world is not unusual – it's been common practice throughout the Realm's history. But I struggle to recall from Nuala and Benny's teachings how many times that arrangement has had such a public face.

'What's your best guess as to how long we've got?' he asks.

'I don't think we have any time at all, Loch. She takes that Throne in two cycles, or none of us can guarantee what Airlie's future looks like.'

He nods. The consummate, unruffled soldier.

'Have you told her what Kailoh wants?' I ask as gently as I can.

His shoulders tense slightly and Lish glances over as if she knows something troubles him. We watch as she returns her attention to Rory's arm, her brow furrowed in frustration. I can see the curse she's holding back as the blood continues to drip into the grass, her healing powers the same pace as the day she healed Loch in the forest. Not the torrent of power she would have required in the throne room. I sigh. I'll need to talk to Nuala and, as much as I value her, encouraging her to think I am interested in the path she thinks I should take is always tiring. But she's the best possible source – Manorynxes like her are rare and she is the last in Airlie.

'He might not,' he says.

I can't bring myself to respond.

Kailoh will want. Kailoh does want. And no one says no to Kailoh.

Not even me.

'Stop pacing,' Rory admonishes gently.

Nuala gestures to the worn armchair in the corner of her living room. It has the best view of the window and door so I can monitor the comings and goings from her little house. She knows it's the only place I can relax here. Or attempt to. I've lost count of the number of times I've been in this room, slumped in this very chair while she tried to convince me of another path. The times I listened to the lessons she insisted I know about the Realm. The times she wanted to impart more knowledge to me than I was prepared to carry.

'Drink this,' her rich voice instructs me, handing me my favourite mug. One worn with the shape of my hand. 'It will soothe—'

'No chance.'

'I said *soothe*, Aeyva, not sedate. Drink.'

She forces the hot cup into my hands, and I carefully sniff the ingredients she's put in there. She waits. Sighing, I take a sip and lower myself further into the armchair. Hastily I drain the rest, recognising one of Nuala's specialties, and she pats my arm before taking the still warm mug from my hands.

'Tomorrow will be here soon enough,' she says quietly. I glance at her, knowing just how clearly Nuala can read me. 'You have some hard edges, my girl, but she won't let you down. Neither of them will. And you won't let yourself down if your heart is open.'

Rory helps himself to the plate of cakes Nuala hovers in his direction without looking at him and I stifle the urge to narrow my eyes as her meaning sinks in. My destiny and Ciara – two topics Nuala has very specific views on. She watches me, my teacup still held in her hand. I know that look well enough to understand there is something she wants to tell me. I sigh again and open my mind to one of the most powerful Manorynxes in the Realm.

'The Blue Pointed Star must remain her priority, Aeyva,' she says just to me. '*Being the formal ruler of Airlie is merely the first step in a long, difficult process. Do not let her be distracted by focusing only on the Givings. You, me, and Kailoh, along with Lish, are our best chance at finding the Star.*'

'She will be able to stop the Givings as Queen,' she continues out loud, 'that's important but temporary. Do you understand?'

'Thank the Mother for that,' Rory says from his spot on the floor, his long legs stretched in front of him. It's more habit than anything that he's here. Nuala has helped us both – together and separately – in more ways than I can count, both during and after our romantic relationship. Now it seems the three of us are almost a package deal. The night before such an important moment, with all the preparations in place, I found I wanted to spend it with Ciara.

So I came here instead.

I nod slowly in response to Nuala's question, I do understand. Whether Lish stops the Givings or not, our world is still dying. Our magic is not replenishing itself as it should and, all the while, the human world drains too much life that doesn't belong to it. And we have let them. Our inaction has made us complicit.

'I'd like your help with her magic, Nuala,' I say, unable to ignore the flicker of appreciation in her eyes. 'There's ... more to it than I understand yet, but she hasn't been able to tap into it the same way she did at the Challenge.'

'Of course,' Nuala says. 'I'm confident that will form part of the search for the Blue Pointed Star, or what we do with it when we find it. There is much Roisin's line can do.'

I glance outside, the moon little more than a sliver in the sky, as if she knows this phase is ending for us, too. I say my goodbyes, leaving Rory with Nuala.

Ciara is just reaching the end of the garden path that winds up to Nuala's house as I make my way down to go home. My breath catches in my throat. Her dark hair is heaped on her head, mutinous strands dancing around her face and catching the lights of Nuala's garden. She watches me for a long moment.

'I thought you'd be here,' she says, and I can only nod as I join her on the path. She falls into step with me as we walk back towards Nuala's front gate. My heart quickens as I note she clearly didn't come here for Nuala.

'You've been quiet,' I say softly, sparing her a quick glance.

'Since when?' she's being purposefully obtuse, so I wait. Her breathing shallows slightly. 'I know, I -'

'What?' I ask.

'I think I may have'—she takes a shuddering breath and won't meet my eye as she appears to reshuffle her thoughts—'I don't want it to be a distraction.'

I blanch, but force my expression, and voice, to sound neutral. 'How so, Kiki?'

I clear my throat, wishing I didn't know where she is going with this. The same place I know it should go. There is nothing I can offer her but darkness.

'This – with Lish – is a beginning, Aeyva. One you're not fully stepping into.' She draws a deep breath and I find myself desperately hoping she won't continue. That I can stay in this in-between place with her. 'That night – with us – it's been dominating all my thoughts,' she says quietly. I imagine her eyes going dark, and I'm relieved I don't have to look at them as I focus on where we walk, a hard rivulet of pain running down the centre of my body. 'We need to focus on the task at hand. You need to focus on doing your part ... to choose your place. You're allowed to be happy, Aeyva.'

There's a weight on my chest I've never experienced before. She doesn't know how badly I want to be good enough to choose what she's asking. To choose what Nuala wants to share. To be the Calahi she and Ciara think I should be. But the weight still presses into me because now I know she saw the glimmer of a beginning with me, too, and I'm not good enough for her to let myself see it through.

I nod, still unable to say what she wants to hear. 'Time for that crown to come out of its box.'

CHAPTER SIX

LISH

Lochlain breathes heavily next to me and I roll over to face him, watching the sleep ease from his face before consciousness comes. As I let my gaze trail the freckles that run over the bridge of his nose, and down to the wolf that spans the breadth of his chest, I think about the ways nature has changed around me without my notice. The little bluebird I'd saved once, a species I haven't seen in years; a small, red fruit my mother used to grow, the name of which I can no longer remember; the storms that were so many seasons apart, I'd almost forgotten what it felt like to feel rain on my skin. Until they became superstorms that bludgeoned Rhyton multiple times a year.

But, today, I can start to find a solution.

Because today is claiming day, the day I will present myself to the Custodian and claim my Crown and my Throne. In reality, I will claim much more than that. I will be taking my birthright. Repossessing the life my mother should have had. I will be fulfilling the role I was born for, and doing so on behalf of us both. And I will be starting the process of bringing the Custodian to justice.

I breathe deeply into that knowledge, unable to ignore the weight of it. Not because I don't want it, or even because of the expectations that come with it, but because of the very real threat both the Realm and Driarn are facing. Whether nature is really 'the Mother' or not, the accelerating death of it around us is a reality none of us can hide from, a threat that all indicators seem to point at being almost completely irreversible. Unless, that is, I find the Blue Pointed Star.

And it holds the key to some long-lost secret that will give us our futures back.

During all of the change I saw and lived through on the continent, the people of Driarn went about their days ... not quite oblivious – there have been protests and rallies and petitions, some of which I have been loosely involved in – but the focus always seemed to be on adapting, making the most of what we could do with every day. But actually accepting responsibility and committing to fundamental change was a constant debate – debate instead of action. Yet, here, the Calahi have been doing exactly that for longer than I even know. Trying to shoulder the burden for all of us, without knowing how effective it will be.

But at least they're trying.

Lochlain releases another long sigh as he blinks his eyes open and smiles lazily at me, our stone-coloured bedspread running across his hips.

'You okay?' he asks sleepily, reaching out to tuck a strand of hair behind my ear.

I smile. 'I'm fine, just ready for today,' I say.

He shifts a little so he can look down into my face, his dark eyes framed by even darker lashes. 'Me too.'

He tips my chin up and kisses me deeply. I wish his confidence would seep through me along with the warmth his kisses bring. But I don't let myself be carried away on the sensation of his soft, hot tongue on mine. Instead, I remind myself of the immediate task, of the Calahi who will be with me as I walk into the Airlie Palace, and the Prominent Families who will be ready to stand once I'm there. This is Airlie's system and I am simply stepping into my role and taking the helm.

'You will make a fine Queen, Lish,' he whispers against my mouth. 'I can't wait to bow to you.'

I laugh in spite of the impatience knotting its way through my core. 'I am not at all queenly'—I pause—'and under no circumstances will you bow to me.'

Lochlain pulls away from me and examines me seriously. The black in his eyes swallows the copper flecks as he stares at me.

'I'm your General, Lish,' he says, 'I will always bow to you.'

Niamh whinnies at me as I pause in her stables on the way out the back gate. A lush vine trails the entrance, its flowers just about to turn and fall. On a whim, and with a tinge of desperation, I bury a hand in the fine foliage and breathe out. Not dissimilar to when I healed Lochlain. Aeyva has had me practising my magic with Rory but, so far, I haven't been able to access it the same as I did at Lochlain's Challenge and it's left me feeling ... lacking. My skin still registers the emotions of my Rhyton friends and Lochlain, and I have been able to maintain my rudimentary healing skills. But using so much power my knees want to give out isn't something I have been able to do again.

A handful of flowers bloom bright once more, the colours returning to their former brilliance like soft gems in the grass, the leaves that frame them glossy. I blink, half expecting them to return to normal as I remove my hand. They remain, and I wonder what happened to the white flowers I accidentally created in Althea Forest. But the knowledge I can still do it releases the pressure in my chest a little.

I am of this world.

And I will find a way to stop the Calahi giving up all their magic.

Lochlain joins me and I focus on the lingering sensation of Niamh's soft nose in my palm as I walk the cobbled streets of Elenlea towards the Palace. Lochlain flanks me, a light cloak thrown over his General's uniform. The Calahi of Airlie know his face, but the lack of obvious uniform means we can move a little less conspicuously – mostly because the citizens of Airlie try to be respectful of his personal time. And no uniform is supposed to indicate he's not working. But, even in my relatively short time here, I know that's a thin principle – it's the same as the Commissioner of the

Guard in Rhyton is always the Commissioner, regardless what shirt he wears.

He is one unknown for today. He was present at Lochlain's Challenge but I don't know what happened to him in the aftermath. As far as I'm aware, he hasn't been back to Elenlea. But I will find out what his connection is to this world, and if he really looked the other way when General Siosal took women from the continent. There may be more pressing steps for me to take today, but I will absolutely find out.

I think of the Throne I saw in the Challenge room, the crown in a box on its seat. Imagining that crown on my head is nothing short of preposterous. I can't even imagine it on my mother's head. What I can remember of my mother is someone warm and funny, someone who crawled on the floor with me as we played. But she was not someone regal, not to me.

Without her, it's my faith in the process – and the support I have – that's helping me put one foot in front of the other. That, and the drive to find an alternative to the Givings. The other unknowns crowd alongside the Commissioner in my mind. What is the solution to the Givings? And what, exactly, will finding the Blue Pointed Star require of me? What if, once we do find it, I can't do whatever it will ask? Or, perhaps worse, it doesn't actually do anything? The questions that bubble forth are too sharp to think about too closely. It's the hope that the path will illuminate more greatly with every step I take that keeps me moving in the direction of the Palace. To my Throne. To my crown. To helping the people and Calahi I care about.

So, I walk to the Palace where my mother's portrait will bear witness to what I'm about to do.

The Calahi we pass dress just as vibrantly as they did when I first arrived, and I still marvel at how liberating it is not to dress for the heat alone. But there's a dullness to them despite their colour, as if their wavering trust in the Custodian is tainting Elenlea. Literally.

Lochlain is close but doesn't touch me. We agreed it was best not to make a public display of our relationship and allow it to raise questions about Lochlain's role in my claim, and his loyalty to Airlie, as opposed to himself.

I clasp my shaking hands in front of me as we wander; the only physical comfort I will get is from myself today. But Lochlain's energy buzzes along mine and his presence is soothing as he sends me a very gentle, calming sensation I let wash over me. Focusing on the stones that press into the soles of my tall boots, I watch the city around us. I haven't walked this route in its entirety, but I feel I know it by heart thanks to Aeyva. She was very clear about the specific path to draw the least attention – lest the Calahi of Airlie think Lochlain was about to publicly declare me as his Soul Accord. It's not a distraction we can allow, not when there is so much more at stake. It's a thought that tugs at me as I recall the night we lay in front of the fire at Ciara's – the night before the challenge – when he told me Soul Accords' magic talked to each other. But I force myself to push it aside. I can't give it space when I need to prove, with my blood, that I am the owner of the boxed crown.

Lochlain's tension that skims along my skin increases and, when I look up, his expression is hard. Following his stare, I find a Calahi in a dark green uniform heading towards us – a Royal Watchman. I don't recall seeing one of them out on their own before, I believe they normally work in teams of four like when they monitor the Givings. But I know from my last visit here that their uniform means they serve the Court of Airlie and, therefore, the Custodian until they serve me. I wonder what Palace business he's on that would agitate Lochlain.

I want to talk about something, anything, that will take the edge off, but my voice won't come. Taking the Crown, and the Throne, might be what I want, but it doesn't mean my limbs aren't tingling with nerves. I'm anxious about the reception I will receive and angry that the easiest way to remove the Calahi who killed my mother is, effectively, to ask him for permission to prove myself. My teeth start to ache where I clench them.

Lochlain stretches his right hand out slightly and gently guides me half a step behind, his eyes never leaving the Royal Watchman.

The uniform clad stranger disappears down a lane way to our left and Lochlain abruptly directs us the same way. In the shadows ahead, the stranger waits with his palms held skyward. Lochlain relaxes only marginally. Despite their diminished magic, the Calahi can be lethal with magic alone, particularly those strong enough to be in positions of authority; but the show of no weapons is still symbolically important.

'General,' the stranger whispers, the relief on his breath clear. 'You need to leave. Now.' He nods respectfully at me. 'You need to take her away.'

Lochlain looks down his nose slightly, inspecting the stranger intently. To his credit, the Watchman doesn't cower.

'And why might that be?' Lochlain's voice is threat enough.

'I'm sorry, General, but – but the Custodian has just announced to the Palace that the Queen is dead and that he knows who killed her.'

The blood in my veins runs hot, and I grip Lochlain's arm. That Calahi knows full well what happened to my mother.

And yet I already know that's not what he's announced.

'What else?' Lochlain asks, his own anger simmering under the surface and sparking on my skin.

The Watchman looks at me. The rings in his eyes are a pale quartz, making the coloured parts of his eyes seem quite small.

'I know who she is, General,' he pauses. 'I know who I fight for. But it is she who the Custodian is claiming killed Queen Catriona.'

The ground starts to shift beneath me, and I become overly aware of the smell of the food being served in the establishments on the road we just left, where we would have passed before this Watchman brought us into the alley and threw our entire plan off course.

Lochlain pulls me into his side, and I inhale deeply as the stranger glances between us.

'The search for you begins now,' the Watchman says, looking at me. 'I came as soon as I heard, but I will be missed – the Custodian is preparing to make the announcement to the Court.' He glances back down the laneway. 'I'm being noticed on the streets, I must return. The orders are to kill on sight. He wants to make sure you never get a chance to make your claim.'

Regret swims in his features before he hurries back out of the lane and turns towards the Palace.

I stare at Lochlain, his eyes wholly black, rage rippling from him. Slowly, his anger rights me and I pull away slightly, needing to stand on my own. My breath comes in shallow gulps and I force myself to steady. To draw long, cool inhales before breathing hard out my nose.

My mind whirls, searching for a next step, the next rung on the ladder to hold on to, but I find none. Nowhere in my planning, learning the ways of the Realm or talking with the Prominent Families did this come up as an option. That I would be a wanted fugitive of Airlie. For the death of my own mother.

But as the plan falls apart before my eyes, I know I need something, anything, to help me work out the next steps – and I know where to get it.

'We need a new plan,' I breathe.

CHAPTER SEVEN

LISH

The last time I was in Lochlain's cabin was a life altering moment, perhaps for both of us, as we looked at my reflection with the yellow flower crown and him with his wolf tattoo.

My second visit feels just as monumental, and not for the better.

'Who the fuck does he think he is?' I storm at Lochlain as I pace the small living room. Will staggers up the backstairs, followed closely by Sofia, who looks as composed as ever, and Nico, who's grinning from ear to ear.

'Can we do that again?' he asks cheerfully.

'Not if I can help it,' Will grumbles, flopping himself on the couch. Nico jumps on his stomach, whooshing the air from his lungs.

'But it was so fun!' he exclaims.

His enthusiasm creates a tiny crack in the anger that's been brewing since I left Elenlea, and I cross my arms as if I can contain it. Or maybe hide it from him. Nico's world has been in enough turmoil. But seeing the innocence on his face only serves to remind me of my own. The innocence the Custodian stole from me when he killed my mother. And now he wants to take my life too – wants the Calahi of Airlie to believe *I* killed her. Meeting the Custodian at Lochlain's swearing in ceremony brought a whisper of recognition for me, but I hadn't considered he'd know exactly who I was. My mother has been gone so long, I no longer remember her in her entirety – can't recall the sound of her voice or the shape of her face.

Just pieces of a life I barely had time to experience for reasons I don't fully comprehend.

But perhaps I look far more like her than I'd considered. Or maybe Siosal was more open with him than I'd expected.

Rory is in the process of ferrying everyone here, and my nerves jangle louder with every passing moment. If the Custodian recognised me at the ceremony, it means he's been biding his time to position himself for this announcement, working up a plan I can only guess at. And it means he will also know who is associated with me. My Rhyton team were obviously not from the Realm when they too stood with Lochlain – the Custodian even called that out – and the thought of him finding them, to locate me, makes my blood run cold. Lochlain grabs my wrist gently as I pass him once more and pulls me towards him.

'Breathe, Lish,' he whispers in my ear. Closing my eyes, I turn my face into his chest and do as instructed. His hand cups the back of my neck for a moment and my nose fills with the smell of him, like mulled wine. 'We'll figure it out.'

'Lish,' Will says from the couch. Taking a last inhale of Lochlain, I turn to face him. 'What's going on?'

Riley is the last to arrive and she strides in several paces in front of Rory.

'We've had a complication,' I tell the group, my gaze flicking to Nico long enough for Sofia to redirect him with a book she's pulled from her bag. 'The Custodian is about to publicly announce that he knows the Queen is dead ... and that I killed her.'

Lochlain picks up where I left off. 'Lish's image is about to be all over the Court – and soon the whole Realm – as the one who murdered Queen Catriona.'

Hearing him say it out loud, even though I just did, creates a sharp burn in the back of my throat. This was her world. A world whose rules and processes I have tried to follow, only to find myself on the wrong side of the law. Nowhere near where I need to be.

'Damn it,' Aeyva whispers. Her voice is murder.

'That's ridiculous,' Will says. 'Surely not even the Calahi would believe a six-year-old would kill their own mother?' He frowns slightly, as if suddenly remembering the power of the Calahi. 'Well, not willingly anyway.'

Blaire glances at him, her brow furrowed.

'He won't tell them Lish is her daughter,' Ciara says, looking at Lochlain, concern pinching her face. 'The Calahi of Airlie will have no idea of the familial connection and will probably assume this is a recent event. So her age, or that she wasn't an adult when her mother died, won't come into it. I don't think the question on how Lish ages compared to Calahi will even come up.'

'Wait, what?' The confusion in Phoenix's voice mirrors the looks on my friends' faces.

'Suffice to say,' Aeyva says, 'we are older than you probably thought and not as old as you're thinking now. But yes, the Calahi will imagine Lish looking almost exactly as she does now when she supposedly killed the Queen. Because, for all they know, it was yesterday.'

'This place makes no sense,' Phoenix says quietly.

'It's immaterial really,' Aeyva says. 'We're not immortal, nor do we live excessively longer than you.'

'We do, however,' Rory chips in, 'keep our solid good looks for decades on end and gain ... invaluable experience if we use our time wisely.' He winks at me, but I can only summon a shadow of a smile. More of an acknowledgment of his attempt to lighten the mood.

Blaire's concern is clear from across the room, gently buffeting my senses, but it's Sofia that breaks the brief silence that descends. Her hazel eyes clouded with worry.

'So, what do we do?'

Even Nico is quiet as we look at each other, wondering exactly what the answer to that question is, and I think about what I did when I was his age – run.

'It doesn't change that we need to find the Star,' Ciara says quietly. 'Unfortunately, the Mother isn't in a position to wait for you to be crowned Queen - she's dying as we speak.'

Meaning we all are, too; beginning with the Calahi and ending with the human world. I clench my fists, digging my nails into my palms.

'That still needs to be the plan,' Aeyva says.

'The plan,' Riley replies, 'was for Lish to take her Throne and then lock in the alliance with that other King. How exactly do you propose we get someone wanted for murder on it?'

'Don't we literally need the sapphire in the crown? Isn't it part of the Star?' Phoenix asks.

'We need it on her head,' Aeyva says.

I click my teeth together as I think. The pieces swirling in my mind. I was supposed to go to King Kailoh and forge an alliance – one based on being the leader of Airlie, Court to Court. That alliance was also intended to encourage him to share his knowledge of the location of the rest of the Star. Something not even the Manorynxes, Benny or Nuala, knew or know. Something Aeyva insists Kailoh will, but won't give for nothing.

I search the room for blue eyes, the ones that will be putting this together. Until a pang behind my ribs reminds me Hayes isn't here. I swallow against the thickness in my throat. What would he do?

'The path has changed, not the plan,' Aeyva continues. 'We go to Mercasia and forge the alliance with Kailoh. Then have Lish claim the Throne with his support and get the sapphire from the crown.' She looks at me. 'There is no way the Custodian, or anyone in the Royal Watch, will risk killing you with members of Kailoh's Court in tow. At least not until he knows why they're with you.' She addresses us all as she talks now. 'We need that alliance now more than ever. Kailoh ... thinks there's something more happening in the Realm, something we need to be ready to go to war over.'

My head pounds. 'Like what?'

'I don't know yet – neither does he. But when Kailoh's senses are raised, it's normally for good reason.'

'Being prepared to defend Airlie,' Lochlain says from where he stands beside me, 'is what we've been working towards, regardless. Training the Royalists, positioning me as General so I have control of the Whispers'—he runs a hand down the back of my arm but doesn't take my hand, as if he can tell I'm too pent up to fold yet—'ensuring we can defend Airlie against an attack is normal practice for us. I don't think we can let that throw us off course just yet.' He looks back to Aeyva. 'But we do need to know what's coming.'

'Which brings us back to aligning with Kailoh and finding the pieces of the Star. That's it,' she says.

'That's it?' I ask, aware my voice sounds suddenly high. 'You're saying that I, a crownless half-Calahi, am supposed to win over one of the most powerful Calahi Kings in history and convince him to help defend Airlie, in addition to his own Court, against an unknown threat? Not only that, but elicit his support in my claim as Queen and find pieces of a sapphire that have been scattered to the winds for ... something we have absolutely no idea about? Other than a dead librarian thought it will show us how to heal the world?'

'Correct,' Aeyva says, looking at me, not backing down.

Correct. That's all she says.

My vision flickers as the room begins to fill with a new image. One of the Custodian seated next to the Throne. My limbs feel heavy, and I don't register the others' reaction to this means of communication. I've only seen it once before myself, when his broadcast filled Ciara's living room after Lochlain was sworn in as General. When I remembered who he really is.

'Citizens of Airlie,' the Custodian says in that sickening melodic voice. 'It is with a heavy heart that I bring you this news.' My eyes burn with anger, a constricting band running across my chest. 'Just this morning I have received confirmation that ...'—he draws a breath, false emotion flickering across his features—'that our Queen, Catriona, now graces the halls of our Mother.'

Lochlain's cabin is deadly quiet, only the Custodian's voice fills the panel-walled room. His hands clasp the staff he holds in front of him, black gloves like a second skin.

'I am sorry to say she was taken from us in the most savage of ways,' he says, and Aeyva's lip lifts in a snarl. 'But do not despair. We may have lost our Queen, but I will continue to lead you to the better future I have always promised. A future ripe with our gifts, a future restored of balance, and a future of safety.'

He stands and moves in front of the Throne.

My Throne.

Gesturing to the side, he bows low as another figure walks onto the dais. A tall, willowy woman in a dark coloured dress that fans out behind her as she walks.

'Fuck,' Rory mutters.

Lochlain's grip on my hand tightens.

'I know who ripped our world apart at the seams,' the Custodian continues. I brace myself against Lochlain's outrage, my own emotions emptying away. Like the tide sucked out before a tidal wave. 'I know who killed our Queen. And I will make her pay.'

The Custodian turns to the woman beside him. She wears a tall, pale crown that towers up behind the back of her head. As they stand together in a room filled with images of the history of Airlie and the rulers that came before, it's hard to imagine the Custodian wanting anything more than to be where he is. He looks so at home.

'Queen Nakiasha has generously offered her full support to Airlie in our time of need. We will bring this individual to justice.'

There is no audience in the throne room, but I imagine the Calahi of Airlie raging in their homes as the message is broadcast. At me. Their rightful, innocent, Queen. And the least capable person of murdering my mother.

Gasps sound from around me as my face fills the room. An image of me in a torn dress with blood on my face and in my hair. An image of me with violence in my eyes. But still, clearly an image of me. I shudder at the visual reminder of my time in Siosal's compound – one I didn't think was recorded in any way.

'I don't understand,' Will says. 'How did they get that? And how does he even know you?'

I can't look at any of them as I leave the room and walk down the back stairs. The Custodian has taken so much from me and now he wants to poison the love I had for her, too. And he's doing so with Queen Nakiasha already by his side. I don't fully understand the power of the Court of Rothani, but instinctively I know it was something we needed to avoid. I cross the grass, past the horse stables and around to the meadow in front of the house – towards the most open space I can find.

The Custodian has just taken a very big, public step in cementing their alliance and painting me as the villain. One that will make it even harder for me to convince anyone I am the rightful Queen. Even if I could prove the Custodian killed my Mother, why would the Calahi of Airlie trust me with the Court? I am a foreigner to this land versus two experienced Calahi leaders.

A small voice in the back of my mind tells me to remember the Prominent Families, the ones who agreed to stand by me. To remember that I am, in fact, innocent. But I can't see a path to follow to show them that. And what if they believe him?

My eyes burn with angry tears and a scream builds in my chest. Even in the open, the world is compressing around me.

It's Rory who comes for me and I chide myself for not keeping better composure. But he's not the one facing execution for murdering a parent. A royal parent. His eyes, normally full of cheek, watch me wear a path in the green grass. The yellow wildflowers that crowned me last time I was here have almost all disappeared - yet another reminder of what's at stake and how quickly it's all disappearing. Rory joins me and we walk together, as if he knows trying to get me to stay still is pointless.

'It's a shitty thing, sweetheart, I know,' he says, easily keeping pace with me.

My chest is aflame. 'I can't fight him, Rory, this is not my world.' He doesn't answer and I move faster, trying to outrun the emotions that chase me. 'Shit, Rory. I want to go home.' My breath comes faster now, and my hands tingle. 'I don't know enough, I - I can't do this. And Nakiasha is with the Custodian. What does that mean? And the Commissioner? I keep coming back to him—'

Rory shushes me gently and reaches for my arm.

My ears start to hum and my flame surges with something unfamiliar.

And then I'm screaming.

The world flies past in green and blue before I can only see black. A roaring wind rages in my ears and my voice is torn away.

Dimly I hear Rory yelling at me. 'Let go, Lish! Let go!'

Numbly, I fight to raise my hands in the wind that barrels into me and discover Rory locked on to my elbow. But there's nothing in my hands to let go of. Rory yanks me hard and spins me to face him. Gripping my face in his free hand, he shouts again.

'Close your eyes! Breathe!'

My lungs aren't strong enough to suck in a full breath of the air that's racing past, and my chest heaves with silent sobs. Rory talks to me softly and I can't make out the words but still, the wind around us calms and my breathing begins to come more slowly. The gale stops completely and we land in the meadow, the impact hard enough to bruise.

I stare at Rory, who's crawled to his knees and rests his forehead on the ground. I ignore the others running towards us.

'Was that supposed to be a joke?' I gasp.

'That,' he says, his voice muffled against the ground. 'Was not me.'

Lochlain slides on his knees next to me and gathers me up, inspecting me. 'Mother above, are you okay? What was that?' His eyes flash with concern, but I push his emotions back.

'I'm fine,' I say, gingerly picking myself up and glancing uncertainly at Rory. I will definitely have bruises along my left hip where I slammed into the ground. I'm momentarily thankful I didn't hit my head.

Confusion dusts Lochlain's features. 'Ror?'

Rory staggers to his feet. 'Not me.' He takes a few deep breaths. 'I officially apologise for making you sick the first time I took you, sweetheart. Is that how it feels for you every time?' He gapes at me.

'I ...' I trail off. The others are now all here, staring, and I have no explanation for what just happened either.

'Did you guys see the whirly whirly?' Nico asks. 'It was huge!'

'Going by the look on Lish's face, I think she was the whirly whirly,' Blaire says, frowning.

'Well, I don't know what a 'whirly whirly' is, but it certainly feels about right,' Rory says, finally standing to his full height.

Aeyva's all-knowing, pale blue and grey eyes look between us and I can almost see the thoughts turning behind them. Lochlain looks to her too and I notice the others do the same. Except my Rhyton team who move in towards me, Will gripping my shoulder.

'That looked exactly how it felt to have Rory ... deposit me here,' he says.

Pushing away the thought, and the sensation, I lean into Will's hold, and remember what we would have done in the Guard when we weren't sure of all the facts – interrogate all the options until we did.

Kailoh doesn't have answers and I have no crown. So perhaps I can give him answers instead. The Custodian might think he's played the distraught little girl whose mother he slaughtered. He might think he's manoeuvred me out of my crown with the Court of Rothani on his side.

But I'm not just that little girl anymore.

CHAPTER EIGHT

AEYVA

Most would be overwhelmed by the obstacles ahead of us. But, both individually and as a team, we have faced the insurmountable before and come out the other side. Not always intact, but we always came through. I remind myself none of the humans have been to war. We may not yet know exactly what threat we're facing, outside of the loss of the Mother, but battling for our home is not something completely foreign to us. The Realm has had its share of battles – both internal, and from external forces whose histories we changed to erase the knowledge of our existence. And, of course, we have all fought battles closer to home.

Siosal and the Whispers that were loyal to him being the most recent.

But it sets my nerves on edge in a way that's new for me. I've never needed to know all the answers like they seem to – I'm clearly far more prepared to walk into any unknowns, blades out. So, instead of making an immediate exit for Kailoh and the Court of Mercasia, their voices fill the cabin, and I try not to show my impatience at allowing them space to discuss what they've just seen, what it means. Nico bounces on the timber floor on his toes exclaiming loudly. His excitement is palpable and elicits a small smile from me when he skips past.

A memory of Nuala is quick to assert itself. One in which she held me, cradled in her arms on the floor of her living room as I broke. Shattered. There were flower petals on her thick rug that I'd walked in on my boots. The smell of one of her teas filling the room. And no sound but mine.

Some years later we'd had a conversation in that same room about what else I would do with my life – serve the crown. And I have, just not always in the way either of us expected.

Will catches my eye and lifts his brows in expectation. I have a deep respect for humans, despite how blindly they've screwed up their world and, in turn, mine. There is no doubt the lack of care for their own is causing the demise of ours. But to have them treated as something less, something other, by so many Calahi has always grated on me. It's people like Will that solidify my belief they should be treated better than they have been.

Phoenix looks between Loch and Lish, ultimately landing on me as well. I study him and Will – neither fidget under my gaze. They're both handsome. Different, and very human. At one point in time, I would have considered a life with a man like one of those in front of me now. Kind, reliable, attractive. But then my life took a different course and not even the strongest Calahi could withstand the darkness I harbour. But here, in this version of myself, I can be somewhat kind.

'What do you need?' I ask Lish, interrupting her discussion with Blaire and Riley.

Will visibly exhales, his gaze flicking momentarily to Sofia and Nico, and I wonder what he was expecting me to say.

'I want to know why,' she says after a moment. 'How did it get to this?'

The room seems to pause. Not because, after everything, anyone would consider not having this discussion. Or that we don't understand what she's referring to. It just feels like ... a lot.

Loch drops a hand to her knee. 'Initially, we believed Siosal was acting on his own – searching for you to make good on the bonding he'd anticipated with Catriona. We'—he glances around at us—'didn't have reason to think the Custodian was involved in any way.'

'I think it's clear,' Blaire cuts in, 'that the Custodian is quite a masterful manipulator. I would imagine it's not a huge leap to say he was probably completely aware of Siosal methods. The question, then, would have been if he would have actually let the bonding Siosal thought he was owed proceed, and what he would have done with you instead.'

Ciara nods gently as Blaire, quite neatly, sums up the likely relationships between the two male Calahi.

'Now,' Ciara continues for Blaire, 'it's safe to assume the Custodian doesn't want you anywhere near his position. He wasn't able to dispose of you quietly using Siosal, so he's gone public – to make it almost impossible for you to replace him.'

Lish is quiet for longer than I expect and I almost think there is something else she's considering asking. Or if we haven't properly answered her question.

'What else do you need?' I prompt softly.

'Time,' she says, sighing. 'Time and information. I don't want to go to Kailoh as a fugitive, but it looks like I won't have a choice. But I can choose how wilfully ignorant we are of what's happening around us. I want to know as much as we possibly can before we go.'

'Meaning,' Will adds, 'we need to know what our opponents are doing. I want to do reconnaissance in both the other Courts and Rhyton to establish how real, and advanced, those different threats are – waltzing into Mercasia with the little information we have now could be suicide for all we know. Especially with Lish's new status as 'wanted' in this Court. We also need to know as much as possible about this Star and its relevance to what we're doing here – what will it do when we put it together and how will it help Airlie?'

'I want to know everything you do about that Star before we leave this room,' Lish says, steely determination in her voice. 'There may not be a Crown of Airlie for me to show Kailoh as proof of my place in this world, but I can give him information – we just need to find it first.'

I run the scenarios through my mind. Even as I know the trip to Mercasia will not be suicide – Kailoh is barely containing himself in his excitement to meet Lish – they have a point. And it's not really my call to make as Sentinel, it's Loch's role as General to make some of these overarching decisions when the safety of the Queen and Airlie are at stake. Previous Queens have been comfortable letting their warriors do what they do best. But Lish is also a warrior, one that isn't accustomed to understanding the vast skills of the Manorynxes and heeding their advice – she hasn't had the time to develop those trusted relationships. For now, she just has us.

A warrior, hand-tied in a foreign land.

I look at Lochlain. 'We have a couple of days, at most,' I say, 'before it will be untenable to get Lish into Mercasia and a public audience with Kailoh.

Even he will draw the line at publicly aiding Queen Catriona's supposed killer.'

Lish's green eyes flash before the faint relief on her face washes through the rest of the group and she looks at me. 'I know we don't know all the pieces,' she says, 'but I want to run them through and fill as many gaps as possible before we go to Kailoh.'

Reasonable enough.

'We have very little time,' I warn again. She just nods, but I can see a little of her confidence creeping back in.

'Then we take the days we can,' Lochlain says.

Phoenix moves from where he was standing behind Lish, gripping the back of Lochlain's couch.

'Let's start with the Star,' he says. 'We know there are four pieces, of which we have one.' He points at Lish's chest where we all know the Wolverton Pendant sits. 'That leaves three pieces to locate, and attain, so we can put it together and get the instructions to save ... nature. Am I right so far?'

A small chorus of murmurs confirm his view.

'So, for one piece – in the Airlie crown – we know its approximate location but have no way of getting it right now. What do you know of the other two pieces?' he asks.

Ciara settles herself in the couch cushions next to Lish as she sighs. 'Not a huge amount. Kailoh is one of the greatest Kings in our history not only because of how he leads Mercasia, but because he is uniquely knowledgeable of so much of our history.' She tucks her legs up underneath her as she talks, and I force myself to look away from the curve of her thighs. 'The Realm used to be one, with Roisin the Queen of all of it. When she fell, the Realm split – violently – into the three Courts we have today. Of all the current serving monarchs, Kailoh has been on his Throne the longest. That, plus all the research he's done over his lifetime, means he's our best chance at finding the location of the other two pieces.'

Lish closes her eyes briefly and inhales. I watch her for any sign of drawing on anyone else's magic like she obviously did with Rory's in the meadow, but I don't see any. If she's doing it, no one in this room is aware. But I know there is more to unpack there. Far more.

'There is ... a theory,' I say and Ciara's gaze flicks to mine, expectant. There's always a sliver of hope shining from her when I talk of the knowledge Nuala and Benny have shared with me. She's almost as bad as Nuala. 'Legend says the four pieces are symbolic of the different ... ingredients the person who finds the Star will need to have to enact whatever the Star shows them.'

'This is new to us,' Riley says, frowning from where she sits on the floor drawing with Nico. I have no idea where she got the pencils and paper from.

'The stories suggest that only a person of Roisin's line,' Rory chips in, 'can make the Star burn again – someone who is a rightful bearer of the Airlie crown, like Lish. The other pieces that person is to gather are meant to symbolise the support and power of the Wolvertons,' Lish looks to Lochlain, a slight awe in her face, 'and a great partnership with a Manorynx.'

I clear my throat.

'So Nuala should be able to help?' Will asks.

'She doesn't know where they are, so not on the locations directly,' I say. 'But Rory is talking about the theories on the meaning of each of the pieces. Why they symbolise those things and what it will do when we put them together isn't clear. And yes, Nuala will definitely support Lish as required – all her power as Manorynx will be at Lish's disposal should we need it.'

There are a few moments of silence, the sound of Nico's pencils scratching on the paper the only noise.

'So, that's the Star,' Sofia says. She's now also joined Nico and Riley in their colouring and there's something oddly mesmerising about watching the colour etch onto the page. 'Two bits we know the location of, only one of which we have. And two bits that Kailoh is, hopefully, the key to finding. So ... he still holds the balance of power there.'

'Yes,' Lish agrees. 'But does he know what the Commissioner's up to? How Rhyton is connected to Airlie? Whether or not what he thinks is brewing is starting over there?'

'No,' I say.

'Then he doesn't know why the Commissioner was at Lochlain's Challenge,' she says, 'and we're going to find out. I can't believe it was simply a thank you from the Custodian for helping cover up the missing women.'

'And what about the Custodian and the other Queen?' Blaire asks. 'Will he know the details of that arrangement?'

'It's likely he will know that, yes,' Lochlain says but he turns to me, a question on his face. A long time ago, I was appointed the unofficial liaison to Kailoh's Court, and it's felt natural since the beginning.

'There is an internal source I can try for anything additional,' I say, 'particularly for information on Queen Nakiasha.'

'Aeyv ...' Rory starts softly, 'what if we track down the Eternal Queen?'

My heart stops.

'For what, exactly?' I ask slowly, his question the very last one I expected. Riley looks between us.

'To take out the Custodian ... quietly,' he says. 'None of us will get close enough now, save maybe Loch.' His eyes dance as he entertains that idea.

'No,' I say, clearing my throat in an attempt to get my heart going again. 'As tempting as that might be, Lish needs to be seen to legitimately take her Throne. Otherwise, Airlie will be left just as unstable, or more so, than it is now. The Calahi of Airlie need to be behind her.'

Rory nods.

'Who the hell is the *Eternal* Queen?' Riley asks, her grey eyes wide, before she mutters, 'What a stupid name.'

'A ghost story,' I say, 'and not one we want to know about our search for the sapphire.'

'Why's that?'

'The Eternal Queen effectively runs our ... underworld, I guess you could call it,' Rory says when it's clear I won't talk. 'She's someone that's haunted the Realm for longer than anyone really knows – and represents everything that is the worst of the Calahi. At least, according to the Wolvertons.' Rory gives me a knowing look as Loch and Ciara each nod and my heart sinks a little. 'She is turned to for all manner of reasons, mostly nefarious in nature, but no one her Society targets walks out alive.'

'Exactly,' Loch says. 'Associating Lish taking the Throne with her help in any way will immediately disqualify her from the Throne in the eyes of Airlie.'

I try not to think about the conversation I had with Kailoh. That he had a way for me to get out and disable some of her power in the process. A way that will likely get me killed. But, once Lish is in her place as Queen, if I can't formally be a Sentinel without the shackles of the Society, it's a sacrifice I will gladly make.

'So,' I pause. 'Any other views on how we do this?' I ask, meeting Phoenix's gaze.

It's unusual for me to work in a team nowadays and even more unusual to ask for input. In the Society, I lead teams. But only when absolutely impossible for me to do an assignment on my own. Phoenix is clearly not entirely over the fact Lish left him – and for a bigger, stronger, magical Calahi. So, while it's not only him I talk to, I look to him as I ask. An invitation in acknowledgment of his efforts to make this work for us all.

'Yes.' It's Blaire who pipes up instead. 'Phoenix and I will go to Rhyton and find out what we can about the Commissioner's involvement.'

Lish shifts forwards in her seat and opens her mouth to speak, but seems to think better of it and her lips snap shut. Phoenix looks between the two of them.

'You know it may not be safe?' Ciara asks. 'Particularly if your Commissioner recognised you at the Challenge.'

'I know,' Blaire responds. 'And he will more than recognise me, but we need to find out what's going on – why the Commissioner is involved in Airlie. I'm best placed to do that. I can get close to him ... again.'

Silently, Phoenix crosses the room and stands beside Blaire. 'Let's do this,' he says.

'Okay,' Ciara agrees. 'I'll go with you.'

'I'll go to my other sources,' I say, 'see if there's anything more I can find out about the Custodian and his involvement with the Court of Rothani that Kailoh doesn't already know.'

Ciara glances at me but only nods.

Lish puts her hand on Loch's that has remained on her thigh. 'And I'll go to Rhyton.' His head whips around to her, and she shakes hers slowly at him. 'I can't very well stay here with the Royal Watch after me, can I?'

'Fine,' he says, his voice low. 'Lish and I go to Rhyton.'

'No,' Lish and I say at the same time.

'No,' I say again. 'You are needed here in the Palace with the Custodian; we need eyes on him at all times.'

'You know you need to be visible, Loch,' Ciara says gently. 'Elenlea's hope will crumble quickly without their General.'

'You don't think he will be implicated in the whole 'Lish is a killer' thing?' Riley asks.

'It will be tricky,' I say, 'but the Custodian has only just sworn him in, it would look very bad to suddenly lose his General. Particularly a Wolverton who was destined for the role – the city almost rioted over getting him formally appointed. And the very fact Lochlain shows back up at the Palace without Lish will give the Custodian some false indication of where his loyalties lie.' I look between Loch and Lish, wondering if she's aware of just how skilled a warrior – and General – he is. But, then, she does know he was working covertly under Siosal. 'He's been in trickier spots.'

We eventually agree that the best place for Will and his family is Elenlea, with Lochlain and Nuala to watch over them, and Rory and Riley would go with me. I feel more comfortable with a Calahi in each group. The humans don't like to be minded by us but, as skilled they may be, my current responsibility is as Lish's Sentinel and protecting her at all costs. That includes those she loves, whether they like it or not.

'Two days,' Ciara says. 'Then we meet back here with whatever information we have gathered in that time, and Lish leaves for Mercasia.'

'One last thing, Lish,' I say.

She shifts her gaze to me slowly, and I'm sure she knows what I'm about to say. The alliance Kailoh wants is important. In its own right, it's less important than the Star but, given how vital his help is in finding half of it, it's critical Lish meets his expectations. If having more information helps her feel she can do that, I'll support her in any way I can. But if we can't ...

'When we return, we are working out that magic of yours. If we fail with Kailoh for any reason ... it might be all we have.'

The room seems to still for a moment as everyone looks to Lish, Nico included.

'I know,' she says.

CHAPTER NINE

LISH

'They'll believe him, won't they?' I ask Lochlain.

I couldn't risk returning to Elenlea myself, knowing the Royal Watchmen would be looking for me – even if not all of them want to. Openly defying the Custodian, with no guarantee I will be crowned, could mean they pay a price I'm not prepared for. Cold-blooded murder, no matter how long ago, makes him dangerous and I don't know enough about how his mind works to take the risk with more innocent lives. So, Lochlain and I wait at the cabin while the others gather our supplies and hide Will, Sofia, and Nico away.

'At first, yes. They have no reason not to at this stage,' he says, watching me where we still stand in the living room, irritation flickering under my ribs. 'The Prominent Families already know the truth, of course, and this will just be one more piece of evidence against him in the end.'

'But what is that end now?'

The copper in Lochlain's eyes burns as he looks at me. 'With you as Queen. Me as your General. I will never stop fighting for that, Lish.' The conviction in his voice feels like it transfers to my chest where a warmth starts to bloom, before a helpless sort of anger starts to wash over me.

Not long ago, Blaire questioned the truths we're told. This is the second untruth the Custodian has been singularly responsible for that's shaping the direction of my life. I force hard breaths through my nose as I grit my teeth. What he doesn't know, though, is that while he took the most important person from my life, he also delivered me a family I never would have had otherwise. With my mum still alive, I never would have ended up in that orphanage, never met Will, and never had him deliver me to the front door of the dance class Blaire was teaching that day – events that started a domino effect that led me here.

But it still doesn't help me understand.

I make myself unclench my jaw, the dull ache hard to let go of. No, the Custodian doesn't know what he gave me – despite his best efforts. He might think he's denied me my rightful place in this world, but he also doesn't know how hard my family of friends will work to right the wrongs we see each and every day. That we are hardwired to find solutions, even if I no longer have Hayes on my side.

The need to see Rhyton and the Commissioner for myself tingles in my palms. Because Rhyton is my home, too, and investigating there is second nature. King Kailoh is a Calahi that, so I'm told, values facts and loyalty above all else. Loyalty will be hard to prove, and for him to earn, but facts I can give. I just need to find them first.

'There's so much for us to undo here,' I say. 'The truth about my mother, me ... understanding the Givings ...'

He circles my wrist with his fingers, and I let him tug me closer, over the well-worn rug.

'And we will,' he says, his voice soft. 'You're a leader in the Rhyton Guard. You know how to find the things people hide. You know how to sort the real from the false. And'—I watch his throat move as he clears it—'the King will appreciate that.'

'I was a Team Leader in the Guard. Now, I'm a fugitive.'

'One with the full support of General Wolverton of Airlie.' There's a rough grumble in his tone as he tips my face up to meet his gaze, his fingers warm where they press into my chin. 'That's no small thing in the Realm, Lish. It might be trumped by Kailoh's support, when you get it, but it's still ... powerful.'

'But not powerful enough for the two of us to overthrow him on our own?'

A sting of regret flashes against my skin and he cups my face in his hand.

'Your mother was so well loved here,' he says. 'It will take a lot to convince the Court to give you an opportunity if there is any doubt of your innocence. Having Kailoh by your side will all but eliminate that.'

'Is that why he killed her? Because she was too well loved?'

Lochlain's mouth tightens slightly.

'I think ... in hindsight, the Custodian had become so used to his input into the running of Airlie being highly valued that the thought of Catriona expanding her team of expertise sat uncomfortably.'

I frown, the inadequacy of that response diminishing the steady burn of the flame in my chest.

'He was an adviser of hers,' he continues. 'Not a Manorynx, but someone – a friend – who was very knowledgeable about the Realm and its history, and they were rarely seen without the other. There was never any suggestion that they were romantically involved, but she leaned heavily on him for strategic input into the running and direction of Airlie.'

'And bonding Siosal would have upset that,' I muse quietly. The words are almost emotionless, but I can tell Lochlain can see the weight of this conversation on my face and my skin flickers with his concern. My meeting with the Prominent Families, and now this, is the most I have learned about my mother as a person in a long time. It's both welcome and painful.

'Yes,' he agrees. 'But I've been thinking about it, and I can't imagine the suggestion of Siosal as her partner would have passed the Custodian if he wasn't on board. She didn't want it, so if he agreed it wasn't suitable, they would have found a way out.' His black and copper eyes seek mine out and he holds my gaze. 'I think it has more to do with your father.'

My pulse thrums in my ears. I know literally nothing about my father. Except that Siosal killed him. That my mother loved him.

'How so?' I make myself ask. 'If there was nothing romantic between her and the Custodian, why did it matter?'

'Your father was human,' Lochlain says gently. 'And Catriona was nothing if not a dreamer of a better world. We know she wanted to change the structure of how she received council, what if she saw the joining of our worlds as the solution to each of our downfalls and the Custodian disagreed?'

'Because he has a different view on what Airlie's future looks like,' I say, matter-of-fact.

We watch each other for a moment as my thoughts whirl. Part of me thinks I could talk about this for hours, around and around, trying to make it fit, to force it to make sense. But, as I reflect on what Lochlain has told me, I wonder what else I could know that would make it better. And the truth is, nothing will. The only thing I can do from here is move forward.

'As General, do you agree this is the right plan? Gather information and go to Kailoh?' I ask. 'You didn't want me to go to Rhyton without you.'

His brows quirk downwards. 'I don't. But, you and me, we're the pillars that Airlie stands on – the Queen and her General. As much as I don't want you to go without me, I trust you'll be in safe hands. That you will make sure you're safe. Because we will be in the places that play to our strengths. You in Rhyton to work out the connection to here, and me in Airlie to learn about the Givings and watch over the crown.'

I sigh, letting the anger shift away. I wouldn't ask Lochlain to leave Airlie without their new General, but that doesn't mean I'm looking forward to being away from him.

'I'll miss you,' I say quietly.

Lochlain's soft smile is impossible not to return and the fire he creates in my belly is just as compelling.

'How long do you think you'll look at me like that?' I ask, pushing aside the curls that fall across his forehead as he looks down at me.

He cocks his head quizzically, those ringed eyes of his that peek out underneath are my own personal kindling. 'Like what?'

'Both like I'm a treasure beyond compare, and one you'd like to devour,' I whisper, running my fingertips down his neck.

His smile broadens and he lazily winds his arms around my back, pressing me against his body, my heels lifting off the floor as I stretch up into him.

'Given each of those are, in fact, true – for now, I will say never. But a part of me is thankful to have been given this extra time outside the Palace.'

'For now you will say never?' My eyebrows shoot up and he laughs, picking me up so I can loop my legs around his hips.

Lochlain walks slowly with me still around his waist to a bedroom. His soft lips trail my neck and nip my ear as we go, and it doesn't take long for my thoughts to wash away. My body presses harder into his of its own accord as his hands explore my back and the roundness of my ass. He takes the back of my head in one hand and pulls my hair back gently so I look at him, my scalp tingling pleasantly.

Touching his mouth to mine, he's slow and gentle and far more contained than the heat that's rising in me. Dropping my feet back to the floor, I pull him over to the bed and seat him in front of me. Standing between his knees, I lift his shirt to expose the wolf who's crossed with weapon straps. Lochlain's chest is slightly sweaty underneath the leather where they are tightest on his skin, but I leave them on. He's pure power and my heart rate quickens at having some over him, too.

I push him back to lie on his elbows and then allow my pants to slide to the floor as he watches greedily. Sitting astride his hips, I press myself against him gently until his shoulders tremble and he closes his eyes. Undoing his pants just enough to free him, I slowly ease myself down where I wait for a beat or two before pushing hard and taking the entirety of him within me. I grin as he inhales sharply. His beauty never ceases to amaze me and having him here, underneath me where I am in total control, is a heady sensation. I rock my hips back and forth as I move on him, my breath coming more quickly. Looking at his weapons straps, and knowing I have control because he feels safe enough to give it to me, is what ultimately starts to tip me over the edge.

Lochlain reaches his hand to where we join and pushes a thumb against me as I move around him. The tension in my core is almost unbearable and I reach back to support myself on his legs as I arch into his touch and take him at the same time. His thighs start to contract under my fingers, and I rock harder.

Lifting my head from where it's fallen back, I watch his release play out across his features and my name slip from his lips. He never stops the pressure of his hand for me and I shatter around him, collapsing on his chest.

He pulls my face closer and kisses me deeply, his breathing still ragged. As I lie my head on his chest and listen to his breathing even out, I know he doesn't doze off. There's alertness to both of us as we wait for the others to return, the ticking down of the time remaining beating in time with my pulse.

I think on the words Lochlain used earlier. About having extra time. About us being two pillars of the Court. But, as I think about what I am aiming to do with the information I can gather for Kailoh and myself, and the expression on the faces of the Airlie Calahi when they look at Lochlain, I can't bring myself to ask him what he meant. What being in the Palace together, with me as Queen, will mean for us.

Because pillars stand on their own.

Ciara, Phoenix, Blaire, and I are taken to the edge of Rhyton by Rory, leaving us just inside the tree line. Not far from the point where I'd sat on my way to the coastal towns, ready to leave Driarn. Instead, I'd opened my mother's box and cried – ready to surrender myself to the Whispers.

It's easy to let Elenlea take priority over Rhyton when I'm in the Realm. Elenlea is all-consuming and, with my family and Lochlain there, there is little immediate need for me to focus on the woes of Driarn. Outside of trying to puzzle out the Commissioner's connection. But the suffocating heat, and the faces of those relegated to the dock slums, bring it all crashing back. Long ago, I'd sworn an oath to protect these people – even from themselves.

Instead, I have abandoned them for another cause, another love.

When we make our way through the dockside slums and up the stone road to the city gates, a hunched figure watches. Drawing closer, sapphire and hazel eyes find mine. She smiles sadly at me as we continue our approach in the dwindling light of day, nodding at Ciara.

'You found them, I see,' she says in a brittle voice.

Help them, they're dying. You must help them. Her words from our first meeting flash in my memory and I realise she knew, it was me she was missing. I glance at Ciara, a little wide-eyed, and she kneels before the woman and offers her water flask.

'Thank you, you have given us much hope,' she says.

The woman laughs. 'You were always such a sweet girl. How's the cross one?'

'Aeyva?' Ciara asks, but no surprise shows on her face.

The woman makes a noncommittal sound in the back of her throat.

'She's well, thank you.'

'I don't believe that for a moment, and neither do you.' The woman looks pointedly at Ciara. 'You know the key that will release her happiness and yet you refuse to give it to her.' Ciara looks torn between walking away, and her reluctance to be rude. 'Despite it being the very same thing that will release your happiness.'

Abruptly, Ciara stands and dusts off her pants. 'It was lovely to see you, be well. If you ever need help to get home, please let me know,' she says.

She shakes her head. 'These people need us more than ever,' the beggar says as we prepare to walk away. Her eyes light with intensity when she holds my gaze. 'We're all connected, my Queen. The first one knew that, too, but her story has been lost to time.'

My first instinct is to be surprised by her statement, that she would know things. But I find I'm not at all surprised, she just confirms the nagging that's been sitting in the back of my mind. That there is a link between Rhyton and the Realm that's bigger than what I currently understand. I take Ciara's place where she knelt before her and look into her lined face. The grit on the stone road digs into my knees in a way that's completely familiar. I can't even begin to count the number of times I have patrolled this road.

'What can you tell me?' I ask, taking her hands in mine.

'Nothing you don't already know,' she says sadly. 'But you don't have much time. I can feel the life draining out of it all.'

She closes her eyes and it's clear the conversation is over.

'You know her?' I ask Ciara as we walk towards the city gates.

'She was one of the first Royalists, a Manorynx in training.' Ciara looks at me sideways when I don't answer. 'It was our first good piece of information that you might actually be alive. She volunteered to be based here very early on in our search, not unlike Benny. But she insists she's not ready to return – that she doesn't want to leave Rhyton until you're Queen.'

How long the Royalists have looked for my mother and me is overwhelming. These passionate and gifted Calahi, loyal to someone they didn't know. Loyal to an idea. Staring into the face of my city, I can't reconcile the two parts of myself – who I know myself to be, and who I am in their eyes.

There's a tugging in my gut that tells me I need to help them both. As I glance around the shanty town that leads up to the dockside gates, a place that's much quieter at this early hour than normal, I know I can't give up my commitment to them. And Kailoh is still my best hope at helping both Elenlea and Rhyton, at understanding all the linkages between them. Rhyton might not know of his existence, but it doesn't change the reality that having access to his knowledge and resources will make my position stronger. If I'm going to ask him for an alliance, then I will be damn well informed before I do so.

There are answers in this city I intend to find.

CHAPTER TEN

LISH

Blaire's apartment is in tatters. We're not too far outside the leave period she'd requested from Robard, and she was confident they wouldn't have replaced her yet. As far as we can tell, that's correct, but someone obviously thought she was hiding something. I rub my face.

'I'm so sorry, B,' I whisper.

My jaw tightens as I watch Blaire sift through what remains of her belongings. Although another thought pushes through – would we still have Blaire if she had been here?

Phoenix's apartment was the same, although he isn't taking it as hard. There was little he was attached to here apart from the six of us. Particularly me, at one stage, but I can tell that's shifted. The stinging hurt that brushed alongside his desire for me diminishes day by day.

Blaire sniffs slightly and Phoenix gives her shoulder a squeeze. I've blocked out their emotions for this journey but the blush that dusts her cheekbones gives her away. She managed to salvage her dancing shoes and tucks them into her pack now. She looks up to find Ciara watching and shrugs slowly.

'Honestly, it's not so different to what we expected,' she says. 'I think it's safe to say the Commissioner recognised us at the Challenge and they've been looking for what we know. Now, it's our turn.'

'And you have a view on where to start?' My question echoes Aeyva's from earlier, and it dawns on me I should've asked this before we left. But my mind was spinning between the Custodian's claim and the steps ahead of me, including what else my magic can do and how I control it.

'I know the Commissioner, Lish,' she says. 'He was not coerced into being in Elenlea.'

'Knowing him is a bit of a stretch, isn't it?' I ask, remembering shaking his hand at our graduation.

She pauses a fraction of a moment, not enough to make Phoenix look at her but enough for me to understand. To remember what she'd said in Lochlain's cabin about getting close ... again.

'Not really,' she says, holding my gaze. 'He had motive to be in Elenlea and an informed one. He's a smart man, Lish – there was something he was getting from being there. Something more than just keeping the existence of the Realm quiet in Driarn.'

'Captain Robard's office might give us something,' I say.

It feels like a lifetime ago I bristled at Riley stealing his access card to get the missing person files. And here I am, suggesting we break into his office.

'I can do better,' Blaire says quietly. 'I know where the Commissioner lives.'

Blaire leads us through the night covered streets of Rhyton, towards the Commissioner's house. Not his primary home, she explains quietly, but where he spends much of his time. His wife and children live in an apartment on the other side of the city. The memories of Rhyton pull at me as we walk. This is the only home I can remember clearly. Even though I would give many memories of the orphanage away if I could, it's still where I met Will. And, for good or for bad, I wouldn't be who I am today without it. The bar where we celebrated our graduation from the Guard College is just around the corner. Perhaps that's why the Commissioner has chosen this area for his second residence.

The Commissioner's place is a ground floor unit with a garden that's large by Rhyton standards, although very small compared to Elenlea. We just can't grow the same things here. From our vantage point at an outdoor table at the wine bar on the corner, I can see three private security personnel. They appear to watch over the garden primarily, with two in the vegetable section. I imagine the Commissioner has a good garden at his family home and enough money to buy fresh produce when he needs it. So what purpose he has for this garden to be doubly guarded isn't clear. Until a young woman walks down the street with a small bag of potatoes. I can't be sure, but I'd be willing to bet money she came from the Commissioner's place.

I turn to look at Blaire, seated across the wide timber table. Her fawn-coloured eyes flick between mine for a moment.

'It wasn't like that with us,' she whispers, spots of colour appearing on her cheeks.

'Wouldn't matter if it was,' Phoenix says quietly without looking at her, a complex wave of emotion coming from him.

My heart beats loudly in my ears as I watch Phoenix reach out to Blaire and thread his fingers through hers. My breath catches, her cheeks flush deeper. This is what I wanted. For both of them. But there's still a pang in my chest I can't explain.

I slide my eyes to Ciara to find she's watching me in the shadows. I smile at her, willing my awkwardness away and take a sip of the pale gold wine in front of me. Quickly followed by some iced water.

'Where's he likely to be?' I ask Blaire quietly.

'In the office. He would ... ah'—she looks at Phoenix's hand in hers as if she can't believe it's there—'after, he works from his office.' She jerks her head in indication. 'Northern window, near the back. Those three should be the only security.'

'There has to be more than we can see, surely,' I say. 'He's the Commissioner, wouldn't he need more personal security than that?'

'I've never worked on his detail,' Phoenix says, 'but I'm pretty sure he has one.'

Blaire just shrugs slightly. 'It wasn't something I had to worry about.'

Ciara opens her mouth to say something, but my attention snags on a second woman walking away from the direction of the Commissioner's not-so-secret residence. Her auburn hair is ratty and she fiddles nervously with it as she hurries. She's a far cry from the last time I saw her, but I recognise her as Claire. She was on duty at the library the day Benny was killed.

I drop my gaze and subtly duck my head towards Ciara to hide my face as she walks past the wine bar. I'm not sure what makes me do it, but I didn't need to worry. Claire glances around anxiously at everything, but I get the sense she's not seeing anything at all. On a hunch, I give her a moment to get a couple of paces beyond the wine bar before I slip off my stool and motion to the others to follow. Phoenix, Blaire, and I have worked together long enough for them to catch on quickly, and Ciara clearly isn't a stranger to this either.

Claire continues to hurry along the street, unsuccessfully hiding a limp. She's frailer than I remember, and my heart goes out to her. She has clearly suffered some kind of trauma or loss since the last time I saw her as a fresh-faced and eager recruit, optimistic even in the face of a violent murder. We lose sight of her when she ducks into an alley close to the city centre. Ciara grabs for me quickly and motions to us to pause. I listen but keep my eyes glued to the alley. I'm not familiar with it and can't be sure if it's a dead end or not. A little voice in my mind asks if this is sensible and if we should have gone to the Commissioner directly, but everything else screams this is the right path, I cannot let her slip away.

Ciara closes her eyes for a moment before a warm buzz starts to radiate around me, like an orb, and I glance at her.

'It will make us harder to detect,' she explains, her voice quiet. A fraction uncertain.

'Do not try to tell me you've just made us invisible,' Phoenix frowns, looking at his hands.

Ciara huffs quietly, a hint of sadness in the soft sound. 'No, for that I'd have to kill you. I've just given a little cover. You still need to be silent and focused but it should keep anyone's gaze settling on us too long.'

Phoenix stares at her, mouth open slightly.

'I - it's'—she sighs—'I can break down barriers and connections. What you can see and hear, the walls in your mind so I can communicate with you – see what you have seen. And ... between life and death. So, I keep it small.'

None of us respond, and she shifts a little uncomfortably.

'Let's move,' she instructs.

We position ourselves behind a solar control box not far from where Claire is talking animatedly.

'—solution. I can't do this anymore.' Her voice is a harsh whisper and carries faintly on the hot breeze.

Judging by the build, Claire's companion is a woman, but her face is obscured by her large, wide-brimmed hat. It's not really needed at this time of night but it's not unusual for people to still be wearing them after being out in the day.

'I know,' the other woman says sadly. 'I'm so sorry this has been happening to you. Come with me now, don't go back. We can keep you safe.'

'I can't,' Claire stifles a sob. 'If I don't go back, they will take my family. You know that. Don't tell me you can keep me safe, it's a false hope.'

'We'll stop them, Claire.'

'It will be too late for me, but promise you will. That I haven't taken these risks for nothing. It has to stop.'

The second woman takes one of Claire's hands. 'Never for nothing, I will make it count. I promise.'

I furrow my eyebrows in question at Phoenix, hoping his childhood on the streets might shed some light on what this conversation might be about. He shakes his head, scraping his honey-brown hair off his face; he doesn't know what this is about either. The two women look at each other for a moment. Gently, a sense of compassion drifts up the alleyway and I imagine the second woman wanting to hold Claire to give her some small comfort. But wherever Claire has gone, she's too far for that.

Abruptly the women step apart and Claire turns back the way she came. I hold my breath as she passes us crouched together behind the large, grey box.

'How long will your magic hold?' Phoenix whispers to Ciara. I watch the other woman who stands motionless where Claire left her.

'I can keep it up for about half an hour, but you won't be able to stray far.'

Phoenix looks at me expectantly and I nod, breaking away with Ciara to follow Claire, knowing he and Blaire will trail the second woman if, and when, she moves.

Ciara and I follow behind Claire for several minutes before I realise she's heading back to the Guard Residence, not the Commissioner's house like I'd wondered. My lips purse of their own accord. The security at the Residence has been quite light historically but it could still pose a challenge for us to follow Claire.

Instead of heading into the Guard Residence, though, Claire glances around her and keeps walking straight to a fence, beyond which lies vacant land. It had been built up at one point, but the buildings were deemed too expensive to retrofit against the weather. So, they were demolished to make way for more secure dwellings.

She disappears into the darkness.

Scrambling to catch up, Ciara and I reach the fence with no obvious gate.

'Here,' Ciara whispers.

Below a very small dip in the level of the ground, just deep enough for someone to lie in, is a hole in the fence. I hold the wire up so Ciara can wriggle through, the tension in the fence cutting into my palm as I try to give her room. She mimics me so I can follow and we look out over a desolate, will-be construction site. Large chunks of concrete are dotted around the flat expanse that's been excavated into the ground like a huge, shallow hole. Along with a handful of portable building offices covered in solar panels that glint softly in the moonlight.

There's no sign of Claire.

We begin to skirt the perimeter of the site quickly, looking for anything of note. Ciara moves like air, not making a single sound. I have no idea what Calahi vision is like but she seems to be navigating the way in the dark quite well, so I follow her lead. About a third of the way around, Ciara grips my elbow and points down. Just below us is a shadowed area, a bit darker than the rest of the site. As I start to shake my head, not understanding, my eyes adjust a little better and I realise it's not one shadow but a collection of shadows.

People.

And none of them are moving.

From behind a chunk of concrete, Claire creeps forward and fades into the group of people. The darkness snaps at my skin and the hairs on the back of my neck prickle uncomfortably. I glance at Ciara. She's hard to see in the moonlight and I can't make out anything of her eyes, which tells me they must be wholly black, all the gold consumed. Her head is turned towards me, though, and she squeezes my hand gently before tugging me along, closer to the group of people.

We crawl around to the same large concrete boulder Claire appeared from and peer around the side. As my eyes continue to adjust, I make out a cleared, circular space, two rectangular buildings on one side. Before us, in the centre of the cleared space, the shape of the people appear to be mostly in their physical prime, no elderly and no children. Every one of them is chained to the ground. Bile rises in my throat. This is my city, my people. A rough city, and one that turns its eye to the suffering outside its walls, but not an inherently cruel one. Not an evil one. Images of my time with General Siosal spring before my eyes. How they'd shackled Will to the roof and beaten him. I'd never considered similar things could be happening in my childhood home. Not on this scale.

For a time, nothing happens. The people are mostly still with only the occasional shifting of position. The thought of them being out here during the day is like a stone dropping into my stomach. If that's what is happening to them, I'm surprised they've lasted the day. The heat of Rhyton is dangerous even for those that have provisions and shelter.

Boots crunch on the gravel behind us and we shrink back into each other against the boulder as two armed men march into the group. They obviously don't expect to be discovered here and, apart from loosely holding their weapons, don't seem to take any precautions of staying hidden. A small floodlight from one of the buildings comes on, illuminating the space.

'Time for your next dose,' one of the men says in a deep voice, releasing the shackles on the limp figure closest to him. Ciara squeezes my arm and I bite my tongue not to call out.

Claire.

The other man grips her hair at the base of her skull and drags her forward. Her attempts at escape are feeble and he jerks her head to the side, exposing her neck to him.

Her words *too late for me* come back and I understand, in that moment, that she knew. She knew this would be the last time for her, of whatever this is.

'We have to do something,' I whisper to Ciara, palming the pistol I'd taken from Rory – he had no qualms about me using it outside the Realm.

Ciara nods but a scream pierces the air before we can move.

The man roughly shoves a large syringe into Claire, embedding it deep.

I cover my mouth to stifle my own scream as Claire's eyes bulge and her skin burns to black at the injection site. Quickly, the blackness fans out from the syringe, running away from it like a spider's web.

'Fuck,' one of the men mutters. 'She was supposed to be promising.'

The last thing that's recognisable is her right eye as it lifts to the dark night sky in a silent prayer before her lifeless body is dropped into the dirt – at the feet of the men that killed her.

CHAPTER ELEVEN

AEYVA

'The entrance is just around this bend,' I tell Riley as the trees start to thin out a little.

'Thank God for that,' she says.

I look over to her, striding along the stone road. Rory is a step behind her – I'm not the only one noticing how she walks. For different reasons I'd venture. I'd debated bringing a human to Rothani at all but, for better or worse, we're all in this together now, and I have no doubts in mine or Rory's ability to keep her safe. She's confident, Riley, which has served her well in the Realm so far, and I can only assume in Rhyton before that. But Rothani is less welcoming to humans than Airlie and her humanness is hard to hide. It's been some time since I was last in the Court of Rothani, but the memory of watching humans in chains dancing on the stage is vivid. The binds chafed where their skin was dry and slipped where it was wet with blood from the whippings. My companion at the time had laughed heartily, his handsome face twisted by cruelty.

It was the last time he'd watched.

Nakiasha, Queen of Rothani, was renowned for keeping humans as pets and I imagine she hasn't changed – it's her favourite method of punishment for those she blames for the decline of our magic. The knowledge the Custodian already has her support is a complication I'd hoped wouldn't happen so soon. And definitely not when he's put Lish in such a difficult position. If she were to make her claim now, the citizens of Airlie could effectively have two Queens to choose from: one they know, with an established Court who has already promised to support them; or Lish, a half-human they've never seen before whose face is now associated with the murder of our beloved former Queen.

It's not hard to know where their support would go.

The road curves around the edge of the river and the warded entrance to the Rothani capital catches the sunlight ahead. Its tall, slightly arched top reflects like a beacon against the blue sky.

'Does it matter how we go through?' Riley asks.

'With me,' Rory says seriously. 'In here, you are always with me.'

Riley looks back over her shoulder briefly, her eyes flaring.

'Okay,' is her only response as she looks forward again. I glance at Rory just in time to see his shoulders relax slightly.

'Was it this quiet when you last came?' I ask Rory as we keep drawing closer. He looks at me for a long moment and shakes his head.

'There're no guards at the entrance,' he says quietly, glancing around us. 'That's very unusual.'

Rory steers us off the road and into the tree line that runs alongside, the heavy green foliage giving us some cover. There's not a soul in sight as we approach the entrance from the side, Calahi or otherwise, and it's quickly clear why. The magic of the entrance has been sealed. Its normally pale, shimmering veil where we would have walked through is now a solid wall. The borders that run between Courts are always shut, bar the official entrances; there's no simply going around the gate. Some time ago, Keeva had mused that Nakiasha was preparing to tighten her Court, but we couldn't land on a plausible reason why. Now, it seems she was right, even if I still don't know why.

'I know another way in,' I say. 'But we'll need to be careful.'

I explain to Rory where we need to go and, in less than a beat, we are standing in a small clearing beside a large boulder. His hand lingers on Riley's upper arm before he catches me watching and drops it. Riley doesn't appear to notice.

'Under here,' I whisper, this part of the wood is not a place to linger.

Riley's eyebrows rise. '*Under* the rock?'

I ignore her and kneel before the stone, placing both hands palm down in the dirt and grass and speak the words I was taught so long ago. The rock begins to shudder silently, and an entrance opens below it.

'Stay close and quiet.' I eye Rory. 'Both of you. And whatever you see here, you will not breathe a word of it to anyone else. Got it? Not even the others.'

'Who is your source?' Riley asks, instead of giving me her assurance.

I glance at Rory, his face equally determined, and I square my shoulders as I turn to them.

'Their identities are not normally for sharing,' I say tightly. 'But I am meeting my … friend, Keeva, who runs the bar we are about to step into. I mean it though, not one word.'

I don't wait for a response before leading them through. This is the furthest I've ever let anyone come into my other life and my teeth are on edge for how closely my two halves intersect here. We arrive in the dusty storeroom of an old haunt of mine. One full of Society members and one I now avoid at all costs, if only to preserve whatever is left of who I used to be. I suck in the musty air and try not to cough at the intrusion of dust.

The old timber stairs creak under Rory's weight behind me and the small door is swung open before I even reach for the handle.

'Mother above!' Keeva says. 'We were starting to think you were dead. But then the bod—'

'I'm not here for long. I need information,' I say over her.

'You're joking, I assume,' Keeva says. 'Countless turns around the sun with no word at all and now you *want* something from me?'

Her red hair is cut shorter than I saw it last, with a longer fringe that curls attractively around her face. She's still beautiful. But that face hides a darker side that matches my own. At one point in my life, I didn't think darkness and darkness should go together. But I now know darkness doesn't go with light either.

'Yes.'

She scoffs. 'So, nothing's changed then.'

She looks Riley and Rory over, a hungry grin beginning to appear as she assesses Riley in particular.

'She's with me, I'd prefer if you don't look.'

Keeva's emerald, brown-ringed eyes flick back to mine. She cocks her head. 'With you?'

I let the silence stretch out.

'Well then,' she says, turning away.

She's waiting at the bar with four drinks ready when we come into the larger, but still gloomy, room. Timber tables and stools are strewn about haphazardly. A small number of humans, in clothes that have caught the grime of the place, wait tables. Which is a nonsense, really, when everyone in here has enough magic to have the bar run itself. The humans are for entertainment – to remind the patrons they still have some power over another being, despite their bargains, their obligations to the Society.

Rory falls in behind Riley, so close I imagine her hair moves with his breath. I step tight in front as we move through the space. Every face in the place is focused on Riley, and Riley alone. Even in Airlie, a human could warrant a high price – or at least an evening of entertainment. Here, they are even more highly valued ... just not for how well they live. I seat Riley at the bar between Rory and me, Keeva on my other side, her sunset hair a beacon in the dark room. Leaning my back against the bar, I monitor the room in front of me and Riley at my side. She reaches for the drink in front of her and Rory knocks it from her hand. Pungent smelling liquid splashes over the three of us.

'You've heard Nakiasha is lending her support to Airlie, I take it?' I ask Keeva, who's taking in every detail, ignoring the surprise on Riley's face at her spilled drink.

She stares at me.

'I want to know everything you do,' I say.

Her gaze softens slightly, and she reaches out and tucks a stray strand of hair back into the braid at the top of my head. I tense slightly as she runs her fingers over one of the shaved sides, her gaze soft.

'Everything,' I say again.

'You're no fun anymore, you know that? Maybe you should've been dead.' She pouts.

'Maybe I will be soon, if you don't tell me what you know.'

She sighs deeply. 'I guess that wouldn't be so fun, either.'

She clicks her fingers, hiding us from the eyes and ears of the other patrons who grumble loudly as Keeva's shield effectively makes us invisible. They know we're still here, though, and I continue to watch them carefully in Riley's presence.

'You know there's more going on, or you wouldn't be here,' she says.

'Like what?' I ask, not giving away how little I really know.

'What are you going to give me for this exchange, pray tell?' she asks in return, trailing her fingers along the counter.

I smile slowly at her. 'Your life, how about that?'

She quirks an eyebrow, knowing there's no real threat in my words.

'And,' I add, 'maybe, one day, I'd think about a trip down memory lane with you.'

I have no intention of doing anything of the sort.

'That's cheating, you know I can never resist you.' She drains her drink and nods at Rory before looking pointedly to the drink he knocked from Riley. 'That was offensive you know; it was my finest.'

She stares at Riley for a long moment who just watches back, Rory closer than her shadow.

'Interesting company you keep, Aeyva.' She looks out over her patrons. 'I could get a good price for her, you know. I bet she looks fucking good with less on.'

Rory bristles but Riley only scoffs.

'It's a time sensitive offer, Keeva,' I say.

'Fine. Nakiasha has closed her borders to uninvited guests. Thinks she has, anyway – this is the only accessible entrance to Rothani. But she wants to know exactly who is in, and out, of her Court. The only *official* entrance is in her Palace itself.' Her gaze flicks to mine. 'You know she's given her support to your Custodian. But she's also been working on gaining additional resources for some time now. They say they're preparing to bring an army in – she's offered up her Court as their training ground.'

I frown.

'Kailoh's?' I ask, not actually believing he would let his army be given to, or borrowed by, Nakiasha. Not when the value she places on any lives outside her Court is so much lower than his own. And especially not when he knows we have Lish.

But there are only three Courts in the Realm, so he's the only option.

'I'm told it's an outside force.'

'An *outside* force? There haven't been any armies from outside the Realm. Ever.'

'No, but that's how the story goes. Nakiasha's found one that will both fight for her and the Custodian and bring their own magic.'

'And Kailoh doesn't know?' I ask.

'Not yet. I only found out in the last few cycles. I saw him just last week, he asked after—'

'So we're definitely looking at a potential war. You sure you don't know any more about where they're from? Or what they want?'

A human man, who looks much older than I'd guess he is, refills her glass and she drains it, too, before shaking her head. No surprise registers on his face that he can't see who is drinking it. He's either very used to Keeva's magic or has lost all ability to question anything he sees here. I finish my own drink and survey the room again, no one's moved.

'Thanks Keeva, I appreciate it.'

'I thought you said everything?' she asks coyly.

'Spit it out.'

She sighs. Petulance was never a good look on her. 'The Custodian is looking to garner internal support as well. In case this ... army ... falls through.' Keeva circles the bottom edge of her glass on the countertop. 'You are perhaps the only one who can stop that kind of support.' She glances at Rory and Riley before shaking her head slightly. 'I'd suggest the circumstances aren't ideal, but if you want to influence the way it will go, you need to move now.'

I stare at her, my mind going through the options even as I know what Keeva is saying. I know Kailoh isn't supporting Nakiasha or the Custodian, which means there's only one remaining option. I study Keeva's eyes. They don't leave mine, the message there entirely clear.

Shit.

I forbade Riley and Rory to ask questions, but I can see them in their faces as Rory deposits us a short distance from the border of Airlie and Mercasia. Just on the edge of a small village I frequent. His eyes are more knowing than Riley's and I look away, unable to hold his gaze. This little town has always been a favourite of mine and a small amount of tension leaves my shoulders as we walk the dirt main road. It's a place where the Calahi aren't jaded by the bigger players in the Realm. Wholesome, is how I would describe it. Something so different to me but perhaps pieces of it will rub off each time I visit.

I should visit more often.

The inn is a two-storey, white building with a thatched roof. There are still a handful of buildings like this in Elenlea, but not like this village where they have meticulously maintained them. They are fully booked aside from my usual room. Even the Calahi seek out that which is quaint as an escape from their daily lives. But I pay well and they respect my privacy. My room is never disturbed.

'Do I know anything about you?' Rory whispers as we follow Riley up the wooden stairs. Once again, though, his eyes are not on me.

'Hopefully all the things that matter.'

My room is light with large windows and heavy curtains. It's a stretch to call it mine, really. It's not home, but it's a piece of it. Another place that lives in the in-between of my lives. Not quite there, but not totally here, either. There's a generously-sized bed and a cot that comes from underneath – not that I've ever used it. I haven't been here with anyone else before and it feels cramped with Rory and Riley occupying the space that shouldn't be theirs. Not uncomfortable, exactly, I don't do uncomfortable with Rory, but definitely cramped.

Riley sits on the bed and groans as she removes her boots, rubbing her feet. Rory leans back casually in the chair at the small table, his posture at odds with the fact I know he is at full attention in this new place. And the questions I could see in his eyes earlier look like they're about to break free.

In Loch's cabin, I'd said no to finding the Eternal Queen, the thought of doing so winds a hard knot of tension into the base of my neck. But Keeva's thoughts were clear – the Custodian is trying to secure additional internal support and I might be the best Calahi to stop it. That support could only be one individual.

I'm done with the Society, I know that in my bones. I'm just not ready to tell the Eternal Queen. But I do need to ask her not to support the

Custodian. I just wish I didn't have to act now, while I have Rory and Riley in tow.

CHAPTER TWELVE

AEYVA

Rory got us closer to the border of Mercasia after an uneventful night at the inn. He is skilled enough to take us across the borders himself but the Courts have wards in place to alert them of that sort of activity. So, we've spent the day walking through the woods to a rarely used, Society-only entrance close to the largest city of Mercasia – Ilcaena, where Kailoh will be.

The network of entrances I use are known to only a handful of Calahi – those of us in the Society who have served long enough – and showing them so blatantly to Rory and Riley has its own risks. Ones I hope don't come to fruition. But I can't use the main entrance here, either, without publicly alerting Kailoh to my presence and I don't want to see him again yet.

I know how excited Kailoh is for this alliance based on my descriptions of Lish, even though the Custodian's accusation will make it much harder for him to openly make it. But, despite the ripples it might cause in the Realm, I know he'll be too curious to turn her away. When I do arrive publicly, it will be with my Queen.

And I don't trust him not to interfere with what I must do now. Because, in this small space between the borders of the Courts, I will walk a fine line with the Eternal Queen and sometimes his good intentions can bring more trouble than they're worth. Keeva's words have played on repeat since I saw her. The Custodian is looking for additional support, and this one could obliterate Airlie just for the fun of it.

The portal, concealed behind a waterfall, is not the ideal entrance to a city much colder than ours and I shiver once we're through. Beyond the trees ahead of us, the outskirts of the city begin with small timber houses whose chimneys puff white smoke. Their primitive appearance is deceptive though; the interior of many of these houses is quite modern, and warm.

'Just here,' I say, walking further into the wood and away from the houses before us.

'This place is incredible,' Riley breathes with a puff of white air as she hugs herself for warmth. We're dry, but I should have prepared her for the cold. I forget humans are a shade more sensitive to it than Calahi. Or, perhaps, it's just because they have less time to acclimatise. Rory takes a step towards Riley that's so subtle I'm not sure he even knows he makes it. But she turns into him slightly, soaking up his warmth by proximity anyway.

The cabin is nestled in a thicket of trees almost entirely hidden from view. If I wasn't looking for it, it would be very hard to find; the shields assist with making it difficult, of course. It can only be found by those given permission to do so. I turn to Rory.

'You two should—'

'No,' he says, his face torn with worry. Riley watches us quietly.

'Ror—'

'You said no questions, Aeyva, and I'm trying to honour that, but you are putting me in an impossible situation. I either let you go on alone – you think I can't feel how powerful the magic here is? – or take ... my Queen's Riley into whatever craziness this is.' He points at me. 'Whatever happens, I have eyes on both of you at all times.'

There's a faint popping as one of the shields is lowered.

'This is a pleasant surprise.'

The voice filters through the trees.

My palms itch, desperate for my knives. I close my eyes for a moment, praying I could take it back. That I could be here without Rory and Riley. I draw my shoulders back, tension rippling through my limbs.

I try to smile.

Rory and Riley follow silently behind me as I turn once more and approach the cabin, something neither Lish or Lochlain would have done. I don't even want to think what Ciara would be doing if she were here. The door opens as we ascend the handful of wooden stairs and closes softly behind Rory once we're across the threshold. Three steaming mugs of coffee appear on the kitchen table and Riley frowns at them suspiciously.

'You normally come alone,' the soft voice echoes around us.

'I apologise for the intrusion,' I say, inclining my head slightly as is proper.

'You know what happens to those who betray me, Aeyva Kaylneau. Do your companions understand the risk?'

Two sets of eyes narrow at me.

'They do,' I lie.

They'll get the gist of it, even if I didn't tell them before we came. Betray her location and end up worse than dead – your family too. Pretty standard for our line of work, even if her methods are a touch more unusual.

I wave a heavy hand at Rory and Riley.

'We do,' they say in hesitant unison.

There's no response for a moment or two, and I force myself to release a slow breath.

'Know I only ignore this infraction,' her voice bounces gently around the empty kitchen, 'due to who escorts you. Arrive here without Aeyva, and you will not find me so accommodating.'

The tension in the room rises markedly, along with the sharpness in her tone.

Riley ducks her head, mimicking my earlier action, even as her eyes flick around the room. Looking for the source of the voice. 'Understood,' she says. She's a fast learner and, thankfully, Rory follows a beat later.

'My Eternal Queen,' I begin. Rory's stare flies to me and I ignore the burn it leaves on my skin. 'I have come to ask a favour of you.'

A gentle laugh chuckles around us and Riley rubs her arm. The dappled sunlight through the kitchen window catching the hairs that now stand on end on her limbs.

'You have come to the right place, Aeyva, you know that. I do so enjoy fulfilling favours.'

I open my mouth but she cuts me off.

'I know you are distancing yourself from me though.' My stomach clenches. 'And I understand, I do,' she continues gently. My heart slams in my chest, her understanding is often worse than her wrath. 'But I assume you are here to ask me not to supply forces to your Custodian and Queen Nakiasha?'

I nod, the confirmation they are working together not lost on me. 'Yes, Eternal One. What need should they have for additional forces? If they are granted, I fear what will happen to all the Realm if we find ourselves in a position of war.'

'I have a Society to keep employed, Aeyva. You know full well the opportunities war presents. Yet you ask me to turn them down? All while ignoring the space you put between us.'

'I know, Eternal One,' I say quietly. 'But the Society is supposed to be neutral. Supposed to stop those that would bring us down – not be part of it. I know war has been part of our past. But it is our past and it should remain so.'

'Is it not the natural order though, Aeyva? There is no leader in Airlie, so she is prime for the taking. It's simply the way the sands shift.'

I slowly turn in the kitchen as I talk, not knowing exactly where to rest my eyes but knowing she will see my face wherever I look. Riley and Rory are silent, and a small sliver of relief runs through me as they stay that way.

'There could still be a leader for Airlie, you know there are rumours an heir is still out there,' I say.

A cold mist creeps into the kitchen and begins to weave around our feet.

'You know something,' she says.

'I know it's still a possibility, yes.'

I breathe slowly, but not too deeply. I don't want her to know I am trying to calm myself. Trying to hide the knife edge I am standing on. She cannot know we have Lish. A fledgling Queen would be attractive enough for her to take under her wing, but I've heard enough rumours of her hatred for Roisin's line to not risk exposing Lish just yet.

A tendril of mist caresses my throat, leaving a slight wash of dampness on my skin in its wake. 'Nothing else you should share, my dear?'

I shake my head. Not much frightens me anymore, but I would be a fool if I didn't watch myself in her presence. Especially as I lie to her.

'Nothing more, my Eternal Queen.'

'I will consider your request, but I do not give my assistance lightly, Aeyva.'

I already knew there would be a cost if she agrees not to join this battle, but the reminder still makes my throat tighten. 'Thank you Eternal One, I am forever grateful.'

I turn back towards the door.

'The dead should stay that way, you know,' she says, and I stop short. Nuala has said something similar to me more than once. But more question than statement.

'Who?' I try to keep the demand from my voice.

'The one you do not wish me to know you seek.'

'I—' I don't know what to make of it.

'She will never be found, Aeyva. This true motive of yours is a fool's errand.' The mist almost dances around us as it darkens, the cold trying to bite at my clothes. Riley shivers. 'I suggest you occupy yourself with current matters of the Airlie Throne – and current only.'

I blink and the mist is white again.

'He is a fine specimen, Aeyva,' she says. 'I am pleased I was to meet him, in the end. He would have grown into a very good father.'

Riley's eyebrows shoot to the sky. Evidently, Lish was discrete. Rory bows deeply this time.

'Thank you, Eternal One,' he says.

I spin on my heel and walk away, trusting the others to follow.

Having gathered as much information as I can about Nakiasha's plans, we return to Lochlain's cabin. The cosy little house radiates a feeling of welcome and stirs a sense of unrest in me. It's a picture of a parallel life, one that might have been. One in which I would have raised my daughter to be wild and free. Where I'd have fallen in love with my best friend and we lived out our time – defending our Court by day and sitting in front of open fires by night. But that life didn't eventuate, and instead I am a visitor here. One without young, and a soul much darker than the one I started out with.

'You need to focus,' I say, returning my own mind to the task at hand.

I'd negotiated half a day with Ciara – half a day to test Lish and see what I can bring forth to show Kailoh when we go to him. Half a day for me, and then Nuala arrives. The Eternal Queen's comments about who we seek have played on my mind constantly since we left her cottage. We're searching for the Star. But the Star belonged to our First Queen, Roisin. Is that who she was referring to? I shouldn't really be surprised she knows a lot about our Realm, but there are three Calahi I will abide knowing more of our history and our path than me. Two of them are Manorynxes; one is a king. And only two of them still live.

Lish levels me with her green, ringless eyes. It still strikes me as odd that the Calahi rings didn't carry through to her, despite being of Roisin's line.

'I don't think my focus is the issue, Aeyva. I don't have the sort of magic you think I do. I don't know what happened with Rory, but I am telling you, it can't have been me,' she says.

I know without doubt that's not correct, and there's a glimmer of that understanding in her face, too. I also know Rory, and I know what he can do. And he is always, always, in control. Not since the days he first began his training has his magic looked like it did when Lish accessed it in the meadow – so obviously chaotic. I also know Lish was running high that day. She'd felt boxed in by her choices, and the Custodian's declaration she was wanted for her mother's death struck her in a vulnerable place. Somehow, I need to push her back there.

In another time, I would feel badly for what I need to do to make that happen. But, if Lish really does have powerful magic, magic that hasn't been seen in the Realm for a long time, we need her to access it. Taking a half-Calahi with no magic and no formal crown to Kailoh, and publicly asking for his alliance, would be madness. A madness I'm sure both Kailoh and I will face if we have to; but I would certainly prefer a magically intimidating Queen on my side.

There's something about Lish's abilities that nag at me. The way she was able to summon all that power at Lochlain's Challenge, accessing Rory's. It's not impossible – the history of it in our Realm is something I once had the opportunity to know better than anyone – I am sure of that much. But I pushed access to that knowledge aside in favour of the Society. Now,

I have to live with the gaps in my understanding, and figure it out another way.

'Try again,' I instruct. 'Imagine that flame you've talked about, and push it outwards.'

Lish stifles a sigh and reaches out to take Rory's arm once more. She closes her eyes and I hold my inhale. We've been at this for hours and Lish shifts slightly on her feet as if they're aching. Nothing more happens.

'Her name was Claire, right?' I ask.

Lish's eyes fly open but while there's a hint of steel there, her face remains relaxed.

'That won't work,' she says.

'Reminding you of what we're fighting?'

'We don't know what that was, or what we're going to do about it.'

'Perhaps,' I say. 'But if you stepped further into your magic, Lish, we could stop it,' I say. 'If you can do what we think you can do, you could almost be the most powerful person in the Realm.'

'Except that I'm not and I won't be, and you won't piss me off enough to tap into some non-existent "super magic".'

She drops Rory's arm and holds her hands together at her front. Patiently waiting for me to try again.

The weight of my knife tingles at my side. Physically, I could make Lish tap into her fear and overwhelm and trigger this part of her magic. She's talented, but far less brutal than me, and that means she would not be able to best me. But that shows her, and Rory, exactly who the Society has turned me into. I'm not that desperate.

Yet.

'Again,' I nod at her. Rory calmly pats her hand as she takes his arm once more.

'You can do this, sweetheart,' he says. 'I'll pour you a wine after.'

She smiles at him. 'If only it was that easy.' She closes her eyes again and sighs.

'Do you think Lochlain imagines a crown on your head when you're together?'

'Aeyva,' Rory warns, his tone telling me it's more than my management of Lish that's irked him. There's still the sting that I didn't tell him about my connection to the Eternal Queen's Society.

Lish keeps her eyes closed. The first sign I've hit a nerve.

'She's not my Queen yet, Ror, but Loch wants her to be his, doesn't he?' I continue.

Her breathing remains even.

'Don't be unkind, my love,' he says, and I ignore him.

'Does it worry you?' I ask. 'Not knowing how much of his feelings are for you instead of the crown? Do you know what the future holds for the Queen and a General?'

'Enough, Aeyva,' Rory snaps.

Lish says nothing. But she's so focused on ignoring me, she doesn't notice the slight blurring of her outline as she moves an inch towards Rory.

Without taking a step.

I hide my smile as I tuck away that piece of information. As for unpacking what it means, and the information the Eternal Queen shared, I need Nuala's help.

CHAPTER THIRTEEN

LISH

The scalding water of the shower beats down on the back of my neck and I relish the way it helps drown out the world. If only it could wash away what I saw in Rhyton and the reality that I leave for Kailoh's so soon. I'm both anxious and impatient to get there and meet the Calahi who has been quietly supporting the search for my mother and me. It would be far easier if she was here to tell me what to expect from him, from his Court, from being a Queen in a foreign world. But it's just me – and the little voice in my mind that tells me there's still so much more to learn.

But then that's not quite fair. It's not all just me, but a team of the best possible people and Calahi, and I will never give them up. Or give up on what they need. Even as Aeyva's words from earlier continue to furrow into my mind. Her objective was clear – tip me over the edge and hope I'd drag on Rory's magic, or my body's memory of it, but it takes more than that to make me lose it. I didn't survive my time in the orphanage by having a hair trigger.

Even if I don't appreciate her methods, I do understand what Aeyva is trying to do. The sensation of being whipped around the meadow, as if I'd been picked up by a tornado, makes my stomach a little uneasy. At the same time, there was something familiar about the way my flame responded ...

Aeyva knows what wounds to pick at, and this one feels raw. Ciara once told me how much Lochlain loved Airlie and how much he would sacrifice for his Court. It's been a thought I've tried to ignore since then – would I be included in those sacrifices? The undercurrent of concern the others have for us is clear in Aeyva's steely gaze as it flicks between us, the sadness in Ciara's. It's the memory of the Royal Watchman taking note of how Lochlain held me when we were told to run that sticks. How the disapproval in Pendita's gaze at the meeting of the Prominent Families made the hair on the back of my neck stand up.

But, running alongside it all, is the image of Claire as she died. I lean my forehead against the tiles. 'Promising' the man had said. Promising for what, exactly?

I let the shower wash my sigh down the drain before I press the heel of my palms into my eyes and attempt to get a grip on my emotions.

The bathroom door creaks open and I gasp as I try to cover myself.

'I'm in here,' I splutter, half choking on the water.

The door shuts again.

'That's what I was hoping for,' Lochlain's deep voice cuts through the steam and I smile despite the thoughts crowding my mind.

'Give me a second and I'll hop out.'

'I'd prefer you to stay where you are,' he says, opening the shower door.

I take an involuntary step back to better take in the sight of his naked form. His broad, dark tanned shoulders dwarf me in the shower and my skin tightens in response. He reaches out and tugs me forward by my hips until I stand flush against him.

'Rory told me about your session with Aeyva,' he says quietly.

'I told you I don't know how that ... wind event happened,' I say, examining his chest and trailing my fingers over the ears of his wolf.

He tips my chin up and gently forces me to look at him, the water running down his cheeks and over his lips.

'That's not what I was referring to.'

Great, just what I needed him to know.

'And?' I whisper.

He leans down towards me, dark curls dripping with water, and fixes me with his black and copper eyes.

'I can't say I haven't imagined you in that crown,' he says as he strokes my jaw. 'But the crown is not all I see.'

'Oh?'

'I see you, Lish. You don't need a crown for me to see you.' He kisses me deeply and I pull myself harder against him, savouring his ridges on my skin. 'This is a risk for me too,' he breathes. 'By all that is right, you should take your crown and be swept off your feet by some foreign King. By—'

I shake my head. 'Not possible.'

'No? Then perhaps you'll be a Queen who'll have a lover in every Court.'

I think on that for a moment. 'I can work with that vision.'

His eyes flash copper and he presses me against the cold wall of the shower. Lochlain drops his head to my neck and drags his teeth along my collarbone before kissing his way back up my neck and running his tongue along my bottom lip. He grips my ass and lifts me so my legs wrap around his hips, my weight pinned between him and the wall. My cheeks flush as heat courses its way through my chest and core. I tip my pelvis towards him to better feel the length that teases me. I could stay here forever. With the steaming water pounding down on us and washing away all sense of the outside world. My heart wants to beat out of my chest with what I feel for Lochlain and my physical reaction to him.

'Just know,' he breathes in my ear, sending lightning between my legs. 'There is no one – no one – who will make you feel like I do.'

I squeeze my thighs around him and slide my fingers into his wet hair as I kiss him again. His tongue sweeps mine and I groan into his mouth.

'Show me,' I whisper, and I lose myself in him. Throwing my head back on the cold wall as he does exactly that.

I hope the cabin has a magical hot water system as Lochlain and I reluctantly leave the intimate sanctuary of the shower. A pang of guilt hits me uncomfortably as I think of the scarcity of water in Rhyton, and I remember I don't understand enough of how this world works compared to my home. Nor how the two of them fit together when one doesn't know the other exists.

My towel wrapped around my wet body, I motion for Lochlain to sit on the edge of the tub. My gaze follows along his skin where I drag the plush towel. He has more scars than I can count, but they're mostly quite subtle. His natural healing ability combined with his magic makes it harder for him to permanently injure. The wound I healed, though, is more prominent along his side, clearly not as skilfully done.

He watches me take him in.

'I can't decide if you want to explore me or nurse me.'

I look back to his face expecting to find laughter there but he's genuinely curious. I smile softly.

'I guess both, really.' I shrug one shoulder. 'The day of the Challenge ... is hard to shake.' I close my eyes briefly, there is more than one nightmare I have about that day. 'What others like that are to come in this fight for Airlie?'

He takes my hands in his. 'I'm not going anywhere, Lish.'

'Promise?'

'Of course.' He pulls me closer and takes a deep breath. 'But there's something I need to tell you.'

'I'm not up for managing another wife of yours.'

He chuckles darkly and the sound electrifies the crackle that exists between us. 'No more bonded partners in the wings, of that I can definitely assure you. But,' his face turns serious, and I try to ignore the rise in the static on my skin, 'the Realm is a place of tradition and ...'

I wait, my pulse thundering in my ears.

'It will be ... difficult for us to be together when you become Queen. I can't be General and ... overtly ... yours.'

I frown at him, even though understanding is pressing on the edges of my mind. 'What do you mean?'

'You could have me as a lover, of course—'

'Lover?' My back teeth press closed and I force a breath out my nose.

'Well, the Queen is welcome to do whatever she pleases in that regard.' My stomach tightens in a different manner than it did earlier. 'But a Queen is generally expected to become bonded, if she isn't already.'

Bonded. My heart flutters, but I think it's got the wrong message. I can't bring myself to say anything. He releases one of my hands and runs his through his curls before shaking them loose, little droplets of water landing across my collar bones. 'And she should bond with someone worthy of her.'

'I - I don't understand, Lochlain. I've never even asked you about marriage – bonding. I know you've been bonded before and—'

'I mean the Realm won't like a Queen that's with her General. Not as her bonded partner.'

I stroke his hair and face, willing the possibilities that race through my veins to calm.

'Lucky I don't give a shit what the Realm thinks about that, then, isn't it?' But I can see in his face that he does. He always has.

I kiss him then, not prepared to hear any more about the Realm. Not when I have a Calahi in front of me I would seriously consider giving it all up for. Not that I've told him that in so many words. He draws back and presses his forehead between my breasts and mutters something against me.

It sounds like 'you will'.

The words twist in behind my ribs, taking a space I don't want them to be able to claim as their own. I've been so adamant in my life that I would never be someone's dirty little secret. And now I think Lochlain is saying that's all he can be to me? The thought churns my stomach.

Nico throws cushions at Phoenix, who is doing his best to catch them without doing too much damage to Lochlain's living room, while Aeyva's attention seems torn between Ciara's laugh and Nico's joy, but her face gives nothing away. The sky flashes and the rain that's begun to fall lands a little more heavily on the windows. Rain like this in Rhyton never lasted more than a moment before the heavens unleashed their worst. The city now keeps a tally of how many residents have perished in the superstorms. The numbers are both unimaginable and of no consequence. There comes a point where the numbers no longer represent people and the brain just glosses over them, unable to compute.

That point was passed long ago.

'I want to see Nuala,' I say, the group looking to me in surprise at my sudden statement. 'The Custodian was going to make me prove my lineage, in addition to what Siosal already did,' I continue. 'We've gathered what we can from other sources, I want Nuala to verify my bloodline like she would have done in the Palace.'

Ciara nods in agreement.

'I'll organise it,' Aeyva says.

The next flash turns the sky magenta and everyone's heads turn towards the window that's rattling slightly under the force of the rain. I note the absence of protective shutters as Rory frowns.

'What is that?' Riley asks, eyeing him sideways.

Since our time in Elenlea, she's been trying to hold her emotions from me, something she didn't know to do before. But she's not very skilled at it and I can clearly sense her concern for Rory and her anticipation for whatever he's sensing. As I watch her avoid looking outright at Rory and wait for his response, I wonder if she's even more inclined to this world than she lets on.

Rory, on the other hand, watches her carefully, considering his response. 'There's a storm over Rhyton,' he says.

It's my turn to frown. 'How can you tell that?' I ask.

'The colour of the sky. If the storm's centre is in the Realm, it looks the same as you would be used to. Albeit with less ferocity,' he notes, nodding in my direction.

'When the pink leeches through,' he continues, 'it's the storm buffeting up against the shields we have in place between your world and ours.'

'You have shields?' Riley asks, but I remember the pull of warm silk on my skin as I crossed between Driarn and the Realm.

'How else would we stop you human folk coming through and stealing all our hearts?' he says with a wink at me. A slow smile tugs at my lips as I look at Lochlain.

'I guess you are quite vulnerable to our charms,' I say to Rory, who gives me a little smile himself before turning back to the window. Riley's emotional profile tightens slightly but she still refuses to look at him.

'If this is normal, why the frown?' she asks, returning us to the reaction of Rory's she noticed.

'Because this isn't normal,' Ciara answers. 'We shouldn't actually be able to see the storms at all, and certainly not have rain at the same time. For most of our history, we haven't even known about Driarn's storms. As a pink tinge started to grace the sky, the Realm needed to find out why.' She looks around at each of us. 'Your superstorms are why. Since then, it's been well documented across the Realm that the stronger the storm in the human world, the deeper the colour here. There are some concerns the storms could break through the shields, but it hasn't occurred yet.'

'And if it does?' Will asks, gently taking a cushion from Nico and directing him to a pile of books.

Aeyva walks to the kitchen and grabs a wine bottle by the throat as she pours herself another glass. Her eyes can be so cold, it's impossible not to wonder how often those hands have gripped the throats of the living too.

'That's not a situation you want to happen,' she says.

'Because?' Phoenix prompts.

Of all of us, he has the least patience with the Calahi. I push away the question of how much that has to do with me and his views of Lochlain, who narrows his gaze at him.

'Because,' Ciara starts and I look at her gratefully. 'The magic of the Realm would no longer be contained just to the Realm and the Calahi would not be safe from humans.'

Phoenix laughs. 'Not safe from humans? Are you forgetting it is the Calahi that have preyed on human women for countless years and threatened the very existence of not one but *four* of the people in this room?'

Okay. Definitely not just about me.

Lochlain's resentment rumbles against me but it's not entirely focused on Phoenix. The guilt he feels for putting us in that position is obvious. At the same time, I understand Phoenix's view. It was exactly that behaviour I had set out to stop and found myself in a relationship with one of the strongest of the Calahi.

On paper, it doesn't look good.

'No one has forgotten, Phoenix,' Blaire says quietly and even Nico looks at her.

Her fingers twitch slightly at her sides and it's clear she wants to reach out to Phoenix. I block out the emotions of the humans around me and focus on Blaire. Lochlain's irritation on my skin is distracting enough.

'But,' she continues. 'We also don't know the history of the Calahi and their reasons for avoiding ... humans.' I think it's the first time she's referred to us in this way out loud and it sounds uncomfortable on her tongue. 'You know there's not a lot we can't put past humans, either.'

'Everyone has murderous tendencies if you look hard enough, Phoenix,' Aeyva adds. 'And there are a lot more humans than there are Calahi.'

She's abrupt but there's a grudging sort of respect forming between her, Phoenix, and Will; and I don't interject for fear of disrupting the balance. Phoenix and I have a way to go, given the doubt I planted in his mind and the hurt I caused. But I'm encouraged by his slowly developing relationships with those around me. All but Lochlain, at least, and I'm not fanciful enough to expect that will ever be anything other than what it is.

Phoenix and Blaire trail off into a conversation with Ciara about different events that have ensured humans and Calahi do not normally interact, despite there being a scattering of half-human, half-Calahi throughout history. I listen as Ciara explains not many live past infancy given the dim view both races have of them. At risk from the Calahi because they know what they are; and the humans because they do not. How that won't work against me in my attempt at the Throne, I don't know.

Not wanting to listen to anymore, I turn to Lochlain on the couch next to me. 'What actually happens if the shields come down?'

As if in response, the sky flashes magenta again, painting us all temporarily pink.

'Nothing good,' he says. 'A war of another sort, I suspect. Humans do not like what they cannot understand – so we would either be obliterated, or taken for experimentation. Both of which have been attempted before.'

I frown. I want to object but how can I do that when I have seen so many awful things in the Guard? Saw Claire?

'We had those events written out of your history,' he continues. 'But none of that would happen without the Calahi slaughtering a greater number of humans on our way down. In the end though, however strong we may be, there are simply far more humans than Calahi. With our diminishing magic, and reliance on the shields meaning less are trained in the arts of war, we don't have a lot of defences.'

The implication strikes the same way the numbers of the dead after a superstorm does. At once overwhelming and frightening, while entirely unbelievable. I sink back into the couch next to him and rest my head on his shoulder, conscious of the warmth of his body next to mine that moves with the current of his emotions.

'So, to protect the Realm and Driarn, we need to not only find a way to get me off the execution list, and on the Throne, but stop the weather as well?'

'Weather is nature, Lish,' Ciara says, obviously doing her own listening around the room. 'Finding the Star and a solution to our diminishing magic helps the Mother, too.'

'One step at a time.' Lochlain cups my head and pulls it towards him gently to place a kiss on my hair.

Right. One impossible step at a time.

CHAPTER FOURTEEN

LISH

Nuala's presence in the cabin is soothing as I watch her collect the information we've each gathered over the past two days. The images of those conversations, replayed as if we are watching a movie or were there ourselves, flicker around the room. After a moment, the image settles on one wall as she shares the key bits for the rest of us as well.

It doesn't feel like enough.

The image of Claire succumbing to whatever they plunged into her neck doesn't fade from my mind as it disappears from the timber wall of the cabin, and I send a silent thank you to Phoenix for suggesting Nico not be here for this. But there's a yawning black hole in my mind where the connection should fit.

'Aeyva suggested a quick revisit of what we know of the Star might also be useful,' Nuala says without condescension. 'Aeyva,' she looks at her expectantly. Aeyva just stares back, shaking her head slightly after a long moment.

Nuala seems to draw a deep breath before she turns back to the rest of us, huddled around Lochlain's living room.

'This is what we, Benny, and other sources, have experienced or put together about the Star,' she says before closing her eyes, images flashing up onto the walls around us once more. A limp hand lying in bright green grass; a large sapphire snatched out of its palm; a blinding blue light as the stone splinters into four pieces.

The Wolverton Pendant warms between my breasts as a man with dark brown clothes fills the room, tears silently coursing down his face as he leans over a workbench. A tiny tool in his hand as he carves a wolf into a bit of copper.

I press the pendant to my skin through my shirt, dwarfed by its history – the love, and grief, that helped create it.

Then there's a crown of gold leaves and I suck in a breath as it's placed on the head of a woman with dark hair. Her waves cascade down her back.

Turn around, I plead silently.

But the only thing I can now see is the piece of sapphire that sits in the centre of the tallest crown spire.

Then Nuala is splashed across the walls, handing a small, cloth wrapped package to a tall, auburn-haired Calahi. He bows deeply to her and pats her hand before he turns and walks away. The Nuala in the image turns around and before her is a different Calahi – Benny – in a different room.

'It holds her last message,' Benny says, his voice raspy.

My chest warms beneath the hot pendant.

The image of Nuala says something in return that's not audible and Benny speaks again.

'She was the conduit Nuala, and we lost her. Her sapphire was a gift from a greater being and it holds our last opportunity to make it right. It will show us how to replenish the Mother so we can all prosper once more. We just need to put it back together.'

Benny nods at something Nuala says.

'We still need her,' he says. 'Whatever the message says, I'm convinced it won't work without her.'

The room goes black momentarily before the softness returns and the light orbs bounce back into life in the corners of the ceiling. I blink into the shifting light as I sink into the couch behind me.

'I thought there were supposed to be four stories?' Blaire asks. 'That was only three.'

Nuala, the flesh and bone version, smiles at her and laughs softly. A gentle, heartwarming sound.

'You're correct. We do not know the location of the fourth piece,' she says. 'But I am hopeful Kailoh will have found more leads since we last spoke.'

No one speaks and Nuala simply watches us all for long moments. She clears her throat.

'That's enough of that now. I came here for another reason, too.'

She looks at me and orders all non-essential people and Calahi to return to their business. Lochlain moves to join me.

'You too, General,' she says gently. 'She can choose a human to stay with her, but I'm afraid I can't have any interference from full Calahi blood.' She looks knowingly at him. 'Certainly not a Wolverton's.'

Will and Phoenix step up to my side together and Lochlain's eyes slide to them cautiously.

'I'll stay,' Will says.

Lochlain's uncertainty ripples along my skin. He presses his soft lips to my temple once more and I lean into him gently as his breath tickles my hair.

'I'll see you when you're done,' Lochlain murmurs against me. 'Whatever you see, I will be waiting.'

His words don't erase the nervous knots in my stomach, but they do loosen them a little.

I turn back to Phoenix, who is looking at Nuala.

'Only one,' she says, and he nods.

'Thank you, though,' I say quietly to Phoenix.

'It's what friends do, right?'

I embrace him on impulse. He stiffens a fraction before gripping me tightly. 'I'm sorry Phoenix, for everything,' I whisper.

'I know,' he says, releasing me and watching Lochlain walk away with the others after giving my arm a quick squeeze. 'You've said that.' He winks at me before turning serious again, noting my need for reassurance. 'I ...' he trails off, raising one shoulder slightly.

'Wouldn't change it?' I ask, possibly a dangerous question.

But he gives himself away as he steals a look at Blaire who glances back at him on her way out. A lopsided smile appears on his face, green eyes sparkling.

'Perhaps not, time will tell I guess,' he hedges.

My heart skips in response, not unlike it has done in reaction to that grin before. But this time it's for the possibilities it presents for Blaire.

'Shall we?' Nuala's voice drags me back to her.

Nuala takes Will and me into the meadow outside Lochlain's cabin. The beauty of the night sky, punctuated by the cloudless magenta storm, steals my breath. Both for its beauty and what the bleeding of purple means is happening in Rhyton. The rain beats gently down on us, and I shiver in my increasingly damp clothes.

'Please be seated,' Nuala says, her tightly coiled hair catching the pink tinge of the stars.

There are no seats, and she gestures to the ground. I sit crossed legged beside Will, who sits with his legs stretched in front of him. Fit as he is, flexibility isn't his strong point.

'What should I expect, Nuala?' I ask, hoping the nervous edge in my voice goes unnoticed.

'Unfortunately, "exactly" is not something I can provide, Adelais – the process can be different each time. But your blood can hold memories,' she says gently. 'I will trace it as far back as I can so we have firm evidence for Kailoh, and the Custodian, when the time comes. But we will also see if it has any messages for us.'

'Will it hurt?' I ask, a trickle of fear runs down my spine.

'I will give you something to help you relax, and avoid any pain,' she says softly. 'I will need to make a small incision in each palm during the tracing, but Lochlain will be able to heal you quickly when we're done.'

My chest tightens around the knot that's been building there.

'What do you need me to do?' Will asks, looking at me before shifting this gaze back to Nuala.

'You are here to act as her support and her guide,' she says, not looking away from me. 'Should she need it.'

'And how do I do that?'

'I feel the strength of the bond between the two of you, your presence alone should be enough. If she struggles with lucidity at the end, just talk to her.'

I open my mouth to ask more, but Nuala reaches down and grips my hand and I decide I just want to get it done – I know enough. At her touch, the throne room comes into sharp focus around me, replacing the meadow; my memory of Lochlain's Challenge as clear as the moments I lived it. The feel of the wolf's fur on my palm as I watched him dying on the floor, my fingers gripping it as other fingers held mine.

'You were there,' I say, and she smiles softly at me.

'Not completely,' she says. 'I helped get someone else to you – someone who committed to be with you even in death. Do you remember?'

My mind immediately goes to my mother, but I know that's not right.

I start.

Benny. He promised to be with me in this life and next.

Nuala draws a long, deliberate breath and smiles at me as if she can see the connection I've just made. The vision of the throne room falls away.

I blink at the sparkling ring of silver in her dark eyes.

She gave me Benny so I could draw on his magic. Even in death. Tears prick my eyes.

'The ceremony must be performed when the moon is high in the sky,' she says. 'This is when I can get the greatest clarity and Kailoh will expect nothing less.'

Kailoh. A name I've heard endlessly these past couple of weeks. A name I've thought about endlessly. I clear the tears from my eyes and focus on the task at hand.

'Do not worry my dear, your lover has given me very strict instructions to return you in one piece.'

My heart warms at Lochlain's concern. But I don't miss that she uses the same term as he did – lover. What does that mean here?

'Drink,' she commands, handing me a small, glass vial.

A vibrant orange substance swirls gently in the vessel that's no longer than my thumb. Its similarities to the vials of magic that are drawn during the Givings are not lost on me. A small voice reminds me I can still back out. If I stop now, I will never know for sure. I could ignore the way Siosal pursued me. Push away the knowledge I have discovered about myself here.

But I know I can't walk away. So I pop the tiny cork stopper and the contents of the vial slither down my throat. The sensation of the hot liquid sucks the air from my lungs.

I jump slightly as a low guttural sound begins to emanate from Nuala's throat. Her lips don't move. She glides around Will and me slowly, her full sleeves falling away where she holds her arms wide. A vibration dances across my skin and I find Will's wild eyes. Around and above us, the air shimmers and the rain ceases and I know instinctively Nuala has hidden us beneath a shield of some kind.

Nuala continues to glide slowly around Will and me. I try to watch her feet, but my eyes are increasingly difficult to focus. Gritty. Tiredness creeps along my limbs. I have a vague sense of Will's strong hands guiding my head to the grass beneath me but all I can see is the fathomless night sky. Stars dance around me, and Will and Nuala waver at the edges of my vision.

Nuala's chanting grows louder and my throat hums along with her.

Prickling begins to radiate from the centre of my palms, its intensity increasing into an incessant burn. I want to call out, but the sound catches in my throat. My eyes are full of stars and can make out no other details of the space around me. A single bead of sweat makes its way from my temple towards my ear as I lie in the grass. Someone, Will I think, strokes my hair.

The sound of my skin tearing churns my stomach before the dull pain registers and radiates along my fingers. My palms drip blood onto the ground and it pools under my knuckles in the wet grass. A thick warmth in contrast to the chill of the green blades. The chanting becomes deafening and the sky itself begins to shake. Tears run from the corners of my eyes and join my sweat in their journey across my cheeks. The sky above me blurs. I can no longer feel Will stroking my hair. Four pricks of light fight their way from the unfocused night; growing until all I can see is blinding white light. Even with my eyes closed.

A woman flickers against the white, smiling. Her kind eyes send a pulse of hurt through me like finding an old bruise. The yellow flowers dance around her.

Adelais, Adelais she sings, spinning away from me and disappearing from view.

They are our wolves, my son, a man tells a young boy. He's dressed in old fashioned leathers, a knife at his hip. The boy stands before him with a wooden sword.

They are our wolves, the man says again, *they made us the strongest in the Realm and we are duty bound to protect them. Our line has always protected them, as we protect the Queen. The wolves and the Wolvertons – we are of the one purpose: protect the Queen and the Mother at all costs.*

More faces swim before me, my eyes straining against the harsh white light. The more faces I see, the more the weaponry changes, the clothing changes. Time itself changes.

My head throbs.

Just when I think I can't take any more white light, it recedes. Leaving a meadow, not unlike the one I think I still lie in. An eerily beautiful woman with copper hair flowing down her back, past the curve of her elegant spine, wanders through the grass. Her hand trails the wildflowers that burst to life around her. She flicks her hand to the side and a creek appears, bubbling quietly where it now hugs the meadow. Arms snake around her waist as a man approaches from behind her, the large sapphire at her breast bouncing heavily as she spins to him. The smile on her face brightens the meadow.

Arlo, my love, she says.

The man releases her and looks around. *Did you do this?* he asks.

It's beautiful, isn't it? she says.

You're astonishing.

I did it for them, she says. *To give them somewhere safe to raise their pups.*

At her words, three wolves enter the meadow, cautiously taking in the man. One remains seated at the edge of the meadow, his amber eyes flicking to mine. *Your time has come*. The words beat in my chest, in time with my heart. The wolf faces the woman again and the flame in my chest burns a little hotter in response to the message it's given me. A knowing taking root that these wolves will always look for me. The woman turns back to the man, his deep brown skin glistening in the sunshine.

They have a gift for you, my love, she says. *For protecting me, they have a gift for you. My wolf.*

The meadow remains but now the beautiful woman is with two others.

The man has gone.

They're talking but I can't hear the words. Wolves growl around me, the sound running deep in my bones. The copper-haired woman falls to the ground and the edges of the meadow begin to ripple. Faster it moves. Racing towards the fallen woman. A single flower beside her dies. My limbs shake with the rhythm of the ground under her and thunderclaps overhead.

But the sky is blue where she is until it shatters into a million pieces of sapphire.

The facets of the sapphire glint in the sunlight until they're blinding as well. The brilliant blue flashes at me, a message I need to understand—

My body sings with power, an electric surge that steals the air from my lungs, my fingers tingling—

And then it's gone. They're all gone.

In their place is death. And I'm cold. Empty.

The scent of smoke and rotting flesh clogging my nose and throat. I draw a breath, desperate to leave this place. The flowers are dead, the creek bed is dry. Villages and cities stream past my vision. All deserted. Some burning; most black and deathly quiet. As every place disappears past me, I look for the people. I look for the shelters. Where did they go?

But there are no shelters. None that would withstand whatever this destruction is.

The feeling in my body begins to return, my vision having gone black. My head is pressed roughly against the ground and my arms flung wide from my body. A low throb marks my open hands and the pressure in my head erodes all conscious thought.

And then it's gone too.

Will rolls me to the side and I retch into the grass until everything has left me. The light has eaten away all my sight and from a distance I note a faint panic that it might not return either. I think my eyes are closed as I lie in the grass, defenceless to the emotions of Will that wash over me now like a soft tide. His concern for me brings tears to my eyes again.

The depth of his emotions are mine for the taking now and I breathe them in, letting them fill the aching holes I seem to be made of. Another stream of life pulses beside his, an ancient one that knows much. So much. I reach out to feel it too.

'Lish?' Will asks in a strangled voice. 'Are you doing that?'

My eyes fight open, but I may as well leave them shut. A fluorescent white mark is still imposed on the darkness of the meadow.

Trepidation grates along my skin. I think of Sofia and regret that I brought her here – a knowing I should have—

I breathe out.

Those feelings aren't mine. My head swims and memories of my time in the orphanage come back. When I was first overwhelmed by foreign emotions. Before I learned to tell the difference and so desperately wanted to be filled back up with ... something. Anything.

Will squeezes my hand.

'Lish,' he says again. 'I'm here, Lish, open your eyes.'

With my head in the grass, the world spins around me as I try to do as he says. My gaze catches on a dark figure across the meadow.

The moon sparkles back into the sky and the light catches on the amber eyes that are solely focused on me. *Your time has come.* I reach a hand towards the wolf and it lowers its head. I don't know how long we stay like that, but gradually a warmth returns behind my ribs and under my skin.

Almost as if I can feel myself coming back home.

CHAPTER FIFTEEN

AEYVA

Loch takes Lish's bloody hands in his as they sit on the lounge and she closes her eyes, drawing a deep breath as he heals her.

'What did you see?' I try not to flinch at the hardness in my voice as it cuts through the others who are all talking at once.

I feel Nuala's gaze land on me.

'Her blood led me back to Roisin, the First Queen. Her title is as we thought,' she says, holding my gaze. But I know it's not only that.

Riley flops in the armchair opposite me.

'I'm still not bowing to you,' she says, looking at Lish.

Lish tries to smile softly but she's quite pale, and a little shaky.

'What did you see?' I ask again, a little more softly this time.

'I think—' Lish glances at Nuala who nods. 'I think I saw what the world might be if we don't succeed in Benny's tasks. In finding the Star and harnessing its ... power.' She looks around the room, glancing at Nico playing in the corner. She drops her voice to a whisper. 'There was nothing left.'

Nuala steps towards me, the package of messages held in her hands. I take it gently from her, the white light seeping between my fingers.

'There is more to her magic than we first thought,' Nuala says quietly. She considers me for a moment. 'You already knew that.'

I nod slowly. 'Before you came, she accessed Rory's magic somehow. You delivered her a boost of power at the Challenge, but none of us saw what happened behind Siosal's shield before it fell.' I study Nuala's face as I think. The magic and knowledge she holds swirls in her eyes. 'She's talked about her mother teaching her to borrow magic. But I don't know of anyone with that as an ability in itself. Do you?'

'Not "borrowing" no ...' Nuala trails off. 'I'll give it some thought.'

She turns to stand beside me as we watch the others fall into their own conversations. She's at least a head shorter than me and her shoulder presses into my arm.

'Outside,' she says, looking through the windows and towards the meadow, 'the blood took her through a series of memories and delivered the message she shared – what you now hold for Kailoh, as well. But there was something else ...'

I glance at Nuala as she tries to find the words.

'I've never seen it, only the stories. But it was almost like the memory of the power in the blood was trying to find its way back to her.'

'Roisin's blood?' I ask.

'Benny told us the Star would be useless without the descendants of Roisin, perhaps this is why.'

There's a beat of silence between us and Nuala waits, as if she knows I have more to say. She probably does. 'I ... met with the Eternal Queen recently,' I say.

Nuala lifts her chin slightly but she doesn't comment – just waits for me to go on.

'She seemed to know we're looking for something and told me "the dead should stay that way".' Nuala's gaze slides to me now. 'I can't shake the feeling she was talking about Roisin, but what does the Eternal Queen have to do with her?'

Nuala shakes her head slightly. 'Roisin was Benny's speciality, not mine, I fear. And you know the circumstances of his death mean he couldn't pass me all his knowledge before he left us. In this case, Kailoh might be our best chance at understanding any connection.'

Her comment reminds me of something else I have learned tonight. 'Why did you give Kailoh a piece of the Star?'

Her shoulders drop a little and she looks at me sadly. 'Because, Aeyva, it was a piece entrusted to the Manorynxes of Airlie. After Benny ...' She looks back to Lish. 'I'm the last one left – it needed to be someplace safe.'

An uncomfortable weight settles in my stomach and I look up from Nuala. Only for my gaze to collide with Ciara's all too knowing gold eyes.

'So, we have Nuala's confirmation,' Lish says, addressing us all, 'and as much as I think we'll get from our other sources quickly.' She meets my gaze. 'It's time to take it to Mercasia and present me to Kailoh.'

Lochlain's features tense slightly at her word choice. But it is the right one. We are to present her to Kailoh as the rightful Queen of Airlie and ask for his alliance. Not only does Kailoh want to meet her, for his own motivation of restoring the appropriate balance of power in the Realm; but there is also no one more obsessed with the Realm's history outside of Benny. If the last pieces of the Blue Pointed Star are to be found, Kailoh will know where to start.

I nod. 'Ciara and I will go with you in our place as Sentinels,' I say without looking at Ciara.

She knows that is her role and will not disagree. It's what I decided to do when I first started hunting for the heir – Lish; but it's what Ciara was born to do. But I also don't look at Nuala.

'We need to talk through how we do this,' Will interjects. 'I don't want to be separated from Lish, or Sofia and Nico.'

The conflict is clear on Will's face. It's obvious he has always had Lish's back and his devotion hasn't changed in what is a new, strange world to them. His commitment is admirable. But he also has a great love for Sofia, who is just as clearly not a warrior, and her brother. The little one both Will and Phoenix treat like a son. If only I could laugh at the irony of being surrounded by so many who would make wonderful fathers when I have no young.

'That's not going to work, Will,' Rory says gently. 'Lish has no choice but to go to Kailoh in person and we don't know exactly what we'll find.' He pauses and looks pointedly at Will. 'It's not a situation you can take Nico and Sofia into.'

He doesn't elaborate on this in Nico's presence, but his meaning is clear – humans, particularly vulnerable and untrained humans, will be at greater risk in Mercasia than they are here. Not from Kailoh, but having our attention stretched further than Lish, and perhaps one other, is an unnecessary distraction. Will leans forwards and places his elbows on his knees, holding his head in his hands.

'I don't like this, Lish,' he looks up at her, his entire body tense.

'I know,' she says quietly. 'But it has to be this way. You can't leave them.'

The words she doesn't say is that it would tear Will in two if something should befall his acquired family.

'Will,' I say. 'I'd appreciate your help with the Royalists while I'm gone. Anyone else have a view?'

'Yes, actually, I do.' Blaire says as she glances at Phoenix. 'We do. We're going to find that woman who was trying to help Claire. And I'm going to get back in with David – the Commissioner.'

The Mercasian guards are in their standard, thick, elaborate scarlet uniforms as we make our way onto the bustling lower plateau of the city. I pull my collar a little tighter as I watch them standing still in the cold. The main road through Ilcaena, the city's capital, is highly visible as it winds its way to the Palace. For this reason alone it is not my usual route, but there is more to our announcement of Lish than just presenting her to Kailoh. The performance matters, and the more of his people who see her, the better – gaining a swell of support in Mercasia would be better still.

Ciara and I have taken our positions as Sentinels and walk a single pace ahead and half a step to the side of Lish. Riley and Rory do the same behind her and the Calahi around us keep a polite distance as they wander the food stalls that line the far side. It's a very small escort by Realm standards, but I am banking on the crowd being too curious to cause any trouble. Kailoh is expecting us, of course, but he too has a part to play; it is up to us to make the introduction.

So, we walk among the Calahi of Mercasia who go about their day, and move in and out of the city through what is now a renowned market across the Realm. The gently falling snow doesn't deter any of them. I imagine if they avoided the snow for any reason, they wouldn't get much done in Mercasia.

The main road is much the same as I remember, despite the years since I've been this way. The stone is worn in most places and the turrets on the low walls that run along either side are battle worn. The end of the last war was won and lost here, in the earlier days of Ciara and Lochlain's father's time as General. At the time, Mercasia had expected Kailoh to restore the city to its former glory. He did, on the whole, and then some. But not this road. This he left as a reminder to all that passed of what he fought through, and what he fought for. A reminder that the peace he has brought his Calahi did not come without great sacrifice. And, to the Calahi of Mercasia, there is no greater leader.

We draw nearer to the stone stairs that lead to the second plateau and I remember the stories Benny told me of the gates that used to exist here. How Kailoh made a very public demonstration of taking them down when he became King. The city of Ilcaena was built around a status system – three plateaus, each higher and smaller than the one below, with the Palace at the top and in the centre of the final plateau. Like layers carved around a mountain.

Lish and Riley draw twin breaths in awe. I imagine the cold Mercasian air puffing white as they breathe out and look up at the rest of Ilcaena. I'd instructed them not to react to anything they see here for good or bad and now I can only trust that those breaths are not reflected in their faces. If we had time, I would have smuggled them in to see the Heart of Mercasia under the cover of anonymity so they could absorb it in their own way. But, with the message Lish saw last night, the Calahi of Airlie being drained of their magic, and the not so small issue of my Queen being wanted for murder, that was a luxury I could not give them. In another life, I think to myself, I would fill my days with small luxuries.

Luxuries instead of blood.

There are more Calahi watching us on this plateau than the one below, their interest in the happenings of Mercasia greater. But their observations are not as keen as the third and final plateau, where the Calahi behave more like the creatures who feed on the remains of my dead. Once upon a time, these plateaus in Mercasia reflected the level of privilege – a system Kailoh has worked hard to disassemble, starting with the gates. But there is still an echo of it here and, for the first time, I find myself uncomfortable with where the Mercasians think my place should be. That, if they knew, the Calahi around me would agree my life should be spent in the Society and not by the side of my Queen.

The guards at the Wings that will take us up to the final plateau – and the Palace – are ever watchful, but only one pair of eyes shows any recognition. He nods shallowly at me, his dark hair dusted with fresh snowflakes. He gestures to the egg-shaped Wing closest to him, one of five, instructing those who were about to board to wait.

'You have far more friends than I realised,' Rory whispers after the doors hiss shut with just the five of us inside.

'Don't tell me you don't have friends in every Court, Ror,' I say.

He chuckles as I spin to face them all, now that we are on our own briefly.

I half expect Riley to look up at the sound, but her gaze is firmly pinned to the ground.

'What the fuck are we about to do?' she asks. 'If you expect me not to scream, someone had better fucking warn me. Now.'

Rory laughs again, a different tone this time. It's the deep one that helped me fall in love with him once. I cock my head at her before registering the look on Lish's face as well.

'We're going up,' Ciara says. 'You have contraptions like this in Rhyton, I'm sure?' Her eyebrows furrow slightly with her question, creating a tiny crease between them. One I could gently rub away with my thumb.

Riley's eyes flare. 'Are you talking about a lift?'

Lish breathes out loudly, her eyes travelling towards the sky in the direction we will go.

'Our *lifts*,' Riley continues, 'are nothing like this. They are – they're not entirely made of *glass*, for fuck's sake, and they don't bloody fly!'

I join Rory in his laughter and Ciara smiles at us, blowing on that little kernel of hope in my heart.

'Fly?' Lish asks dubiously.

Riley turns to her. 'Do you see anything holding us in place, Lish? 'Cause I sure as hell don't.'

'You can do this, Lish,' Ciara says. 'You're the Queen of Airlie, with or without your crown. It's literally in your blood to do this – to create alliances, forge Queendoms.' Her face shutters a little at the mention of the alliance and I know she's thinking of Lochlain and his role as General. Of all the things we each have to give up to fulfil the roles the Realm expects of us.

Silently, the Wing begins its ascent. The smooth, curved glass rising effortlessly into the sky. Lish starts to mutter to herself with her eyes closed. Rory moves to take Riley's hand as panic flashes across her face. But Lish reaches blindly behind her and Riley grabs onto her like a lifeline, not seeing the hand she's left hanging in the air. I pretend not to notice as Rory looks away and over the city, his hand dropping back to his side, as we rise up to the third and final plateau.

Where the King of Mercasia will be waiting.

The Calahi here spot us as soon as the top of the Wing breaks even with the plateau. The gold and scarlet arches that curve away from each side beat steadily as it holds its position, like a bird hovering above a meadow, until it's ready to descend again. The doors make their usual hiss as they open us to full view of the spectators. I take the larger step across the drop to the plateau and listen for Ciara to follow. Third out is Rory, who turns back to the Wing and grips Lish as she steps across the void. Ciara and I focus on the crowd in front and any potential threat. Riley's breathing is heavier than Lish's as Rory gently helps her out. I wait two beats longer before I move forward, to give her a moment to catch her breath.

The Calahi milling around the snow dusted gardens naturally give us space as we make our way towards Kailoh's less than humble Palace. All eyes turning to watch us make our way forward. But the message of our public entrance has been received and the ornate white doors in the distance begin to open, the scarlet clad guards spilling out like blood. His soldiers were likely briefed to keep an eye out for a small entourage and to alert him to our presence.

I nod at the guards as I pass through the gaping entrance, ensuring we keep a tight formation around Lish.

'A moment.' A senior guard, discernible by the single gold shoulder plate that covers a small portion of his chest, halts us outside the throne room.

Kailoh knows I wouldn't take this route unless it was formal, and he is meeting me as such. The guard disappears through an open archway before returning a moment later. I smile to myself, Kailoh's curiosity has got the better of him. He hasn't kept us waiting as he was likely to have done for any other visiting party.

'You may enter,' the guard says.

CHAPTER SIXTEEN

AEYVA

I chance a single look at Lish, her soft brown hair pulled back gently in an intricate braid. She takes a moment to straighten the tailored jacket she wears over her usual black attire. I don't want to appear to check on her, but the risk of appearing uncertain of my Queen is better than having her go to pieces in front of Kailoh and his Court. Her face is set and expressionless as she meets my gaze. She nods once, and we move forward into the vaulted room.

The Palace is unusually quiet, I suspect Kailoh has dismissed his regular attendants until he can make his own assessment of Lish. The inside of the throne room hasn't changed, all white and blood red to match the rest of the Palace decor. At the centre of the room sits Kailoh's cold, silver Throne. Kailoh looks the same as I last saw him, although his attire is significantly more formal today. I bow low, once we've crossed enough of the gleaming white floor to see him in detail, and Ciara, Rory, and Riley follow. Lish remains standing as I'd told her to. Kailoh tilts his head, inspecting us.

I wait.

It's customary for the King to speak first in formal situations, inviting another to the conversation. It's not a courtesy I extend him in private. It's not one he would expect, either.

He looks us over, assessing us from head to toe. His gaze flicks from Lish back to me. I keep waiting.

'Welcome,' he says, 'to the Heart of Mercasia.'

'Thank you, Your Majesty,' Ciara replies. 'We are of the Court of Airlie and come with news.'

'Only news?' he asks.

'News and an opportunity,' I clarify.

'Enlighten me, Aeyva of Airlie.'

I hope the note of familiarity in his tone reads as nothing more than that of an entitled King. If the others remark on it ... well, he has been our silent patron in the hunt for Lish, and I was the unofficial emissary. That's explanation enough.

I press the heel of my hand to my chest and lower my head.

'Thank you, Your Majesty,' I say, stepping aside and gesturing to Lish. 'I wish to present someone to you, someone long thought lost.' Behaving so formally with Kailoh feels ... unusual. But he insisted on this display for the benefit of his advisers and even the guards that line the room.

He narrows his eyes at Lish slightly and his nostrils flare as his gaze flicks briefly to Riley.

'If it does not offend, this is perhaps a conversation best held in closed quarters.' I say before he can comment on Riley or Lish's humanness, their slightly smaller stature and ringless eyes. Although there's very little he doesn't know about Lish and her team, I can't always guess how he will play things publicly.

'You are bold, Aeyva of Airlie. But I will allow this, if only to satisfy my curiosity. I hope you do not disappoint.'

A hungry smile graces his face, he's clearly enjoying these false formalities. Nevertheless, I breathe a little easier; Lish has apparently met his first stage of critique.

We're escorted to a smaller, though still opulent, room off the throne room. Six of Kailoh's guards remain and I know this is the best we can hope for at Court. And, if any of his guards are indiscreet, then word of Lish will begin to spread through Mercasia that much sooner. Kailoh gestures for us to begin.

'As you know, the Court of Airlie has been held by a Custodian since the loss of our former Queen. We now know that she is no longer living,' Ciara says.

The guards look steadily at us. Kailoh raises an elegant eyebrow.

'Someone did survive, however,' she continues. 'I present to you Adelais, daughter of Catriona and Queen of the Court of Airlie.'

Kailoh's expression doesn't change. 'That's quite a claim, and I note the absence of a crown. I assume you have proof?'

'We do, Your Majesty,' I say.

'I'd like to hear from her before I see it.'

I bow to Kailoh and wait, hoping Lish can pull this off eloquently. She takes a deep but quiet breath.

'King Kailoh,' she begins, 'it is an honour to meet with you. As my Sentinels have indicated, my mother was Catriona, Queen of Airlie. It saddens me greatly that her life was cut short, but I am now here to pick up the pieces and restore Airlie, following the Custodian's reign.'

'And why would you wish to do that?' Kailoh asks.

'Because the Calahi are hurting, *my people* are hurting, and I believe I can draw them from the uncertain times in which they have been living and give them a brighter future.'

Kailoh considers this for a long moment. 'Your sentiment is sound, Adelais, but you'll forgive me if I wish to see the proof before I take your word.'

'I have heard much about you, King Kailoh, and I would be concerned if you did not do your due diligence,' Lish says evenly. She turns and nods a silent command to me, every bit the regal monarch.

Nuala's orb flickers into life in the palm of my hand and bright white light begins to creep along my fingers as I present it to Kailoh. Beside me, Lish keeps her gaze on Kailoh's face, steadfastly avoiding the orb and what it shows. Perhaps she's seen enough already. Kailoh's eyes, however, remain glued to the light and what it contains.

He blinks several times when it's finished. Despite his prior knowledge, I haven't divulged any information on the nature of her mother's death or her visions from her time with Nuala. So there are some elements of surprise for him still.

'That is certainly an interesting tale, please thank Nuala for me.' His eyes hold mine almost a beat too long before he turns to Lish. 'It is an honour to meet you, Adelais. I am pleased for Airlie that you have returned. I must, of course, ask why you are presenting this to me, however, and not the Custodian?'

'You saw the nature of the Custodian's involvement in my life in the message from Nuala,' Lish says tightly. 'That, in addition to him publicly declaring me responsible for my mother's death, makes it impossible for me to claim my Throne through him.'

'That was an entirely silly move on his behalf, I do not think he would be so excited for me to know the truth.' Kailoh smiles. 'You want the support of Mercasia to claim your crown, I take it?'

'I do. I trust in my,' she betrays the slightest pause at the official title, 'Sentinels and they, along with the General and Manorynx of Airlie, are steadfast in their views that an alliance between our Courts is the most effective way of preventing the vision you hold in your hand from being realised. Both for the Calahi we each represent, and the humans I swore to protect.'

Kailoh's fingers steeple under his chin, regarding her quietly.

Lish assesses Kailoh in return, her shoulders square.

'Your Majesty,' she says. 'From what I understand, you are a King who wants the best for his Court – and the Realm. I want the same thing for my Court, for Airlie, and I am here to formally request your assistance in the form of an alliance between our Courts, so we can save the Realm and the human world.'

Kailoh's eyes sparkle softly and he shifts in his seat.

'I will consider your request, Adelais. But I will not provide an answer until I have a better idea of what's in it for me, and my Court. I don't give myself, or the resources of Mercasia, away for free. I'm sure you understand.'

Lish nods slightly; it's more than I could have hoped for from our first meeting. 'In the meantime,' Kailoh continues, 'we will have a ball in your honour tonight. I should like to get to know Airlie's new Queen better.'

Officially, Ciara has given herself and Riley the night off to enjoy the ball and get to know some of the members of Kailoh's Court. Which simply means they go without their uniforms for the night and keep their weapons concealed in the dresses they wear instead. Rory and I are Lish's very obvious guards; but the other two will remain close. While I remain vigilant in my assessment of the flowing crowd and watchful eyes, I am not expecting anything difficult tonight. Tonight will be an opportunity for Kailoh to observe Lish engaging with the most influential Calahi in his Court.

For some time, I have questioned what Kailoh will want in exchange for his assistance. Why he was invested in finding Lish or her mother. It seems very obvious now that my instincts were correct.

Kailoh wants the Queen of Airlie.

Kailoh wants Lish.

And all she can offer.

Rory and I escort her through the Mercasian Palace, alert for any disturbance. Before we left our suite, Ciara reminded Lish that she must not appear intimidated by the ornate surroundings, or the many scarlet clad guards lining the white walkways.

The wide hallway swells with Mercasians who ebb around us. My hand on the hilt of my sword, ready to draw, is enough of a message to keep the other Calahi at arm's length. Their conversations are light and drift through the air, the nature of their discussions that of a people who have never seen an all-consuming darkness. I imagine myself able to float away on their words. Float away to a place of gentle laughter and polite smiles.

I glance sideways at Rory; he is even quieter than usual. His keen eyes sweep the crowd constantly, ever watchful for anything out of place. *Or perhaps*, I think, sensing the tension radiating from him, *he's looking for a specific someone who is most definitely out of place in this Court.*

'She's with Ciara,' I remind him quietly over Lish's head. His jaw tightens.

'Lish doesn't need to lose another friend, Aeyva.'

'She's not going to, Ror, not tonight.'

'Lish doesn't need either of you talking as if she's not here,' Lish says as she walks between us. Rory smiles softly.

'Apologies, Your Majesty,' he bows his head slightly.

Lish stops dead, her skirts coming to a halt after she does.

Her fist balls at the side of her scarlet dress, worn in honour of Kailoh's Court.

'If anyone calls me "Your Majesty" again,' she grinds out, 'I will act the part of the Queen you wish me to be and happily arrange for your heads to roll.' She looks at us a moment longer and a gleam comes into her green eyes. 'And I will do it regardless of what Riley or Ciara have to say about it.'

Rory and I look stupidly at each other before catching up to Lish as she strides down the hall towards the ballroom. A grin pulls at my face as I register the slight blush that appeared on Rory's cheeks – a subtle deepening of colour most wouldn't notice.

'Ah, but Your *Majesty*,' Rory purrs, 'that's exactly what we're here to call you.'

The ballroom is decked out in Kailoh's signature opulence. Even I can tell he has a great eye for style and detail, and genuine happiness seems to fill the room as members of his Court help themselves to the welcome drinks. Lish stands immediately in front of Rory and me, drawing curious glances from those that pass her. A member of Kailoh's serving staff bows low to her before passing her a drink that she accepts graciously but does not sip. Rory's shoulders finally relax slightly, and I follow his gaze.

Riley and Ciara are talking animatedly with a group of Mercasians. Either they have made firm friends quickly or Ciara knows them. I don't blame Rory for being tense. The many eyes continually flicking towards Lish and Riley are impossible to ignore. Although Kailoh has been swift to stamp out brutality to humans in his Court, I know I'm not the only one who remembers humans being used for 'entertainment' in events just like this.

The hours pass without major event, as expected. Kailoh introduces Lish as his beautiful and intelligent *friend* Adelais, who he hopes his Court would get to know 'very well'. Publicly celebrating a wanted fugitive from another Court could get messy, but even this introduction leaves Lish inundated with Mercasians and visitors desperate to talk with her.

As Kailoh's guest of honour, Lish needs to be here for enough time to allow as many to meet her as possible. And remain visible to Kailoh as she indulges them. Worrying about her tiring, not to mention the shoes she's wearing, I direct her to a tall table and she sits just to my left with Rory standing at her back, facing out. Riley sits across the table and Ciara immediately to my right, where it is impossible to ignore her presence or the sense of peace that her proximity brings.

Between watching the crowd, and being acutely aware of both Lish's and Ciara's locations, I watch Riley. There are many Calahi here who would be considered exceptionally attractive, particularly to a human, but it's Rory's shoulders her eyes keep returning to. I smile grimly to myself. The Calahi in this room would be attractive to me, too, if I wasn't so captured by Ciara; there are none here that can compare to her. Perhaps not anywhere. The last time we were at an event like this, she danced with me with tears on her face. Then hers and Nuala's wishes for me became one and the same – a destiny I'm just not able to live up to – and she asked me to focus on the task at hand. Which is not her.

When the Calahi she's chatting to departs for another drink, leaving us temporarily alone, Lish turns stiffly to us with a smile plastered on her face.

'Please tell me this will be over soon,' she begs.

I open my mouth to answer, but freeze as Ciara's knuckles brush mine on the table. She's put her glass down and her hand stays against my own as she twirls the stem in her fingers. Lish's gaze finds our hands and she looks slowly back to me.

'Okay, now,' a male voice interrupts. I don't recognise it and turn to find a golden Calahi in front of Ciara. She smiles up at him. 'You have denied me all night,' he continues, 'and now I am calling in my debts. You, my friend, owe me a dance.'

'One dance, and all debts are paid?' she quips.

'I guess it depends how good a dancer you've turned out to be, doesn't it?' he says.

She laughs, before looking down at our hands. She glances at me before taking hers away and placing it in the handsome stranger's.

I feel like I've been punched in the middle, and she didn't even say a word. Her actions said it all. *Focus on the task at hand* she'd said. But I guess that only applied to me. Riley stands and Rory is by her side in an instant.

'I need a bathroom break,' Riley says, and I nod in answer to Rory's unasked question as he looks at me.

'What are you doing, Aeyva?' Lish asks when we're alone.

'What? Do you need to go, too?'

'Funny. What are you doing with Ciara?'

'Noth—'

'Don't lie. We're past that,' she says.

'It's not a lie, it's – there's nothing for it, Lish.' Her unwavering regard makes me feel exposed. My hand still tingles where Ciara touched it and I sigh. 'She needs me to direct my energy elsewhere.'

'I would say otherwise. Don't wait, Aeyva,' she says gently. 'Don't wait until there are too many small hurts and misunderstandings between you to get beyond. You have a connection with her, and you know it. Don't blow it, isn't connection the only thing really worth living for?'

It's as if Lish has reached into my chest and gripped my heart in her fist. I blink at the intensity of the sensation and it takes a moment to register the bite in her voice. Perhaps she's not only talking about me.

'I'm not good enough for her,' I whisper. 'For what she wants me to do – expects me to be.'

The music still sounds through the ballroom and as soon as the words are out, I hope she didn't hear them.

'Maybe not, but she's smart enough to make that decision for herself.' She pauses for a moment, lifting her glass towards her mouth. But she continues before it reaches her lips. 'As for what she wants you to do, the Wolvertons seem to have been instrumental in helping me find my way here. Maybe what she wants you to do is, in fact, where you need to be.'

I shake my head. 'There is so much she doesn't know.'

'And yet she's still here, isn't she? She's still trying to gently reach you.' She places the glass back on the table.

Trying to gently reach me. The words echo in my mind. Not much else registers except that Ciara hasn't returned.

Trying to gently reach me.

CHAPTER SEVENTEEN

LISH

The faces of the Calahi I have been talking with all night swim before me. The King introduced me merely as his friend, Adelais, with no surname or context for where I've come from. But with a royal introduction and the deadly expressions of my two uniform clad Sentinels, the members of his Court clearly knew I was something they should sound out.

Being the subject of so many curious and suspicious Calahi for endless hours is draining. I'm normally the watcher and, when I'm not, my life is not of interest to anyone other than my friends, so I move around Rhyton with almost total anonymity. Elenlea was different, especially initially, when Siosal was looking for me. And then Calahi started to recognise me as someone who supported Lochlain at the Challenge. But that was nothing like the attention I am getting here.

As the ballroom begins to quiet and the guests take up positions in the pillowy couches that have appeared, I take the opportunity to observe more of the Mercasians. It's easier to fade into the background now that the only light comes from the brass lanterns floating in place around the cavernous ballroom. Somehow, the effect of the lighting and the changed seating arrangements make the room seem almost cosy despite its size. Opulently dressed Calahi drape themselves on the furniture, the grace in which they move never seeming to lose my fascination.

Another round of drinks, this time molten gold liquid in tiny glasses, dances lightly through the hall. I tentatively pluck one from the air to be polite and I'm surprised to find it's warm underneath my fingertips.

'Is this okay?' I ask Aeyva quietly.

She nods imperceptibly, but I'm bolstered by her acknowledgment that this enticing drink is safe for me to drink. I have experienced firsthand the effects of too many Calahi drinks on a human and it's not something I wish to repeat. Particularly in a strange Court, where I am trying to convince the most powerful ruler in the Realm to partner with me in putting the Star together, and whatever comes next.

Nuala's, or Roisin's, really, message was clear. The Star will show me how to access some greater power that the world desperately needs. Something that without, the Mother will never come back from the downward slide she's currently on. What it didn't show me is what I do with that power once I find it, or exactly how it will prevent the Mother from dying. And it certainly didn't show me how to stop whatever is happening in Rhyton. I think of Blaire and Phoenix, literally a world away from here, but fighting the same battle. Nuala's tracing may not have shown me anything but destruction in the human world, or here, but it would be a mistake to believe they're not connected. The magenta storm showed me what I'd really known all along – the Realm and the human world are intrinsically linked. The potential implications of Blaire getting close to the Commissioner again eats at me. I trust Blaire not to put herself in a position she's uncomfortable with. But what will it cost her and Phoenix?

I let the gold liquid warm the back of my throat and distract me from the realisation that their relationship, however important, needs to take second place to ... saving the world. But the warmth is small comfort in the face of our greater roles.

Aeyva has confirmed the Custodian and Queen Nakiasha are working together in a bigger way than just her showing her public support for him and Airlie. I may have underestimated him initially, but now I know who he is, and what he's done, I know there can't be any doubt he is the driver behind it all. And he's been playing a long game. Not the death of nature perhaps, it would be naive of me to put the decline of the Mother down to a single person. But Siosal's brutal search and the supposed alliance with the Court of Rothani are him. Which has to mean he's connected to what's happening in Rhyton. The Commissioner didn't appear in Elenlea by accident, nor was it just for the sake of him covering up magic in Driarn. I just need Blaire and Phoenix to work out what the link is.

I steer my thoughts back to the ball. Being here is my task – forge a relationship with Kailoh and show him his backing has been worth it. Have him help instate me on my Throne and get our plans to stop the Givings and find the Star back on track. The chatter around me falls silent at the same time the soft tendrils of a rich, exotic aroma fills my nose. Aeyva remains beside me, surveying the crowd.

'Tell me, Adelais'—my heart jerks at the voice behind me—'how are you enjoying the festivities?'

I turn on my stool to face the King. Should I get off and stand before him? The thought of catching my heel in the long dress he sent to my room keeps me seated.

'It's been a wonderful night, Your Majesty. Your hospitality is incredibly generous.'

He stands close to my side watching the room around us, one elbow propped on the tall table. I remind myself I am to be his equal and I don't give in to the temptation to look down. Instead, I take in his profile and the light that bounces off his high cheekbones. He smiles wide.

'I am good at celebrations, that is true.'

He turns to face me fully then, the smile still in place and my own smile grows wider at the openness in his features. 'Let me give you a tour of the Palace,' he says, holding out his arm.

I place my hand in the crook of his elbow and lean on him as I slide off the stool. Aeyva and Rory stand to attention on either side of us, waiting to follow. A quiet murmur of whispers follow us as we exit the ballroom and I hope the King can't hear my heart hammering at the attention of his Court. At his attention. Everything rides on him accepting me as a worthy ally, that I unquestioningly fill the role of Queen of Airlie. Given I have literally nothing but myself to bargain with, the pressure of being up to scratch physically presses on me. A hard breath escapes me at what that might mean.

'Your home is magnificent, Your Majesty,' I say when we're out of the ballroom and back in the main hallway.

The lights here have been dimmed as well, but it's brighter than the ballroom and the glow softens the stark white interior. My red shoes click loudly on the pale stone tiles. We round a corner and the King covers my hand with his free one.

'Please, call me Kailoh,' he says. 'Ruling a Court can be a lonely place, as I am sure you are beginning to discover. We need to keep our friends close.' He gives my hand a light squeeze.

'How do you know I am your friend?' I ask, and immediately regret it. Digging my nails into the palm of my free hand as I silently curse myself and my clumsy tongue.

Kailoh stops and looks at me without releasing my hand, laughter in his features.

'Isn't that what you want to be, Adelais? My friend, so I will accept your plight as my own? Believe that I need to help you take your Throne and find the Star to'—he sighs and waves his hand in the air—'save us all from the fate Nuala showed us both?' He cocks his head at me. 'Did I miss anything?'

I scramble to think of a suitable response, but he's captured it. I need everything from him – knowledge, power, resources, endorsement – and have nothing to offer in return but a vague hope I can help with the Star and ensuring Roisin's message doesn't come about. Something I have no idea how to do. I do have one piece of the Blue Pointed Star, and its absence tonight is heavy, but one without the other three doesn't give me anything.

'Wait,' he says, holding up a long finger. 'Before you respond, I will tell you an important thing about me.'

He turns now and looks over my head, behind me to Rory and Aeyva. I glance back at them, their faces giving nothing away. Kailoh's honey eyes return to mine, their amethyst rings sparkling in the light. He's taller than Lochlain and, while not quite as broad, he fills out his scarlet jacket well.

'For those in my circle, which is where you want to be, I expect authenticity. There are many things I will tolerate ... should I choose. But if you are deceptive with me, you walk a dangerous line. More than one charlatan has not left my Court. You should only need to ask your Sentinel if you need confirmation.' His face grows serious, and he looks over my head once more before his smile finds him again. 'The rest you will have to work out for yourself.' He moves to keep walking, taking me with him by the hand, but I stand still and pull against him lightly. He looks me over, mildly surprised.

'Kailoh.' I push down the nervous flutters that stir in my gut. 'I don't play games. On one condition.'

'And that is?'

'You do the same.'

He laughs softly and its genuineness surprises me. 'I think we're going to have a fun time together, Adelais. Here's to hoping it's fruitful.' He dips his head at me and we continue, hand in arm, through the Palace.

Aeyva wasn't wrong about Kailoh's passion for history, and he talks me through vast numbers of events associated with the different pieces he has collected over time and scattered throughout his Palace. My brain is full to bursting with new knowledge of the Realm and Mercasia when we walk through a guarded door, and the sounds of the Palace and my shoes on the tiles are immediately silenced.

'Oh,' I breathe.

I risk offending Kailoh by finally removing my hand from his warm, firm arm and turning on the spot to take in the room. It's heavily carpeted with rich, jewel-coloured tapestries on each wall and a full-length window overlooking his Court. I'm drawn to the window first and Kailoh trails me. For a moment, I am back in Siosal's compound, looking out at the rolling green hills, a colour I'd never seen so much of, before I started to burn. When I was only a member of the Guard, and not a Queen.

I place my hand on the cold glass to bring myself back to the present, straightening my spine. The multiple panes in the window outline the captivating view in black frames. Far below us, gardens lit with thousands of sparkling lights stretch towards the edge of the plateau before Ilcaena, the Heart of Mercasia, cascades away. I can just make out the gold and scarlet arches of the Wings dipping below the edge of the gardens. Soft, white flakes fall from the sky and settle on the ground.

'I've never seen snow before coming here,' I whisper.

'Not many in Driarn have,' he says quietly. 'Unfortunately, this looks like it's going to be another heavier storm than we're used to.'

'How is it the Calahi know so much about us, and we know nothing about you?' I ask, still watching the snow and marvelling at the cold beneath my fingers. Kailoh moves closer behind me.

'Well,' he starts, considering. 'We have the advantage of time, I suppose. But we have always been invested in knowing our impact on the world around us, and that world's impact on us. How can we thrive if we do not know how?'

'A question Driarn and the rest of the human world could ask, I think.'

'Yes. But some questions cannot be forced.'

'Perhaps they should be.'

'Is that what you will do, Adelais, force them to ask the hard questions?'

I look up at Kailoh, who's now beside me, and notice for the first time that he's not wearing a crown. Not that anyone would mistake who he is, but it surprises me all the same.

'That's a question I now ask myself everyday – am I strong enough to be that person?'

Kailoh looks at me sharply.

'Authentically me, remember?' I ask.

I'm captured in Kailoh's honey and purple gaze for a long moment. Rory shifts on his feet as he watches us, and a warmth begins to make its way across my chest. I pull my eyes away to look back at the falling snow. Far below, a black shape pads across the white carpet. A single howl echoes in the distance and the wolf below raises its head to answer. My scalp prickles and I lean harder against the glass to watch it. It turns to look up at the Palace and I'm hit with an unwavering sense that I'm where I am supposed to be.

'If Nuala's message wasn't enough,' Kailoh says, 'those wolves would tell me all I need to know. Roisin had a very particular ring of protection, including that very wolf down there, I imagine. Now you, the last of her line, are in a foreign Court and making a play for a world on its edge. I'd wager they'd follow you anywhere.'

I drag in a deep breath before I turn and take in the rest of the room Aeyva is not so subtly assessing. Her eyes have landed on a pedestal with a glass top and I walk towards it, my shoes sinking into the lightly patterned carpet.

'What's that?' I ask.

The glass top is gently lit from the inside from some unseen source. Kailoh doesn't respond and I look back to where he still stands by the window, his scarlet pants and jacket striking against the increasingly white view. He gestures to the pedestal with an outstretched hand, quietly encouraging me to look. The only sound as I draw near is that of my breath in my ears. Enclosed in the glass top is a small, ancient-looking book. A picture of a woman has been painted on the front, but the details are too faded for me to make out her face. Her crown though, is still clear.

As is the wolf at her side.

Kailoh's gaze is heavier now but, on impulse, I turn to Aeyva and Rory, my eyes wide. Aeyva stares back at me, urging me on, silently giving me the space here to be Kailoh's equal. I look back to the case.

'This is incredible, Kailoh,' I say quietly. 'What is it?'

'You know the story of Roisin, I assume?'

'Some.'

'Nuala said she traced your blood all the way to her.'

I drag my attention away from the book. 'Yes,' I confirm. 'That's how we got the message you saw earlier. Nuala traced my blood along with its memories and messages.'

Kailoh nods knowingly, his auburn hair shining in the firelight, as if none of that is news to him. Which I suppose it isn't.

'This is her story,' he continues. 'By which I don't mean a story about her, but the story she wrote of her own life. As much of it as she was able to live anyway. She was our First Queen, but I fear the stories about her that remain have been warped with time. This story, I believe, is much closer to the truth – this is who she truly was.'

I let my fingers gingerly trail the glass cover, the amber eyes of the wolf are clear as day and bore into my own. Kailoh's words strike a memory of a conversation with Blaire – about the gaps in what we accept as true. And I find myself desperately wanting to know what Roisin's own truth was.

CHAPTER EIGHTEEN

LISH

'Can I read it?' I dare to ask.

Kailoh places his fingers on the case next to mine.

'I'm afraid not, Adelais, the pages are now far too delicate for touch, even with our skills.' My outward breath gives away my disappointment. 'Fear not, I happen to know her particular story very well.'

The warmth from the fire in the corner caresses my skin.

'Tell me what you know,' he says.

I take a moment, thinking through what I've heard of Roisin.

'I know she was the First Queen of the Realm. That she was ... corrupted, thought to be somehow due to her sapphire. I know that sapphire was smashed, and its pieces distributed throughout the Realm.' I look at Kailoh. 'I know some Manorynxes have questioned the corruption – whatever that means – and that I am supposed to find the pieces of that sapphire for instructions on how to stop the destruction Nuala saw.'

I raise my hand to touch Lochlain's pendant at my chest only to remember it's not there. At the last minute, Ciara had told me it didn't go with my outfit and she now wears it under her clothes instead. Its absence sharpens the knowledge that Lochlain isn't here, either, and I blink away how much I'm missing him. Wherever Ciara is, I know she keeps the pendant safe.

Kailoh nods slowly. 'True enough, I suppose,' he says. 'And you are right, there are questions around Roisin's supposed corruption. But do you not wonder about her? We have these historical figures whose lives are boiled down to fact, often not even true fact, but accepted fact. Yet we know nothing about them.'

'What does her story tell you about her?'

He smiles gently, happy in my genuine curiosity.

'That she was incredibly, unapologetically, loving. That's probably the thing that stood out to me the most.' Kailoh shifts from the window and sits facing me from the settee, his arm draped gracefully over the back.

'She had a partner, a Soul Accord, she loved deeply and young ones she adored – both of her blood, and ones he brought to their union. But it's evident throughout that love sustained her. And, in turn, she sustained the world around her. She is the first example we have of a Calahi whose magic was symbiotic with nature. We know other Calahi from her time were powerful, incredibly so, but they hadn't yet wondered where it came from. Roisin had a gift no one had seen before, and she gave it life like no other had, either.'

Kailoh smiles gently, my face obviously giving away the churning happening in my mind to try and understand. He gestures to the window.

'Roisin effectively made everything you see in the Realm, architecture aside, with her own bare hands. After her death, we were split into the three Courts. Although, there were suggestions at one time that she may still live,' he says, holding my gaze.

A small hole feels like it opens in the bottom of my stomach. If the First Queen lives...

'But,' he continues, 'I have found nothing to support that claim. It's also said, though – and this I do have more faith in – that her power still resides in her final resting place.' He ponders this for a moment, and I swallow the strange sense of disappointment that started to gather at the mention of another living Queen. 'Its location has been lost to time – or perhaps it was never actually revealed – and ... extracting and holding that power may not be the same thing.' Kailoh leans towards me slightly. 'But that doesn't mean that her power wasn't, isn't still, greatly coveted.'

'Could you be wrong about whether she lives?' I ask quietly. Even for a Calahi, it would be an impossible amount of time – but there is still so much I don't know about this world.

Kailoh shakes his head. 'I can assure you, if she does, it is not like we do now. And not enough for her to come back.' His gaze is both sad and pointed. 'Her place of rest must be protected at all costs. As Queen of Airlie, you should make it a priority of yours, also. There are those among us who have been cursed for trying to take a power that wasn't theirs. But, if someone was to succeed in finding the location and ...' I watch as the smile slides from his face. 'Well, let's just say that Roisin's magic had the ability to create. In the wrong hands, how difficult would it be to let it destroy, instead?'

I hold his gaze as I let his words fill the different spaces in my mind. Something nags at me.

'You said "let" it destroy?'

His eyebrows kick up. 'Yes,' he says. 'If hers was the power of creation, and it's currently residing in her final resting place, it's potentially our last tether to the Mother. A last kernel of what's keeping us here – all *this* here.' He gestures out the window. 'If someone was to take that power from there, even if they didn't actively use it to erase what she created, isn't it possible that merely the absence of it would do it anyway?'

My chin drops towards my chest as I study the wolf in the painting. The gravity of what that implies pressing on the back of my head, like someone is trying to push me under the surface of a body of water.

'There are a number of stories about what happened to Roisin when, and after, she was supposedly corrupted.'

'So you don't believe that either?' I ask. His gaze searches my face when I look back at him.

'I know she wasn't,' he says.

We watch each other for a moment, and I let my awareness of Aeyva and Rory fade a little as I assess his handsome face.

'You're wondering what that means,' he says, and I nod. He draws a deep breath. 'It means Roisin's power was taken unfairly from her and, thus, from the world. It means I think her power needs to be returned to us, and to the Mother, but the risk of it going very wrong is high. Wielding another's power, and certainly that much power, is most likely to destroy everything in the bearer's path – as well as the bearer themselves.'

I swallow. Just as the fire light shifts and snags on something small in the corner of the case.

A piece of deep blue sapphire. The piece that Nuala entrusted to him for safe keeping.

Kailoh catches my eye and holds my gaze.

My mind is still snagged on the sapphire, and it takes me a moment too long to answer.

'Maybe Roisin didn't go mad,' I say. 'But she still carried a great weight.'

He spreads his fingers out on the velvet as if he'd like to caress her book.

'She did,' he says quietly. 'And she left a tear in the fabric of the Realm no one has been able to mend. But she lived her life exactly how she wanted. At least until the end.'

He looks like that should be a comfort, but I'm not sure if that makes the fact her life was cut short better or worse. Silently, I move to join him on the small couch.

'I have been mulling over your question of strength – if you are strong enough to make others ask, or perhaps answer, hard questions,' he says when I'm settled, 'and I may have something that can help. Both with proving that to yourself and ... in gathering the pieces of the Star.'

Near the door, Rory and Aeyva both focus on Kailoh with a deathly stillness. The corners of Kailoh's mouth lift slightly. A look that's far too knowing. Of what, though, I don't know.

'How might that be?' I ask.

'If I am correctly informed, you currently hold one piece – the Wolverton Pendant,' he says.

I blink. It's common knowledge that piece was given back to Lochlain after the Challenge. But there's something in Kailoh's tone that makes me think he knows I personally have it, not Lochlain.

'You know one resides in your crown and where I keep the one the Manorynxes entrusted to me.' He lifts a finger from the arm of the seat and gestures to the case with Roisin's book. 'I can tell you where to find the final piece.'

My mouth drops open. 'That,' I start, 'sounds too easy. And are you just going to hand your piece over?'

Kailoh laughs deeply. 'I said I know where it is, Adelais. Not that it would be easy. In fact, now that I know where it is, I know just how hard it will be.'

'What do you mean now that you know?'

He crosses one leg over the other as he shifts towards me again. 'I have researched our origins alongside the best in the Realm,' he says, gaze flicking to Aeyva. 'But it was only today that a certain theory of mine was proven correct.' The soft purple in his eyes sparkles and I wonder how it can be so similar, and yet so different, to the colour in Siosal's. 'When Aeyva showed me the information Nuala collected, there was a memory of three women in a meadow - do you know which I refer to?'

The meadow where she also met with the Calahi she called her wolf, Arlo. The same as Phoenix referred to Lochlain – as 'my' wolf. I nod.

'I recognised those women,' he says. 'They were cursed – by the sapphire or the Mother, I can't be sure – but they were not the same after that day. The day they destroyed our First Queen. The first lost her true form, unable to conjure a corporeality that would allow her to completely live, despite being able to move freely through the Realm. The second was effectively banished, her form mostly intact but unable to live in view of anyone else. Their power was anchored together so the fate that befell one might befall the other, but this theory has never been tested. And one of them became somewhat of a hoarder. I am absolutely confident she will have held the final piece of the sapphire – as a trophy, if you will.'

I blow out a breath, my cheeks puffing in a very unqueenly manner.

'And you know where to find where she would have kept it?' I ask, my voice barely above a whisper.

He nods. 'But I can't go with you, unfortunately. As King, in a time of uncertainty in the Realm, putting myself at risk would be unfair to my Court.'

I stare at him, unsure if he's serious, but there's genuine regret in his face and I suppose it makes sense on one level.

He looks straight at Aeyva. 'Let me talk plainly here,' he says. 'Where I send you is to one of the sisters. A cursed pair whose existence is bolstered by the other – their power runs between the two of them like a circuit.

Take out one and the other's strength is greatly diminished. Almost makes them defeatable, one by one.'

I frown, the expression mirrored on Rory's face.

'Meaning they're not now?' I ask.

'No. The agreement I made with them was to let them be as they are, providing they stayed in bounds. To date, they have done nothing to force my hand.'

My head spins. I'd known Kailoh was powerful in his own right, but just how magical does this mean he is? How powerful are these sisters?

'And which sister will remain after this? Which one becomes defeatable?' Aeyva asks, the colour draining from her face.

'The Eternal Queen.'

Our suite in Kailoh's Palace is impossibly beautiful, with a number of bedrooms off a central sitting room. The pile of the pale-grey carpet is so deep my feet all but disappear as I find the comfiest looking sofa to make my home for this discussion. My eyes are heavy and dry with tiredness, but Aeyva insists we talk now while the details are fresh.

So I sit and watch her wear a path in the carpet.

Kailoh has given us – me – an opportunity to prove myself as a warrior queen. My heart skitters at the thought. But, if I examine it, it's the right one. Being a figurehead Queen is not in my future. If I am going to lead Airlie and the Realm out of uncertainty and into a future filled with magic and life, I will do it by getting my hands dirty. I didn't spend my whole adult life in the Guard for nothing. But, as a lightness takes hold in my chest at really stepping into my place as Queen, it's anchored by Lochlain's comments on being General. The sense of rightness he has at being in the role he was destined for.

Two roles, two destinies. But, according to the Court of Airlie, those two things run in parallel. Never to meet in the middle.

Riley joins us a moment later in her tracksuit pants and t-shirt, all traces of the evening's makeup washed from her face. Rory shifts a cushion on his couch to make room for her, but she passes him by and snuggles in with me.

'I'm better at thinking when I've slept,' she mock whispers. 'Do the Calahi not need sleep? Actually no,' she says, flashing me a grin. 'I do not need to know how much you and Lochlain don't sleep.'

I swat at her with a cushion and she yelps, laughing. Across from me, Rory smirks.

'I should have recognised them,' Aeyva says, irritation in her voice.

'As far as I can recall,' Rory says, 'you didn't finish your training with Nuala. So how could you have recognised them when she didn't?'

She glares at him briefly. 'Because ... perhaps it would have been useful if I'd given her and Benny some more of my time.' Her voice fades in anger as she talks. 'But I'm not surprised Kailoh knows.'

'So you trust him on this?' I ask.

As I search her normally cold face for an answer, I realise how much I am coming to rely on her knowledge. Kailoh has the history. Nuala can guide me with the Court and Prominent Families. But it's Aeyva, and this group, I look to for how to take the very next step.

'Unfortunately.'

'Unfortunately?' Riley asks.

Aeyva sighs. 'Retrieving a piece of sapphire from the Eternal Queen's sister will be no small feat. It's not something I'm happy for any of us to be walking into.'

Her eyes flash with something I can't place. I haven't seen Ciara since the ballroom, and I wonder what else is driving Aeyva's uncertainty.

'We'll do it together, Aeyva, love.' Rory's deep voice is soothing to my tired self, and I rest my head back on the couch and try not to let my eyelids drift closed. 'We retrieve the next piece, discuss alliance details with Kailoh on our return, and add his piece to the mix. Then we travel back to Airlie with his support to seat Lish on the throne and in position to get the final piece in the crown. Easy.'

There's something in their faces, particularly Rory's, that tells me I might not like the discussion with Kailoh about his piece of the Star. I shake away the memory of Lochlain raising his name in our discussion in the cabin. One about who might be *worthy* of me. And I focus on the fact Roisin also had a Soul Accord. Someone her magic talked to – danced with. If that's not the reason Lochlain makes my heart swell and my skin tingle with his emotions, I can't imagine another possibility. Surely the Realm will believe in that above all else, even if it's between a Queen and her General.

Aeyva closes her eyes momentarily and I try not to stare. It's not a tell I've seen her give before and I don't think it's just about Ciara. Opening those steel and aqua eyes, she looks around at us all.

'This will be hard,' she says. 'We do this my way, and we might just pull it off.' She sighs heavily and even Rory looks concerned. 'The price will be memories.'

I frown.

'But each of us here knows too much about the Star, Roisin's Place and our plans – they can't be shared with someone who tried to steal it. So I will need to ask someone else a favour – an impossibly large one.'

I wriggle my way out of the deep couch, letting Riley fall into my spot. Just like that, Aeyva has ensured I won't be sleeping tonight. But I don't share my concerns with the others. They have come so far with me, and for their Court. They at least deserve to try and get a night's sleep without hearing more of my worries that will be so similar to their own.

But, as I walk towards my bedroom, I can't help but feel I am taking a significant step towards gaining the alliance with Kailoh and becoming Queen. And taking one away from Lochlain.

'Great,' I say to cover the sting in my eyes. 'Sleep first, then we raid.'

CHAPTER NINETEEN

AEYVA

I do up my leather vest, jerking the waist strap tightly. After almost a full night of tossing and turning, waiting for any sound Ciara might make as she returned, I didn't hear a single one.

Rory took last guard during the early hours of the morning, meaning I was able to torture myself in the privacy of the bedroom I'd claimed. I don't know if it makes it better or worse that I now know for sure Ciara spent the night elsewhere, and my thoughts pivot between Ciara and what she might be starting with someone else, and the retrieval of the piece of Star.

The sisters have been known throughout our Calahi history as a fearsome pair. Cursed or created was always the discussion, but I never knew the answer – perhaps I would have known if I'd finished my training with Nuala and Benny. But Sentinels don't need that sort of training and, by then, I'd committed to the Eternal Queen anyway; the less I knew about her the better, it seemed. With that decision made, it was all I could do to not be swallowed by my own darkness, I couldn't add the weight of anyone else's.

What I did know was the Eternal Queen was incredibly powerful. But there were – are – restrictions to their existence. I just didn't care what they were, not when she offered me a life to drown away my pain in someone else's – all for a greater cause. My hair is silky where it slips through my fingers as I braid it back, out of my face, and I focus on the sensation.

Now, Kailoh is suggesting I don't let her sister walk away when we bargain for the piece of the sapphire she holds. Not only will we be one step closer to putting the Star together, I'll be able to face a more equally weighted opponent if I need to kill the Eternal Queen as well. Killing her is the only way I will be released from my vows; I knew going in that it was a 'til death' agreement. I just wish I knew then what I do now – that there's hope.

My stomach rolls over. I might be able to play at being Sentinel for now, when Lish isn't formally on the Throne, but the swearing in ceremony for that role will require a commitment I won't be able to make when those vows have been given to the Society instead.

But I *will* be Sentinel. Whatever it takes.

And it will be alongside Ciara. My gut lurches again. A lifetime of working to, and with, the one Calahi I'd give everything in the world for. The one who doesn't want it in return. I'd accepted that – when I couldn't see the steps to get out. Then Kailoh appeared in my villa and told me he had a plan for me to get out of the Society. Now, I have the how to see it through.

I watch over Ilcaena as the sun begins its journey across the sky, the clear skies giving me renewed focus from the swirls my mind takes in the dark of night. When it's fully visible, just leaving the horizon, I turn to the door.

My ribs squeeze as I find Ciara waiting in the sitting room. She's fully kitted out in her black uniform, her dark hair braided similar to my own and hanging down her back. Her eyes find mine immediately. As if she was staring at the exact spot I would appear.

Neither of us moves, but the air almost pulses between us.

'This is a disgraceful hour, you realise?' Riley asks as she joins us, yawning.

I blink and Ciara looks away, something on her face I can't place. Hurt? Disappointment?

Once Lish joins us, we collect Rory from his post outside the doors on the way out. At this time, and following the ball last night, we should be safe from the prying eyes of all but the Palace staff. But it's impossible to keep track of who each one reports to on the side, so I take us to a mostly unused room. The dust whirls slightly as we make our way into what was once a sitting room for visiting, but lesser, Calahi.

'Ror, we need to get to the outer limits of the Heart of Mercasia, behind the Palace. Just before the Range starts,' I tell him.

'Anything for you.' He winks.

He holds his arms out a fraction from his sides, palms up. Ciara takes the hand closest to her as Riley stands on his other side. He looks down at her and holds her gaze as she slowly slides her hand into his. Lish glances at her and smiles softly as she takes Riley's other hand and stands close.

Leaving me with Ciara.

I join the line and she easily slips her hand into mine. A sense of rightness is almost overwhelming and my magic kicks into life, an insistent fizzing in my veins. I may not be right for the role of Manorynx but I will be a damn good Sentinel, and I will serve as well as I can beside this Calahi that owns my heart. My palm tingles and I hold on tightly. Just as the wind of Rory's magic begins to whip around my ears, she returns the pressure around my fingers.

Lish and Riley gape as Rory delivers us softly into a small clearing covered in snow. Not for the first time, I marvel at Rory's accuracy. There are others in the Realm with a similar skill, but none as precise – which could also be a by-product of how long and deep our relationship runs. Despite, or perhaps because of, the hurt that was between us in our early days, our connection will always bind us. Along with the thought of what could have been.

'I wish the others could see this,' Riley says to Lish. She crouches down to brush her fingertips in the snow. 'It's unbelievable.'

Lish joins her. 'Can you imagine the rioting we'd have to sort out over this in Rhyton?'

Riley laughs as I turn in a circle to confirm my bearings.

'This way.' I begin my way through the snow and try, and fail, to see the world through Riley's eyes.

We don't walk very far, but it's still enough for Lish and Riley to fall behind. Each of them stagger through the snow, disappearing up to their knees when they stand in the wrong spot, and it gives way beneath them. Rory follows behind them, dragging them out of the snow as needed.

Ciara walks effortlessly beside me through the trees at the foot of the Range, every bit the powerful Calahi she is. But there's a grace to her that's rare; perhaps it's her Wolverton blood.

'You know Mercasia well,' she says without looking at me. I can't tell what lies beneath the words.

The large tree I have been heading towards comes into view and I glance to Ciara. With her dark braid over her far shoulder, I can see the top of her tattoo before it disappears under her collar. The gold rays of sunshine snake delicately on her skin, the ends running up into her hairline. She deserves to know of the commitments I've made – ones that will impact my role in Lish's Court – whatever the fallout is for me. I won't put her in a position of being the lead Sentinel with a compromised partner. She deserves better than that.

But my voice catches in my throat. Somehow, even though part of me has been desperate for no secrets between us, now I have the opportunity, I can't find the words.

She waits.

The tree is tall and gnarled – strong, despite all the things it's witnessed in our Realm.

'A long time ago,' I say quietly, as I crouch at the base of the trunk, 'I made a decision – a commitment—'

Riley's laboured breathing announces the arrival of the others and I drag my eyes away from Ciara's gold ones, shamefully thankful for the distraction. I don't know what I could have said that wouldn't fundamentally change the way she sees me. To Ciara, I am supposed to be a Manorynx – one of the greatest of our kind. And yet I want to be a Sentinel. But ultimately, I went with being part of the Society.

And, in doing so, have left a vacuum of knowledge to succeed Nuala.

'I thought this shit was supposed to be beautiful,' Riley gripes. 'This,' she says, pointing to her soaked clothes, 'is not beautiful. This is shit.'

Ciara and I laugh, the sound warming me a little on the inside. Poor humans, they could really benefit from some Calahi help at times.

'Everything beautiful bites, sweetheart, the question is how hard?'

'Don't tell me you have a muzzle,' she says.

Rory's chortle bounces around us.

The tree bark is coarse as I run my fingers along the tops of the exposed roots. My memory doesn't fail me – the notch is exactly where I remember and I murmur the words, the entrance shuddering into view at the base of the tree. The rough stairs are dusty at the edges, a well-worn path down the centre. The other members of the Society aren't who I would call my friends, but I don't wish many of them ill-will. They might not all be Calahi who can be free, without cause or purpose, in the Realm, but I still breathe a bit easier to know they are okay. Including Keeva, who, outside of this group and the ones we left behind, is one of the closest things I have to a friend. Her and Kailoh – not that I'd ever admit that to him.

Some things I'd never live down.

'Please tell me there's no more snow on the other side of this one,' Riley says, coming up behind me.

I stand to face them.

'You've been to this establishment before, Riley,' I say. I let my gaze flick over the three of them and stifle a sigh. I draw a breath and try not to focus on each of their calculating stares. Instead, I imagine them as just more soldiers in my team. I clear my throat.

'Kailoh has given us a broad location for the sister,' I tell them. 'But we'll need to get as specific as we can if we're going to catch her by surprise. Down here,' I jerk my thumb at the entrance in the tree, 'is someone who knows Rothani as well as I know Mercasia. If there is anything more we can learn of the sister's location, it's here.'

Ciara searches my face. 'He also said we need memories to tempt her into a trade,' she says. 'Aside from the "gifts" he said the Eternal Queen brings her, being unable to live in view of others means she hasn't been able to have the life she wanted. So, apparently, she lives vicariously through others' memories. But ... the curse, or her nature before it, means I'm going to wager she's not interested in happy ones.'

A sinking feeling tries to settle in my gut.

'It can't be me,' I say, clearing my throat. 'I don't have all of Nuala and Benny's knowledge, but it's too much of a risk to give her access to me.'

'Of course,' Ciara says immediately. 'I can do it.'

That sinking feeling turns cold. I know what she's talking about. A time her magic got too big for her. A time more Calahi died, as her magic burned through the layers between life and death, than I allowed her to count. A time that the only thing that stood between her and complete destruction was me and my own magic. The way our gifts responded to each other. My heart skips a beat at the memory and I clear my throat.

Lish and Riley look between us.

'No,' I say. 'There's someone here who might be willing.'

'And where is this exactly?'

'It's a Society House.'

The gold in her eyes flares and I make myself hold her stare, even as the others watch us. But is it surprise that I know the location of a Society House, or that I've told her that's made them spark?

CHAPTER TWENTY

AEYVA

It's a different way in, but the tunnel leads to the same tavern I brought Riley and Rory previously. My skin crawls having Ciara here. Of all the places I wanted to avoid her being, this was very high on the list.

But, if we are to succeed in getting the fourth piece of the sapphire – and for me to try and kill one of the most powerful beings in the Realm – I need Keeva's help. It's the sapphire that takes priority. Whatever it means for my future, my dreams to get out come second. I can't risk killing her without knowing we have the sapphire.

I allow myself one last look at Ciara and mentally apologise to her, for what feels like complete duplicity, before I lead them all up the stairs, drawing a knife as I go. Slowly, I open the door at the top.

'Stand down,' I say as I walk through, knife at my side. Two large Calahi flank the door. 'Put them away, I have company.'

The smaller one moves, quicker than expected, and latches on to Riley. She doesn't make a sound as she drives her knee into his side. Rory's knife is at his neck before he can recover and Riley steps back, spitting in his face.

'I said, stand down,' I repeat flatly.

I only move again when I can see each of their chosen weapons are returned to their homes. Most of these Calahi have worked under me at different times and are each magically skilled as well. But the show of no weapons is enough for me to continue through the doorway, exposing the others who trail behind me. These two are ones I'd trust to not be under the unquestioning control of the Eternal Queen, but I think of the Society members I've had to ... dispatch, ones that came to enjoy the spilling of others' blood too much, and I'm reminded how many there are that can't be left unchecked.

'I need to see Keeva,' I say to no one in particular, walking to the bar.

I nod at the Calahi who runs the drinks service, several humans scuttling around him doing his bidding. I direct Lish to the seat immediately in front of me, Rory does the same to Riley so he and I stand between them and the rest of the patrons who unashamedly watch our every move. Ciara stands to the side of Rory and Riley, making us appear like any other group chatting at the bar. Except no one else here has brought two humans, one a Queen, into an assassins' den.

'I knew you'd be back quickly,' Keeva's voice sounds from along the bar.

She stands a distance away, one hand propped on the sticky timber top. Her fire-coloured hair is pulled into braids on either side of her head. This morning, they were probably taut. Now, they end in a wild pile of flame at the base of her skull. There was a time I ran my hands through that hair and noticed its coarse curls in a detached way. Now, in Ciara's presence, I wish I'd never even seen it. But that's not fair to Keeva. Especially with what I've come to ask her – that she do what I can't. In my attempts to serve my Realm, and the Court of Airlie, I have somehow become compromised. Not only because my commitment to the Society interferes with my ability to be a Sentinel, but because my partial training as a Manorynx makes it dangerous for me to even fulfil that duty if I want to.

I turn and smile at her, ignoring the way Ciara's now black eyes don't leave my friend and the evidence of my messy role in the Realm.

'It seems nothing can keep me away,' I say.

'But that precious face of yours tells me it's more than the memory of me that's brought you back this time, Aeyva – you're too easy to read.' She watches me for a moment. 'Perhaps we should talk elsewhere.'

The Calahi and humans I came with look intently at me, Ciara's gaze holding questions I don't want to answer.

'Do not move,' I say quietly. 'And neither of these two leave your sides.' I jerk my head at Lish and Riley.

Keeva leads me out of the public room and down a narrow timber hallway to the office she uses most here. It's simple and sparsely furnished.

The Society House is not a place for home comforts, having them here would only encourage complacency.

'I assume it's only a business discussion?' Keeva asks, pouring me a drink after I close the door behind me.

'It's business ... and an opportunity.'

Her attention lifts from the glass in her hand to my face.

'I need something from the Eternal Queen's sister,' I continue, 'and then I intend to kill her. Kailoh thinks her power is linked to the Eternal Queen's. If I take out the sister, I take out the Eternal Queen's power base.'

She blows her breath out loudly. 'You've always had a death wish, Aeyva, but this ...'

'I don't. Not really. But I could release us all from our vows to her.' I search her face, knowing exactly the hope I will find there. 'We could have our own lives, Keeva.'

She places her glass heavily on the timber desk she leans on. 'And what of the ones who need to be kept in check?'

I toss my drink back and nod as I swallow the burning liquid.

'I thought you might like that job. Kailoh agrees.'

'Fuck, Aeyva, this is a bad idea.'

I give her a moment, watching the thoughts running behind her eyes. The assessment that's happening in front of me. She knows my past, knows the Manorynx knowledge I possess – however incomplete – can't be shared with anyone. So she knows it's the pivots in my life that now impact hers.

'Kailoh thinks she's in the capital – or under it somewhere,' I say. 'Have you heard anything more than that?'

She nods shallowly. 'You're going to need more than directions. I can get you as close as I know, but I've never had anyone come back after that point to tell the rest of the way – after that, it will be a hunt for her. What's your plan, though? I highly doubt you'll be able to surprise her enough to take her out unawares.'

Something a lot like guilt tightens itself in my chest. 'I was hoping to use your memories as a trade.'

Keeva stares at me and a flicker of doubt grows in my gut. I'd told the others we couldn't use our memories for this assignment, and I meant it.

Giving the Eternal Queen, through her sister, access to our information is equally as dangerous as engaging them in an outright confrontation.

I'd really thought Keeva would pull through for me on this. Despite that we didn't end up where she'd hoped, I know how she feels about the Society and its Queen. And I know how fearless she can be.

She pours herself another drink and downs it in a single swallow. A third one chases it.

'A really fucking bad idea, Keeva,' she says to herself.

And then she slides off the desk and stands. 'Let's do this madness. I need a future that's my own.'

Rory takes us, with Keeva's directions, to the outskirts of the capital of Rothani – Dechua, a city I try and avoid whenever possible. It's only ever Society work that brings me here. If Airlie is the fairest of our Courts, the one that still glows in the light of being Roisin's birthplace, Rothani is the opposite. It's not awful – not compared to places in the human world – but it's rougher. More brutal. Particularly to those that can't defend themselves. Had I lived here when I was expecting my young one, not even my bonding to Lochlain would have saved me from being vilified.

The city itself looks the same as I last saw it. Charcoal buildings that blend in beautifully with the green surrounds. Dechua is full of lush greenery with plainer architecture, compared to Elenlea's vibrant colours, but it doesn't diminish its beauty. It's more timeless, somehow, even as it provides a background for a more violent Court.

Keeva looks Rory over. 'Skills like yours could be handy in my crew, gorgeous.'

'He's not looking for a crew,' I say without looking away from the cityscape.

Beside me, Riley shivers slightly despite the warmer temperature of the Rothani sky. She's still soaked from her stumbles through the snow, as is Lish.

Rory's soft chuckle registers dimly. 'I have my hands plenty full enough with the crew I have, but I'll take the compliment.'

'Where to from here?' Ciara cuts in.

Keeva assesses her coolly. 'Wherever I lead you.'

Ciara steps towards her casually, a move I know belies the tension underneath, one that screams Sentinel, and I brush my palm over the knife at my side.

'Let me make this clear,' she says, her eyes completely black. 'You are here because Aeyva seems to trust you. But I will not think twice about putting you in the ground should I feel the need.'

Keeva laughs. 'Don't fret, darling, the feeling is entirely mutual.'

Ciara steps back so she can face us all again and I lower my hand as I breathe out. Killing Keeva because she makes a move on Ciara is not on my agenda today.

'We go in and retrieve this piece of the sapphire. Nothing else happens until we've got it. Understood?' Ciara asks, levelling me with her gaze before she takes in the rest of the group.

'Understood,' I say.

'Then,' she continues, now not looking at me at all, 'if we have an opportunity to neutralise her, we take it.'

My heart skips a beat. Does she know I need this? Or is this part of her duty to Lish?

We loosely separate into groups of four and two to draw less attention to ourselves as we make our way through Dechua. Ciara and I trail behind Keeva, who's leading Rory, Riley, and Lish. The Calahi around us wear colours the same as those in Airlie, but the trend here seems to be more muted.

'She knows everything, I take it?' Ciara asks as we walk, carefully watching the group in front of us. The implied statement is that Keeva knows more than she does. Which is true. It creates a band of tension around my chest. That's not the way it's supposed to be.

'She does. She is the only one I know who can get us close and she's willing to share the memories that will be asked of us.'

'That's ... good of her,' she says. 'I assume she agreed because of you?'

I steal a glance at her, finding her face impassive. But is that jealousy in her voice?

'She's an old friend,' I say carefully. There's an undercurrent to our conversation that feels dangerously close to revealing exactly how I feel about Ciara and the mess I've made of my path to Sentinel.

'We all need friends, Aeyva. But if she compromises what we need to do here today, or Lish's safety, she's finished.'

We head closer to the city centre, Keeva never wavering in her direction. Her red hair disappears off the crowded street and down a flight of stairs to the Flyer station. Calahi mill around us as we descend into the brightly lit station that's unique to Dechua – the rest of the Realm's transportation is above ground. Making our way through the throng, I'm reminded how many Calahi there are whose lives continue on, oblivious to the threats that surround them.

Keeva strides down the landing and the crowds thin out around us – then the four of them disappear altogether.

I grab Ciara's hand and drag her forward in a half jog, breaking through Keeva's shield. Only because she lets me. The activity on the landing continues as if we were never there and, for any Calahi who might look this way, we're not.

Keeva glances at us once, as if accounting for our presence, before running her hands along the smooth, pale blue wall. The lower portion gives way beneath her touch and slides to the side. Lish is about to duck through when Keeva throws out her arm to block the way.

She looks solely at me.

'Are you sure about this? There's no turning back once we're inside.'

'I need that bit of sapphire, Keeva,' Lish says, as if the question was directed at her.

I can only nod.

'And then we deal with the sister,' Riley says. There's a fire in her eyes that tells me she knows exactly what she's saying. That she sees the way out I need and wants to help me get it. Why, I can't be sure. But then I guess that's one of the things about the Calahi, the people, who have ended up in my life – we all want something better.

I just hope I can be whatever that is.

CHAPTER TWENTY-ONE

LISH

The stench of the tunnel brings tears to my eyes. The Calahi do sewerage differently to how we do it in Driarn and that's not the smell that greets me, but the sweet rot of decomposition. I slip on something underfoot and force myself not to try and see what. Ciara said Kailoh talked about 'gifts' the Eternal Queen gave her sister and the queasiness in my gut is almost as much from the knowledge I now possess of what they must be, as the smell itself. Were they alive or already dead when they were brought down here? The reason for Keeva's presence in our group suggests they were alive – but how long did they live after their memories were taken? I can't see the walls and keep my limbs tucked closely to my body to avoid brushing up against anything.

Someone gags behind me.

'Welcome to the hive,' Keeva says, her voice muffled, I assume because of the hand she covers her mouth with. 'You'll never get used to the odour. Form a chain and follow me. A little further in, I can give us some light – it's best not to do it here. After that ... well, I fucking hope you've got good tracking skills, Aeyva.'

She waits for a moment, every beat of silence and darkness pulsing through me.

'My knowledge of what happens from here is purely theoretical,' Aeyva says quietly. 'No one Keeva or I know has been beyond this point and told the tale before.'

Rory curses softly.

We grapple around in the dark for a few minutes as we attempt to form a single line with Keeva in the front and Rory at the back. I have a handful of Riley's shirt in front of me, and Ciara's slipped her fingers in my belt from behind. Slowly, we each start to put one foot in front of the other and move further into the darkness, into the smell that's so thick I can taste it.

Keeva eventually summons a soft ball of light in the palm of her hand like I've seen Lochlain do before.

My head starts to swim with the decay that fills my nose.

'Wait,' Riley whispers hoarsely, the muscles in her back clench with the effort of throwing up as I run my palm up and down her spine.

'Sorry,' she croaks when she's done.

I watch the soft light Keeva holds aloft from over Riley's shoulder.

The minutes pass slowly, the only sounds our collective breathing and the crunching squelch from beneath our feet. I've seen my share of disturbing scenes in the Guard, both intentional and accidental, and there's a sinisterness to the intentional ones that permeates the air – as if it eddies differently around whatever is left behind. That same sensation fills the tunnel now. I focus on the sounds around us, how they move, what I can see and smell, the emotions running over my skin. These all form part of my Guard trained instincts and I slip them on easily. With them, and this team, I know I can manage whatever lies at the other end of this tunnel of decay.

Riley comes to a stop and I squint to see we're standing in a wider portion of the tunnels, surrounded by several black openings.

'This is as far as I know,' Keeva says quietly. 'The Calahi I brought down here ... this is where I left them.'

Aeyva and Keeva share a look, one of some shared understanding I can only guess at.

'*This* is as far as you know?' I ask. 'Which one do we take?'

A strange sound echoes down one and I shudder.

Aeyva straightens in the dim light and closes her eyes. Ciara watches her intently, as if something will magically appear in her place. She looks so like Nuala did the night she took me into the meadow that I suppose something might. Her eyes open slowly, as if she's pulling herself from a trance, and she turns to the right of the tight circle we've made.

'I think it's one of those,' she says, pointing to two of the five black holes.

The hairs on the back of my neck stand up as the sound comes again. Riley shifts on her feet.

'Can you hear that?' she whispers.

A tingle runs down my spine as the sound becomes clear.

A howl.

For the first time since we left Kailoh's to find this piece, *take* this piece, a feeling of surety washes over me. The black space on the left of the two Aeyva pointed out draws all my attention and I step away from Riley, almost as if I'm being dragged towards the blackness.

The howl sounds again and I look back to the others to find Ciara has drifted close to my side, the gold of her tattoo seeming to glow in the low light.

'This one,' she murmurs.

'We need to mark our way back,' Riley says, drawing the knife from the sheath at her side and scratching a mark into the wall, it comes away covered in gore. A memory of Will doing the same thing to the trees in Althea Forest flashes in my mind. I push back the dull ache that winds its way through me at the reminder of the permanent goodbye I almost had to make with him. And the one I did have to do with Hayes.

'I'll be able to get us out, Riley,' Rory says, his voice bouncing gently in the small, rounded room.

'We need to expect that she will know we're coming,' Aeyva says, joining us as we crowd around the entrance to the next tunnel, a low, wolfish grumble emitting from the space. 'Our first priority is to trade Keeva's memories for the sapphire.'

Something in Aeyva's face reminds me of the conversation we had with Kailoh – how killing this sister would weaken the Eternal Queen, and the look on Aeyva's face then. An expression of terror ... and hope.

'Aeyva,' I say, reaching out and taking her arm in my hand. The wolf howls again and, for some reason, I think it has more to do with Aeyva than the tunnel this time. 'Kailoh said we could do two things here – retrieve the sapphire and weaken the Eternal Queen.'

She nods sharply. 'The Star is the priority,' she says. She's looking at me so she doesn't see the pain on Ciara's face when she looks between us. I pretend not to notice. But right now, as I stand with them in this dark, rank space, I know the Calahi we are about to bargain with needs to die.

There is no 'if'.

As we move into the tunnel the howl came from, my ears hum with the sound of small bones cracking under our feet, the wet smack of boots lifting in and out of what remains beneath us.

The wolves will guide you, my mother told me. *The wolves will guard your path*, Benny said. Could this be the same wolf I saw from Kailoh's Palace? Or the one from Nuala's tracing that said now is my time? Perhaps they are one and the same. As I follow the tunnel with a quietening howl echoing around, and a Wolverton has once again positioned herself at my back, the gold flame in my chest burns a little hotter.

Our human chain starts to slow and the faint glow of a light appears up ahead, seeping around the rough shape of a door. One made of the brittle white and yellow of bones with what looks like a finger of bone protruding as the handle.

As I watch, the finger slowly spins so it faces upwards and beckons in a 'come closer' motion. I swallow. Ciara grips the back of my pants tighter, but I don't miss the sound of blades being drawn around me. I step in front of Riley, twisting so I can pull Ciara off me and forcing them behind. Until it's just me, facing the bone door, flanked by my team.

I turn for a moment, searching for Keeva. 'Are you sure?' I ask as our eyes lock.

'Here's to a better me,' she says quietly.

I reach out to the finger bones but the door swings open before I make contact. We file into the circular room, weapons still drawn.

Empty.

Not what I expected from the Calahi Kailoh described as a hoarder. But I've seen enough to know that people, and I can only assume Calahi, don't always have their treasure readily on display. Aeyva studies every inch of the room, no surprise gracing her features either.

'What an unexpected surprise,' an almost child-like voice echoes around the room.

Chills run down my spine. Not at the voice, but the way Aeyva flinched when it spoke.

Lochlain's pendant begins to heat against my skin.

'Stay at the exit,' Ciara instructs Rory, and he and Riley take up positions on either side of the bone door.

'I so rarely get visitors,' the voice continues, 'and certainly not this many. Not still standing, at least.' A laugh reverberates through the room. Shifting my feet, I note the floor here is bare – no rotting corpses. For some reason, that makes me more wary.

'I have something for you,' Keeva says, her voice steely.

'Oh! I love presents!' the voice squeals, then pauses. 'And yet you want something in return?' It's almost feminine, but edged in so much darkness it's hard to tell.

'A simple trade is all I ask,' Keeva responds.

Laughter surges throughout the small room. 'If only it was simple. What do you seek?'

'There is a piece of sapphire, from Roisin's original, that is in these walls. That is what I want,' Keeva says.

Ciara's voice sounds in my head. '*There's more to this room than we can see*,' she says, the pendant at my chest growing hotter.

I fight the urge to react, but it's the first time anyone has communicated with me this way. For a moment, I think how handy it would have been in Rhyton. But I also know there is something that keeps Ciara from fully using her magic.

Aeyva nods almost imperceptibly, and I understand Ciara has spoken to all of us.

'That is certainly a prize ... should it be here. I assume you have brought me something worthy of exchange?'

'I have brought you more than one – a series of the hardest memories I could find,' Keeva says.

The owner of the voice inhales in excitement and the room around me wavers. Ciara looks knowingly at me.

'Are they your own?' the voice, that's edging back to child-like, asks. She sighs heavily, dreamily. 'It's so much better when they're your own.'

'They're mine.' Keeva's voice is bitter.

I watch the others as the voice 'tsks' around us. 'At least you had the opportunity to make them yourself,' she says. There's a pout in her voice as Keeva raises a brow – the only sign she's not convinced the memories she has to share are something worth fighting for.

'Show yourself, and let us make the exchange,' Keeva says.

The room is plunged into momentary darkness, fast enough for my stomach to plummet.

'Remember whose house you are in, young one, and who has the right to make demands.'

The light returns gradually, and Riley steps away from where she'd stepped closer to me, and back towards the door.

'You are right, however, I should like to see what you have brought me and, if I deem it an equal exchange, I will give you what you seek.'

A woman appears in front of Keeva, who steps back in response. The woman is bent in the middle and doesn't reach Keeva's shoulders. Long, white hair is tied loosely down her back and wisps fly around her heavily lined face. Eyes that might have once been colourful immediately find mine.

'Oh,' she says, 'hello, there.' She breathes in deeply through her nose and my stomach churns a little. 'I thought I recognised the scent of your blood.' She licks her lips. 'Delicious.'

Keeva steps back in front of her, trying to conceal her swallow. 'Show me the sapphire, and I'm ready when you are.'

Slowly, she looks back to Keeva. A spark of blue appears on an empty shelf above me, almost close enough to pluck from the air. The Wolverton Pendant, still hanging where it belongs at my chest, starts to pulse. Aeyva grips my hand and subtly shakes her head before I can reach for it. Not yet. She nods at Keeva and presses the palm of her hand to her chest. The two women look at each other for a long moment, Ciara glancing between the two of them before Keeva drops to her knees in front of the ancient woman.

The light seeps out through the walls and darkness drenches the room once more.

Then the screaming starts.

A young girl's pleas echo around the room and desperately I want to look for her, my vision straining in the dark. The screaming pierces into the deepest parts of me. But I know where she is. Who she is.

No, please no.

I promise I'll be good.

I won't do it again, I'm sorry, please.

I'm sorry—

Keeva's own screams join the girl's and white light flashes across the empty walls. The old woman grips Keeva's temples, a grin on her wrinkled face as she stares blankly at the heavens that seem so very far away. Keeva sobs in unison with the young girl I can't see as she is dragged through what sound like the worst memories of her life. Memories she is giving in exchange for the piece we need.

You will pay for what you did to me.

For what you made me into.

Did you mean for pain to become pleasure? Because that's certainly what yours is going to bring me.

Blood appears to splash the walls as a man's screams join the others. The pain in Keeva's memories presses on my chest. It's different to how I normally feel emotions; the old woman is somehow making them accessible to us all.

The sister licks her lips again and drops a now motionless Keeva to the floor as the light returns. I draw breath back into my lungs and grab for the sapphire. It's warm in my hand and I slip it into an inside pocket of my vest, close to my heart.

Aeyva watches me tuck it away and then looks towards the bone door – an instruction.

But I have my own agenda here, too. I won't be a queen who doesn't fight for the needs of those that serve her.

Lightly, I brush my palm over the pummel of the sword at my side – the one Rory gave me when we ambushed my first team of Whispers.

'Thank you for your time,' I say, moving towards the woman, trying not to look at Keeva to see if she's breathing.

Ciara scoops her up under the armpits and starts dragging her to the door. The old woman just smiles.

The door slams shut.

The bones rattle in their places.

The ancient one cackles, and I lift my chin as I meet her gaze.

CHAPTER TWENTY-TWO

LISH

'Oh,' she says. 'Please tell me you really thought that would work?' She laughs again and my pendant and flame burn hot. 'Surely you understand no one leaves here – those that are unfortunate enough to end up here sustain me in their misfortune. And that part of Roisin's Star will never leave here.' She points a gnarled finger straight at me, as if she could stab it into my chest from where she stands.

Aeyva flings her arms wide.

'No!' The woman screams as the room around us flickers and the illusion of emptiness starts to crack.

She holds a hand out to Aeyva and slams her against the wall next to me, Aeyva's head bouncing. The power of the sister's magic seems to suck the air from the room. The old woman stalks to her, the room darkening around us. Whatever magic she has is old, and dark. It makes my hair stand on end in a way no other Calahi magic has so far. Not even Siosal's.

'How dare you use your magic against me, you spiteful child,' she spits.

Rory grips his sword, stalking towards the old woman.

'Your blood is mine,' she says to Aeyva. 'And you wasted it for a piece of a whole you will never have.'

She throws her other hand out, towards Rory without looking at him, and he's thrown backwards. Shattering the bone door.

The sister pins Aeyva with her magic. I close my eyes for a moment and can hear it humming along my skin. Aeyva gasps for breath next to me, close enough for me to feel her breath on my cheek. The old woman's steps creep closer.

I look to Ciara and silently beg her to open her mind, to find mine.

'*Get out,*' I try to tell her. If she can hear me. '*Get out.*'

'*I can't leave you, or the sapphire,*' she says, a bead of sweat dripping down her forehead. She takes a quiet step to the woman but I can't have four compromised Calahi on my team. Rory has disappeared into the dark of the outside tunnel and I send up a prayer he can recover enough to get us out.

I have one shot.

My mind eddies. To have come this far to fall now is not an option. I won't lose anyone here today. But Rory is too far away for me to try and drag on his magic like I must have in the meadow, like Aeyva tried to drive me to use again with words designed to get under my skin.

I focus on Aeyva and the breath that's fading against my cheek. Silently, I crawl my fingers along the dark wall, ignoring what runs along my palm and catches my sleeve. Studiously ignoring that the woman could see what I'm planning. But maybe she's picked up on the human in my blood, and not my connection to Roisin. I can barely make out her shape in the darkening room and I hope her vision is worse than mine.

The woman is still talking, lecturing Aeyva, but I don't take it in.

There.

Aeyva's fingers are now beneath mine. I empty my thoughts, and close my eyes. Everything I am is now focused on Aeyva. Imagining I hold her hand, and her magic, like I did with the wolf and Benny. And I pray to the wolves that led me here to help me do this.

Aeyva's power surges through me, my flame surging, and I bite the inside of my cheeks until I taste blood. I tuck her power into a ball in my gut, one that sits under the golden flame in my chest, and let the sounds of the room back in. The old woman is just in front and to the side of me, still talking.

Aeyva's magic is warm in my veins – it feels like a wall. One made of stone, with iron barbs running down the outside.

I open my eyes and throw my hands out, pushing Aeyva's magical wall away from me. The illusion of the empty room cracks, Aeyva's magic slamming into it all and driving it backwards.

The room flickers between light and dark as I churn through Aeyva's power. Ciara drops Keeva with Riley just outside the room and runs back towards me.

'Go!' I scream.

Ciara stops in her tracks, her head whipping around behind her.

I'm struggling to remain standing against the force of the magic flowing from my hands. It's different and yet the same as what I did in the Challenge room with Lochlain. But, then, I knew what I needed to do. I don't really know what Aeyva's magic does or what to ask of it. The sister stays down but I don't know how long I will be able to keep her that way. I let my body remember it, learn how it feels, and I pummel it at the woman. The barbs hook into her like claws and she screams. Aeyva tries to crawl towards the sister who's crumpled on the ground, attempting, and failing, to stand.

Ciara turns her back to us and steps to the side of the tunnel.

'Lish,' Aeyva gasps, reaching for the knife at her calf. 'Get out.'

The power falters with my attention and the old woman turns her head to me and smiles. Her mouth is full of black, rotting teeth.

'You think you can steal from me? Defeat me?' her voice is ragged.

She laughs suddenly, throwing her head back on the cluttered floor. 'You will not win, you cannot beat us. Not the Eternal Queens. Not even Roisin,' she spits the name like poison, 'could beat us. She, who created the world in her image, was defeated. One day'—she coughs—'it will be remade in ours. We will take what we need.'

She drags herself to her knees, pushing against Aeyva's power that is slowing its ebb from me.

Focus Lish, focus on what you can control, I tell myself.

I look towards the tunnel, knowing full well she could follow me through there. If she did, I would die in the dark – just another corpse. But one of a queen who failed. The final nail in the coffin of her people.

The old woman is on her feet now. Aeyva is shouting at me and forcing her way forward, knife drawn but her strength hasn't returned. Or did I take it?

Instead of retreating to the tunnel, I take two steps closer to the now standing old woman. One more and she will be in arms' reach.

I let go of Aeyva's power and feel it leave my bloodstream, enough to hope the sister thinks I have nothing left. The laughter that fills the room is icy.

'Oh, you've made this such fun, little one – what happened to all your strength? I shall so enjoy the delicacies of each of you. But you, in particular,' she says approaching me. 'I know from where you hail. And you'll taste so good.'

I grip the sword at my offside with both hands and draw. Twisting my hips, I swing. Driving my weight forward with my back foot. The sound it makes as the blade sinks into the old woman's neck is haunting. And yet I hope it's enough. I push harder into the buried blade. She stops mid-step and her eyes flare. Blood leaks from the wound, slowly at first, and then it bubbles out her mouth and down her neck as she drops to the ground, taking my blade with her. I step forward and place a foot on her chest as I heave the sword out.

Two wolves stalk into the room, past Ciara, and my scalp prickles at their presence. Two pairs of eyes find me, one a striking amber just like the wolf from a lifetime ago in the forest, when Will and I were taken. Like in the vision Nuala showed me. They circle the sister who lies crumpled and bleeding on the floor.

Before I can blink, the second one sinks its teeth into her neck and rips out her throat, blood dripping into its fur as it drops the chunk of flesh from its mouth.

But it is the first wolf, the one with amber eyes, that I follow with my gaze. Frozen where I stand.

It moves further into the room, that's now bursting at the seams with things I don't want to name, before looking back at me intently.

Instinctively, I search the space around it, my heart pounding in my chest. There are boxes and boxes made of dark timber, shelves overflowing with jars and jewels and clothes, what looks to be an auburn braid, skin still attached at the top. I try not to gag.

The walls start to shudder.

The wolf watches me, dipping its head a fraction before it turns and slinks out of the room.

The other trailing behind it.

I look back at the sister. Her mostly detached head lolls and I shudder in time with the tunnels as Aeyva grabs my arm.

'Run,' she breathes.

We launch ourselves back towards the tunnel that led us here. The floor trembles underneath me, the very foundations starting to fail.

'Ciara!' I shout. 'Run! We're behind you!'

Gripping my belt like Ciara did, Aeyva all but shoves me through the tunnel.

My foot twists on something and I go down. The pommel of my sword jamming into my hip, my knees sinking into the blood and filth that coats the ground. Aeyva wrenches me to standing and pushes once more. A boom sounds from behind us, and grit begins to build in my eyes as the tunnel starts to go to pieces.

I stagger again on the littered ground and my hands sink into something wet and sticky as I fall. A new density of stench suffocates me. The rumble around us grows just as we burst into the pod shaped room we paused in before. The dark mouths of other tunnels swirling around me. As if they laugh, just like the sister when she thought she'd trap us here.

Maybe she still will.

Ciara screams at us from somewhere I can't see.

'Run! Run!'

The marks, I think frantically. *Where are the fucking marks.*

'Light, Aeyva. Light!'

She immediately douses the room with light and I spot them.

'Here,' I say, running.

The light all but disappears as Aeyva's breathing starts to come heavily.

I run, Aeyva on my heels.

There's a light ahead.

'Run!' Ciara screams.

I focus on her distorted face, both Rory and Riley are holding her back from re-entering the tunnel. The floor slips away under my heels and I pound harder – faster – hoping that the thundering of my weight will crush anything underfoot and I won't fall again. Aeyva's breathing and grip on my belt tell me she's still with me but my body strains against where she pulls me back.

She's flagging. And the floor of the tunnel is disintegrating quickly behind me, right where she is.

Ciara grows in my vision. The world around me slows as I realise I can't close the gap. Ciara's face seems to morph into Lochlain's and regret stings in my chest that I won't get to say goodbye to him. That I have failed in this queenly test so early. That I will die being known as the murderer of my mother. That Airlie will never know what a damn good Queen I would have been.

I look over my shoulder to Aeyva as I run.

'No!' she screams. 'We can do this. Move!'

Her face has my body reacting before my brain and I spin. Gripping her arm and taking her with me. I let her go as she regains her footing in front of me and slam both hands into her lower back. Pushing her towards Ciara's outstretched hands, using the last of her magic in my veins to propel her forward.

I close my eyes as I continue to run, my heart sinking. I still have the sapphire. And the pendant.

They will be with me when I die.

Fuck.

'Lish!' Rory's voice drowns out Riley's.

I know what will come.

But I can't stand still to greet it. Every beat of my heart screams to get out.

I want out.

So I run as the howls of wolves echo around me in the dark.

The back of my head slams into something hard, the crack snapping my teeth so forcefully I expect them to choke me.

'You with us, sweetheart?' The worry in Rory's voice doesn't match his casual words.

The smell that pervaded every inch of me returns and coats the back of my throat. My stomach rolls.

'What—?' I croak as I struggle to sit up.

I blink in the bright lights of the landing for transport I can't remember the name of. Other Calahi walk around us as if we don't exist. I stare, uncomprehending, at the others until I see Ciara monitoring closely to see how her magic shields are holding.

Rory and Riley compress me in a squeeze as they each breathe a sigh of relief.

'Don't you *ever* fucking do that again,' Riley says.

'I am not telling Loch I lost you on my watch,' Rory adds.

Riley pulls my head back and holds my face.

'Are you okay?' she asks. 'How—'

I look at where I've gripped her wrists, and the gore I've left there. Her voice disappears as I look down at myself. My fingers start to tremble, my stomach hollows out.

'I need – oh god, get it off. Please, get it off.' I rip at my blood-stained vest and shirt. Pieces of skin and hair come away as I tear at my clothes, sticking to my hands.

'I can't. Get me out. I – Oh, fuck. Off. Get it off!'

Rory barks a command at others that has them crowding me and then I'm immersed in freezing water. Gasping for breath, Ciara grips my elbow and floats me momentarily on my back.

'I'm here, Lish, I'm here. I'm taking it off.'

Her voice is soothing. At least, a quiet one in my own mind knows it's supposed to be. She tips me vertical in the water again and I find I can touch the bottom as she unzips my vest and tosses it to shore where the others wash themselves. Aeyva scrubs the blood from my sword and the water turns pink at her feet.

My jaw chatters as I shake in Ciara's grip. She lifts my arms up over my head and removes my shirt, using her hands to scrub away any remaining traces of blood. I try to undo my own pants but my hands tremble so much I can't grip the button. Instead, Ciara lifts each leg and removes my boots before struggling with my pants and throwing it all to the bank. She grips my hands as I stand before her, freezing and soaked to the bone in my underwear. Vaguely, I notice Rory turn his back to me and whisper to Aeyva before he disappears and reappears in the same spot a moment later.

'It's shock, Lish,' she says. 'You hit your head pretty hard, but I think this is shock.'

I stare at her.

The soft sand gives way beneath me as we walk out, Ciara holding my elbow. Rory hands me a small towel and a pile of dry clothes I ungracefully drag over my wet skin.

'I'm sorry,' I say. 'I didn't expect—'

'Don't apologise,' Riley says. 'That was messed up.' She glances at my clothes, that sit in a wet pile at her feet, and shudders. I notice the others drip themselves.

'The sapphi—' My hand automatically flies to Lochlain's Wolverton Pendant that sits between my breasts.

'Got it,' Ciara says, opening her hand.

I look around at the lake that's surrounded by trees on the side closest to us as I let the events wash over me. We did it. We not only recovered the sapphire but I – the wolves – killed the sister. Succeeded in weakening the Eternal Queen that I know was important to Aeyva and Ciara, even if they won't say it to each other. Now, I need to get it back to Kailoh so he can help me get my crown.

I frown. Where did she go? I look to Ciara, who understands my question without it being asked.

'Keeva almost didn't make it,' she says quietly. 'Aeyva's with her.'

CHAPTER TWENTY-THREE

AEYVA

I try to tell myself it was her choice. That she knew what she was coming to do. But that doesn't change that Keeva almost died reliving the worst moments of her life.

'It's okay, Aeyva,' she says as she struggles to sit up in the dry leaves. We're still within the borders of Rothani and the sound of the crunch below Keeva's hands – different to the sound of breaking bones – is unsettling. This dryness is on a scale I haven't seen in the Realm before. 'We both know Kailoh is right – that was the only way we could have weakened the Eternal Queen enough to give us a fighting chance.' She shakes her head, her red hair falling softly around her face, and part of me wishes I still felt something more than friendship for her. It would be easier.

'Now,' she says, 'we really have a shot at another life Aeyv. We might act the part, but I know how bad we both want it.'

There's a long pause and I can't think what to say. But it's not an uncomfortable silence. Keeva and Kailoh, outside Rory and the Wolvertons, are the only true friends I have. The King and an assassin – an incredibly unlikely duo. Between them, I fit somewhere – an assassin, would-be-Manorynx desperately trying to fit into the role of Sentinel.

Except ... I remember the sensation of Lish shoving me towards the exit of that tunnel, before herself, and Riley screaming at me to run. Perhaps the group I can rely on has ... expanded somewhat.

Keeva picks up a leaf and breaks it apart in her fingers as I watch.

'Will you come back with me?' she asks.

I try not to look back at Ciara but it's impossible. I shake my head.

'She's lucky,' she says. 'She doesn't think you should be a Sentinel, does she?' she asks a long moment after.

I sigh. 'She thinks I was destined for something ... different.'

'Are you?'

Her face is soft as I consider her. 'Perhaps if I'd finished my training with Nuala and Benny. If I'd known more, I could have saved you from what you went through today. I could have found another way.'

Keeva sits back to lean on her hands, her legs crossed in front of her. 'Maybe. But maybe this is what you needed to help you make the choice. You've always had a foot in both camps, Aeyv, but you're beyond good enough for either. You need to stop punishing yourself for the choices you made in pain. You did the best you could, and you've served our Realm in a harder way than anyone could imagine. Now, maybe it's time you stood in the light.'

Ciara is helping Lish dress as I watch them; it's clear from here that Lish is still shaking.

'Perhaps we all can,' I say quietly.

'Does she turn into a wolf?' she asks. 'Is that the attraction?'

I laugh. 'No. Lochlain claims to have done it once, but, really, the ability to shift mostly died out with their father and grandfather.'

'But they're still connected, or the wolves wouldn't have come today.'

I nod. 'And to Lish. The wolves, and the Wolvertons, vowed to protect Roisin's line – and she's what's left.'

'Sounds like a legendary romance in the making.'

I glance back at her. The Wolvertons and the Queen have always been the most important roles in Airlie and tradition says they were never supposed to join. But thinking of Kailoh's comments about how love sustained Roison, I wonder why it's become the standard. We know Roisin and her Wolverton lover never had young together – only separately, never bonded – so it's been purely the potential risk of complicating the safety or running of the Court that's borne that expectation. A tradition I have made sure Lochlain was very well aware of.

Along with my own understanding that the role of Manorynx of Airlie would never be held by one such as myself – not a Calahi with rumours of carrying young without a bonded partner. No matter that I ultimately bonded with Loch ... and lost my young.

As I look at Lish and what she's going through for this Court, I wonder why she has to give up her shot at love as well.

Perhaps neither of those assumptions about what is good for this Court is correct.

Ciara watches me carefully as I return to the group, but I can't return her gaze. If I'm starting to believe Lochlain and Lish should be able to fight to be together, why are Ciara and I so different? What if Lish is right and I shouldn't be deciding for her? Why am I fighting Nuala so hard on what my role is when I trust her with literally everything else?

'We need to go,' I say when Rory has returned from taking Keeva back to the Society House to rest. I'd tried to get her to come to Kailoh's with us. But she said if she really was going to take it over when I killed the Eternal Queen, she needed to be visible.

I didn't tell her I have no idea how I am supposed to do that.

Quietly, we assemble around Rory. This time, though, instead of waiting for Riley to hold his hand, he reaches out and pulls her to him, her face lighting with surprise. She gives a small nod in understanding as he tucks her against his side.

The wind whips around my ears as Rory starts to take us back to Kailoh's Court.

A scream cuts the air around us. 'I know what you did! And I know where you're going, Aeyva Kaylneau.'

Rory has taken us too far back to Kailoh's for me to change his course.

I feel the mist before I see it in the unused sitting room. It grips my ankles and wrenches me from Rory's magic. My wrists jar as I throw them in front of me, not fast enough to stop my chin connecting with the corner of a low table and splitting on impact.

'Aeyva!' My heart leaps at the alarm in Ciara's voice.

'What did you do?' The voice I know so well seeps into my head. It's always been laced with violence, but not often directed at me.

'What. Did. You. Do?' she asks again.

I push myself to standing, ignoring the impulse to cup my chin, letting the blood run down my throat. I turn around the room slowly, allowing her to see me as I make sure everyone else is accounted for. Rory and Riley look around warily, Rory's hand hovering over his sword. He knows better than to draw it. Lish gapes at me uncomprehending. Ciara is enraged.

The mist thickens, obscuring my view of them.

'You know what occurred, My Eternal Queen,' I say quietly.

For a manic moment, I wish I had succeeded. That I killed her magical anchor – her counter that made her so strong. Instead, it was Lish. The Queen whose spine I once doubted. And now I've brought the attention of the Eternal Queen on us all.

An uncharacteristic flutter starts in my gut.

'And do you have any idea what you've cost me?' Her voice slices through me.

Ciara moves to step towards me, but I desperately, silently, plead with her to stay where she is. Her face shutters.

This was the risk. I am accustomed to risk. I draw a deep breath.

The mist swirls menacingly around the room, blocking most of the light.

'I do, my Queen,' I say quietly, the title grating when Lish stands in the room.

'And so you accept your fate without a fight? That is not like you, Aeyva Kaylneau.'

'She said she understands the penalty.' Lish appears beside me through the grey. 'Not that she committed any act that would affect a penalty.'

Genuine laughter rings around the room. I shudder, imagining her claws dragging down my skin, and move to push Lish away. She holds firm.

'And who, exactly, might you be to talk to me in such a manner?' the Eternal Queen asks.

'Oh, I'm sorry,' Lish replies, her voice heavy with sarcasm. 'I didn't have time to introduce myself before you assaulted my Sentinel without question.'

The room blackens. I shake my head at Lish but she's not looking at me. She's moving to stand in front of me where I'm frozen to the spot, my limbs refusing to cooperate.

'Your *Sentinel*?' the Eternal Queen repeats.

A fraction of light returns to the room as the density of the mist recedes.

The door is pushed open with such force it slams into the wall.

'No,' Kailoh's voice booms through me.

I glance at Rory, who is physically restraining Ciara. He and Riley know enough to know we cannot get out of this by force. Even if they do not know I will not get out of it at all.

'This is absolutely *unacceptable*.' Kailoh slashes his hand through the mist to emphasise his point.

I remain frozen. If I'd finished my training with Nuala, I never would have been here. Never would have failed so magnificently at being a First Sentinel.

'You,' he points his finger to something I can't see but I know who he talks to – not even Nuala knows the depth of Kailoh's magic. 'Are not welcome here. Your *business* does not belong here. Not in my house.'

'Oh, Kailoh,' the mist purrs. 'I was only meeting your most recent guest. She's been involved in events that interest me and I thought I'd pop in to say hello ... ask a question. She claims this one as her Sentinel,' she says as the mist weaves around me. 'That would imply she fancies herself a queen, but—'

Kailoh strides further into the room, four of his Sentinels on his heels. The door slams behind them, the walls trembling with the weight of Kailoh's power as it starts to pulse.

'Ask your question and get out,' Kailoh says through gritted teeth.

The room darkens again and the temperature plummets. I look once more at Ciara. Is she beginning to understand she's out of her depth here?

'Which of you did it?' the Eternal Queen asks.

Silence falls and the mist gathers more densely around me, leaving the others, readying to suck the air from my lungs. But only long enough for me to pass out and be taken elsewhere. I draw my last free breath—

'I am responsible for the actions of this group,' Lish says, lifting her chin. My stomach drops. 'Perhaps you could enlighten me as to what exactly you are referring to?'

'A death,' the mist spits.

'Of whom?' Lish drawls slowly, sounding every bit an irritated queen.

Her fists are clenched at her sides. If I didn't know it was to cover her shaking hands, I would say it was in anger. I want to refute her claim of responsibility, it's possibly the worst thing she could have chosen to say, but I have no way to back us out of this path now. All words sticking in my throat, hemmed in by the stinging in my chin.

'My sister!' she screams.

'Again, I can tell you I am directly responsible. So you can take your issue up with me.'

Shit.

I look to Rory and Ciara. I will do anything to stop her taking anyone in this room. Including killing them myself.

Kailoh is at Lish's side now and I still can't voice my objections. The band around my chest is like a vice. *This must be what terror is like*, I think from far away.

'You have your answer, your time is up,' he says.

'She,' the mist wraps around Lish's throat. Lish's eyes flare slightly but she doesn't show any other sign of fear, 'will answer for her actions.'

'I,' Lish responds, showing no outward sign of discomfort to the hold the Eternal Queen has on her. 'Will do no such thing. I am Adelais Wolverton, Queen of the Court of Airlie, and I do not answer to you.'

'We're done here,' Kailoh says as he takes Lish's elbow and guides her to the door.

His Sentinels light the arrows on the bows they've drawn and aim into the room.

'Burn it,' he says from the door.

Rory and Riley hurry to follow but my feet won't move. It's Ciara who drags me from the spot I have been rooted and shuffles me out the door as the arrows fly.

An angry shriek echoes around the room behind us and my only clear thoughts are how many questions Lish will have – and how badly I need Nuala to help answer them.

CHAPTER TWENTY-FOUR

AEYVA

'I want to know what it was for,' Lish says when only the two of us are left in the sitting room. The others have gone to wash, and I crave the steaming water myself.

Lish holds the part of the Star in the palm of her hand and she watches it as she waits for me to talk. Gently she rolls it around her hand with a finger, as if she's examining every corner. Then looks straight at me.

'I'll go first,' she says. 'You will find I am a person who fights for those around her – those I care about. I may not be able to feel your emotions like I can others', Aeyva, but one look at your face in those tunnels and I knew something else had to happen there. Retrieving this'—she lifts her flat hand, the sapphire a small, blue mound on top—'wasn't going to be enough.'

I stare at her, my body suddenly feeling very heavy. She might be someone who fights for those she cares about but so am I – and exposing them to all my secrets wasn't what I wanted to do. Letting Lish take sole responsibility for the death of the sister is something I never should have allowed to happen. I still feel numb after the visit from the Eternal Queen, shocked at the sudden change in direction in my life. Even though it's something I've thought about for so long, the options have opened up much faster than I expected. With one, huge, obstacle left – the Eternal Queen herself.

'But it was Ciara's face that confirmed it,' she says.

I frown, my heart kicking behind my ribs. 'What do you mean?' I ask, aware how tired my voice sounds.

She moves from in front of the fireplace and sits across from me on the sofas, her elbows propped on her knees. The clothes Rory snatched for her are still damp in places.

'When we talked about killing the sister in the tunnels, your face was ... resigned. Resigned to the fact it wasn't possible. Ciara's ... there was a desperation there I've felt before. Like when I watched Lochlain present himself to the Custodian.'

Her voice grows softer as she sits back and I try not to gape at her. At the meaning underneath her words.

'So,' she says, 'I know it was necessary. And the ... sister, made it much easier by trying to lock us in there. But I want to know why.'

There's no question in her voice. There hasn't been since the conversation started and, for the first time, I turn over our similarities in our mind. I would have at least expected judgement from her but she knows, whatever the cost – opportunity – to myself, I never would have endangered them in those tunnels. She made that decision for me. In doing so, opened a door to gaining the freedom to choose.

I let out a slow breath and hope I can find adequate words.

'I belong to the Eternal Queen's Society.' The words taste sour in my mouth as I tell them to my actual Queen. 'The vows I made to her mean I won't be able to swear myself to you as Sentinel in the eyes of Airlie, not unless I am out somehow. But no one's gotten out alive before.'

'Why?' she asks.

'The vows are for all our functional years. If there are none of those left, we're ... expired.'

She nods as if this isn't news and I can readily imagine her in her human city, listening to all the wrongdoings of humans. Making sure none of her reactions show. Her green eyes are kind as she waits for me to continue.

'With the sister dead, the Eternal Queen is slightly less formidable. It means, if there's an opportunity, I might have a shot at officially getting out.'

'Officially?'

'You saw her reaction today,' I say. 'I won't be able to go back without her killing me for the infraction, but I'm still bound. She'll take every chance to make us pay.'

'And Kailoh knows her too,' she says, confirming it for herself. 'Is that why you two are close?'

I wait for a moment. We're not supposed to disclose our clients to anyone but I think, now with what she knows and has seen, Lish can be an exception.

'In addition to his support in our search for you,' I say, 'Kailoh ... engages my services when he needs them. I almost exclusively do his assignments. Because I trust him.'

'Okay,' she says, and I can tell she's filing the information away, compartmentalising the threat of the Eternal Queen and my relationship to Kailoh. 'There's something else.'

I wait.

'In the tunnels,' she says. 'You did something that was just like Nuala – then you narrowed down the entrances. How did you do that?'

I think back on the way I'd shifted through my old knowledge, categorised in a way I wouldn't be able to explain in words. Knowledge Nuala and Benny shared with me. Knowledge I discovered on my own and added into the right places. But knowledge that's still so full of holes.

'Before,' I start, the words feeling too big for this conversation that's already been so full. 'Before ... everything, I was training to be a Manorynx.' Lish's eyes sparkle a little. 'Nuala and Benny were the last Manorynxes in Airlie and they chose me to take their place when the time came. But then—'

'You lost your daughter,' she says gently and I nod.

'I turned to the dark instead. The Society offered a way to still help the Realm and smother myself at the same time.'

Her brows lift at that, and our conversation starts to feel more like friends than a gentle interrogation. Something warms in my chest at the thought.

'Nuala has been trying to train others as well but ... she and Ciara – fuck, I think everyone, including Kailoh – think I should be letting Nuala pass it to me and not be a Sentinel.'

'And should you?'

'The Queen's Manorynx is a position of honour, Lish, but it's also one of light.'

She stands slowly, closing her fist around the sapphire.

'And you're the only one who doesn't think you're fit for it,' she says. 'Sometimes, Aeyva, it's those closest to us that know us best. Sometimes they know us better than ourselves. It's time you had a choice. Because'—she dips her chin a fraction to level me with her human gaze—'one way or another, you *will* serve in my Court.'

She watches as I let that settle over me and I think about how it felt in the tunnels today. That moment when I thought I'd have the answers to lead us. When all the information wasn't there, and it could have been if I'd finished my training. Then the wolves stepped in. The Queen, the Wolvertons, and their wolves. My heart beats a little faster as I realise that, perhaps, today I did execute the role of Manorynx well. That I worked in tandem with the wolves and, between us, we got us where we needed.

Did what was needed.

Kailoh smiles, but it hides a worry about something. He'd sent a message to Lish and me not long after we'd washed and dressed, looking for all the world as if we didn't crawl out of the Rothani tunnel system today. He'd asked me to use his private entrance so we could talk without his Sentinels. It's not something most of his guards know we do when he wants to talk about something he doesn't want whispered in the halls of his Palace. It's also now the only way I can talk freely and not have to conform to the constraints of being a Sentinel, one behind Ciara in authority, in the presence of his.

'You succeeded, it seems,' he says.

Gently, Lish places the sapphire on the small table between the low chairs we sit in and Kailoh picks it up in his long fingers, turning it over. Wordlessly, he hands it back.

'Halfway,' he says.

'Hopefully closer than half,' Lish replies instantly.

I look between them. They're definitely getting along – differently to how I expected, but well. My heart sinks a bit for Loch. To have the whole of Airlie weighing in on the appropriateness of his relationship isn't something I'd wish on him. That somehow the Wolvertons are good enough to be the protectors of our Queen but not her life partner. Not officially. But here we are. To save our Realm, and the human world, we need Kailoh's piece. Whatever the ask. The look on Lish's face says she knows that, too.

Kailoh chuckles a little but his mood still appears damp.

'I should think so,' he says. 'There are some other members of my Court I'd like you to meet tonight.' I try not to groan at the prospect of another ball. 'Then it's just the crown to go.'

He shifts in his low backed chair and switches which leg he has crossed over the top.

'The Eternal Queen, though,' he says, looking at us both. 'You know she won't rest now, I assume?'

Lish nods.

'If it comes to it,' she says, 'how do we kill her?'

'I would guess that you'll need to do it together. Or, at least, Aeyva will need to partner with another to have enough power to stop her. She's now quite a risk to what you are trying to do,' he says. He looks at me and raises a brow slightly, as if asking if he can talk about this with Lish. I nod, suddenly full of cool relief that I have been honest with her. 'Not only because of Aeyva's relationship to the Society but because of who the Eternal Queen is.'

The enormity of who she is, what she and her sister did, and what it's meant for the Realm is bigger than I can process. Not to mention how old that means she is. I knew there were rumours of the curse of the Mother – now so much about the Eternal Queen and her sister makes sense. Why there are no others like them in the Realm, the Eternal Queen's rumoured hatred for Roisin's line, why she told me not to look for the Star.

'I assume you think she's going to actively interfere with us putting together the Star?' Lish asks.

'Yes,' I say, 'or with whatever comes after. The Star is supposed to show us something, right? Where to go, what to do, etcetera, but it's not the solution in its own right. So, perhaps she doesn't care as much about the Star itself but what it will show.'

'I think that's a reasonable assumption,' Kailoh says. 'But you need to be on guard for her.'

I turn in my chair to properly look at Lish as my last conversation with the Eternal Queen comes back. 'She's also likely to offer her services to the Custodian.'

I stand and pour us each a drink from the crystal decanter Kailoh always keeps on the timber buffet. This, his private study, is small compared to the rest of the rooms in the Palace and one very few people get to see.

'Also,' Kailoh says, 'there have been raids in my Court – in the small villages that border here and Rothani. My scouts tell me they don't know who is carrying them out, but they seem to be operating under the instruction of the Custodian.'

I turn that over, pushing the Eternal Queen aside for the moment. If the Custodian was legitimately striking against a dangerous force, he'd have Loch lead as General. But I know Loch would have sent us a message if there was a new threat. Instead, he's looking for the magic we Give – trying to understand what happens to it.

I shake my head. 'Loch would never lead Airlie in attacks like that. Could it be Nakiasha? She and the Custodian are aligned.'

'Nakiasha is clever enough to give support without getting her hands dirty or having anything pinned on her,' he says. 'And I already know it's not your General leading the forces. On the ground, they are answering to a Rothani soldier. But he's reporting back to Zadicus, not Nakiasha.'

'Keeva said they were bringing in an outside force,' I say, my mind still grappling with what that means.

Lish looks at me sharply. 'An outside force?'

Kailoh looks a bit pale. 'He's got a human army.'

I force myself to swallow. Lish freezes next to me. This news would have angered me regardless of who the Queen of Airlie was. But hearing it while sitting with a half-human one makes my shame all the sharper.

'I thought humans weren't welcome here?' she asks.

'What do you mean he has a human army?' I ask at the same time, incredulous. 'What Calahi in the history of the Realm has ever led a human army?'

Kailoh cocks his head at each of us. 'You mean outside the Great Battle of—'

'Fine, fine,' I say, waving a hand. 'But in all *reasonable* history of the Realm. This must be a first.'

'It does seem to be the first time any Court has proactively sought and utilised a human army. The other occasions'—he emphasises the plural—'it was more of an "end of the world" calamity that drove the alliance.' He sips at his drink, a solemn expression on his chiselled face. 'Although, Nuala's message certainly confirmed we are headed back there faster than any humans are prepared to acknowledge. Again.'

He nods to Lish. 'And no, humans are not normally welcome here. Not like that. Which means they have been given guest status.'

'Why?' Lish asks.

'Nakiasha has never thought humans were appreciative enough of the magic around them,' Kailoh says. 'Present company excluded, on the whole, humans live their lives completely unaware of the incredible things that happen around them. Which means they are equally ignorant of the delicate nature of those things and destroy more than they care for. There are many in this Realm, Nakiasha included, that believe this ignorance is purposeful.'

Lish is quiet as she takes a deep breath and I wonder what she is thinking of. But she doesn't challenge Nakiasha's view.

'So, what are they up to?' I ask, a memory surfacing of Ciara and I talking about the implications of a human life being magic enough to sacrifice at the Givings, in place of our actual magic. The concern about this on a case-by-case basis was enough – the question we argued was what if the Realm did it on a larger scale?

Lish closes her eyes, as if she knows what's coming and needs to brace herself.

Kailoh exhales. 'Testing them,' he says.

CHAPTER TWENTY-FIVE

LISH

The fire crackles in front of me where I watch from the deep couch, a velvet cushion pulled into my lap. The flames hold both good and bad memories and I struggle to look away from what they contain. Not so long ago, I lay with Lochlain in front of a fireplace. A moment that was, in hindsight, instrumental in propelling me along this path. But in that moment my heart was full and excited, although terrified at what he would face the next day, and it leapt as he told me about the dancing magic of Soul Accords. Now, it's full of ... something different. I blink away the memory of the people chained to the ground in Rhyton and look at Riley. Her grey eyes shutter as Aeyva tells them all what we discussed with Kailoh.

'Humans aren't designed for magic,' Riley says.

I almost say I don't understand what's happening, what the different connections are. But that's not quite true. The different pieces are starting to pull together in my mind, like magnets drawn to each other.

'They're injecting magic into the members of the Guard,' I say. 'That's what killed Claire.'

The symmetry in the Calahi having their magic drawn and dying, and humans being injected with magic and dying, is a reality I can't ignore. The activities in Rhyton have hung over all of us since then, at least in part because there was no explanation. Now I have one, I can't say I like it. But it provides a likely explanation for why the Calahi of Airlie don't know what's been happening to the magic they Give, why there's been no impact on the state of the Mother, and why the flowers continue to die and butterflies fall from the sky.

There's a racing of my heart as this thought clicks into place.

The weight of the challenges on all sides is a constant pressure at the base of my skull. The longer it takes me to get the Throne and find the Star, the Calahi of Airlie – and the humans in Rhyton – continue to suffer quietly, and the more damage is being done to a world I need to save. Once, I wondered how I would split myself between my feelings and commitments to Driarn and the Realm. Now, I know they are one and the same. I can't save one without the other. I haven't given up on my oaths in the Guard – I'm just serving them in another way.

I shift in my seat, crushing the cushion beneath my crossed forearms, as if I can squeeze the threats away. Phoenix and Blaire are in Rhyton. In the Guard. Or getting close to it anyway as they try to infiltrate a human rebellion and solve the issue of why the Commissioner is involved in the Realm. My stomach turns as I realise we've just done the last part – he's been giving over Guard members for experimentation.

My throat tightens at the thought, and the risks to my family, and I pull myself back to the conversation just as Kailoh strides into our suite. Two of his Sentinels follow, their scarlet uniforms contrasting against Kailoh's long, dark jacket. A thick white sash tied around his waist highlights his tapered form.

'My guests are expecting us,' he says gently as he looks around the room. Obviously guessing what we've been discussing.

He looks at me and I steel myself for what I need to do. Who I need to be tonight – a queen.

'I'm sorry, Adelais,' he says. 'You will discover that ruling doesn't stop for anyone, or anything. Being visible to your Court is absolutely crucial – being visible to mine is even more so if we want them to literally fight for us.' He draws a deep breath. 'And it seems we are indeed preparing for a fight.'

The ballroom seems smaller tonight than when I was last here, more intimate somehow. The same brass lanterns bob gently, casting their enchanting light. Of all the incredible things here and the grandeur of Kailoh's Palace, these whimsical lanterns are my favourite.

Rory and Riley stand at my back in their black uniforms. Tonight, Ciara and Aeyva wander the room outfitted in impeccable dresses, but ones they can move in easily should the need arise. They check in with us every now and then, as if to remind the room that while they may not be on duty, their attention very much remains on me.

I feel no threat here in Kailoh's Court, but I understand the need to keep up appearances of my importance and protection. To maintain the mystery of my standing while winning over the members of Kailoh's Court so they will stand with him, and with me, when the time comes.

As if I've conjured him with my thoughts, Kailoh appears at my side. He's resplendent in fitted black pants with a long, white jacket – different to the one he was wearing earlier. Its cuffs are a deep red velvet along with the collar that stands tall along his neck, the velvet brushing his skin as he moves.

'Come, dance with me.'

I almost choke. As familiar as Kailoh has become with me in a short period, publicly dancing with the King of Mercasia ...

He holds out his hand and some of the Calahi women nearby openly glare at me. Too late for me to decline, I take his cool hand in mine and follow him to the centre of the ballroom. No one else is dancing. Based on the small amount of time I have spent here, I assume they wait for Kailoh to indicate when dancing may begin. The crowd parts around us and the four Sentinels that closely follow, creating a small, open space. My gold shoes sparkle against the smooth white flooring and I don't know whether to be thankful or not that my dress skims my ankles. I won't be able to trip on it, but the unskilled movements of my feet are going to be painfully clear.

We move gently around the space that surrounds us, the Calahi watching from behind the boundary each of the Sentinels has created. Riley smiles but Rory's expression is guarded. Like he knows something's coming, and he doesn't like it. I swallow. We need this. I know we do. But I still can't quite bring myself to really consider what he might want from an alliance with us.

Kailoh's tall, lithe frame envelopes me and he holds my hand gently as he guides me around the room. He pulls me a little closer so he can talk quietly in my ear.

'Having fun?'

I force a smile. 'I'm trying to. The events of the past few days have left their mark, but yes, this is ... fun. Thank you, Kailoh.' I pull back a little so I can catch his honey and purple eyes and try not to think on how much I'm missing Lochlain. 'Why do you ask?'

He looks back across my shoulder, watching the sea of Calahi around us. The music is soothing and carefree and, in true Calahi fashion, winds its way into my soul.

'What do you mean?' he asks.

'Why do you care if I'm having fun? Why help me at all?'

His grip on my fingers tightens a little.

'Honestly, Adelais, this is a tough subject when I need to keep smiling.' I can hear that his royal one is still in place. 'But there are things at play I wish to stop, and I believe you have the power to do so. I also believe you have a better chance of doing it with me by your side.'

A familiar prickle runs over my skin.

So softly I might have imagined it. But the caress along my bare arms is enough to light me from the inside and I know my smile is wide when I catch Rory frowning as we spin past him. Kailoh twirls me out and back in, pressing me up against his side.

He grins down at me.

Another song starts up and other Calahi join the dancing outside the circle our Sentinels have created. Kailoh maintains hold of my hand as he guides me out of the circle, leaving the Calahi to enjoy themselves. He bends down to talk once more.

'There is a visitor to my Court that you should know about.' My stomach tightens in anticipation. 'I do believe this one is on our side. He certainly was but ... I noted his recent absence.'

I scan the room but don't see who I want – need. I look up at Kailoh. 'Please, just tell me who it is.'

One of his Sentinels jerks his head to me in question. But Kailoh merely smiles.

'General Wolverton,' he confirms.

'Oh,' I breathe, my grin impossible to hold back.

The static on my skin intensifies and I force myself to focus on Kailoh and not desperately search the room. Kailoh turns to face me, still holding my hand. A spike of understanding and uncertainty that doesn't belong to me runs along my limbs.

'It's a name that's familiar to you, I know. I remember very clearly how you used it with the Eternal Queen,' he says, raising an eyebrow at me.

'I didn't think my human name would have much sway with the death mist,' I say. Kailoh throws his head back and laughs, members of his Court glancing at us curiously. 'In seriousness, though,' I continue, 'I appreciate you checking but, yes, General Wolverton is with me.'

'Well, look at you, already winning influential friends in your own Court,' he says, smiling.

And then he's there. My heart leaps into my throat but something in his face and the way Kailoh grips my hand stops me from throwing myself at him. The ache of missing him, that I've pushed far down, breaks the surface.

'General,' Kailoh says, the smile gone, but there's no animosity in his face. Just the expression of a king who knows his place in the world.

'Your Majesty,' Lochlain bows low, his focus catching on my hand in Kailoh's. My skin itches with the need to touch him.

'Welcome to Mercasia. I trust you will find my hospitality warm.' Kailoh lowers his voice in a mock whisper. 'Although there are some very attractive Calahi here you might find even warmer still.' He grins.

Lochlain rises, meeting Kailoh's stare. 'I think very highly of your Court,' he says seriously. A wave of uncertainty bubbles beneath my ribs.

'My Queen,' Lochlain says to me, and I try not to look confused.

'General,' I say quietly, searching his face.

'I look forward to hearing of your time here. I have some updates from Airlie I should like to share with you in due course.'

He bows to us each once more before turning on his heel and disappearing into the throng of Calahi. I can see where he travels by watching the hungry gazes of those around us as they follow his progress through the crowd. The sensation on my skin diminishes with his retreat, leaving only my burning in its wake.

It's an effort to return my attention to Kailoh. What just happened there? Is that what Lochlain meant when he said I could keep him as a lover? That everything between us would need to be a secret? I catch Rory's gaze as I spin slowly on my heel and the conflict on his face seems to reflect the irregular beating in my chest.

But the message is clear. Whatever it means for Lochlain and me, I can't jeopardise my relationship with Kailoh – not with so much at stake. The uncertainty sitting in the base of my gut sours into nausea.

Am I really expected to give him up?

'Your majesty,' a vaguely familiar voice says. I start as I recognise Mulriarty from my meeting with Airlie's Prominent Families.

'It's lovely to see you,' I say, recovering and returning his warm smile. 'What brings you here?'

The light in his eyes takes on a mischievous gleam. 'I came with two goals,' he says. 'To show Pendita just how well you're doing.' He shoots a look towards the edge of the ballroom, where Pendita subtly dips her chin at me. 'And,' Mulriarty continues, 'I promised an old friend of mine an introduction.'

He waves over a Calahi who looks to be about Haryk's age with long, almost lilac coloured hair tied at the base of his skull.

'Ah,' Kailoh says as the third Calahi joins us, taking Mulriarty's introduction from him. 'Adelais, this is Peadat, one of my most valued representatives of the Prominent Families of Mercasia.'

Mulriarty winks at me when I glance at him and I smile, his support and gentle manoeuvring warming me from the inside. But, as I focus on the conversation, I can't help but feel someone like Mulriarty wouldn't ask me to leave Lochlain.

I endure as much more small talk with Kailoh's various advisers and family representatives as I can. I do my best to focus on the conversations, but it's difficult when the connection between Lochlain and I is a constant hum beneath my skin, telling me how close or far away he is. I try to catch his eye several times but every time I look his way, he is deep in conversation, or smiling at something one of the many overly attractive Calahi are saying to him. I try not to be jealous but it's hard not to think about what these Calahi have to offer him. All without the complication of being a half-human Queen.

But it's more than that playing on my mind. He is a natural in his role as General and I don't need to feel his pride licking against my skin to see it in his face. General Wolverton is not only who he was born to be, but who he *is*.

As I watch him talk with an older Calahi male, one who presses his palm to his chest in reverence of Lochlain, I know I will never ask him to give up his role as General in order to be with me.

And I know I need to be Queen. The Realm needs me to be.

Kailoh notices my attention wandering. 'He's quite the attraction, isn't he?' he whispers between conversations. 'I've heard many tales of his loyalty, and his father's before him. You've done well to get him in your corner.' He looks at me intently.

I grip my glittering, empty glass a little harder and swallow, unsure how to answer.

Kailoh plucks two of the gold drinks that circle the air around us, indicating the more formal part of the evening is drawing to a close and soon I can make my escape. I sigh gently as the warm liquid fills my mouth.

'Delicious, aren't they?' Kailoh says, raising his glass to me. He smirks. 'You have a little—'

Rory steps forward as Kailoh raises a hand and brushes my lower lip with his thumb. I blink at him as Rory tries to calm the storm on his face and steps back. A spike of possession that's not mine flares across my skin and Kailoh lifts his questioning eyes to Rory.

I take Kailoh's hand that hovers in the air.

'Come, let's find another of these and then I'm off to bed.'

I don't dare look in the direction of Lochlain or Rory.

CHAPTER TWENTY-SIX

LISH

I pace the sitting room, desperate for sleep but knowing every nerve will jangle until I can talk to Lochlain. Touch Lochlain. Remind myself he's really here.

'What was that back there, at the ball?' I ask Rory.

He and Riley have left their formal stances and are both sprawled on the couches in front of the fire, but there's a slight dullness to Rory's usual sparkle. Riley's emotions, when I lower my barrier, are also muted with sadness. Even as there's an undercurrent of something else – something more undefined – that runs alongside. A feeling that often seems to be with Riley when she's in close proximity to Rory.

'A Calahi,' he says quietly. 'A very clever, powerful Calahi, with designs on my Queen raised his hand to her. Exactly what did you expect me to do, sweetheart?'

I laugh softly.

'Firstly, Kailoh does not have *designs* on me. Secondly, if you really thought he was going to hurt me, he would've lost the hand before he could've even touched my face.' I narrow my eyes at him in a way I think conveys I'm not buying it. 'I've seen you in action, Rory, I know what you can do. What is this really about?'

He sits up and sighs. Riley watches him sideways as he rubs his face.

'It's just hard to watch him engage with you knowing how much we need that alliance and his sapphire – what the likely ask will be.'

The memory of the spiking against my skin when Lochlain watched Kailoh trace my mouth comes back to me. My heart races a little faster.

'I'm going to take a stab in the dark and say I don't think it's me you're worried about here.'

Riley looks at Rory in question.

'Not *only* you,' Rory says, no sign of the characteristic buoyancy in his tone. 'But you need to remember I have seen what the expectations of the Realm can do to a Calahi. The lengths they will go to fit it and, when it doesn't work, what they will give up – regardless of how important it is to them.'

It takes me a moment to work out he's talking about Aeyva. I remember her saying that his parents didn't approve of her and the family they were about to start. But there's something else in what he's saying.

'Do you mean she didn't pursue being a Manorynx because of the pressures of the Court?' I ask.

He lets out a slow breath. 'She didn't come up with the fact she wasn't good enough on her own,' he says. 'And then she let herself try and prove them right by joining the Society.'

An uncomfortable heat creeps out from the centre of my chest and my breathing gets tighter as I think on who else the Realm has expectations of.

'Would Airlie – the Realm – really not accept Lochlain and me? If that's the case, why would he have let us get this far?' There's a crack in my words as my voice shakes.

'Lish,' Riley says. 'You might not have realised it, but you were already in love with him when you came back to Rhyton on the run. We can only assume the feeling was mutual.'

Unwanted tears try to push free and I blink fiercely to clear them.

'It was mutual,' Rory confirms, staring intently at me.

'Which means it was too late for both of you,' she says.

'I need to understand,' I say, looking at Rory, his cheekbones catching the firelight. I know whatever he will say won't change the knowing in my heart that Lochlain is right, but I need to know why.

'The General of Airlie is a highly respected position in our Court – in any Court. The General leads the Royal Watch and the Whispers, you lead the Sentinels, and the Manorynx of Airlie is the liaison for the Prominent Families, essentially creating three pillars of influence in Airlie. While you have the deciding say in any decisions, between the Manorynx and General, you are supposed to have unbiased advisers on both sides.' Rory's onyx, mahogany ringed, eyes look up at me as his shoulders drop a little. 'Having an official, romantic connection with one or the other unfairly sways the balance. As you'd be the Queen of the Court, it would be Lochlain, mostly, who is compromised – the Prominent Families may even pressure him to relinquish the role – but you would also never get their sincere backing. Not without some massive other display of loyalty to Airlie.'

'Why isn't the Custodian subject to this ... scrutiny of supposed morals?' I grind out.

Rory huffs out a loud breath. 'Honestly? He had the favour of your mother for a long, long time – he solidified his position in Airlie as one of trusted adviser well before you were born. He had Siosal on his side and the Givings seemed sensible ... at the time. I don't think the Prominent Families thought there was anything to scrutinise until now.'

'Which would mean I am also to pay for their complacency – with Lochlain.' The tears I'd tried to clear away come back in double force. 'And, yet, he said we could be lovers. I now know that would be in secret, but doesn't that equate to the same thing – this apparent swaying of the balance?'

'Think about Driarn, Lish,' Riley says gently. Either her understanding is faster than mine, or she's talked with Rory about this already. Maybe it's just harder for me to grasp because I don't want to. 'Perception is reality.'

I want to rage against it. Let the hot, angry bubbles in my chest burst free. But Nuala's message from Roisin presses in my mind. The destruction if I don't find the Star, if I can't follow what it tells me to do.

And then I think of my married ex and what it felt like to be the secret. To realise I'd been living only in the shadows of his life. And while it makes my chest feel like it's being shredded from the inside, I know there's no world in which I will make Lochlain anything less than the incredible Calahi he is. He deserves to live his life in the open. Unrestrained.

Meaning unshackled to me, a queen who could never publicly acknowledge him.

The tears are starting to thicken the back of my throat. I look between Rory and Riley and I wonder if they know how lucky they are to have nothing standing in their way. If they will be receptive enough to let this simmering tension between them play out.

'I'm off to bed,' I say and clear my throat. 'Tomorrow, I have to find a way to ask Kailoh for his piece of the sapphire.' I slowly walk away, my jaw tight with need to see Lochlain, even as my heart aches.

But perhaps it would be useful if Kailoh does have designs on me, after all.

There is no way sleep is coming for me tonight. Not now that Lochlain, the person I have fallen asleep next to, or wished I had, for almost this entire chapter of my life is now here. And not with me. He's busy showing Mercasia what an impressive General he is, another integral part of the team that will be in place when the Custodian is removed. Between Lochlain, my 'security' here, and Mulriarty turning up, I can see what this is. A way to show the depth and breadth of my support – that I am more than just a long-lost figurehead. I am a fully functioning, and supported, queen.

But Rory's words echo in my mind. Lochlain was right about the views of others in the Realm. They believe I can't have a proper relationship with him and their respect at the same time.

The door to the bedroom opens slowly.

The connection between us snaps taut as he steals my breath. The figure he cuts in his General's uniform, with both the forest green and sapphire, is striking. His soft dark curls are slightly ruffled and I immediately want to unravel them, the muscles in my stomach clenching gently. He pauses after closing the door and watches me; a slow, predatory smile spreading on his face. The night sky is bright with stars outside the window and a lantern bobs gently by the bed, casting him in partial shadow.

My skin is hot where his emotions run along me and a shiver trickles down my spine as a pool of heat begins to swirl low in my belly.

He takes a single step towards me and I fly across the room to him, crushing myself against his chest as I weave my hands around his neck and cling to him. Lochlain's arms return my pressure where they wrap around my waist, his fingers digging pleasantly into the soft flesh of my sides.

'I missed you,' he murmurs into my neck, his breath warm.

I take his face with both my hands and kiss him, deep and slow, unable to get enough of the taste of him. Lochlain shuffles me towards the bed, his tongue pressing against mine, my hands in those lustrous curls. He lowers me to the bed, gently, even as it seems to pain him to show such restraint. His desperation matches my own. My thin, white silk dressing gown falls open slightly, exposing my bare skin, and a low growl sounds in the base of his throat. His eyes flash copper as they slowly sweep the length of my body.

I prop myself up on my elbows as he drags his hands down my sides and the outside of my legs and back up, leaning down to leave a line of kisses along my collarbones. He cups both of my breasts as his kisses continue over the centre of my stomach. My insides shimmy underneath the path he draws.

Those large, warm hands find my thighs again and he kneels before me, not wasting any time in spreading them wide. A thrill runs through me at how clearly he knows what he wants – and how ready I am to give it to him. I lift my hips, biting my lip as his mouth trails the inside of one thigh and then the other. Travelling so far, and yet not far enough. He sinks his teeth into the vulnerable spot at the top of my right thigh and need flares through me. Finally, his tongue takes its target and I cover my mouth, stifling a moan.

'You are perfection,' he says against me, the vibration of his voice winding me higher. 'I want to taste every inch of you.'

He drags lazy circles with his tongue, slowly edging me to the brink, but never over.

'Please tell me you've still been taking your tonic,' I say quietly, pushing away the thought of what an unrestricted future with Lochlain could look like.

'Of course,' he murmurs.

I close my eyes and give myself to the moment.

'Now,' I say, breathlessly tugging at his shoulders to pull him up.

He obliges and I fumble with the opening of his pants before he takes over, removing them with one hand while the other traces the path his tongue had been taking moments before. My whole body hums and heat prickles my skin. His hands leave me momentarily while he strips out of his jacket and shirt.

'Now, Lochlain,' I beg, my voice rough.

In a single movement, he buries himself in me and breathes my name. I clutch the bed covers as he grips my hips and holds them high as he finds his rhythm. I try to watch him and how the muscles across his torso ripple with the movement. But the sensation of his thrusting pulls me under until I can't breathe and I close my eyes, gasping. His breath comes faster as the speed of his thrusts increases and a groan rumbles in his chest. The sound of his pleasure brings my own and I grip him with my core and thighs as I ride the wave and, together, we let it crash over us.

I trail my fingers on the skin of his broad shoulders and chest, over the wolf, as we catch our breath. It's copper and black fur seeming to dance as my fingers move through it. The weight of his arm across my ribs tucks me in against him and he gently plays with the ends of my hair that have come loose.

'I missed you too,' I say quietly into the wolf.

He stops stroking my hair and looks down at me.

'Nuala had an update from Blaire and Phoenix in the last couple of days,' he says and my chest squeezes. I miss them too. 'They found the woman you saw in the alley and confirmed she's part of a human rebellion against what's happening in Driarn. They're working with her now – trying to work out how much they can trust her with.

'The Custodian is having regular meetings with a member of Nakiasha's Watch,' he continues, and I nod a little.

'We think they are coordinating the attacks on the border of Mercasia,' I say, taking a deep breath. 'Numerous villages have been raided with a human army. It seems they are taking members of the Guard – that's what the rebels in Rhyton will be fighting – injecting them with magic and setting them on Kailoh's Court.'

Lochlain swears. 'That would explain why I didn't find the magic that's Given.'

We lie in silence for a moment and the nervous whirl in my gut returns as he tries to pull his emotions away from me. 'So, things with Kailoh are going well?' he asks, almost inaudibly.

Instinctively I press harder into my barrier even though I know it doesn't work as well with him and his emotions make my heart sink. I lay my hand flat in the middle of his chest where it feels like tiny fireworks explode between his skin and mine, like the beat of a dance. His hand covers mine and grips my fingers.

'I think so,' I say, shifting my head so I'm no longer looking up at him but across his chest.

'He's a good King, Lish. One ... deserving of a Queen like you.'

My stomach feels like it's just dropped out. Leaving a cold void in its place.

'What if that's not what I want?' I ask, my voice somewhere between hurt and angry. Both, really.

'We both know that's not true,' he says. 'You want what's best for Airlie. Kailoh is it.'

I lift my hand from his chest, and it hovers over his skin. He presses it back to his heart.

'This is not – it's not good enough for you. He can give you so much more than I can,' he says, his voice breaking. 'And he's better for the—'

'Please don't say Realm,' I whisper.

I sit up, pulling my hand from his and shifting away. The sheets puddle at my waist and I feel overly exposed, where only moments ago I revelled in our nakedness. Numbly, I take the robe from where it was discarded on the floor and hide beneath the small protection it offers as it slides back over my skin and I sit back on the bed. His face reflects my own heartbreak.

'This ... is our reality,' he says. 'But I can't apologise for coming this far with you. Even if we can't have everything. Some of you is better than none.'

I stare at him, my head spinning and my heart refusing to believe the message he is trying to give me. Hurt and rage fuel each other behind my ribs.

'I have upended everything for this Realm,' I say. 'One of my best friends gave his *life* for this Realm, my *mother* gave her life for this Realm.' My voice is louder than I intended and my chest starts to heave with how unfair this feels. 'They took her choice, Lochlain, she should have been allowed to love who she wanted. I want the choice. I'm ... I'm giving everything. I just'—my words crack—'I just want this choice.'

'I've never wanted anything more in my life, Lish—'

'Then why can't you take it, Lochlain?' I ask, tears beginning their course down my cheeks. But they're not only tears of pain and longing. They're tears of inevitability. Of the knowledge that it's not his choice, just as much as it's not mine. We were both born for the roles we fill, at least the one I am going to fill, and we are both powerless to do anything but keep moving forward. For the Realm. And for Driarn.

I crawl towards him until I'm a hair's breadth away, my body trembling but not touching his, despite the desperate ache I feel.

'I'm right here,' I whisper. 'Take me.'

And then the air is forced from my lungs as he throws his arms around me and holds me to him, hard.

'I don't ever want to let you go,' he says quietly. Desperately.

He spreads his fingers along my ribs and runs his hand down my back to my ass. He cups my cheek and pulls me tighter to him before lying us back down and collecting my thigh, bringing it to rest over his hips. My skin tingles down the length of my body where our skin meets, and he pushes my robe back open.

We lie together several more times, as if trying to wipe away the hurt of the exchange. But sleep doesn't come for me even as Lochlain slumbers. I'm curled into his body and enveloped by him, his arms circling my chest from behind. I try to focus on the heat of him but the reality that's coming between us gnaws at me all the same.

Because despite how we fit together here – how my heart feels at home when he's with me – we both know. We know that Airlie, the Realm,

Driarn – all of those places and the Calahi and people that occupy them – demand more from us. Instead of our love, they need our sacrifice.

So, I count his breaths as I lie in a bed in Kailoh's Palace and try to ignore the fact they are now a countdown for when I will have to let him go.

CHAPTER TWENTY-SEVEN

AEYVA

Loch's arrival all but confirms to Kailoh's Court that we are from Airlie. There are often visitors from Airlie in Kailoh's Court but very rarely do two Wolvertons, including a General, and a member of the Prominent Families, come together and clearly show deference to someone the Mercasians think of as a stranger. Even more rarely do they have such a public display of Kailoh's approval, and curiosity.

Rory and Riley were the official Sentinels for Lish tonight and I would have left the same time as them, had Ciara not stayed behind. The pull to her is as strong as it is to protect Lish. Ciara can protect herself – easily – but sometimes it's protection from herself she needs. I shake off the memory of the day she let her magic go, how it felt so different against mine compared to the destruction it was bringing to others, and lean against the tall table at my back. It's cool, rounded marble digging into my spine.

'She's impressive,' Mulriarty says as he joins me. For a moment I think he means Ciara, whose long, dark hair is swept over one shoulder, exposing her richly tanned skin. The sparkle of the markings on her neck. But when I glance at him, his eyes are on me.

'Kailoh seems very taken,' he continues, 'genuinely so. Something the Calahi of Airlie will certainly notice if he is to support her claim as Queen.'

I nod. Kailoh's support is almost a done deal. He now just needs to ask Lish to bond with him and give her the piece of Star that's sitting in that glass case.

'She's doing well,' I say. I turn to Mulriarty, giving him my full attention. Lish once said he reminded her of Benny and I can see that. But there are so many differences when you really know a person and it almost makes me sad that he's not more like Benny. Not that I dislike Mulriarty – he's one of the best of the Prominent Families. Benny was just ... Benny.

'It was good of you to come,' I say, knowing the open support of the Prominent Families will do nothing but help our case when we return to the Realm. Even if the Mercasians don't know who she is yet, they will. And they'll realise how much they liked her. How much they want their King to be with her.

'I was hoping to help speed things along – I fear we are running short on time.'

I think of the time we've spent here: locating two pieces of sapphire, gaining one, weakening the Eternal Queen to open up my freedom, winning over Kailoh and his Court. It's a lot. But I catch the pinch in his tone.

'Why?'

'The Custodian is sending the Royal Watch on patrols looking for her every day. In a matter of days, they will be doing house ... calls. But it's only a matter of time before someone says they've seen her with one of you. She was at the Challenge after all – someone, outside of all of us, will know she hasn't gone home.' He lets out a deep sigh. 'And he's starting to keep things from Nuala and the Families, our influence is getting harder to exercise. I fear he will stop at nothing to get his hands on her.'

'So he knows something,' I say, quickly trying to think through what. Or how much.

'I can't think what he could know that wasn't already obvious – even coming here shouldn't have been out of his speculation of what she'd do. He doesn't know how much or how little she knows of the Realm.'

The air I drag into my lungs turns sharp. There is something he didn't know before, couldn't have known, because it wasn't even in our plans when we left.

Lish killed the Eternal Queen's sister.

Leaving someone who will offer her services to the highest bidder, perhaps one that can offer her revenge, or justice, for the loss of her sister. And now two of the most powerful Calahi in the Realm, one because of his position and the other her power, both have motivation to keep Lish from that Throne. Or worse.

And he's about to start house calls – in a city that currently houses Will and his family.

Mulriarty pales as I tell him, in whispers hidden under the sound of the music, of what occurred in the tunnels. But there is a spark of connection in his face when he looks at me.

'There were rumours, long ago – Benny told me – that whoever smashed Roisin's sapphire, under the guise of protecting future Calahi from her madness, were cursed. He said that whoever it had cursed probably knew the secret of how to hold Roisin's power.' He looks at me and I frown, not understanding.

'Because it didn't work on them. What if they'd tried to take her power and were cursed for that, not because they smashed the sapphire, or maybe both.' He waves a hand. 'I don't know. The point is, we'd thought those that were cursed were lost. But'—he trails off a bit as he looks back at me and my inability to breathe properly becomes a secondary issue as my heart beats rapidly—'what if that's what he's going to try? To claim Roisin's power, armed with the knowledge of what *not* to do, from her resting place – if he can find it – and, in turn, rule Airlie permanently. With Roisin's power, there'd be nothing stopping him making a play for the whole Realm.'

I swallow. 'Particularly if he has a disposable human army jacked up on magic.'

'I knew,' he says slowly, 'he was a Calahi always intent on power and pushing Airlie forward. At the time, I agreed he was an invaluable support to Catriona. Now, it seems abundantly clear they had a major severing of views at some point.'

I glance at him as he continues watching the ballroom.

'But today, I'm not sure if he simply wants to stop Adelais from taking over the rule of our Court, or if he wants her to watch him prove her mother wrong. In whatever that may have been.'

He meets my gaze and holds it for a long moment. 'Maybe this time we need a Manorynx who can wield a sword on our side.'

My mind is reeling as I send Mulriarty to fill in the others. His parting comment spinning among the crowding thoughts. There was no cheek in his voice – more like a desperation. Nuala is the best of us – kind, knowing, and firm. She will be the best Manorynx for Lish to have at her side. But, for the first time, I consider that perhaps one Manorynx isn't enough anymore.

Ciara moves like grace itself as she dances with her old friend. The one she disappeared with for hours before we went to the tunnels. He's attractive enough, I'll give him that, but otherwise he's about as interesting as the muck I wash off my shoes when I've completed a job. A by-product of a more significant event. But at least he gives me somewhere to focus my disquiet after my conversation with Mulriarty – the time it has taken from getting Lish on the throne before the Custodian can raid Roisin's Resting Place for her power. Because, while the location of where she lies has been a secret guarded so long the location is no longer known to us, if the Eternal Queen really did kill her, then she knows where it is.

Finally, the dance ends and Ciara returns to the table without her partner. Her composure is impeccable as I tell her of my conversation with Mulriarty.

'We need to get back,' she says, looking around the ballroom.

'If we go without Kailoh's piece and support, we're in no better position than we are now.'

Her shoulders drop a fraction. 'Lish will be with Kailoh again in the morning, we'll know his stance then – for better or worse.'

I take a deep breath and try to calm my nerves. There's nothing that can be done about it right now, and there are enough eyes on us here that jumping into any kind of action will be noticed. We need to make a show of strength and resilience. So, instead, I lean back against the table and make a show of complacence.

The Calahi who's tried to occupy as much of Ciara's time as he can weaves his way through the guests. Ciara glances at me before looking back to him, her smile wide.

'We just need to get through tonight and tomorrow,' she says under her breath, 'and then we go back.'

'One more?' she asks as he reaches our table, and she leads him back to the dance floor.

Kailoh's lavish events are excruciating with Ciara here. On past occasions, I have been able to let go of the deeds I've completed elsewhere and enjoy the never-ending parties Kailoh has thrown. These in the ballroom are the ones the public sees, where those who desire to be seen come. But there is always, always, another room, in another part of the Palace, for those of us who do not need the social validation, and simply wish to enjoy the company of others – in whatever capacity that may take. Keeva was often with me and she, Kailoh, and I were never the first to leave. Tonight, I wish I could go back to those days. When the things that weighed on me were of my own making and the entire Realm wasn't at stake.

Lochlain had arrived just as Lish was dancing with Kailoh, and I'd dug an elbow into his ribs in an attempt to drive the thunder from his face. He knows as well as I do that he can't publicly claim her; he circled her for the rest of the evening, staying almost entirely out of sight.

I don't know how to look at the love that's clearly between the two of them. Not when I know what it's like to love a Wolverton – and that there's no way Lish and Lochlain are going to be able to keep what they've found. Having watched Kailoh's response to Lish the last few days, and knowing his desperation for a partner – a solid, appropriately equal, partner – I know without doubt what he is going to ask of her. And how steadily the Court of Airlie believes in *protect without claim*. A sentiment that includes formal romantic attachments.

A tiny voice in my mind wonders if I should chase what I want. How can I turn down the very thing Lish is being denied, if it's within my reach? But one devastated Wolverton is enough – we can't afford to have two. Not if they are to play their destined roles in the carriage of Airlie; the General and lead Sentinel are crucial in establishing Lish's rule over Airlie. The Queen and the Wolvertons is a partnership the Realm has only been without since Catriona was killed. If we are to have any hope of restoring the Mother, that partnership needs to be fully reinstated. And I worry what impact broken hearts might have on it. I might be slowly nudging towards doing what Ciara wants of me – completing my training as a Manorynx in support of Nuala – but I fear that won't be enough. Ciara's intentions are so good, so ... pure. If she really knew how unsuited I am for the position, she'd never insist I take it. And what would that do to her?

Only Ciara and I remain here now, the others all having retired for the evening. Ciara's deep navy dress spins around her ankles as she's twirled around the dance floor, her forehead glistening. There are others who have joined them, but none are as captivating as her and I'm not the only one who notices. The male she dances with grins from ear to ear. How I'd like to follow that line with my blade.

Instead, I throw back my drink and hold it up for the refill.

'Resplendent, isn't she?' Ciara's dance partner joins me at the table, panting, after she excuses herself for the bathroom.

The few dances they've shared have taken it out of him. I remind myself I don't know what she feels for this one. If it's something deep, and I want to keep her in my life, I will need to be civil. Even if small talk has never been my forte. I don't listen to anything else he says but am conscious to laugh and smile in the right places. He is the sort of Calahi who would normally be intimidated by me and it's hard not to draw on that now. But Ciara introduced us, and now he thinks we're friends.

She joins us after a little while and the three of us talk and laugh as the drinks keep coming. I'm desperate to escape the vapidness of the room but I won't leave until I know where Ciara will be. It's the only way I have any chance of rest.

Ciara and the male – whose name I don't want to remember – stand close on the other side of the tall table. He nudges her and looks meaningfully at the door. Her black and gold eyes flick to mine, the gold the most prominent until they look to me. I bet he hasn't even noticed how they change. Or that there is currently no desire for him in them. The sounds of the ballroom thicken around me while she holds my gaze, assessing whatever she finds there.

'We're going to call it a night,' she says, dragging her attention back to her dance partner. He smiles enthusiastically and the stone in my chest drops to my stomach.

'Night,' he says to me as he worms his hand around her waist and leads her out of the ballroom.

'Night,' I say tightly to their backs. 'Enjoy.'

I give them a few moments to get ahead of me before following behind. I won't interrupt, but I need to know where she goes in case she needs me. I pray it's not out of the Palace.

They link elbows as they wander through the thinning crowds in Kailoh's white hallways, never once looking back. Ciara's smile when she turns to face him looks forced from where I trail them. But perhaps that's wishful thinking. A small edge is knocked off the tension in my shoulders when it's clear he is a guest of the Palace.

Maybe we need a Manorynx who can wield a sword. I shake my head. Could I really be both? Nuala will know. Maybe she will know what to do about Ciara, too.

He leads us to a slightly older part of the Palace where Kailoh has installed various works of art in alcoves dotted along the hallways. Most of these have their curtains pulled open in the soft light of night-time. No other Calahi join us in the dark hallway, those that stay here likely having retired long before.

I duck into one of the alcoves when Ciara and her companion stop two doors up. He fumbles with the opening before letting himself in. Ciara says something into the room and pauses in the doorway.

'I know you're there, Aeyva,' she says more loudly without turning around. The wine courses through my veins and my vision blurs in my desperation for her not to take this path. Not with one she is so clearly not interested in.

'Don't go with him, Kiki, please.' My voice is nothing more than a whisper, I'm not even sure I've spoken aloud. She turns on her heel slowly and pins me with a look.

'Why?'

Because it should be me, I think but I press my lips together.

'Why, Aeyva?' she asks again when I don't respond. Can't respond. I want to, but the words are trapped behind my teeth.

She takes purposeful strides to close the space between us.

'Tell me, Aeyva,' she demands, her face inches from mine.

I open my mouth to speak but the words die before I can sound them. I try to draw a breath to recover myself and then her hands are in my hair. She pushes me against the back of the alcove with her hips as she crushes me with her mouth. Her tongue presses against mine, her jasmine and honey scent filling my nose as I grapple to make sense of what she's doing. Before I can return her kiss, she breaks away. Gasping, my mouth still can't form the words that are desperate to find their way out.

'Tell me, and I won't go,' she says. 'Say it. Tell me who you are and what you want.'

I burn with how undeserving I am of her.

'You'll never say it,' she spits, angrier than I've seen her in a long time. I flinch at the knowledge that it's driven by hurt. That by staying in this halfway place with her, in an attempt not to hurt her with all that I am – and am not – I've done exactly that.

She watches me for a moment as my heart breaks before her. Then she turns and walks away, back towards someone who won't ever be good enough for her but won't hurt her, either. And I realise, even with my possible change in direction – my growing need to talk with Nuala and support her in whatever way she needs – the damage to Ciara has already been done.

I took too long.

But I won't let her down in the tasks ahead of us, in saving the Realm. Now is the time for me to act, to become the sword-wielding Manorynx Mulriarty spoke of. To go to Kailoh and demand he ask Lish to bond, if that's what he's going to do, but to support us in Lish's quest for the Throne and let us go back to Airlie.

I stand in the empty hallway, staring at the back of Ciara as she continues down the hall, pausing at the door in front of her. And I understand that all the renewed focus in the world won't save me from the pain of hurting her. That I won't destroy her goodness is my only solace as I return to the shadows of the alcove. The pads of my fingers rest on my bruised lips as I stand guard and watch her close the door behind her.

CHAPTER TWENTY-EIGHT

LISH

Our morning debrief is like having all the walls press in on me. Every face I turn to knows what I am about to do – talk about bonding to someone other than the Calahi male at my side. In a way, it feels strange that I find it so offensive. Lochlain and I have never talked about bonding together. Now, as I look back, I think that was because it was all so new and then, when we both knew who I was, he knew it would never be an option anyway.

But everything, from my heart to my skin that prickles warmly in his presence, knows he is the only one I would ever consider marrying. Or bonding. But my head knows that we live in a world where hearts and dancing magic aren't the only factors.

So, I stand here, looking at my team, thinking about bonding with the King, what I will say to him to get him to commit to supporting my play for the Throne. Do I lead with the bonding? Do I make it friendly? A business discussion? Do I just raise having his support and the sapphire and hope he doesn't bring up bonding in exchange?

The memory of Lochlain's warmth around me when I woke up is both a balm and a wound. But I breathe into it to steady my racing heart and focus on what I need to do – become Queen of Airlie. To do that, and get around the Royal Watch that are looking for me, I need Kailoh. I need to walk into Airlie under his protection so I can get an audience with the

Custodian and force him to acknowledge me and my blood. Then, I will show the Court who really killed my mother.

Before he starts searching houses for me, and finds Will.

The reality of what I'm being asked to sacrifice, and the tiny amount of time I have to do it, starts to sink in. I want to talk it through with Lochlain, have him help me find a way out. But how to get Kailoh's part of the Star, avoid capture by the Custodian, have Airlie listen to me when they think I killed their Queen – not to mention gaining the numbers in our forces to protect my Calahi against the human army that's being put together, and stop the pillaging of Roisin's magic – my head pounds trying to work out how to do it without Kailoh. Without bonding with him.

At the same time, another thought sneaks in. Is bonding him contrary to our agreement to be authentic?

'Let's get this over with,' Rory says, clamping a hand on Lochlain's shoulder.

My skin prickles warmly and Lochlain tucks me into his side, kissing my head and running a hand up my arm. I close my eyes and lean into him. Tipping my head up and blindly finding his soft lips, I taste salt, my tears falling unbidden.

'I'll always belong to you,' I whisper when I open my eyes again, his grip on my arm almost painful. 'But Airlie needs you, General.'

'Everything alright, Adelais?' Kailoh asks.

There's genuine concern in his kind face and I take a moment to observe him. He's dressed more casually today, with only him and me and the four Sentinels between us – two each. But, despite the lack of a long jacket and the crown I've never seen him wear, there is no doubt of who and what he is. It's in how he holds himself, how the words fall from his tongue. I have no doubt he plays games when he deems it necessary, but I believe he hasn't with me.

'Fine, just focused on what we need to achieve,' I flash him what I hope is a confident smile.

'Yes, your task is not an easy one – Nuala's message certainly made that clear. What you, and your allies, are due to stop is ... immense. But you've made progress here, Adelais, that has to be good.' There's a hint of question on his face.

'It is, definitely,' I say, thinking of the pieces of sapphire and not the backwards steps between Lochlain and me. 'But there are still two pieces of the sapphire that are yet to be in my possession and'—I tilt my head slightly at Kailoh—'an alliance to forge. We both know it will be all but impossible for me to make a claim for the Throne without your support and protection. And, if I can't get that Throne, I don't get the crown and I can't put the Star together.'

'And then,' Kailoh picks up and continues the list of challenges, 'we have no way of knowing the details of the Star's message, stopping the testing on humans and removing the Custodian from his path of draining all of Airlie and Driarn.'

'So, really, without those pieces of the Star, we may as well start saying our goodbyes now.'

Kailoh's brows lift in amusement but there's an understanding there as well.

'So, a realist as well as authentic,' he notes.

'When you've seen what I have – both in Rhyton and from when Nuala traced my blood – it's hard not to be.' I don't tell him the slight bite in my tone is also because of what it's costing me personally.

Kailoh smiles sadly, his sensual lips drawing back gently. 'No, it's no small feat. That much is for certain. But you're right, they are each elements I can assist with, or you wouldn't be here. Unless it's my company you find so attractive?' He winks at me, and I smile in response. There's something comforting in making light of the monumental obstacles ahead.

'The company helps.'

He quietens as food appears on the small table between us, an act that never ceases to amaze me. The ceramic bowls of colourful fruits seem too good to be true and I run my finger along a plump, oval shaped one with glistening pink skin. Elaborate, shimmering pastries appear next, along with a blue and green drink of some sort for Kailoh, and coffee for me. Kailoh lifts his drink.

'For my health apparently.' He grimaces as he gulps it down. Laughter bubbles from my throat.

'That face means it cannot possibly be good for you.'

'You don't want one, I take it?'

'I'm good with my steaming cup of human magic, but thank you.'

He banishes his empty glass with a flick of his hand, his honey gaze not leaving my face.

'Your company's not so bad either, you know. I likely would have had you beheaded before now if it wasn't.'

I almost choke on my coffee.

'How do you know I wouldn't just come back to haunt you?'

'Oh, now there's an idea.' He taps his chin in mock thoughtfulness.

Aeyva and Rory are with me this morning, Rory behind me and Aeyva behind Kailoh where I can see her. They each monitor different parts of the room. Kailoh's Sentinels mimic the action. But where the Sentinels of Kailoh's appear to stare at nothing, Aeyva shares a meaningful, but warning, look with Rory at our exchange.

I look back to Kailoh who's still watching me carefully, his auburn framed face more serious now.

'Listen, Adelais, I've been thinking.'

My heart starts to beat a bit faster.

'I will give you a formal alliance,' he says. I want to breathe a sigh of relief, but the feeling is short-lived. 'If we make our union official.'

'Official?' It sounds like a question even though I knew what we would discuss this morning. And I can't help but remember Siosal asking me for something very similar. He wanted it for very different reasons than Kailoh, but I still want to object that I should be allowed to bond for my own reasons.

He nods and my fingertips go numb.

'It's well past time I was bonded, but finding the right candidate has been difficult. Very few have the right motivations and if they do'—he gestures vaguely—'there are other elements that are not compatible. If we bond, we will formally unite the Courts of Mercasia and Airlie. My resources will be at your disposal and, together, we can ensure the safety and ongoing stability of the Realm.' He pauses. 'And stop the Custodian experimenting with humans that are very quickly becoming a threat to all Calahi.'

The room comes to a halt. This is it.

All the details I couldn't previously focus on come into stark focus. The crisp, white tablecloth with the intricate brass cutlery. The pale blue mug with the gold handle that now shakes slightly in my right hand. The gilded frame that hosts a painting of a stunning Calahi woman. The impossible smoothness of Kailoh's chin. Aeyva's face, which practically screams at me to say yes.

I place my mug down gently, the sound ringing around the room as it makes contact.

'Kailoh—' I start quietly.

'I know now you have a lover, of course, and I realise this is a bit unusual to the human way of thinking when you have one of those. But you also know he will never be acceptable to your Court.'

It's his words that make my decision for me. Not about having a lover, but that he will never be acceptable as such to the Court. That, somehow, the two of us being involved makes him less of a General – makes me less of a Queen. But Kailoh is right, it is *my* Court. And I will rule it in the best way I know how – transparently.

I take a halting breath. 'Kailoh, I am beyond honoured ...'

Aeyva's mouth drops open slightly at whatever she hears in my voice, but she is bound to act as a Sentinel today. And that doesn't include sharing her opinions in front of Kailoh and his.

Kailoh kicks up a dark auburn brow, asking the unsaid *but*?

'... but I cannot be bonded to you,' I continue. 'You're right, you can help me, greatly, with what I need to achieve. But aligning our Courts is not a one-sided endeavour, it will be to your benefit as well.'

I look at him and desperately hope I am making the right decision, and not condemning us all. The destruction in Nuala's vision flashes before my eyes. If I fail in putting together all the pieces of the sapphire, I have no hope of saving any of us from that future.

'If this is because of your lover, I'm sure we can make some arrange—'

'No,' I say, 'it's not.' Well, not entirely, but I don't say that.

He steeples his fingers beneath his chin. 'You've intrigued me, Adelais, and this is of course a negotiation. Enlighten me as to why you would decline the very thing you came here for.'

My stomach turns over itself and my palms start to sweat.

'I promised you I wouldn't play games,' I say. 'That you would get my authentic self. And that is what I have done. I did not come here to lure you into bonding with me for the sake of my goals. I have enjoyed your company, and the hospitality of your Court, genuinely.'

'Where then, lies the issue in my offer?'

I consider this for a moment. My heart will never belong to him and a small part of it revolts at his suggestion because of who it does claim, and the tiny hopes that lie there. But there's another reason tapping away at my mind.

'It's not the offer, Kailoh,' I say. 'It's an incredible offer, one I feel incredibly privileged to have received. But I need to decline, and I do not do that lightly.' I draw a steadying breath and grip my hands together. 'If I am going to succeed in taking the Throne of Airlie and finding the Star ... I need to do it because of me. I need the Calahi to believe in me because of who I am, and not who I am bonded to. I fear that if the Calahi of Airlie do not have faith in me, and the future of their Court, they will not have enough faith to fight at all.'

Kailoh sits back in his chair and crosses his legs.

Long moments pass and I can't bring myself to look away from his assessing gaze. Aeyva's stare brands my skin.

'Well ... that didn't turn out how I expected,' he says, releasing a breath and glancing back at Aeyva.

Have I just made a terrible mistake? The faces of different Calahi I have seen in Elenlea swim around me, the little girl who looked at Lochlain with such awe when he walked the streets to the Challenge. What have I just condemned them all to?

Sweat starts to prickle at my hairline.

'I have something for you,' Kailoh says.

I swallow, my mouth drying and tacky. I need water.

Kailoh stands and I tip my head back to watch him as he unfurls to his full height. I make to stand as well, looking to Aeyva and Rory for a hint as to what this exchange might be about now. But their faces offer no clues. When I look back, Kailoh is on bended knee before me. I collapse back in my chair with a gasp.

Not this, please.

'Adelais *Wolverton*.' He winks at me and takes my hand. 'You came to my Court as a surprise, something I don't encounter very often. You have proven yourself to be loyal, kind, and smart – with a brave and lethal edge to protect those you care about. And you clearly know how to stick to your values.' He smiles.

The heat in my chest races to my cheeks. His words fill my heart but they, and his posture, are coming from the wrong Calahi. Did he not understand that I said no? Am I going to have to say it twice? Or is this an opportunity to correct my selfishness?

'With my Sentinels, and yours, as witness, I pledge my allegiance to you. I will support you in your quest for the Star and restoring balance to our world. I will help you claim the Court of Airlie and save your people, as well as my own, and the humans from the Custodian.'

'Oh my god,' I breathe, 'Kailoh, I—'

'I know, I know, I'm *incredible*. But you haven't waited for the best bit.' He pulls something from his pocket and opens his palm. 'My piece of Roisin's Star belongs in Airlie.'

I stare at him, understanding the warmth at my chest is at least partly from Lochlain's pendant. I reach forward to wordlessly take the glimmering piece of sapphire. Kailoh snaps his hand shut and grabs my fingers before I can take it. He plants a soft kiss on my knuckles.

'Should you ever change your mind about bonding with me,' he looks up and I'm struck again by how attractive he is, 'let me know. But, at the end of the day,' he says slowly, 'I understand we need to be able to fight for ourselves.'

I open my mouth, but no words come out.

Gently he moves his hand from mine, dragging the sapphire with him.

'But I can't give this to you,' he says, standing once more. I gape up at him until I feel my face morph into a frown.

'You agreed it belongs in Airlie,' I say finally.

'And it does. But you must understand that this piece was entrusted to me by one of the Realm's greatest Manorynxes. A line of Calahi who were given this piece to care for throughout all our modern times.' He looks at the piece as I remember the vision of Nuala giving it to him for safekeeping.

Behind him, Aeyva has begun to pale.

Kailoh turns to her and she meets his gaze head on. Lochlain's pendant burns almost to the point of pain, as if it's giving me a message. That a piece bigger than just the sapphire is finally falling into place. That Kailoh is giving Aeyva the permission she doesn't need to take the place she deserves. And I am about to walk into Airlie, under the protection of Mercasia, to take mine.

'Aeyva Kaylneau,' he says. 'I now entrust you with this part of Roisin's Star. For pure and good doings.' Aeyva blinks at him. 'And for freedom.'

CHAPTER TWENTY-NINE

LISH

Rory and I leave Aeyva to discuss the specifics with Kailoh's lead Sentinel. There are some details I just don't have the capacity to absorb at the moment. On one hand, my goals are progressing with success. On the other, my heart feels like it's breaking. My walking slows as we near our room. Where I will tell the waiting team we have the alliance, and it's time to leave the Palace so we can work out the details of how I try again. How I retake the same steps in Elenlea as I did before the Custodian announced me a murderer.

The heat in my blood rises as I think about that day. It's an anger that spurs me on.

Always. For her, and for me, I will clear my name and lead Airlie as she should have done.

A realisation slams into me as I think about my father, someone I don't give a lot of thought to – he was never a factor in our lives. It wasn't until I was older that I understood the difference in how my mother spoke about him compared to many others who didn't have a father. There was no hate, no discontent. Just love. A nameless, faceless love.

But when I now think about the hole Hayes left, and the tearing I feel at making the choice to let Lochlain go, I wonder at how she did it. How alone she must have felt, with no one but a young daughter, who had no idea what she'd lost and given up. No idea what was at stake.

'You're not going to tell him, are you?' Rory asks, breaking into my thoughts, and I realise I've stopped outside the door.

I close my eyes briefly against all the implications of telling him. And not telling him. The memory of Rory's conflicted gaze when I danced with Kailoh makes me turn to face him. Other Calahi mill around us and I lower my voice to a whisper.

'I don't think I can,' I whisper.

'He'll be proud of you, Lish,' Rory says, and I have to swallow so I don't cry.

I nod. 'But then he'll feel pressured to risk his position, too, and you know as well as I do we can't risk that. It's easier for the moment that he thinks I am bonding with Kailoh – it lets me make the hard choice for him. And we go to Airlie unattached.'

Rory reaches out and pulls me into a hug.

'I think you will find you'll always be attached,' he says into my hair. 'But I understand.'

His arms are warm and strong around me, and they do deliver a certain comfort. But I wish they were Will's, instead. Someone who would tell me what I want is also worth fighting for. Someone who would tell me that it's not impeccably selfish to want to have the Calahi I love. That maybe it's the Calahi of Airlie who need an expectation shift and not me.

But it's not the Calahi of Airlie who have been born to rule. Who hail from the line of their First Queen, and are critical to the Star in some way.

So, it's me who needs to do the adjusting. The letting go.

I pull back from Rory and take a bracing breath before pushing the door open. Anger and disappointment roll off both Lochlain and Riley as they stop mid-conversation to look at me. It's clear Riley has been giving Lochlain a piece of her mind, but it's not something I have the space to take on right now. The weight of Lochlain's splintering emotions mixing with my own makes my knees tremble and I take the closest chair to hide my unease.

'Well?' Riley asks softly, letting the tension in her shoulders ease out of her.

'She did it,' Rory says dully when it's clear I won't – can't – answer. 'She got the alliance with Kailoh. He pledged his support to her and all of Airlie. We have the sapphire, too.'

Riley's hands fly to her face and cover her open mouth. Lochlain pushes himself off the couch and hovers where he stands. The distance between us now a physical bridge that takes more effort to cross.

'Congratulations, Lish.' His voice is thick as he makes his way to me, his General's uniform feeling like a smack in the face. But I don't think it would be easier if he wasn't wearing it. His warm, soft lips press to my forehead, my arms hanging limply by my sides. 'I knew you could do this. You were born for this.'

I wish that felt like an encouraging thing. Instead, it feels like I'm being hemmed in. Being forced to fill a space that doesn't fit me. Not because I don't want to be Queen, but because I'm not the Queen that Airlie expects.

I look at Lochlain's chest, and not his blazing eyes. But the memory of my hands there last night doesn't ease the blistering ache in mine.

'We need to pack,' I say, finding my voice. 'The Custodian is going to hear of this from me.'

Because I might not be the Queen they expect, but I am their Queen and I will prove how well I can do it, if it's the last thing I do.

The freezing air of Mercasia shivers my bones in the dark of night. Riley and I press against each other as we sit side by side and watch the fire in the centre of our group. Before we left, Kailoh informed me that word had finally reached his kingdom of the price on my head. It wasn't surprising, Lochlain and Mulriarty had already confirmed how intently the Royal Watch is looking for me in Airlie. It was only a matter of time before that spread. But it did mean the normal openings between Courts were no longer safe and I don't need this whole endeavour to come crashing down because some Society bounty hunter got lucky. So, I accepted Kailoh's suggestion of laying low in the forest for a night so we can discuss our next steps and move into Airlie fully prepared.

Two of Kailoh's Sentinels join us, with more to follow. While Daire and Callie now wear black like the rest of us, I know they have packed their deep red uniforms. Uniforms they will wear when we appear at the Palace and demand to see the Custodian. The same uniforms that will signal we are there on business of Mercasia as well – something the Custodian won't be able to deny. At least not publicly. The fact this is still our most straightforward path rattles something deep inside and my flame flickers in discomfort.

Ciara has taken the lead and I observe the way she engages with the Sentinels from Mercasia. Initially, I'd thought she and Aeyva were equal, or that perhaps Aeyva was the lead given her role with the Royalists. But it's actually Ciara that Aeyva – and Rory and Riley, when they are in uniform – defer to. Her style is kind and empathetic, but there's a spine of steel underneath. There is no doubt in my mind that she and Lochlain deserve every bit of reverence they receive for being Wolvertons. But, as she talks with Daire and Callie, I can tell there's something worrying her. Something she is trying not to let distract her, much like I am with Lochlain.

The gentle scrape of Lochlain's emotions on my skin oscillates between angry, hurt, and sad. All things I don't think he believes he should be entitled to feel. Because he believes he can't be my 'official' partner. Does that mean he only deserves whatever scraps a queen might bestow upon him? I can't work through how to make that not be so right now. So, it's easier if he thinks I have made the call that we won't be together at all, and his position isn't compromised by my affection.

What a bunch of bullshit these traditions are, I think to myself. There is a lot I love about this Realm – but these backwards views are not one of them. Something that needs addressing. *Add it to the list, Lish.*

Callie's loud gasp draws me from my downward heading thoughts, and I look away from the flames. Perhaps it's them and their memories, both good and bad – but all pointing to Lochlain – that dampen my mood. Or, perhaps more likely, it's the reality I've let him go that burns. Because my heart is arguing that it will never let him go.

'Do you see that?' she asks quietly, turning on the spot.

A twig snaps to my right, in the darkness outside our circle, and I jerk my head in that direction. Reaching for my blade.

A pair of amber eyes stares back at me from the trees.

My flame surges in response and I press my blade back into its sheath. 'It's okay,' I say quietly, 'it won't hurt us.'

'There's more than one,' Aeyva says levelly, but I note there is no trace of uncertainty in her voice. Outside myself and the Wolvertons, she would be most familiar with the stories of the wolves and Roisin's line. She also saw what unfolded in the tunnels.

Following the direction of Aeyva's gaze, I find at least two more wolves surrounding us, just visible on the edge of the light. The third shadow could be a tree. Slowly, I look back to the wolf closest to me and I incline my head, a smile tugging at the corner of my lips. There's something about its presence that tells me it's the lead. Do they call that an alpha? I try to remember. But maybe these wolves don't follow any of the rules about animals I learned in school. They certainly didn't teach magic there, and that it could have been shared by these remarkable beasts.

The wolf blinks at me in recognition and lowers its head to sniff the ground, its eyes never leaving my face.

'This is incredible,' Daire says. 'I'd heard stories but ...'

My gold flame is warm under Lochlain's pendant as I watch the wolves, a steady heat that seems to be unique to when they're near. Absently, I wonder if I should give it back. But, either way, it would be temporary. So, I'll keep it until we put the Star together. There's only so much I can give up right now.

The wolves don't make any indication that they are just passing through, they're more like a secondary ring of protection. Or maybe it's the first.

'So, tomorrow,' Ciara says, looking at each of us and not the wolves. 'We'll head straight to the Royalists training ground and gather Will and the most solid team he's been training. The others will return to their homes. We go straight from there to the Palace, led by Daire and Callie and backed – literally – by the Royalists.' She looks at me. 'You'll have two Wolvertons and your Sentinels by your side.'

A tendril of nervousness licks up my spine. Is Ciara expecting we may face a fight even getting to the Palace? A fight against the Royal Watch, I can only assume. Lochlain controls the Whispers so it won't be them. But I can't bring myself to ask. If I will be fighting Calahi I am supposed to lead and care for, I'd prefer not to know who I might be killing.

I nod at the waiting Ciara.

'Tomorrow, you'll be Queen,' Riley says.

I look to Lochlain, who's watching me intently from across the fire, the air between us taut with everything that could be. Everything I need to say but can't is hovering above the flames.

'I'll take the first watch,' Aeyva announces quietly to the group.

I tear my gaze away from Lochlain and glance back at the amber-eyed wolf as I unroll my bedding. Riley and I stay near the fire, too cold to move further away, and I wriggle in, white puffing from my mouth. I pile the furs on top of both of us as we snuggle together. Riley grunts and shuffles until she finds my hand and grips it. I stare at her, watching her features in the flickering firelight, and will the tears not to come.

In her furrowed face, and the sorrow caressing my skin, I can see everything she wants to say. That she's sorry I'm hurting. Sorry I can't have what I want. Sorry that I am bonding someone I don't love. Sorry so much of this is on my – our – shoulders and not someone else's.

And the weight of the secret unlatches my hold on my tears.

They stream down my face, hot and fast, and I sob silently, desperately trying to conceal the wracking of my body. I squeeze her cold hand, the only thing stopping me from crumbling.

'He loves you, Lish, I know he does,' she whispers.

'It was my choice,' I choke out. 'I just'—my breath shudders—'I said no,' I whisper so only Riley can hear me. She grips my hand in return.

'Oh my god,' she breathes. 'You have to tell him.'

'I can't,' I sniffle, trying to steady my gulping breaths. 'You've seen him, Riles. You saw what we went through to get him where he is. There's no possible way I can ask him to give that up. Equally impossible is asking me to let him be my secret. An on-demand lover, as if he doesn't deserve anything more from me. I just—why does it have to be so unfair?'

'Maybe you can't yet,' she says slowly. 'We do have some particularly big problems to solve right now. But, look at this.' She indicates the camp with a small movement of her head. 'Here you have two Courts with a formal alliance, a part-Calahi queen with magic in her veins, surrounded by a human and Calahi team that love her ... in a ring of wolves.' Her eyes widen. 'Like, if this is possible, maybe anything is.'

It's the 'yet' in her sentence I hang onto. The one I so desperately wanted someone to tell me.

I know I am right not to tell him now. The presence of the wolves around us as we prepare to move on the Custodian is more than enough evidence for me to know I am the rightful ruler of Airlie. I need to be on that Throne, and I am going to do it without compromising any of the foundations Airlie will judge me on.

But maybe after ...

Tomorrow I will be Queen. I just need to get through tomorrow and then we can work it out.

The gentle voices of the others die away, and sleep pulls to me. The static on my skin softening into a caress as I shiver under the furs.

I open my eyes groggily as my furs are jostled by Rory sliding his bed roll closer to Riley in what I assume is an attempt to keep her warmer with his superior body heat.

I roll over and find myself face-to-face with Lochlain. He inches towards me, my breath held. The lump in my throat grows until I can't swallow past it anymore and my tears come once more. Softly this time. As if they have also resigned to the hurt, particularly now I have a plan to make it temporary. Lochlain pries away the hands I bury my face in and lifts my chin. His soft lips kiss my tears away before he holds me tight against his chest and murmurs in my ear until my tears subside.

Whatever he says, it's too quiet for me to make out but, in this moment, I know what it is to have a love I will do everything in my power to fight for.

I imagine I now know how my mother loved my father.

So, I close my eyes, knowing tomorrow I will take back her crown.

And Lochlain.

CHAPTER THIRTY

AEYVA

I turn onto my other side, the cold seeping up from the ground making it uncomfortable despite the excessive amount of furs Kailoh sent with us. A shiver takes me, and I can't tell if it's from how much colder it is than the last time I stayed in this forest or the cold itself. But the fact we are starting to be more and more impacted by the cold in Mercasia, tells me the same thing the heat tells those in Rhyton. The Mother is broken and we need to stop her decline before it becomes ours as well.

More than it already is.

Grunting as I throw back the top layer of furs, I decide I might as well embrace it now and get up. Today is a big day. But Ciara stops me with a firm hand on my thigh, over the covers. I hadn't realised we'd gotten so close in the night. It takes me less than a heartbeat to understand what she's saying.

The wolves are still here.

Seeing them arrive last night was one of the most incredible things I've ever seen. I've always known about them. But knowing they follow the Queen and seeing it are two different things – watching one of them tear out of the throat of the Eternal Queen's sister felt like a dream until now. The one closest to Ciara and I looks between us for a long moment before it saunters closer to the tree line – but not out of sight.

Twisting around, I look to Loch and Lish across the still burning fire – one of Loch's specialities. A larger, greyer wolf with black markings on its face lies between their legs. Loch shifts as he wakes and the wolf moves away before I think he's noticed. But the image reminds me of a theory

Benny had about why the sapphire split into four pieces and what they each meant.

One piece represented Roisin's line on the Throne; another the support and protection of a Wolverton. The connection between the Wolvertons and Roisin's line has been renowned throughout history – the protector and the protected – so seeing the wolf between Loch and Lish, in that sense, isn't completely surprising.

It hurts me to watch the pain that's between them, but I understand Lish's reasoning. I wouldn't ask Lochlain to give up his role either.

I think on the rest of Benny's four components – one was about the partnership with a Manorynx, the other unknown – as I pack away my bedding and listen to the sounds of rural Mercasia echo gently around us. The same but different to those in Airlie.

'I'm sorry I kissed you,' Ciara says quietly. The pain her words rouse drags me back to the present and away from my memories with Benny. I slide my eyes to her but she's not looking at me.

The others rise quietly and finish their packing, Lish the only one who glances in our direction.

'I shouldn't have done that,' she says, her voice the quietest whisper.

I watch her stare at the flames, almost as hypnotised as I was.

'I wasn't with him,' she says and my heart kicks.

'Do you regret it?' I ask.

'Not being with him?' Her eyebrows furrow slightly but she remains watching the flames.

'The kiss,' I force myself to say. She draws a deep breath and looks slowly to me, the fire burning hot beside us.

'I regret the way I went about it, yes.'

She looks up at me then and our gazes clash. There's a 'but' she's not saying and I desperately want her to. What is it? But I'm not sorry I did? But I want to do it again? But ...?

The moment thaws the cold in my fingers and I lean towards her. Itching to reach out and take her hand. I know how undeserving of her I am, but at the same time that unsaid 'but' is screaming in my head. I wonder again how stupid I am not to take an opportunity to be with her, when Loch and

Lish can't be with each other. How many of us have to give up the Calahi we love?

'Please tell me we have coffee,' Riley says and Rory laughs.

Slowly, the sound of the rest of the crew comes back to me and I glance around to see the wolves still on the treeline closest to us, the soft snow settling on their fur. I look back to find Ciara has moved away and the same soft snow is now dusted in her dark braid.

I'd decided at Kailoh's I was going to talk with Nuala about completing my Manorynx training and the transfer of knowledge, but now I know it's not just for me. I also want to complete it for the Calahi who have unfailingly seen the best in me. Ciara is on that list. Even when I wanted her to stop looking, she found the good in me.

'Everyone clear on the plan?' Ciara asks when we all assemble around the no longer burning fire.

The team's only response is the automatic checking of weapons and tightening of straps. Lish draws my attention again as I look around the group. She makes me uncomfortable, in a way – I've never had a relationship like this with a queen. But, like the others, she knows the plan, and they're ready for the Custodian. With Kailoh's support and Nuala's message, this will be the easy bit – there's no way the Custodian can refute what we have to show him and the Court of Airlie. It's the uncertainty of what the Star will show us that grates on me. Lish and that Star are our last known hope of saving the Mother, and thus ourselves.

Callie has the same ability as Rory, and we split into two groups to travel. Unsurprisingly, Rory and Lochlain reach for the two humans. I look to Ciara and shrug away how much I empathise with that impulse. The wind gust Callie creates as she takes us to the field I'd described is slightly sharper than Rory's.

When my feet reach the soil of the training field, and my ears are met with an eerie silence, I know something is wrong.

Very wrong.

'Ciara.' I nod sharply at Callie, and she immediately understands my instruction, her hand lifting to the side of Callie's face to show her where we need to go. If things have gone badly in Elenlea, there is only one other place Will and his family know. One other place Nuala would have taken them without abandoning Airlie.

'Now.'

I don't have to ask twice, Callie taking the image Ciara has shown her, and we arrive at Lochlain's cabin. Lish flies up the stairs with Riley hot on her heels. Ciara sends Daire and Callie to check the perimeter before circling round and entering the house from the opposite side to Lish and Riley. I throw my senses out as I breach the entrance but there's nothing unexpected here.

Lish is just releasing Will as I come into the living area, Riley ruffling the hair on Nico's head.

'What's happened?' Ciara asks Will. He glances at Nico briefly and back to her. Rory steps forward.

'Have you been practising?' he asks Nico who smiles coyly before racing out the door. Rory following to witness whatever it is without looking back.

Sofia, her dark hair tied low and hanging over her shoulder, comes to take Will's hand.

'The Custodian sent soldiers – the ones in green uniforms – to look for you,' he says, looking at Lish. She doesn't react, we knew that would happen. 'They started going door to door ... Nuala wasn't able to stop them coming in.'

A vibration starts to wind its way up the back of my skull. A warning. I know what he's about to say.

Mulriarty told me the Royal Watch was gearing up to go door to door.

Looking for Lish.

Which also means looking for anyone that may have supported her.

'She sent us here,' Will says. I tie the loose ends of my hair back, quickly plaiting them together. Preparing. 'I don't know how – like Rory. But she refused to come. She said it is how it's supposed to be.' He turns his kind brown eyes on me. 'I'm sorry, Aeyva,' he says. 'She said you're not to go after her.'

I sweep my hands over my head, catching any stray strands and I let myself focus for a moment on the feel of the shaved hair above my ears on my palms. Above the commitments I have tattooed there. I don't let his gaze go as I do a mental count of my weapons and drop my hand to my favourite blade, its handle smooth from use. The weight of Ciara's stare is heavy, and I half listen to the rest of his unhappy update.

'- something else.' I'm not the only one who picks up the additional worry in his tone.

'We haven't heard from Blaire and Phoenix in three days,' he says. 'Nuala was our connection to them, so we've had nothing.' His expression is pained.

Riley's hands go to her head and she starts pacing, Rory watching her every step. Lish mirrors me and her fingers lightly touch the various weapons she carries, despite them being fewer than my own. She looks to me, an unspoken message flowing between us, and I nod slightly. As selfless as I know we both desperately want to be. There is a limit. And we've reached it – we each have loved ones to retrieve. The crown will have to wait.

I turn to Rory for transport. Ciara steps between us.

'She said not to go after her, Aeyva, she knows what she's asking.' She reaches for me, gripping my fingers tightly in her own. I slip my fingers between hers without hesitation. It's both a daring pushing at our boundaries, and the most natural thing I can do with her.

'Please, Aeyva, you can't go after her.'

I give her hand a squeeze and let my fingers fall from hers, a door coming down on anything outside of what I need to do. Of the saviour – my saviour – I now need to save.

'Watch me.'

We haven't been gone from Elenlea long, but I can already see the differences from the increased Givings we've missed while in Mercasia. The life our city usually hums with is slowly seeping away, the impact now clear in everything I can see. Particularly in comparison to those in Mercasia. The small numbers of Calahi I pass are slower, almost fumbling in their movements. And they all file towards the centre of the city, summoned by a message I didn't hear. But I know it's the same reason Will wasn't with the Royalists when we arrived.

I keep to the shadows, thrown by the cloudy sky, and follow the thin crowd. Despite the darker day, there are no lights on in the houses I pass. The low murmur of a congregation builds the closer I get to the Palace.

'—the promise I made to you.'

The Custodian's projected voice reverberates through the city, the empty streets doing nothing to absorb the sound.

'Those responsible for the death of our Queen will be punished!'

A quiet cheer ripples through the Calahi who have gathered. As far as they know, Lish killed their beloved Queen and the Custodian is about to deliver them some sort of justice. The rage I'd found when I started working for the Society quickly starts to simmer. I scale the building closest to me and shimmy up the peaked roof on my stomach to peer over the crowd. The Custodian stands on a platform that's been erected outside the Palace gates. One that wasn't there when we left, but it's clear he wants a face-to-face interaction with the Calahi in Elenlea. Why not just let them in the Palace?

'I have evidence one of our dearest treasures has colluded with the perpetrator of Airlie's most serious crime.'

My stomach clenches, even though I know what this is. It's rare that living things are referred to as treasures in the Realm. And when they are ... it's normally a Manorynx.

'And she will pay.'

Six Royal Watch guards drag a dark figure to the platform. I know who it is just by the shape of her, the breath leaving my lungs. The guards press Nuala to her knees before the Custodian, facing out to the crowd. But if he was hoping for them to validate his targeting of her, he thought wrong.

The crowd gasps collectively, soft cries of objection rising to meet me. Someone starts throwing stones in the direction of the Custodian. A shadow crosses his face, but he is not deterred.

On her knees, the hood of her dark cloak thrown back, Nuala should look like the older Calahi she is, her dusk approaching. But instead, or perhaps because of her age, she's magnificent. Her head raised to the sky and not a tremor in sight. I follow her gaze and a spark of blue winks back before disappearing as quickly as it came, telling me something I don't understand. I look back to Nuala to find her looking straight at me, disapproval now clear on her face. But a tiny flicker of relief is there, too.

Not on my watch.

I summon my power, at the same time willing Nuala to fight back. She's strong. Powerful. She might not carry blades like I do but she can bring him down. But there's no chance the Custodian is a match for me – he will be the one to pay tonight. My veins surge with their familiar throb of magic and a smile tugs at my lips.

Another familiar sensation grazes my temples.

'*No, Aeyva*,' she says softly in a voice only I can hear. Her piercing gaze still holds my face even though she shouldn't be able to see me from her position.

'It's okay,' I whisper. 'I've got this.'

'*You cannot stop this, Aeyva, it is what must come to pass.*'

'What are you talking about? I can stop this. You know I can.'

'*I do. And I know it will take more of your strength to let it happen than to stop it. But I need you for another purpose – your true purpose – and that does not include saving me.*'

I gape at her. Her magic brushes more forcefully against the sides of my head.

'*Trust me, Aeyva*,' she insists.

'No, Nuala, this isn't right. I can help you. We need you.'

The Custodian continues his drone below but his voice is now lost to me. My mind spinning in time with the sickness growing in my stomach. Some Calahi have dropped to their knees, others are weakly pressing against the guards that keep them from the platform. Others still have simply turned their backs and begun walking away. Uncertainty shutters in the Custodian's face.

'*See them, Aeyva, see how they turn from him. Even now, many are believing he will end this. That it's a show, a warning only. But they must see for themselves. You hunt in the shadows, I know. Protecting us all from the demons we can't see and taking them on yourself. But they must see. You must respect them enough to let them see. Let them choose, Aeyva. Let them see, and let them choose her.'*

'But – you're asking me to let you die?'

My magic grips the Custodian's as it shields Nuala, red pricks of blood gathering at the black talons of my magic gripping his. Blocking his ability to drag Nuala's magic, and thus her life, from deep within. He looks around, hesitantly. The need to end him is almost strangling me but I make myself listen to Nuala. Listen to her now like I haven't listened to her before.

'I have a burdensome gift for you – one I had hoped to give you well before now. But now I need you to carry it without my help. It will give you everything I have to understand what the Star needs of you. But know you are worthy of what I give, Aeyva. I wouldn't have trained you all those years if you were not.'

Her resolve seeps into me and I understand what she's asking. Slowly, reluctantly, I release my hold on the Custodian and he shakes his limbs, his magic surging as its constriction eases. Vomit pushes up into the back of my throat.

'Okay,' I breathe, swallowing, and carefully I open my mind to her. Memories of my young days flood back to me, the endless lessons on how to do just this. Being tutored by the Manorynx was an honour more than one Calahi didn't appreciate her giving me. It was for families like Lochlain and Ciara's.

The force with which Nuala sends me her gift – her knowledge and her truths escorted to me by butterflies of every colour – nearly tumbles me off the roof and I grip the tiles, hard.

'*There's beauty and strength in fragility,*' she says as coloured wings stream in my vision. '*And hope.*'

The image of her in the meadow with Lish barrels into my mind. Wolvertons of time long ago.

My fingers bleed with the force of holding on. And still the torrent flows.

Faces and texts and locations I may one day need to revisit. Queen Catriona at her coronation. Lish kneeling before her Throne. A man sobbing over a sapphire pendant. A Manorynx in traditional dress pocketing a stone. The crown circling an image of a family tree. What looks like a mass grave.

Behind her, the Custodian smiles, he thinks he is destroying the last person who can reveal his truth. He doesn't know she is, under his very nose, creating another teller.

'It's time, Aeyva. We cannot have life without death.'

'Please no, Nuala, I—'

I can feel his grip on her through the connection we've made. The claws of his magic sink deep into her chest. She shows no outward sign of pain, she won't give him that satisfaction.

'Show them, Nuala, show them what he did.' I beg her, my voice cracking along with something deep within. Cracking along the lines of poorly healed grief that reluctantly knows its turn has come again. The sky sparkles blue again and I know it's telling me to listen. To let her go.

'This is enough for them, for now. They are too weak to withstand more shock. To learn now that all these years of Giving have been a lie. That the nature of Catriona's death was a lie. That will come after you succeed. Because if you don't, none of this will matter, anyway.'

She presses her palms together and raises them to the sky before lowering them back down to hover together at her chest. And then she inclines her head to the crowd. In a movement of farewell, and thanks, to the Calahi of Airlie.

The now silent group before her remains still.

Towards the heart of the group, a single male drops to one knee and places the heel of his palm to his chest. One by one other Calahi follow, until the small sea of Elenlea is bowed before Nuala.

The Custodian roars in his throat and pulls.

The essence of Nuala is dragged from her bones.

He takes it all. Slowly her head lowers further until her forehead touches the platform she's on.

'Go well, Nuala, hold a space for me where you go.' I whisper. 'They'll let me in if you say so.'

The weight in my own body is almost too much as I watch her fade away. My own head trying to bow to the roof I lie on. But I force the tide of grief back down, and I watch. One bleeding hand now pressed against my chest. I owe her far more than that.

I can no longer see her face, but I feel the ghost of a smile before she lets me go, too.

As what is left of her slumps to the ground, I realise I am now what Mulriarty talked of.

I am the Manorynx who can wield a sword.

CHAPTER THIRTY-ONE

LISH

Aeyva's face is pale, like cold stone, when she returns and the sound in Lochlain's cabin falls away as she moves into the room. Helplessly, as helplessly as I can imagine Aeyva ever looking, she raises her eyes from the floor and looks around. Her jaw is clenched and I worry she's pressing her teeth together so hard they might crack.

Rory moves first. Striding to her and scooping her up in his arms just as her knees start to buckle. He murmurs to her as she buries her head into his chest. I'm not sure I should be witnessing this private moment between them, two Calahi who already share so much heartache.

Quietly, Ciara slips next to her and takes her hand, their fingers sliding effortlessly together, and I brush away the tears that start to fall.

'I'm sorry,' Will says to no one in particular.

The room is still for a long moment before Aeyva pulls herself away from Rory and Ciara and turns to face us all, without quite meeting anyone's gaze.

'He made an example of her,' she says, clearing her throat. 'But I think it turned more Calahi from him than he was expecting.'

'She's a huge loss for Airlie, the Realm, and all of us in this room,' Lochlain says heavily. 'Go well, Nuala,' he whispers, hand on his chest, and the others follow.

I look at Lochlain, the weight of both my sadness for the loss of Nuala and the desperate worry for what all of this means for Blaire and Phoenix eating away at me from the inside. Along with the knowledge we never know how much time we have, and I don't want to spend whatever I have left without Lochlain.

But I also know I need to stop the Custodian.

Need to uphold my duty.

And, suddenly, I feel as helpless as Aeyva looked.

Because I know I can't take another step towards that Throne if I don't know they're okay.

'We need your heart, remember?' Lochlain says to me gently. 'Your family's yours. We'll find them.'

He must know he's also my heart, though. And maybe he's right, he just doesn't know why. Maybe Airlie needs my heart – him included, even as General.

We look to Will at the same time, the conflict on his face as clear as his emotions running over my skin. He didn't choose who to love, but there's no way he can bring Sofia and Nico with us.

'I'll stay.'

I glance back to Aeyva, who's volunteered. 'The Mercasians and I will stay,' she says. Her voice is flat, she's a woman rebuilding a wall before our eyes. 'Find your friends, Will.'

A moment's hesitation brushes Will's features as he looks to Sofia. But he is a man of action, these past weeks and months have pulled him in opposing directions. Sofia turns into him.

'We're fine here.' She runs a finger down his cheek.

Will almost sags with relief before his shoulders set with resolve and he looks to me. If the situation were different, if there wasn't a biting worry in my mind, I'd be pleased to go work with him again and feel the familiar thrum of our operating rhythm. I give them a moment for their goodbyes. It's painfully short but I need to find Blaire and Phoenix. I nod to Rory without saying my own farewell.

Because I know without doubt that Lochlain is coming with me.

Dark smoke drifts past us on the stone road I've travelled so many times before with Will, the smell cloying. It's not unusual for the lightning of the superstorms to start fires that smoulder for days, sometimes weeks, before discovery. But there is so little fuel left around the city that any dead trees that still stand are left to burn themselves out.

These fires are different. Too ordered throughout what remains of the small shantytown to be of natural causes. Not that it seems to matter. While the smell I never got used to remains, oozing from the stones beneath our feet and the towering city wall itself, what is left of the slums of Rhyton are deserted. I think of the faces I used to see on my patrols here, hoping it's not them that have been taken by the Custodian.

We peel off into two groups. Will, Lochlain, and I take the left side of the makeshift street and Riley, Rory, and Ciara the right. Glancing across the uneven stone road, the deepening grey helps to obscure us from view. Ciara faces away from the city, protecting Rory and Riley from behind. I know Lochlain is doing the same for Will and me.

Two wolves keeping the pack together.

The hair on the back of my neck prickles as a low grumble pierces the air. I let out a breath and look at Will as the shape of three wolves moves across the stone road.

'Pieter's Place?' I ask, wondering where we should start looking.

A small crease appears between his brows, a shadow collecting there.

'Blaire knew the Commissioner, right?' he asks and I nod. 'Didn't you say there was a place near there?'

The wine bar.

I try to push aside the knowledge of Blaire's previous relationship with the Commissioner and what she might do to rekindle it for information, what sacrifices it might mean she's making ... there's so much we're all having to give up. But now I know what the Custodian is up to, I know the Commissioner is the contact in Driarn – there is no other reason he would have been in Elenlea with the Custodian at the Challenge. If Blaire and Phoenix have put that together as well, there is nothing she wouldn't do to make sure she had access to him.

On the other side of the gate, making our way through the city, my consciousness starts to pick up the presence of others. What I can feel now in the streets beyond the wall is not people going about their usual, regular activities. It's people afraid of the night. I whisper to Will who fills in the others as I keep moving. The smell inside the city is different too.

Stale.

The gardens we pass either no longer nurture any produce, or have had their security doubled. The private security guards – at the few apartment buildings that still have them – now do their watch from inside barred doors. They watch us as we move through the quiet, but don't engage.

Tonight is slightly cooler than many nights in Rhyton, but there is not the usual throng of people milling around, iced drinks in hand and taking advantage of the fresh night air. Instead, the streets are almost completely still, dark figures scuttling around us and ducking in and out of view.

Smoke billows from the train station.

The neighbourhood of the wine bar, and the Commissioner, comes into view at the end of the street. Lights and music mark the start of what is now clearly a different territory.

'Lish,' Lochlain murmurs behind me, gently tugging me by my elbow further into the shadows. 'It's patrolled.'

It takes me a moment to process his hesitation – something I never would have worried about before, a patrol in Rhyton. But now, Lochlain's right, I have no idea what this is.

I look again and can just make out the stature of the people standing at intervals across the street. Their uniforms, if they wear them, are too hard to make out from this distance, and I can't tell if they belong to the Guard. But the shape of the rifles slung across their backs are clear.

'Can you get us in, Ror?' I ask.

We appear in a shadowed alcove just up the street from the wine bar. Here, the profiles I pick up as I lower my walls are primarily normal. A standard mix of happiness, or as close as most people allow themselves to get at any given time, discontentment, and lust, and everything in between. I don't wait for a discussion and move straight for the wine bar. In this part of Rhyton, I can almost make myself believe I'd imagined the rest. The door is heavy under my hand as I press to open it, Lochlain almost on top of me from behind. I spin quickly on my heel, my stomach and chest flush against him, letting the door close behind me again. Placing a hand on his chest, the warmth there pulls me into him.

'You can't come in here, Lochlain,' I whisper. 'And they *certainly* can't.' I look to the wolves in the shadows.

His proximity clouds my focus. I don't want to be distant from him – physically or emotionally. But, until I am Queen, I need Airlie to see him as an independent General and, right now, I need to focus on getting my friends out of whatever has stopped them making contact.

His eyes narrow and he opens his mouth—

'Lochlain,' I say firmly, 'you're too conspicuous. It's one thing to wander the streets with us but having you, or the other Calahi for that matter, openly in our venues will start a riot.' I smile thinly at him.

'We have no idea what you're walking into in there,' he says. He gestures to the city around him. 'We have no idea of anything that's happening here right now.'

Rory appears at Lochlain's shoulder.

'She's right, Loch,' he says. 'We might not know what's going on, but having the three of us right in the middle of it isn't going to simplify the situation. We can see through the windows anyway, let her go.'

Lochlain places a hand over mine at his heart and, for a moment, nothing else exists. I drag my hand away leaving him standing in the entrance with his palm still on his heart.

Riley blows a breath when we enter the bar, her cheeks puffing out.

'It's them,' she says.

I turn to move towards them, but she grabs my upper arm, forcing me to face her before dropping it quickly.

'Something is off,' she says, so only we can hear. Although the noise in the wine bar is such we are probably not in a lot of danger of being overheard. She squints slightly. 'They're wearing officer uniforms.'

Warmth starts to unwind as I take in her words and I let my barrier down. Ignoring the others in the room, and Lochlain just outside, I make a dedicated effort to take in Phoenix and Blaire only. Phoenix's jealousy and anger simmers under a thin layer of celebration – something that is taking a lot of energy for him to keep up. Blaire, on the other hand, is more resigned. She's playing her part, whatever that is, with a quiet confidence and determination.

I manoeuvre myself surreptitiously to take in the group, the knot in my stomach establishing itself between my ribs again. Blaire and Phoenix sit side by side, with their backs to us. I take in the blonde hair Blaire's left cascading in waves down her back and Phoenix's broad shoulders. My stomach tenses slightly at the sight of them despite my overwhelming relief. They look every bit the picture of enjoyment in the corner of this pub while the situation around them declines.

But, if all was well, neither of them would ignore the woman who is holding her face – where another has landed her backhand – or the patron who is loudly refusing to pay for his drinks.

Or the palpable unrest boiling over throughout the city.

Which means they know something worse.

Finally, their companions begin to quieten slightly and thump each other's backs in preparation to call it a night. Their farewells take long enough for me to bite my tongue in impatience but, eventually, they all stand. Blaire's face shows only the faintest surprise as she turns and finds us. She says something to the man that had been sitting on the other side of her and ducks to the bathroom without looking back to us.

The temptation to follow is strong, but I can't lose sight of Phoenix either. Not yet. He doesn't betray any sign of recognition as he turns away from his chair and takes in the room. He's been looking for us. He hangs back, talking to one of the group, and lets the others move out in front of him. One officer I worked with on a particular case looks at me, the beginning of recognition igniting in his face. The person next to him says something that pulls his attention away and I drop my gaze.

I look up again just as Blaire is coming back from the bathrooms. She still doesn't look at me and I follow her lead. Instead, I turn to Riley and try not to absorb her concern on top of my own. *Hayes would be able to work this out*, I think, a shadow passing over my chest. He would see what's lying beneath the surface of the new relationships, the promotions, and the purposeful ignorance of Rhyton falling around them.

Blaire is almost level with our table now and I stare hard at Riley. Clenching my fist in my desperation to reach out and touch my friend, to make sure she's okay. My other hand loosely grips the drink Will brought over earlier to help us blend in. She stumbles as she approaches, a move her graceful dancer's body would never make, her shoulder crashing into mine.

'Sorry,' she mumbles and keeps walking. I still, not wanting to draw any further attention to myself.

Or the note she's pressed into my hand.

Will watches them leave over my shoulder – his face tight as he watches Blaire leave and I close myself off to him and Riley. I don't need to feel their emotions to know how worried they are.

Phoenix watches Blaire leave, his face uncertain. The other man, one I don't know, places his hand on Phoenix's shoulder and pulls him in close to talk. He whispers excitedly to Phoenix who nods in agreement. A handshake closes their conversation and Phoenix also leaves the wine bar, the three of us left to stare at each other.

'Mother, those bastards can talk,' Rory curses as we find them in the shadows.

'Sorry, Rory,' I say. We might have been anxiously bored inside, but it was better than being stuck in a bush for half the night.

A faint rustle sounds in the bushes and in a single blink Lochlain's knives are drawn and held against the throat of someone else.

'Loch,' Ciara says gently, her hand on his. 'Wait.'

Phoenix stills in Lochlain's grip, he knows as well as any of us it's the only chance of staying alive. Not that Lochlain would ever hurt him intentionally, but Phoenix doesn't need a demonstration to know what Lochlain is capable of.

He glances around when Lochlain releases him, rubbing softly at his neck, before looking at me. 'You got her note?'

Carefully, I unfold the crumpled note Blaire left. The paper trembles slightly as I read her words.

He knows about you. Wants to meet.

CHAPTER THIRTY-TWO

LISH

The waves pound on the rocks below, oblivious to the destruction in the city just to the south of us – or perhaps completely aware and hungry to claim more of the coast as their own. The picture Phoenix paints is beyond grim. Worse than I had imagined, even though the memory of Claire's demise hasn't left me. But it confirms our suspicions. The Guard is compromised at all levels and Rhyton is in free-fall. The Premier is scrambling to regain control but, with no force under his command, it's proving fruitless. And the city is almost literally fruitless as well. The community gardens have been all but destroyed, any produce looted as Rhyton stood divided on whether or not the Guard was the enemy.

Now, it seems the people of Rhyton have all but been abandoned by the Guard who now serve someone else – the Custodian. A Calahi who can offer them, even if it's an unfulfilled promise, access to food and housing and a chance at a better life for their families. All the things I have witnessed in the Realm firsthand. Although the Realm suffers too, the comparison to what is available throughout Driarn is stark.

'And the uniforms? Blaire?' I ask. Phoenix looks to me, no longer hiding his disgust at what's occurring in our home, to people we swore an oath to protect.

'Robard is gone,' he says. 'So I spoke to the Commissioner's Chief of Staff and told him Blaire and I had just returned from leave and were looking for our unit.'

His hands clench at his sides and Will places a hand on his shoulder but doesn't interrupt. Phoenix looks at him, the vulnerability in that one look ... I clench my jaw.

'Numbers in the Guard have fallen significantly, so we were immediately promoted to officers – no questions asked. The perks'—he takes a breath—'the perks are even better than before. While the people of Rhyton are struggling more than ever, and junior recruits are often forcibly inducted, the officers are living their best lives. It's sick.'

The division I saw, and felt, in Rhyton now makes sense. There was once a very obvious line between those who could afford food and shelter, and those who could not. Now, the divide might as well be a canyon down the centre. The members of the Guard, who are apparently gaining these basics from the Realm – at this point I'd be willing to bet many of them are staying, or believe they will be, in the Mercasian villages they're raiding – on the one side, and the rest of the city, who no longer even have access to any essentials, on the other.

'We need to know about Blaire, mate.' Will prompts gently.

Phoenix looks at me again, his hair whipping around his face in the coastal wind. Lochlain attempts to soothe the sickening tension I can't shake, and I take it gratefully.

'The Commissioner requested her on his personal team,' he says softly. 'I tried to convince her that I go in her place. But once we heard the new recruits that made it through the induction were going to Mercasia, she insisted it had to be her. That only she could get close enough, fast enough, to find out what's going on.'

It doesn't surprise me that Blaire is willingly putting herself within reach of the Commissioner for me. Us. But I wish she didn't have to. My gaze slides to Lochlain, who is watching me. Someone else prepared to make a monumental sacrifice. I hold tighter to the sense of calm he is sending me, and his face softens minutely under his hood. My heart clenches in my chest.

'So, the Commissioner is definitely working with the Custodian to get him numbers,' Ciara says. 'To what end?'

'Was,' Phoenix says. 'Now, he's leading the rebellion.'

I frown.

'Why would the Commissioner suddenly stand against the Custodian if he's the one that volunteered them in the first place?' Ciara asks, her dark eyes intent on Phoenix.

'I think it's easiest if he explains that himself,' Phoenix says, his attention caught for a moment by the presence of the wolves that lurk just outside our huddle.

It seems clear now that they're not going away; their numbers seem to change between two and four at any given time, but they're also not quite with us. Distant but connected somehow. Like Driarn and the Realm. My mother talked about following the wolf. But, right now, I can't be sure who is following who.

There are so many pieces to understand and I turn them over in my mind, wondering what Hayes would have looked for.

'So ...' I say slowly as the thoughts come, some much slipperier than others. 'Aeyva thinks the Custodian is after Roisin's magic so he can rule the Realm ... essentially going back to when it had a single ruler.'

'Which doesn't really explain why Nakiasha is helping him,' Rory says. 'I can't imagine she'd simply hand over her Court.'

'No. But perhaps the Custodian has offered her something bigger. And the help she's been giving is indirect at best,' Lochlain says. 'Mostly managed through one of her senior soldiers – the female the Custodian has been meeting with. I'd say she's just hedging her bets against Kailoh and the Custodian.'

'Not me?' I ask. Not offended, but wondering where I fit in this suggestion.

'You're still too much of an unknown to her in your own right. But she will know, if the Custodian's claims are unfounded, Kailoh will find a way to align with you.' My skin stings suddenly with his disquiet at his statement. 'If they're true, then she has an in with Zadicus, if not, there's little to connect her to him at this point.'

Meaning the Custodian is still the primary driver behind all of this. And his long game of dominating the Realm is starting to come to its conclusion. I shift the weight between my feet. We shouldn't be standing still. The Custodian is collecting the magic of Airlie, to pump into humans he's going to use to help him get Roisin's magic. He's going to take it – our only chance of righting the Mother – for his own purposes and let us continue this downward spiral. I think of Roisin's message, of the lack of food, the devastating weather, the complete destruction.

Why is holding all her magic more important than giving every other living thing a chance?

To top it all off, I still don't have the Star to tell me how to stop him, how to stop the death of our worlds and the loss of all magic completely.

I start to pace.

I know people have always been obsessed with what they can't have, so rarely do they appreciate what they do have. I've seen it in the small scuffles Will and I spent our days breaking up. Someone's space was larger than another; someone stole someone else's shirt; someone was disrespectful and they tried to solve it with fists and blades and taking what they could. So much of what we saw was fuelled by a desperation to survive.

An uncomfortable sense of pressure sits over my sternum as I realise that, in a different way, they are the same things I have fought for in my life. For a place in the orphanage; for the Team Leader role so I could increase my food allowance and salary, and increase the stability for me and my team; to take my rightful position as Queen so I can better the lives of the people and Calahi around me.

And, as the personal circumstances improve, the want gets bigger. Some of this was harder to see in Driarn – business deals done under the table or behind closed doors – but, sooner or later, we found out. It was discovered how much more protected land was sold for development, what natural resources were being exhausted for profits, the species of animals lost as their habitat was torn down because it cost less than saving them.

Vaguely, I recall that the Commissioner's wife was involved in one of the highest profile businesses trying to do good for Driarn and lobby the government for change.

Is that what set him on this path? Or corrected it? Because I still don't understand why he started handing over Guard members for fodder.

But, as I examine these pieces as I walk on the rocks, I think I might know why the Custodian wants Roisin's magic. In Driarn, money is power. In the Realm, it's literally magic.

The more he has, the more he can control.

Which is exactly what the humans in Driarn have wanted for themselves.

It's what I wanted for myself and my team in Rhyton.

It's what I want now.

The sea wind dries my eyes as they widen with the realisation. I've stopped pacing with my back to my team and when I turn back I look between the Calahi and humans that make it up.

We all need to fight for ourselves, Kailoh said when I refused to bond with him.

It dawns on me that the humans of Driarn don't only need someone to save them, and nor do the Calahi of Airlie and the Realm. They need someone to give them an opportunity to fight for what they need so they can go after what they want. And to do it in a way that will actually deliver it if we win. A way that will ultimately benefit the many and not just a select few – that will improve lives and not damage them beyond repair.

Which means the human rebels belong with me.

'They're here,' Ciara says. Every one of us draws a weapon as two figures make their way to the point we stand on, overlooking the dark sea.

The Commissioner's stride is purposeful, never faltering as he makes his way to us. He doesn't wear a uniform but it's clear he is a man of discipline. Authority radiates off him in waves. Blaire walks beside him, but I can feel the slight uncertainty in her as she gets closer. I let my barrier down a little more than normal as I watch them, apprehension climbing slowly towards my throat. She opens her palms to the sky and the Commissioner does the same.

When they're three paces away, Lochlain and Rory block them from further approach and I lose my line of sight. Ciara flanks me, Will and Riley close in behind. Phoenix doesn't move into any sort of defensive stance.

'Are you sure this is her?' A voice I have only ever heard from a distance asks.

'I know it is,' Blaire responds. 'Please, let us speak with the Queen.' She doesn't use their names. Or mine.

No one moves.

'It's alright,' I say to Lochlain and Rory's broad backs.

It takes another beat for either of them to move, and not before the shape of Lochlain's shoulders expands with a deep breath. The Commissioner's face, when I finally see it between the wall of Calahi warrior, is slightly more lined than I'd imagined. His short beard is jet black against his face in the darkness. Between the maturity in his face, and the confidence in his stance, it doesn't take long to see why Blaire would have been attracted to him.

He nods at me, completely unfazed by Lochlain and Rory. 'Thank you for meeting with me,' he says, his voice gravelly.

One of the wolves moves to a standing position and the Commissioner starts slightly before schooling his features and looking back to me.

I wait.

'You have seen what's happening in Rhyton, I take it?' he asks.

'I've seen Rhyton, yes. I can't say I completely understand what is happening there, perhaps you can fill me in?'

He falters. 'I—' He rubs a palm over his beard.

'Just start at the beginning, David,' Blaire says. *David*, not *Commissioner*.

He sighs and drops his hands to his sides, some of the commanding figure creeping back in.

'The dangers in Rhyton were steadily increasing, the scarcity of food, resources, and employment for so many takes its toll. We were starting to see a downward spiral for multiple generations – violence, poverty, chronic health issues – and I didn't have enough resources to bolster the Guard. Nowhere near enough to keep the city safe.'

'We were managing okay,' Will says, confused. Defensive.

The Commissioner shakes his head. 'No. That's what we wanted you to see, the Premier and me. I needed you to stay motivated in your patrols of the city.' He draws a deep breath. 'When you know how close the line to destitution is, and you can see the city hurtling towards it at breakneck speed ... you know what people will do. I needed you to believe you could keep them from that. But you didn't see the clean-up crews that operated under a covert section of the Guard. Those responsible for actively sweeping through the worst of the worst.'

An ugly feeling rushes through my chest as I let this sink in. This was the man I served – who spoke at my graduation to a full member of the Guard, who was supposed to represent peace, safety, and stability in my city. Yet he's also been selectively 'sweeping' out those deemed most unfit.

I stare at him.

'Fuck,' Riley says.

Lochlain watches the Commissioner, his face illuminated by twin light orbs that dance close to our heads without blinding. Absently, I note I don't know who they belong to. I can't process his emotions and mine, but my skin warms and I think I see something like understanding on his face. One General hearing another.

'Then what?' I ask.

'I met someone who showed me how I could make the Guard stronger.'

The Commissioner's gaze flicks to mine and he holds it – appearing every bit a man torn between his shame and his pride.

'With magic,' I say.

He nods.

To my side, Ciara cocks her head just enough for my mind to catch onto the query in her posture.

'Who was it?' I ask.

His face shutters and I can feel the sense of shame run along my skin. But it's tinged with more than that - hurt and regret as well.

'A woman,' he says. 'She refused to tell me her name, but she told me she ruled a place that could see the power in us. A place that had the ability to amplify our power to help the greater good.'

'Tell me you didn't really think it would work,' Rory says.

'I don't think I understand why you'd do this – believe that,' Will says at the same time.

'I needed hope,' the Commissioner says quietly. '*We* needed hope. And someone offered it to me. Instead, they're either dying or becoming numbed out of their minds – worse than addicts.'

'And that's why you're leading a rebellion.' Riley says and I fight the urge to close my eyes. Because I understand the need for hope.

'It's not quite a rebellion,' he says. 'There's no one in Rhyton to rebel against.' He looks at Blaire and Phoenix. 'We've been trying to get as many people out as we can, before they're collected, and gathering anyone prepared to fight. That's where you come in.'

We stand quietly, looking at each other for a moment, as the meaning of his words washes over me. He, and the people he's now leading, want to fight Calahi and the mindless human army the Custodian is creating.

Nakiasha found the Commissioner, Ciara says in my head and I nod slightly, some of the pieces starting to fall together.

She planted the seeds of hope, I say back, *and led the humans to the Custodian. But why?*

Ciara's chest rises and falls heavily and I can't tell if I can hear her sigh in my head or I just know she's done it because of what I can see.

Nakiasha thinks humans are a species deserving much punishment for their role in our decline – she is renowned for her views on what she would do if she had control of the humans. That she would stop their destruction of our world in its tracks. And we know the Custodian cares nothing for your world, and wants no semblance of an equal relationship between the two. Perhaps he offered her the human world, providing he gets to keep and replenish his army.

I let the long silence stretch out a little more as I process the words of each the Commissioner and Ciara.

'I swore an oath to protect the people of Rhyton,' I say in response to both, and the Commissioner's gaze bores into mine.

He squares his shoulders. 'As did I. I made a mistake, letting it start this way. But I wasn't wrong that we need hope. We need to correct the course of our world before we lose it all.'

Something painful rushes over my skin and I know there's more to what he's saying.

'You need to tell them everything, David,' Blaire says gently.

His shoulders drop, the strength seeming to drop out of his spine.

'They took my family as collateral.' Despite his posture, his voice is hard when he says it, not broken.

'And yet you're fighting anyway?' Will asks.

The Commissioner looks at Blaire. I can't see the expression on his face, but I can feel a deep respect from him.

'I was convinced that if I don't stop this, there will be nothing to bring my girls back to, anyway.' He holds his long look at Blaire who turns to him and nods with a grim smile. Phoenix bristles and I work harder to block him out, but my own energy is draining.

'Lish,' Blaire says carefully but clearly. 'Our intelligence says they're almost done in Mercasia, they're going to stay ahead of Kailoh's forces. Elenlea is their next target.'

'We have a better chance at stopping them together,' I say.

The roar of the waves below is the only sound as we each process the conversation in our own way. I tuck the strands of my hair that have blown free behind my ears, knowing they won't stay there. Watching Blaire walk away was hard for all of us, but mostly Phoenix, whose eyes remained closed for a moment longer than anyone else's.

My feet pace again over the rocks without instruction but I can't go far. Will comes with me.

'I didn't want to bring more people into this,' I say, spinning to him. 'And yet, somehow, I know we need them. Is that awful?'

He steps towards me.

'They're already in it, Lish,' he says.

We keep moving, back towards the others and find them talking as if I never moved away.

'I've given Blaire a way to communicate with me when she needs to,' Ciara says.

'How?' Phoenix asks warily.

Ciara shifts her weight. 'By ... removing some of the barriers in her mind.'

'Fuck. Will it hurt her?' he asks.

'No.' Ciara clears her throat. 'And we can keep her up to date on our movements, too.'

My mind catches on the fact the Commissioner effectively handed over the Guard to the Custodian for testing magic – magic that is killing innocent people or wiping away any sense of freewill – all so the Custodian can take Roisin's magic. Does he think having the additional force will help him? Or is there something about the combination of human and magic that appeals to him? Is that why he worked so hard to find me? Is that why my mother ran?

'I'm staying, too,' Phoenix says. My feet stop pacing as abruptly as they'd started. 'I won't leave her.'

There's a pulling in my chest that I think might be heartbreak for Phoenix. At how much he really understands what might be between Blaire and the Commissioner now.

'But you know what—'

'I know,' he says. 'And this is what she chose. So I stay, too.'

'Shit. This'—I throw my hands in the air—'everything is just shit.' Tears build pressure behind my eyes, and I squeeze them shut. Not just because of Phoenix and Blaire and what I wish they could explore. But for Lochlain and me, for Will who's left Sofia behind, for all the Calahi and humans who are doing the same thing. All to fight for a future we might not get if the Custodian takes Roisin's magic. There's a reason she's the key. She was the Creator, after all, the conduit for the Mother. And we desperately need her again.

Breathing hurts.

'Lish,' Ciara cuts in. 'With all due respect, this is not all on you. We'—she gestures to Lochlain and Rory—'fight for our Court. For our home and for ourselves. Your friends – our friends,' she adds with a glance at the huddle that Phoenix, Riley, and Will make, 'also fight for their own, and their continent – and you. But you are a part of that cause, not the whole.'

The weight she takes from my shoulders releases the tears I've been holding back, and a handful slip silently down my face. Ciara wipes them away with her thumb.

I breathe in the salt air and let it steady me.

Ground me.

I straighten my spine, the rhythm of the growling waves building my resolve. I can do this for them.

The largest wolf with the amber eyes watches me.

Be together, I think unbidden. What I want – what I need – is for all of us to be together again. There are too many parts of me spread too far.

My fingers find the shape of the Wolverton Pendant under my vest where it slips slightly on my sweaty skin. Something else that's part of a whole, the same as Driarn and Rhyton.

A shiver of understanding prickles in my palms. The Prominent Families talked about protecting without claim. I know this isn't what they meant but I wonder ...

'We don't have time for me to claim the Throne. We just need that crown,' I say.

CHAPTER THIRTY-THREE

AEYVA

My chest throbs with the loss of Nuala and I rub where the ache is the sharpest. It doesn't help. I haven't told the others what occurred on that rooftop. What she finished making me into.

There hasn't been the time.

Or the words.

Lochlain looks up from the map he's been drawing, papers strewn across the table in the centre of his cabin, and directly at Lish – like he knows she has something to say.

'Are we absolutely sure he's not going to be there? What's to stop him killing me on sight if we're wrong?' she asks.

'As sure as we can be, and nothing,' I respond for him.

They stare at each other. The depth of his feelings for our Queen is palpable.

'Nothing,' I say again. 'He killed one of the greatest Manorynxes of all time. But our information says he is in Rothani tonight, so it's our best shot.'

I look back to the map and place my finger where Lochlain said the crown should be – the Custodian hasn't kept its location a secret from those inside the Palace.

'We follow the path Lochlain has laid out,' I say. 'No diversions, no distractions.'

The Custodian's human army is on its way to Elenlea and we need to get in and out before they arrive.

I look at the four of them, dressed in fitted black suits from head to boot, and wait for Ciara's go ahead. While Kailoh's Sentinels stay with Will and the rest of his family, Will will start to get word to the Royalists, with the aid of Haryk.

'Ready?' Ciara asks.

Lochlain reaches impulsively for Lish, freer in his movement with Callie and Daire out on Ciara's command, and gently tugs her towards him by a buckle on her vest. He checks Lish's vest, spending a fraction more time on the left-hand side. A blade of some sort catches the light as he slides it into one of the holders without looking at her face. He doesn't see the words she almost speaks, and I give her another moment to tell him. But she looks back to the rest of us and says nothing. Doesn't tell him she's not being bonded to someone else.

That his heartache is for nothing.

But I did say no distractions.

Ciara obscures us from sound and sight, her magic dissolving the barriers in minds and changing the ability for those around to see or hear us. As it does, my own magic almost shimmies in response. I glance sideways at her, taking in the soft sheen on her forehead, how taxing it is to hold her magic back.

We circle round to approach the Palace from the side. With the building I scaled while Nuala was executed just visible up ahead, the image of her bowing to the crowd as she left this world burns behind my eyes. The Palace curves up and away to my right, obscuring the platform itself, but it's still there. I can feel the imprint Nuala left. We stop several paces away from the black and gold gates triggered for alarm if any magic is used too close. For the moment, Ciara keeps us hidden but we will have to risk exposure to get across soon. Rory's magic is useless with the wards that envelope the Palace.

Lochlain points to where the wards are weakest, a section above the fence where they were created and powered by different magic wielders and the crossover isn't quite complete. Members of the Royal Watch patrol just on the inside of the gate, their footsteps quiet in the grass of the Palace gardens. Two pass each other just below the gap we're aiming for. It's a leap only the most highly trained Calahi could make and it's definitely not one Lish will complete. Not without bringing every Royal Watchman screaming down on us.

She will need to be thrown.

'Now,' Lochlain says.

Ciara drops her shielding and we scurry forward to run along the fence, crouching low to the ground. At the last few paces, I straighten up and run head on to the fence. Pushing hard off the ball of my left foot, I launch myself into the air and sail over the fence, dropping like a pin through the faint gap I can sense in the wards.

First hurdle down.

Ciara lands softly next to me before we hurry to the nearest hedge and roll ourselves underneath to wait for the others. The Palace gardens are immaculate but there is still enough foliage on the undersides to prickle the small amounts of bare skin I have exposed. Ciara presses hard along the length of me, keeping herself far under the hedge to give me room to stay out of sight. For less than a beat, the only sound is that of our breathing.

A gentle thud sounds and I know Lochlain has landed. Turning my head in the leaves and dirt, I watch as Rory thrusts Lish into the air. The fence isn't high, but she didn't even seem to take a steadying breath. Ciara twists beside me so she can see and grips my wrist as we watch Lish free-fall. She tucks herself into an inverted shape at the last moment and drops into Lochlain's waiting arms. The force of the catch sends him stumbling backwards and slamming into the ground with Lish sitting atop him. She would have completely flattened a human.

Lish pauses where she lies against Lochlain, muttering something into his neck and my heart rate kicks up. They need to get off the grass.

Ciara and I exhale in unison as Lish and Lochlain separate, removing his hand from the back of her head and rolling her off. A moment later, Rory has joined them and they crouch at the hedge while Ciara and I crawl out.

'Run,' Lochlain says quietly, taking Lish's hand and running for the balcony that curves around the inside of the Palace, hugging the gardens. Lish sprints alongside him, working hard to keep up. I knew having a human with us would be slower, but the additional moments move by painfully.

We press against the stone wall underneath the black metal balcony.

'You okay?' Ciara whispers.

I look to her, surprised, but it's Lish she's talking to. Lish's breathing is returning to normal after our run, despite its noise. I glance around to make sure the Royal Watchmen haven't heard her. The forest green uniforms making them particularly hard to see in the dark with the garden as a backdrop.

Rory throws a small rock over the balcony above us. It falls back down as dust. Lochlain lifts Ciara off the ground and towards the edge of the balcony. Rory hovers to catch her, should she fall, but I have seen these two in action numerous times before. She braces her knees on Lochlain's chest as he holds the back of her thighs, Rory's hand on the small of her back, and she grips the edge, closing her eyes. The next rock Rory throws goes straight through. Immediately, I take a small running start and use the wall to propel my leap to hang on to the edge of the balcony. I'm careful not to dislodge her hands, but I need to be as close as possible to where Ciara's touch dissolves a space in the shield. I tense for a moment, waiting for the use of magic inside the gates to send anyone running.

No one comes.

My arms burn a fraction as I pull myself up in silence, crouching against the wall. The two guards on the balcony walk quietly around its curve. One approaches me, focused on the gardens below. Not once does he look down and it's almost too easy to push myself to standing, using my momentum to drive my knife in – but I pull myself up and hold it to his heart instead.

His face as it turns to me, eyes wide, is familiar but I can't place his name. He holds my wrist and gives it three quick squeezes. A Royalist. He inclines his head slowly at the other guard and almost imperceptibly shakes his head. I nod, releasing him and silently pad my way to the second guard where my blade finds the base of his skull. The others are all up when I turn back, Lish and Ciara's gazes are lingering on the body I've dropped.

'Only this man would keep the crown that doesn't belong to him in here,' Rory whispers as we enter the Custodian's bedroom a little further along the balcony.

In a shelf, built into the wall directly over his bed, is the Crown of Airlie, its intricate gold pieces heavily engraved with a pattern I've never seen. A large, unusually shaped piece of sapphire is held high by gold leaves. Lish looks at each of us and back to Lochlain, like she's dreaming. But she takes slow, steady steps towards the edge of the bed, Ciara following her with her hand, stretching the bubble.

The room stills as Lish crawls onto the empty bed, as if none of us are breathing. Slowly, she reaches into the small alcove and Rory steps forward.

I brace myself for an alarm.

Staring at the crown as Lish's fingers curl around it is like a dream. But the room, and the Palace, remains silent.

Suddenly Lish is off the bed, retreating back to us with the crown in her shaking hand. She stares at it for a moment before handing it to Rory, blinking. He's a good choice, I would have given it to him, too, in case he needs to get out with it quicker than we can – the wards won't stop us from leaving now we're in. Ciara and I already hold the other two pieces. I turn to leave back the way we came, my body still singing with anticipation of what's to come. But maybe the Custodian is just arrogant enough for it to have been this simple.

'Wait,' Lish whispers. 'Do you feel that?' Her hand presses against the pendant she wears under her clothes.

We each shake our heads at her.

'There's something else here,' she says.

A soft grumble sounds in the room, and I find a wolf at the Custodian's bedroom door. Fuck, those things are turning up everywhere. My magic shivers in response to Ciara's – or the wolf. Or both.

'We need to go.' Ciara's brow is beading with sweat with the effort of holding her magic back.

'No.' Lish looks around, moving away from our exit and towards the waiting wolf.

'Lish,' I warn. She ignores me. Lochlain takes a step towards her.

'We need to follow it,' she says, clutching her chest where the pendant is.

Lochlain takes another tentative step, and she moves again towards the internal door of the Custodian's bedroom. She holds both hands in front of her, palms down.

'What is that?' she whispers, looking at the wolf as if it might have the answers as she takes several more steps towards the door – where there will be at least another two guards stationed.

'Mother above. Remind me never to bring a queen on a mission again,' Rory whispers. 'And definitely not one with rogue wolves.'

Ciara's bubble stretches with Lish and she grunts softly, walking automatically in time with Lish in an attempt to keep her magic close. Contained.

'Lish!' I whisper hoarsely. But her hand is on the handle and Lochlain is behind her.

Dammit.

I take Ciara's hand.

'We're on the move,' I tell her. 'You need to keep us tight.'

Ciara opens her eyes but they glaze over as she focuses on her magic, on not killing everyone in the Palace – including us. I focus on where I lead her. Lochlain takes out the two guards at the bedroom door as Lish opens it. No chance to see if they were Royalists and loyal to Lish or not. We don't have the time to ask the question.

We half run, half walk through the dark hallways, led by the wolf and Lish and her outstretched palms. She flies down a large, curved staircase that leaves us horribly exposed – even with Ciara's magic – chasing the wolf that's racing through the Palace. The fact that we haven't set anything off yet is a miracle in itself.

Lish runs now, her searching frantic.

'I'm coming,' she says quietly. 'Where are you?'

She comes to a fast halt at the elaborate gold doors that lead to the throne room, the wolf at her side. She shoves them open and races to the Throne, where she drops to her knees. But it's not the Throne she's interested in. After wildly searching the tapestries of former rulers that adorn the walls, she focuses her attention on the floor. Her mother, I realise, she was looking for her mother. But, in this moment, whatever is calling to her is stronger.

'How do I – you need to tell me,' she says to herself, running her hands across the marble. The wolf stands beside her, its gaze boring into her. Expectant.

I take a step back – I've seen this before.

Nuala showed me Lish kneeling before the Throne and assumed it was after we'd won. On impulse, I kneel with Lish and take her hand, drawing my blade across it. She inhales sharply before placing her hands, slow and steady now, back on the marble.

The floor groans and drops away, sliding under itself. I scramble backwards to clear the gaping hole that's opened up.

'Oh, Mother,' Rory says. Lochlain's face snaps back to the gold doors, towards a sound on the other side.

'We need to move,' he says, taking two paces back towards the entrance and drawing his sword.

A shimmer from below catches my eye and I peer down into the black hole Lish has opened. I click my fingers at Rory.

'Light.'

He drops a single ball of light and it hovers in the centre of what is clearly a room. A room with countless shelves. For the third time in my life, my hands tremble slightly as I try to take in what I'm seeing.

'What is it?' Ciara asks, her voice strained. She hasn't moved far from Lish, Rory, and me where we peer into the hole and has an arm extended to Lochlain.

'It's—' I start.

Lish sits back on her heels, a grin on her face. 'We found the magic of Airlie.'

I stare at her, and she just keeps smiling back.

'The magic of Airlie,' she says again. 'This is where the Custodian's been stashing your magic before he gives it to the Guard.'

Rory comes to the edge of the hole and peers in. Lish looks around the room, vacantly, like she's thinking. Or remembering.

'Rory,' she says sharply. 'At the Challenge, you said Siosal was stronger than he should have been.' He breathes in deeply, understanding starting to flicker on his face. 'Could he have been given some of this to ... top up his magic as well?'

A finger of cold snakes its way down my spine. If Siosal used magic from the Givings to make himself more powerful, it would have been at the Custodian's discretion. I'm confident Zadicus would have taken the same liberty for himself – and who knows how many others he has fighting for him.

The sound registers before the sight does.

Hordes of soldiers marching into the throne room, as if they were waiting for us.

The wolf growls.

Lish lifts her hands from the floor and it closes. Soundless this time. I press Ciara behind me, Rory and Lish joining our huddle and going for their weapons. Shoulder to shoulder we face the soldiers – the human Guards from Rhyton.

Already in Elenlea.

Ciara forces herself out and beside me, a foot sliding gently on the floor, smudging away Lish's blood.

Rory's eyes flick to Lochlain, calculating the steps between us as talons sink into my magic, holding it in place. Ciara's growl and Rory's clenched jaw tells me the same has happened to them. The Custodian is preparing to pull our magic from us, just like Lish did to me in the tunnels. The same way he killed Nuala.

'I think you've got something that belongs to me,' he says. He folds his hands in front of the gold thread that runs down the length of his grey jacket as he glances at the floor, a small frown appearing. He looks back at his forces and nods at Lochlain.

Two guards step forward, pressing their swords into his sides.

He doesn't move.

'No,' Lish whimpers.

The hairs on the back of my neck stand on end at the sound the wolf makes.

Lochlain stares at her and I can feel the weight of her desperation pressing into the room. I look around, scanning for an option. But we are vastly outnumbered here, and the Custodian knows it. He walks towards

Lochlain and grips his hair in his fist, tucking a short blade into his neck, glaring at the wolf. Everyone of us, save the Guard, know Lochlain could get out of this easily.

But he won't.

Because he knows the risk to Lish if the Custodian orders a full-fledged attack. Time seems to slow as we stare at each other.

'I spent a long time, and a lot of resources, looking for you,' he says, looking at Lish. 'But I won't make the same mistake I did with your mother and believe you are worth more than you are. You have very few choices here. I will have the crown and a Wolverton.'

Lish flinches.

'Give the crown to me,' he says again, 'and I won't tell the Eternal Queen you're here.'

Lochlain shakes his head at her, and Ciara sucks in a breath.

Anger heats under my skin. This Calahi is supposed to represent the Court I love. The Court I have killed for, stained my soul for. But it's the same Court that never thought I was good enough to serve as Manorynx. I always thought Nuala and Benny were outriders in their belief in me. But, maybe, it wasn't just me they believed in, but that we deserve more than those that will only ever fight for the status quo – the one that gives them more and more power.

They knew we deserve more. Slowly, I look at Lish and I can see it written on her face as well. I know she won't give it up. Not even for Loch. Not at the cost of everyone else.

She looks at Lochlain, just a handful of steps out of her reach.

'I'm so sorry,' she says, voice breaking. Too anguished to cry. 'I wanted to tell you—'

Her voice is cut off by the wind she whips up as she grips Ciara's arm. I catch a last glimpse of Lochlain before I lunge for her, Rory and I crashing into each other, and Lish takes us away with Rory's magic.

Lochlain's eyes burn with pride and hurt.

And goodbye.

CHAPTER THIRTY-FOUR

LISH

I get us over the gate with Rory's magic. Somehow, my body remembered its rhythm and as I held on to Ciara, I could feel her magic dissolve the hold the Custodian had on me. Giving me the space to dive down into myself, where sparkling obsidian rose up to meet me. A process I was far more aware of this time, not like I did out of desperation in the tunnels.

But I left my heart behind on the cold marble.

The very floor I saved him on before.

Where I once vowed to never leave him.

Our landing was rough. I'd aimed for the shadows of the buildings I recalled from the street outside the Palace, hidden from view. But I was too fast and blood now trickles down my face where I slammed my head into the wall. The others are unscathed. The tether of the magic that held them in the throne room broken with distance, and able to defend themselves from my inexperience – I could feel when their own magic came back – while I was lost in Rory's magic and the numb, uncomprehending place my mind disappeared to.

I wipe slowly at the blood on my cheek, my fingers trembling.

I look at Rory, his stunning face marred with emotion. But at least it wasn't his choice.

It was mine.

'What did I do?' My voice is hoarse as I look away from him and turn back to the Palace, already wanting to take it back.

I made a mistake. The ramifications start to swirl wildly in my mind. I was so focused on the sapphire in the crown. The end goal. Being the Queen I thought Airlie deserved. And I let myself take the look in his eyes to say that he agreed, the emotions of his I could feel on my skin as confirmation this was the right path.

But I need him.

This can't be the right path without him. I choke on the knowledge I was comfortable enough to give him up, even temporarily, to make sure Airlie saw me as a legitimate queen. I'd told him we needed to talk when he caught me – as I knew he would – inside the Palace gates. But I didn't tell him why.

But I don't want Airlie without him.

I can make this right. I prepare to dive once more. My lungs expand—

It gutters out. Where once Rory's magic lay is nothing.

I open my eyes.

Ciara's face is in front of mine, her fingers gripping my elbow. Her magic eats away the ability to use my own and I find I can't use her own against her.

'No,' she says through clenched teeth, sweat running down her neck. 'Please,' she grinds out. 'Don't.'

'I—'

'Lish.' Aeyva's voice is sharp, focused on Ciara. 'Stay.'

The air leaves me entirely and I press the heels of my hands into my eyes hoping the pressure will erase it. The decision I just made.

Eventually, I drop my arms to my side and nod. Ciara's grip slips from my arm. She braces her hands on her knees with exertion and Rory moves to her.

'We have to leave him, Lish,' Aeyva says, her own voice thick. 'You know that's what we have to do.' My skin is silent, Lochlain too far from my reach. Aeyva glances behind her. 'We need to go. There is a lot of force that's about to come out of that Palace. The Eternal—'

'I want to know,' I say, my gaze pulling back to the Palace again, the black and gold gates that mock me in the darkness. My stomach hollows out.

Confusion dusts her features. 'What?'

'What it was for,' I say. 'We have all the pieces now, I want to know what they show.'

'We don't have—'

I turn to look Aeyva full in the face. Once, it might have been reckless, but her steel and blue eyes hold no fear for me now. My voice is low and quiet when I drag it out, rumbling slightly under the warmth of Lochlain's pendant.

'I am not leaving the possibility of getting him unless I know what the fuck it's for, Aeyva.'

She watches me for a moment, and I don't drop my gaze. The gravity of what I've done presses in from all sides, demanding to be known.

Aeyva holds out a hand to Rory and Ciara, who watch us, Ciara trembling slightly.

We make a small circle, the pieces of sapphire Aeyva and Ciara have responsibility for lying in the palms of their upturned hands – the piece Kailoh held on behalf of the Manorynxes, and the piece we got from a place that crawled of death. Rory pulls out the crown, holding it gingerly.

'Break it,' I say.

Rory's eyes fly to my face but he doesn't hesitate. The gold bends and cracks under his hands as he numbly removes the sapphire. The pendant at my chest warms almost to the point of pain. Pleasant pain that reminds me I'm not dreaming.

I wish I was.

'Let's do this,' Ciara says. 'Put it together.'

Rory gently takes each of the pieces from Ciara and Aeyva to join with his, and jostles them around until they vaguely make a single, larger shape, almost the size of Rory's palm.

'Lish,' he says, demanding my attention away from the memory of Lochlain's face. The way all the faces of the previous leaders of Airlie looked down on us in that room. One of them would have been my mother.

The sky sparkles with blue as I dig in my clothes for Lochlain's pendant, and it swings in the night air as I take it off my neck. Moving so close to Rory we're almost occupying the same space, I peer at the larger sapphire he's made, its cracks clear. A narrow hole peeks back at me. I drop the sapphire of the Wolverton Pendant into the gap, holding tight to the chain it's on, and the fissures in the sapphire crackle and dissolve. Lightning runs up the chain I hold and burns my palm.

I don't let go. I know it's part of the whole, but I can't let go. I want this piece for myself.

My head fills with visions, not unlike what Nuala showed me. The woman in the meadow. The wolves. The stream. The lover. Then it shows me a place. Empty of all people with a lake, and electric blue and purple flowers and thousands of butterflies gently swarming.

And then it dies, leaving just a concrete tomb behind. Over and over I see this place, vibrant and alive and then dead. Somewhere, a wolf howls.

Go to the Resting Place, a voice says as a map fills my vision. Release them. Open the tomb and release them. The butterflies will be the first to find life, as they will be the first to die as it goes – you must release them before all the butterflies fall.

I didn't even notice Rory taking me under his arm and transporting us back to Lochlain's cabin. Not until we're standing in the dark meadow, staring at what was once a welcoming, soothing, building. Now, it's a ghostly reminder of what I might have lost.

Logically, I know we had no chance of success if I'd taken us back into that Palace.

But his face as he held the knife to Lochlain's throat ...

Another layer of unease settles on my shoulders as I recall the vast number of Guard members under his command. If he'd wanted the crown, he could have taken it by force. Even if he didn't expect me to get us out, he didn't have to delay by talking to us.

No. The crown was secondary.

Tonight, he wanted a Wolverton.

Wanted Lochlain.

Someone shakes me and I look up to find Ciara's wild eyes. So similar to someone else I love. I blink, my own are gritty.

'I need him back,' I say, unsure if they can hear me. I can't hear myself.

I stand as I say them over and over until my voice doesn't work. Ciara takes my face in her hands and pulls me into a fierce embrace. Her brother. I forced her to leave him there. He's going to die thinking I was going to be bonded with someone else. And knowing I left him willingly. I left him for a vision of a tomb.

I press my forehead into Ciara's shoulder and let the contact anchor me. To help me focus on the steps in front of me and not those I've already taken. We need to regroup.

If I fall here, I will never be able to right what I've done. I no longer care about being in that room, my image on a portrait with the crown on my head. The crown is broken and I'm starting to fall apart. And I know, beyond all doubt, this is not what my mother would have wanted for me. To be a queen with an empty heart. Whatever my role in the world we are saving is, I can't do it without all the pieces that hold me together.

I'm going to protect every little part of me.

Lochlain, Elenlea, and the Mother included.

'Lish.'

Nico's quiet voice is shaky but determined, and I try to make my face soften as I look down at him from where I stand in Lochlain's living room.

Swallowing against the tightening of my chest, I meet Nico's dark gaze and my heart feels like it's going to break in two. Despite the distance we've all tried to put between him and our search for the Star, he's still seen too much. Has too much worry in his little face, his brown brows pulled low. He is one person I don't have to lower my barrier for – his emotions are clear from here and I gently send a push of calmness over him. Similar to the day we first met. A day his world was torn apart just like mine has been. Again.

'Yes, sweetheart?' I say. Even to me, my voice sounds hollow.

He walks to me and I crouch down in front of him. I'm nearly toppled backwards when he throws his arms around my neck, but I lean into his weight, taking the comfort he gives.

I squeeze him tighter, as if that will help my tears from falling too.

'I'm sorry he's gone,' he says into the side of my neck.

'Me too,' I whisper.

We're quiet for a moment and I listen to the sounds of the others busying themselves around the house. Will appears at the end of the hallway but doesn't approach, as if he doesn't want to interrupt our moment.

'The wolves brought Sofia back from the Star,' Nico says, his voice muffled, 'they'll take your wish there too.'

I let Nico cling to me as I look around at the others in the room.

'You saw it?' I ask. I take the lack of response as a 'yes', those that were there saw the message of the sapphire.

'It's a significant step forward,' Rory says. 'We know the next step and how to get there.'

'Two things I assume the Custodian doesn't?' Will asks.

Someone answers in confirmation but I don't look up. For a moment, the only thing I hear is the sound of my heart beating in my ears, as if in protest.

'He'd be stupid to kill him,' Ciara says hoarsely. 'Not if he is still trying to hold Airlie.'

I shake my head. The sound of my mother's skull cracking is a dull reminder of exactly what the Custodian is capable of.

'We'd be stupid to underestimate him,' I counter, standing from Nico's hold and slipping his hand into mine.

I glance outside to where the sky is still dark; I think less time has passed than it feels like.

'There's a reason he wanted Lochlain over any of us. Over the crown. And I don't think it's one we can allow to pass – we need to get him back,' I say. 'Before we go to the Resting Place.'

'Not one of us is going to disagree with that, Lish,' Rory says, gently reminding me I'm not the only one with my heart on the line tonight.

'We need to move fast,' I say. 'Before he's taken to another loca—'

A knock at the door makes me flinch and Will looks warily at it.

'Has anyone ever knocked on that door before?' he asks quietly.

'Only those with urgent messages,' Aeyva says as she moves towards it. 'That aren't us,' she adds as an afterthought.

A moment later she reappears in the living space of the cabin with another Calahi following behind. She gestures to the newcomer to speak without introducing her.

'The Custodian,' the female Calahi says, 'is assembling the Calahi of Elenlea outside the Palace gates. He's using the humans to force us from our homes and into the Square.'

Riley curses softly. The stranger – a Royalist I presume – glances nervously around.

'He-he said we're to bear witness to the punishment of another traitor.'

For a beat, the room is silent, my attention caught only by the flash in Aeyva's face – she's seen his punishment of 'traitors' firsthand. And then it's filled with the gentle sounds of weapons being tapped, blades slid in and out of their homes as they're double checked for their presence. A steady sense of relief settling over me.

We're going back.

'I'll get word to Kailoh,' Ciara says, her eyes immediately closing in concentration.

Riley moves towards me.

'You know this could be a trap, don't you?' she asks, worry clear in her voice.

My body feels coiled too tightly and I nod.

'I can't leave him there, Riles.'

CHAPTER THIRTY-FIVE

LISH

I let the sound of footfalls in until they beat in my chest. Muffled cries begin to join them, that of a particularly young child twists in my gut. It sounds just like Nico. The floating street lights still illuminate Elenlea and I recognise the bar we approach as the one Lochlain dragged me out of – that feels like a lifetime ago. Peering up the flower lined street, Guard members march towards the centre of the city.

In pairs, they peel off at the houses they pass, forcing the inhabitants to join the column of Calahi being herded away from their homes. As they stumble along the cobbles, I recognise some of the faces among them. From the fruit stall at the Square, a musician I've seen playing on a street corner, a male who turned away when Lochlain carried me kicking and screaming up this very street, and a young one who'd smiled so broadly at me I thought she might be sunshine itself.

Ciara presses her fingers to her temple lightly.

I look back around the corner, my heart racing. They no longer wear Guard uniforms, but the men and women in front of me are clearly human. And they have guns. An image so familiar, but entirely out of place here.

'There are too many of them for us to take on our own,' I say. Heat starting to ripple from beneath my pendant that has nothing to do with Roisin's sapphire but my gold flame burning at the injustice. For the Calahi but also for the members of the Guard who were promised something so different to this. I look back at Ciara.

'Kailoh's on his way,' she says.

The Calahi who walk with us are drawn, in contrast to their colourful night clothes – clothes that no longer fit the atmosphere of Airlie. The Guard moves them towards the Palace and we follow along, the armed soldiers taking no interest in us. At the Palace gates, the Calahi move as far away from the Guard as possible but they're pinned in the square – between the gates and the Guard who block all the roads that lead away. A Calahi close to me slaps the soldier trying to shove her through the crowd. He grins at her and she dissolves into sobs.

'Maeve! Maeve!' A voice calls but there's no answer I can hear. I run my tongue over the edges of my teeth, hard.

A large Calahi spots Aeyva from across the crowd and subtly makes his way over. She remains still as he meets her and begins talking quietly in her ear. She glances around at the Guard briefly and nods once. The only sign she's heard him before he disappears in the crowd once more.

'Citizens of Airlie,' the Custodian's voice booms around the centre of Elenlea. 'Thank you for joining me tonight. For too long we have been weakened, our warriors few and their strength dwindling. But this night marks a new era – one that bolsters our resources. With a force like this,' he throws his arms out, indicating the Guard, 'none of our young ones will need to take up arms against our enemies.'

The crowd is silent, the lanterns that still hang in the sky catching their uncomprehending stares.

Aeyva sucks in a sharp breath, fighting her way to the front as something captures her attention.

My stomach knots beyond the point of pain and I surge after her, pushing the weakened Calahi out of my way. Rory and Ciara not far behind. I don't need to know what she's seen to know the sickening in my stomach is right.

I feel Ciara's magic encompass us as we stand one Calahi back from the platform, her breathing heavy but shielding us from view of the Custodian.

'I have news for you,' the Custodian says solemnly before pausing for dramatic effect. 'Another traitor has been apprehended.'

Lochlain, his face almost unrecognisable under its swelling and bleeding, is dragged to the platform.

A young Calahi behind us starts to cry.

'Sacrilege.' Another mutters.

'I know this is a shock,' he says. 'For us to have been so badly betrayed from the inside. That our own Manorynx and General would work with a traitor, would-be queen, for their own gain. To kill our loved Catriona.'

A ripple of disbelief moves through the crowd but, hemmed in as they are, I wonder if the Custodian can see the doubt in their faces. Has he told himself this story so many times he believes it?

'I have shown you,' the Custodian continues, 'the lengths I will go to, to remove these stains from our Court. My power will continue to grow, and I will be able to make you stronger with me. Together, we can—'

I stop listening, it's clear where this is going, and I won't let him take someone else from me. Aeyva is drawing deep breaths and I steady myself, searching within for something I can use. I have used Aeyva's magic before, I can do it again. I feel it powering through my limbs and I guide it to the flame in my chest, ready to let it fuel the magic that doesn't belong to me. I glance to Aeyva and she holds out a hand, for us to do this together – kill the Custodian and save Lochlain.

A tendril of mist snakes around Ciara's bubble, through the Calahi, and they flinch away.

A chill runs along my skin.

Aeyva swears.

'Adelais *Wolverton*. You'll come with me, now.' The familiar, female voice echoes around us. 'Or I lay waste to this glorious symbol of Roisin's reign – this city you are so desperate to save.' A voice I last heard in Kailoh's Palace, a cold and ancient power.

The Eternal Queen.

Automatically Rory, Ciara, and Aeyva back towards me. Closing me inside a circle of Calahi warrior. A cold mist rises around my legs, clawing at my clothes.

'Oh, A-lice.'

The violence is thinly veiled under her sing-song tone. Sweat beads between my shoulder blades, absorbed by my suit. Quickly, I slip the Wolverton Pendant off my neck once more and press it into Ciara's hands.

'Roisin's Resting Place,' I say. 'You must get there before him and open the tomb.'

Ciara nods. There's a resignation in the set of her jaw, as if she knows she's almost the last Wolverton.

One that's about to be the last stand for the Realm.

'I know you didn't think it would be easy,' the Eternal Queen says, her voice echoing quietly around me. She may have had a physical form once, but there seems almost nothing Calahi about her now. Her presence is like an all-consuming fear with no one focus point. 'Show me where you are.'

On the platform, Lochlain doesn't move, but I can feel the faint prickle of him against my skin. The need to run to him buckles my knees. Only Rory's grip on my upper arm keeps me standing. I try to send Lochlain a wave of what I feel for him. To let him know what I failed to say.

Not a single muscle flickers in recognition.

I turn into Rory. 'You need to save him,' I say, the bubble Ciara created starting to bend under the pressure of the mist encircling it. 'And tell him – tell him I will forever regret not telling him about Kailoh straight away—'

I can't bring myself to finish.

'Lish, ' Rory starts, 'I said I wouldn't lose you on my watch. Kailoh is coming—'

'But he's not here yet. So this is the step for now,' I say. 'We can't let her kill everyone here. And then you will get to the tomb.'

He reaches for me, but I duck around the Calahi closest to me and out of the magic of Ciara's bubble.

I look back to Lochlain, a sob wracking my chest. I want to memorise him. His posture is defiant to the Custodian but so loving as he gazes out on the Calahi of Airlie, without seeing us through his swollen eyes.

But there's blood in his curls, sticking them to his head. I can't see his freckles. And I don't want this to be my last memory of him. Amber eyes flash through the mist and a tiny flicker of hope sparks in me. *The wolves will guard your path*, Benny had said. Perhaps—

The mist parts as it laughs and then dives at me, creating binds at my ankles and wrists so cold they burn. My eyes water with the memories of burning and my throat swells as she raises me a head above the crowd.

Some of the Calahi glance up, but most still huddle against each other or bury their faces into the stone road, away from the Guard and the Eternal Queen. A flash of blue catches my eye but it's too far away to make out. Lochlain is behind me somewhere. A wolf prowls around the base of the platform, as if it's waiting.

Beside me, someone gasps. 'The true Queen,' they say, the voice young. 'She's here – the wolf—'

'What is this?' An unfamiliar voice echoes around the Square and I strain against my binds to see where it's coming from, but all I see are the panicked faces of the Calahi. More voices join in the objections, the sounds ricocheting off the buildings around us.

'The true Queen?' the mist laughs as the binds cut into my skin. 'You are no asset to the Realm, I am the only Queen here.'

A heaviness presses into my ribs as I look at the Custodian's face. He's a Calahi who will die by his lies. And he has no intention of bending to the will of Airlie today, even as they start to revolt, start to push back against something they don't completely understand. With a disposable Guard and the Eternal Queen on his side, he has no reason to. But he glares at the mist, as if he doesn't like the attention that's being drawn to me.

'Traitors must pay!' the Custodian screams across the crowd. 'You will watch them die.'

He moves towards Lochlain and a light catches on the blade in his hand.

Around me, the Guard start to divide the Calahi into groups and the sound of protesting rises. Bonded partners are separated, young ones, some as tiny as newborns, are pulled from their parents' arms. I see myself in each of the young, tear drenched faces around me.

The black mass of the Guard push into the Calahi of Airlie from every side. The crying of the Court I have accepted as my own crowds my hearing. I strain against the binds of the Eternal Queen and the cold singes my skin.

'Airlie does not accept this!' someone cries again. This time the voice strikes a chord of familiarity, but I can't see through the desperate crowd to be sure.

The Eternal Queen raises me on her mist slightly above the rest of Elenlea, floating just above their heads.

'This woman killed our Queen!' the Custodian shouts, loud enough to cut through the noise of the crowd.

'It's fun watching them try to understand isn't it?' the Eternal Queen whispers.

'He's our General!'

It sounds like that voice is in support of us, too. As the Eternal Queen ushers me higher over their heads and towards the platform, I realise it's not me the Calahi are focused on as their villain, but the Custodian, the Eternal Queen. His face thunders. The Eternal Queen's menacing voice starts again but my attention catches on the scarlet pouring into the crowd and I can't focus on her words. Under me, in the screaming and pushing and the chaos, the sound of metal on metal begins to ring.

And the Guard start to fall to those of Mercasia.

I can no longer see Rory and I pray he has gone for Lochlain. More blue flashes through the crowd and the Calahi of Airlie start to fight back, bolstered by the scarlet throng of soldiers who are so clearly on their side. By the wolf among them. A howl reverberates through me. A sea of deep red with a smattering of blue cuts down the Guards who herded them and burn the mist that screeches in my ears.

A scarlet clad archer fires burning gold arrows at the bonds that bind me and I flinch as one hand slips free. But I feel no burn.

'You fools!' the mist, the Eternal Queen, screams.

'No,' a deep voice sounds from below. 'I'm afraid it is you who is foolish here. Your time is up.'

Kailoh.

The air leaves my chest in a whoosh. He came. For no other reason than the betterment of our world, he came.

'I will not allow you to harm my friend, and Queen of Airlie,' he continues. 'Release her, and the Calahi of Airlie.'

'Roisin and her offspring have always held too much, Kailoh. You will pay for this,' the mist says as it constricts my still bound limbs and grazes my throat.

'Not today.' Kailoh lifts his hands but I don't see what his magic does.

The Eternal Queen drops me like a bomb, and I plummet to the ground below.

CHAPTER THIRTY-SIX

AEYVA

'No!'

Ciara saw the Custodian move for Loch's throat and let go of her magic. But, instead of killing everyone in her path, it weaves around the Calahi of Airlie and Mercasia, around the wolves that are tearing into the mist of the Eternal Queen. Here is the destruction of barriers Ciara tries so desperately to hide from. But she can't escape her gifts, her ability to remove the gap between life and death.

I'm reminded of the beauty in destruction, Ciara in its centre. Dark hair falling from its binds and flying around her face that's turned up to the sky. The almost graceful way the bodies of the Guard around her fall to the ground like an elaborately timed dance as she screams, her eyes closed tight.

Ciara's magic races towards the Eternal Queen, the wolves keeping pace with it as they run into the mist. Her magic and the wolves suddenly seem to be as one. The mist screams as her magic and the teeth of the wolves find their mark.

The ground shakes and buildings fall as a blast warps its way through Elenlea, a wave of destruction racing away from the Palace as the Eternal Queen's power is ripped from her. A whoosh of a huge, scarlet shield flies into place and the gates of the Palace fly through the air. I duck, watching as a chunk of debris narrowly misses Ciara.

'Stop!' I scream as I race to her, shields up. Desperate to try to call her back to herself. The pull of Ciara's magic has always been too strong, too powerful. I can understand why she fears it, and that one day she will lose herself to it.

The rubble bites my skin as I slide the last few paces to her. I grip a blade in my right hand, the pain keeping me present. My shields start to buckle under the pull of her magic as they race to contain hers, my own barrier moving around the chaos hers can bring. I take her chin in my hand as her magic strokes along mine. Curious, and almost uniquely designed to take mine apart, just as mine is designed to immobilise hers. But the way our magic engages is more than just that. She pauses, her magic skittering against my own where it closes in.

A tremor runs through me as that thought settles in and I let Ciara's magic run over me, seeing who I am.

'Ciara,' I bark. 'Stop. Look at me and stop.'

Gripping my blade harder, I let my shield go a fraction. Letting Ciara's magic in, closer to me. Until it entwines with mine, and they weave around each other. She sucks in a sharp breath.

Her eyes find mine slowly and the gold fights for its position. And then she cracks as the rush takes her. Her magic races back, pulled in tight, and I press a hand to her chest in a feeble attempt to keep it there. To hold her together because I know what's to come.

Her hands find her face and colour drains from her like she's bleeding out. On impulse, I check her for wounds but there are no fatal ones.

'What did I do?' she mouths.

The same words Lish said when she got us out of the Palace, leaving Lochlain. I have only seen Ciara completely unleash her magic once before and she's never forgotten it. She starts to splinter before my eyes.

'You saved us, Kiki,' I say. 'You stopped them. The Eternal Queen is dead.'

She's shaking her head, my words bouncing off her. All she sees is the death, the irreparable damage she's caused.

A broken Elenlea.

'You saved us,' I say again, pulling her to me. She droops against my chest, not enough strength left to resist.

I get her on her feet and to Rory, who's dragged Lish from wherever he found her, tear tracks clear on her face.

'She cannot see this, Ror,' I say quietly.

He doesn't have to nod in understanding, it's written on his face – we're at significant risk of losing two wolves in one night.

Lish limps towards a group of Calahi survivors, huddled amongst the rubble that was Elenlea, and I follow. A young one lies in the middle of the group, a section of the Palace gate speared straight through her middle. She's grey, breath rattling in her chest. The mother's tears fall on the dying girl's face as she whispers to her that it will be okay.

'May I?' Lish asks, kneeling beside the girl.

Uncertainty flashes on the mother's face but she relents, and Lish rolls the girl to her side.

'Hold her.' Lish's voice is steadier than she looks. 'This will hurt, and she will likely pass out.'

She grips the end of the metal post and pulls. It moves a fraction and the girl cries out, the mother unable to help herself from pushing Lish's hands away.

'Stop!' she yells between sobs.

'Please,' Lish pleads, looking at me.

I crouch beside her and take the post, waiting for the reluctant nod from the mother. The girl sags in her mother's arms, as the post comes free, sinking into unconsciousness. I hope she stays there until a painless end.

Lish places her hands over the wound and bows her head in concentration. She hasn't been able to do this before, not without Lochlain's magic to draw on. A single bead of sweat drops from her nose and the mother covers her mouth as she understands what Lish is trying to do. The gift of healing is not common amongst the Calahi, particularly for wounds such as these. And even for those who can, so much of the magic has been taken at the Givings, I imagine it would be almost impossible for them to succeed.

But Lish hasn't ever had to Give, and the girl's breathing slowly starts to even out. She blinks groggily, the colour slowly returning to her cheeks. The mother, whose nightgown is torn from one shoulder, looks agape between Lish and her young one before clutching the girl to her chest. She reaches out with one hand to grip Lish's, looking over the shoulder of her daughter.

'Thank you,' she whispers.

The 'what ifs' push their way forward in my mind. But there was no Lish then, and no guarantee she would have been able to do it, anyway.

'Lochlain?' Lish asks in a choking voice as they walk away, and I have to shake my head. As I watch, she seems to push it all aside, swallowing her pain. Her panic. And she turns to take in the injured Calahi around us.

A wolf prowls through the stunned Calahi and sits at Lish's side. Absently, she drops a hand and runs her fingers in its fur as if it's the most natural thing in the world.

A presence makes itself known behind me and I twist to find Haryk looking down at us, Pendita by his side. It takes me a moment to realise he's wearing a blue shirt. It's torn and bloodied now, but the blue shines through all the same. I raise my eyebrows at him in question and he gestures around us silently. Over half the Calahi here, either standing or fallen, are wearing blue in one way or another. Haryk nods when I look back to him and the air escapes my lungs.

The Calahi of Airlie are wearing Lish's colours.

Pendita looks, wide-eyed, between me, Lish, the wolf at her side, and the others that stalk through what remains, before her gaze drifts to the young one Lish healed as she's helped away by her mother. Wordlessly, she raises her hand to her chest in recognition of Lish, who looks out over the wreckage for Lochlain.

We set up a triage system and Haryk rounds up all those with any healing ability, no matter how small – Lish and three others. Two in their middle years and one closer to dusk. One of the younger ones, a male with rich dark skin and tight hair, is especially skilled for his age and waning magic. He and Lish work together on the most difficult injuries, not all of which are successful. For every one that shifts into the next space, the male says a Calahi prayer. By the third, Lish joins him and their mouths move in unison as they murmur over those they cannot save.

I move amongst the remains of the Palace and the streets that once held some of my favourite places, now filled with the fallen Guard and the Calahi from Airlie who were lost. There is a scattering of scarlet uniforms of Kailoh's unit too. I will be forever grateful Kailoh arrived when he did and I look at him now, talking with his soldiers and offering help and support. But we lost a lot. Our city is gone and, while most of the bodies are those of the humans of Rhyton – Kailoh having saved as many of Airlie as he could with his own shields – they didn't deserve this, either.

Dust continues to fall from above, illuminated by the few lanterns that remain in position, coating my hair and clothes. Squinting into the darkness, I climb over the chunks of stone and marble that cover the streets and search. For survivors who I instruct other Royalists to collect and triage; for the dead who I sit with and say my own prayer; and for Lochlain. There are few survivors, and their injuries are such I am not hopeful they will hold on.

Of the dead, there are more than I can count.

Of Lochlain, there is no trace and, slowly, the cracks deep in my chest begin to reappear.

But I haven't found the Custodian either and, whatever he is enduring, if Lochlain isn't here, there is a possibility he remains.

The hope in Lish's face as I approach, the dark of the sky just giving way to light, is enough to twist my heart in two. I shake my head at her again, still unable to find the words, and it takes her a moment before she can drop her gaze back to the Calahi she's working on. She wipes her cheek on her shoulder, smudging the dark spots on the side of her face and mixing them with the blood. She's covered in a myriad of cuts and grazes herself.

The last of the survivors that needed attention from a healer walks slowly away from Lish and the young male. The other two healers are now checking each other for minor injuries. The male working with Lish rises unsteadily to his feet and bows low to her, his hand at his heart, black hair glinting in the low lantern light. She mimics the action before he fades away into the distance, amongst the remaining Calahi who stand aimlessly in their city, most now without homes.

Lish slides down the edge of stone she'd made to sit on and doesn't move, save to rest her head against it. Her eyes remain open but how much she takes in of what's happening around her I can't tell.

'You should rest,' I say, after picking my way across the rubble to her.

She closes her eyes briefly. 'No,' she says on an exhale. 'There is so much—' she takes a deep inhale. 'We need to find these people –

Calahi – somewhere to sleep. They've lost'—Lish's head drops onto her arms—'they need to rest.'

I hold out my hand to help her to her feet, squeezing her hand for a moment.

We work through the morning with Haryk, who I appoint as lead for the Royalists, and Daire, who is the main point of contact for Kailoh's unit. Those Calahi who discovered they still have homes, or partial homes, left that are sound enough to house others, have sorted into groups based on how many they can accommodate and their location in the city. Those without homes are matched as closely as possible to those groups, doing our best to keep families together. That still leaves a large number of Calahi with nothing and, with the help of numerous Royalists and Mercasians, we clear out several restaurants and public buildings further from the main blast for temporary shelter.

By the time the sun is starting to wane into the afternoon, I know we can do no more without rest. Daire and Callie switch places and I leave Haryk to select his stand in for the Royalists before dragging Lish away. She mumbles a protest, but her words are clumsy and I don't catch them.

We walk in silence through the ruined streets of Elenlea, needing to see the rest for ourselves. A smattering of houses that still stand is the only real reminder of what this rubble once was. If I look closely, I can see the remains of kitchen curtains, a child's toy poking out from under a piece of stone, what looks like a photograph and a pile of books. But I try not to see the scraps of what was once a full life here. Where my life was once held.

Lish pauses in what was the yard of Ciara's house, we've found ourselves in the laneway at the back. Without saying a word, she scrambles over the pieces of wood and stone and takes a plant in her hands. I stare at her. I've seen shock more times than I can count, and she is well on her way down that road. She closes her eyes and breathes, and the pulverised foliage stitches together before my eyes, the soft pink and yellow of the flowers bursting back to life. Sparkling colours dancing over the remains of Ciara's home.

I imagine Lochlain's cabin as a dream. A welcome relief from the chaos of Elenlea as Lish uses the last of her strength to get us here. Instead, it's more of the same destruction.

Lish swallows a quiet cry beside me.

'Will,' she breathes, just as the chestnut-brown haired human appears from the tree line with Riley, and she sinks to her knees.

Will gathers her to him, rocking her like a child.

'He's gone. I lost him.' She cries into his chest, and he strokes her hair while looking to me for confirmation. 'I lost him. It's all gone.'

Will closes his eyes and holds her tighter. The gesture makes me wish for someone to hold my pieces together. So I turn on my heel and keep walking.

'Niamh,' Lish says suddenly, forcing herself out of Will's embrace and to her feet. Another weight is added to the centre of my chest. Lish breaks into a stumbling run towards the house and I follow behind, not willing to rush too quickly and find what might be left of Niamh.

The roof of the small stables has come down, pinning Niamh in a tight corner where she has still managed to pace herself into a froth. Lish talks quietly to her as she approaches, as both Lochlain and Ciara have done on more occasions than I can count. Together, we move the pieces of roof that have kept her in place and she bursts free, racing around the available space.

I slip my belt off and, holding it behind my back, I approach Niamh quietly, aiming for her shoulder. She eyes me suspiciously, her whole body trembling, but she doesn't shy away. I slip the belt around her neck in a makeshift halter to help keep her in place. The quivering of her muscles slows gradually as I stroke her shoulder and down her flank.

'Where is she?' I ask Rory as I approach the house, leaving Niamh to graze.

He angles his head backwards, indicating the trees.

'With Sofia,' he says.

I peek through the trees to where Ciara and Sofia sit with their backs to me. Someone has made them a small fire, even though the day is warm enough without one, and they both gaze into it. They don't talk, as far as I can tell, but Sofia is close enough to Ciara to be resting her hand on Ciara's thigh. And I'm struck by the peaceful combination of human and Calahi.

Lish's face as she made the decision to leave Loch comes back to me, the regret of all the things she should have told him, and I realise I don't want any secrets between Ciara and me anymore. There are only so many regrets I can live with, and she's not one of them. Lish was strong enough to make the hardest choice when she got us out of that throne room. And again with the Eternal Queen, when she must have known she was going to her death. Replaying it in my mind fuels my belief we can do this. We were saved today by Kailoh and by the wolves – and Ciara. Saved so we can stay together on this course of saving the Mother.

The sounds of the destruction of Elenlea still ring in my ears. But I know where the Custodian has gone – to get Roisin's power – and we have to beat him to it.

So, to gather our strength and regroup, there is only one place left for us to go.

CHAPTER THIRTY-SEVEN

AEYVA

'What is this place?' Rory asks as he delivers us all, in a slightly bumpy landing, into the sparse living room of my villa.

The one no one was supposed to see. But, today, our need for shelter and safety trumps any desire for secret keepings. It was Nico that ultimately decided it for me – and Ciara. None of the rest of us, save Sofia perhaps, would have been totally unaccustomed to sleeping outside if necessary. But while I watched Nico's half-hearted playing with Rory, the thought of telling him we were staying in the same woods that surrounded the city he just saw explode was jarring.

As I look at the dirty, shell-shocked group around me, I realise perhaps I also needed to let them in. As I look at it now through their eyes, it could be quite lovely with its peaked ceilings and encased by the woods at every window, but it's nothing but bare bones. I'd furnished it minimally more out of process than desire and a small part of me warms at having them here ... notes that I need more places to sit, if this will happen again.

'There are bedrooms and a bathroom back there.' I point a thumb over my shoulder. 'And another over there.' I gesture across the other side of the living space.

Rory raises his brows at me.

'Food,' I say, frowning at the kitchen. 'There's no food ...' I look back to Rory.

'Got it,' he says and breathes heavily before disappearing. With so much of Elenlea gone, I don't know how far he's going to go.

Sofia leads Ciara, who remains silent, down the hall towards the bathroom and I dig out clothes from the cupboard for everyone to change into.

'Lish?' I ask as she looks around her. She seems like a woman caught in the moment before she decides to fight or flee. Someone processing that her options right now are severely limited and neither whom she wants to fight, nor flee to, are here.

'I need to see it again,' I say. 'The message in the Star.'

Her blinking is too rapid, she needs a drink.

'Ciara has the pieces,' she says dully, staring at the dark couch. I watch as she drops her chin to her chest and visibly tries to rally herself.

The sound of running water stops from down the hall and Ciara returns a few minutes later, a renewed focus in her gait.

'Where are we at?' she asks.

'I need to see the message again.'

She hands over the three pieces of the sapphire along with Loch's pendant. I can't bring myself to think that it belongs to her now, that Loch is permanently gone. The stones are warm when I cup them in my hands – alive with a gentle hum of magic and they almost vibrate towards each other. Letting them fall together between my palms, they arrange themselves to fit as one once more.

Immediately, an image of a flower-ringed lake fills my villa and the butterflies take flight.

Open it, sounds from the message. *Open the tomb and release them.*

Transferring the Star to my left hand, I hold out my right to pause it, twisting my fingers to focus on the tomb. There are footprints around it, and drag markings in the sand it sits in. No name marks the resting place but I know with certainty that it's Roisin's. It's where the sisters stashed her after they killed her. But, if the Eternal Queen and her sister were cursed, one having no form and the other unable to live above ground after they tried to take her magic, who left those prints?

I let the message play again, the butterflies taking flight only to drop and fall like rain again, and again. As I watch, it's always the butterflies that die first, caught by the net of death before they reach the top – what might be the way out – and the flowers follow. It's as if they are the first to succumb to the loss of the magic, the life, that fuels them. The parallels between that and the human world and the Realm seem clear. That the humans are the fragile, but vibrant, butterflies that so desperately want to shine they don't look at what's beneath them – the lake that's starting to boil.

One thing is absolutely certain, though; the flowers, the butterflies, the death, they are connected.

Lish walks closer to the image, crossing the black rug on the floor, as if she can get the answers by proximity alone. Small white particles of dust fall from her clothing as she moves.

Moving through the message, I find the map, a path marked from the outskirts of Elenlea and through the wilderness of the Realm. There's a pulsing blue light at the northern end that can only be our destination. A lump grows in my throat – Benny would have been beside himself to know how to get there.

'It's definitely Roisin's Resting Place,' I say out loud. 'I recognise it from Nuala.'

'So, who's there that needs releasing?' Rory asks as he magics different, simple plates for us.

'It can only be her magic, right?' Riley asks from her spot on my hard lounge. 'She was the one that created the world, and the power of creation has been trapped there with her. No creation, we stay in this death spiral.'

I turn on my heel slowly to look at Riley, really look at her.

'I think she's right,' I say, looking again at the butterflies paused in mid-drop. 'We've been worried about the Custodian taking Roisin's power because of what it means he will be able to control in the Realm. I've been thinking that meant we had to defend it.'

Ciara's stares at me, comprehension dawning on her too as I continue, 'What if it doesn't just need releasing, but harnessing?'

We both look at Lish.

'I think you're supposed to take Roisin's power,' Ciara says.

'So much for winning the favour of the Realm, I'll just raid the tomb of your First Queen,' she says quietly, but she's still focused on the image before her. 'There are markings on it,' she says, pointing, and I grip the air and tug the image in tighter.

Along the lid of the grey, mostly rectangular tomb are three indentations.

'Are they supposed to be keyholes?' Will asks.

We fall silent, every one of us aware we don't have anything that resembles three keys.

'I hope I'm not interrupting?' Kailoh asks as he strides in from the balcony, the only sign he's been in a hurry to join us are the loose strands of hair that sway around his face as he breezes in.

Everyone in the room stares at him, amazed that he would turn up here. Except Ciara, whose eyes slide to mine as if she wonders what other secrets I hold. I pour him a drink and gesture to the only vacant chair – the one he sat in last time he was here.

'Have you heard anything?' Lish asks without preamble. Kailoh knew of her affair with Lochlain, so I guess there's no point pretending where she's at right now.

There's genuine sadness in his face when he looks at her. 'I haven't, Adelais, I'm sorry. But I have some of my best Sentinels looking for him.'

She nods once and clears her throat.

'The sapphire has given us directions to Roisin's Place,' she says, still looking at Kailoh. 'We're ... surmising that we need to beat the Custodian there and stop him from taking her power – and that I need to take it instead.'

Kailoh sips at his drink, nodding slightly as he absorbs what she's saying. 'Roisin's power still resides with her, we know that, and I agree it's better with you than Zadicus. But to what end?' he asks. He shifts forward in his seat suddenly, tossing the remains of his drink down his throat and swallowing. 'We know that the sisters tried to take her power once and were cursed for it. To try it again, the Custodian must think he has something different this time.'

Will stands a bit straighter. 'The Guard – humans with magic. That's different.'

Kailoh's gaze is sharp and considering when he looks at Will. 'That *is* different ... a combination of worlds.' Slowly, he turns to look full at Lish, his face lighting with understanding. 'That's why he was so keen to find you. You're part Roisin's line and part human. Now he can't have you, I think he's going for human-magic blends on a larger scale. What was Benny's theory on the meaning of each piece of the Star?' he asks, looking back to me.

Quickly, I scan my memories and shift through the knowledge Nuala shared with me, at the same time I try to process this new understanding. 'That one holds the support of the Manorynxes of the Realm; the crown symbolises that Roisin's line is on the Throne where it belongs; and the love and power of a Wolverton.'

I try not to look at Lish at the last statement but it's impossible to ignore how her heart seems to crack a little further before us.

'And the fourth has been an unknown,' Kailoh says and I nod.

'So it's entirely possible for the Guard to represent the coming together of the two worlds as the fourth element,' Will adds, 'despite how poorly that's turning out.'

'But how does any of that help him?' Rory asks. 'We have the sapphire – it gave us the only directions to the Resting Place known to the Realm. He can't find it without us.'

I squeeze my hand around the stone on impulse, its hard edges pressing into my skin.

'Because,' I say, 'he had access to the Eternal Queen, one of the two only other beings who knew where it is. He's going to try and open the tomb with or without the Star – there could be another way to open it that only she and her sister knew, who knows. If he succeeds, then we have no way of using the power of creation for good and the Mother, and us, remain in this "death spiral".' I glance to Riley in acknowledgment of her earlier statement. 'And if he doesn't succeed, hundreds of human soldiers are likely to die while he tries.'

As I say the words out loud, I understand how little it has made sense to think we were ever separate. Just as the faces around me say that I am not separate to them, no matter how hard I tried.

'So,' Lish says, 'either way, we're taking the Star to the tomb.'

When everyone's eaten – Lish no more than a few bites – I leave them all to select their own rooms after directing Will and his family to the largest.

We have limited time to rest while we wait for Kailoh's Sentinels to arrive, so Rory and Callie can get the human Commissioner's rebels into place. Haryk is leading the Royalists while we go ahead and we'll converge at Roisin's Resting Place.

But, instead of thinking through the strategy for when we arrive as I should be, my mind churns through where the Custodian could have taken Lochlain.

Something nags in the forgotten places of my mind, something about why the Custodian might need him specifically and not just the Wolverton Pendant. But I can't think straight enough to work out if it's some knowledge of my own, or that Nuala transferred to me. I know it's required, but staying put tonight is making my skin crawl with impatience and it's hard to focus.

Swiping a bottle of Kailoh's favourite drink that he insisted I keep here for his visits, along with its matching glass, I move out to the deck. The glass fits in the palm of my hand and the light dances around its etching.

What a stupid thing for me to have.

I pitch it over the deck that's two storeys high on this side and listen for the soft smash as it finds the bottom. I move to the edge and look for its pieces. Uncaring if I find them. It's not possible for a Calahi to end their own life by falling, or jumping, from this height. I know because I have tried from higher.

The inhale alone of my drink of choice makes my eyes water when I remove the stopper, and I almost smile at the anticipation of its burn. The heat as it goes down is as good as I'd hoped, and I take mouthful after mouthful. Chasing the sensation until my vision blurs. I recall the brief sensation of flying as I'd leapt, before the realisation of failure set in. I only had regrets when I hit the bottom, alive, and faced a painful healing process.

I'd do it again and again if it meant I'd work out where Loch is. If I didn't have to feel this complete impotence in helping him.

'Hey,' Ciara says as she joins me, the pain in her voice clear. It doubles my own.

I drop my forearms to the balustrade, bottle still in hand as it now dangles over the edge. Steeling myself, I take another mouthful from the bottle before holding it out in invitation.

She takes the bottle and presses her hips against the balustrade next to me, my blood tingling with her proximity.

'What is this place?' she asks, the same as Rory did.

I roll the lingering taste of Kailoh's drink in my mouth.

'I ... would come here. When I needed somewhere to go when I completed an assignment.' The words are less bitter than I thought they'd be. Because, now, I'm no longer part of the Society – an organisation Keeva will run in the wake of the Eternal Queen's demise – and because I know everything I did there was still in service of my Court, even if it wasn't in the way they would have preferred. The same as Lish isn't the Queen the Court thought they wanted, but maybe she's something better.

'I wish you'd have told me,' she says, still looking towards Elenlea.

'I know. I think I just didn't know how,' I say, thinking of the oppressive weight of losing my daughter and the decisions I made in the time that came after. 'It was just easier to manage it separately – consider it as something not really part of me.'

'But it is. The same as being a Manorynx is part of you.' Her face is so beautiful in profile, but it takes my breath away when she looks at me straight on.

She hands me the bottle back and I take another burning mouthful. 'Mulriarty suggested I could be a sword-wielding Manorynx.'

A faint smile dusts her lips. 'I can see that.' Her gaze turns back to the newly fractured skyline of Elenlea, beyond the trees. 'I hurt them, Aeyva. Worse than hurt them. They-they were just people. Humans. And I—'

'I know, but— '

Ciara bends at the waist and rests her head on her arms at the balustrade.

'I just'—she stands up and paces the deck—'I feel like I'm going to explode. Like there's too much. So much.' Her hands wave gently in the air around her face, indicating where there's too much happening. 'I am supposed to be a Wolverton. I am a Wolverton but, Loch and me'—she chokes—'we're supposed to be protecting Lish and Airlie – together. And ... we fucked it.'

I walk to her and take her face in my hands, forcing her to look at me.

'Kiki,' I say firmly. 'You did what you had to do to save us and our Queen. Lish did what she needed to, to give us a chance to save Roisin's power and the Mother.'

'I know it's in my blood, the same as Lish's responsibilities,' she says as she brings her forehead to mine. 'I just thought I'd always have Lochlain to protect her with.'

It would be so easy to slip my hands into her hair from here, to close the gap between our mouths. To kiss her softly enough that it eases some of her heartache. But, as I watch her from up close, she starts to compose herself. I can already see the thinking through of our next steps swirling behind her eyes.

And I can't kiss away her loss, our loss. I can't pretend all of this is okay or promise her we'll find him, not in this new space of no secrets between us. She'd see it for the hollow lie it would be.

'I need to wash up,' I say, pulling away reluctantly.

She gives me a long look, as if there's something she wants to say. We stay like that for a moment before she moves ahead of me. I let my gaze run over the back of her, the curve of her ass as she walks back into the villa, the mention of her Wolverton blood nagging at me.

CHAPTER THIRTY-EIGHT

AEYVA

Dressed in clean, comfortable clothes, I wander through the villa, checking on everyone here. With no one requiring anything from me, I do the only thing left I can do.

The door to the smallest room is still open with no light and I peer in.

Empty.

Sighing, I kick the door gently closed behind me. I don't concern myself with light – the villa is more familiar in the dark – and make for the bed, where I lie back and stare into the darkness. In the dark, it's harder to hide from what we've lost. Loch is gone. Elenlea is gone. And Lish and Ciara are barely holding on. In some moments, I feel like I'm barely holding on.

The Eternal Queen doesn't exist anymore, which I am exceptionally grateful for. But it's the people and Calahi around me that are paying the price, not just me. I throw my arm across my eyes as the memory of Loch's face as Lish took us away burns them. Logically, I know it was the right choice, that none of us would be here if she hadn't.

Which doesn't take the suffocating sting out of losing my best friend.

I can't lie here and do nothing while we wait for aid from Daire and Callie. So, I tuck onto my side and breathe deeply as I delve into Nuala's knowledge, shifting through anything she gave me that might help me understand more about Roisin's Place.

Why the thought of the Wolverton blood keeps making itself known.

Sleep must have found me because I wake with a start to the bed depressing next to me. I expect Rory, but the soft smell of jasmine and honey winds around me and I freeze.

'Did you find anything?' she whispers into the dark. For a fleeting moment, I try to pretend to be asleep, but she knows me too well.

'Not yet,' I say without turning over. 'There's something I need to understand between your line and Roisin's tomb, but I can't find it yet.'

The silence settles between us and I continue winding my way through the slabs of information Nuala imparted to me. The Wolvertons were gifted with magic from the wolves, because of Roisin. To protect Roisin. But was there more to it than that?

The mattress shifts underneath me, and I can feel her searching my back in the dark room. Curled on my side, I can't see the details of her face. I both desperately want to and am suddenly tied with nervousness. She runs a finger down my spine, pulling my shoulder blades towards each other of their own accord and a sharp, cool breath into my lungs.

'I know you love me, Aeyva.'

That cold air shoots back out like I've been punched in the gut. My brain tries to turn over. I don't want to lie to her, not about this. But I'm not sure I deserve to love her.

Her soft finger continues its relentless path, up and down my spine.

'I'm sorry,' I whisper.

And I am sorry. There should be a stronger word for how I feel for distracting her with this when she expressly asked me not to. It feels like a lifetime ago we had that conversation outside Nuala's house.

'Roll over,' she says.

I still further and wait.

'Now, Aeyva.'

Slowly, I turn myself to face her. I can just make out her silhouette in the dark room.

'The time is now,' she says.

I frown against the skittering in my stomach I haven't felt in a long time.

'I don't—'

'To acknowledge it. Acknowledge me,' she says, her voice quiet but even. 'I know you love me, now you just need to confirm it. I need to hear you say it.'

Love. She uses the term so freely. Is that what this is? This all-consuming desire to keep her safe, to fight for her happiness – to make her proud?

But of course it is. I've known I've loved her for longer than I care to recall. I loved her even before then.

I clear my throat.

'You're right, Kiki, I do,' I say, my voice barely audible even to me. 'I'm sor—'

She presses a finger to my lips.

'Sorry and love don't belong in the same sentence if it's the love itself you're trying to apologise for, Aeyva.'

I close my eyes. Her features are becoming clearer as I adjust to looking at her in the dark, and I don't want to remember how her face looks when she says she doesn't feel the same. She removes her finger and I breathe a little easier, waiting for her to go.

Soft as a feather, something brushes my mouth. I squeeze my eyes tighter, the pain in my chest tightening. Even behind my closed lids, the blackness gets darker and I draw a ragged breath. Only to taste her scent. She's too close. Her mouth moves against mine again, more insisting this time, her tongue teasing, fingers lightly tracing just above my ear. A shiver runs down my neck in response.

She stops kissing me for a moment and I hesitantly open my eyes. Her gold ones are laser focused on mine.

'What are you doing?' I ask.

'It's not obvious?' she asks, a tiny smile in her voice.

'I—' my words run out.

No, it's not obvious, I want to say. *You're kissing me when, not so long ago, you apologised for doing exactly that.* And now, no, I don't know what this is. My body knows what it wants this to be, but the uneven hammering of my heart is drowning it out. I can't do a once off with Ciara. I don't think I'd recover from that.

Her hand moves to the back of my head and pulls me closer, our breath mingling. Her full, delicate lips press themselves against mine again and I suck her bottom lip between my teeth without thinking. She inhales sharply and pulls me closer still, our teeth clashing as she deepens the kiss. I reach out and find her shirt, dragging her towards me by the handful I've collected.

Ciara's hips grind on mine and my tongue finds hers. I must be dreaming. Dreams aren't real. I can do this in a dream, dreams are—

'Aeyva,' she says, breaking away and holding my face. 'Are you with me?'

I cover my face with a hand and nod.

'No,' she says gently, 'don't do that. Stay with me.'

'Why?' I whisper.

'Because this is what I want, Aeyva.' My heart stutters and I wonder vaguely what would happen if it stopped in this moment. 'And I think it's what you want.' She kisses me softly. 'Is this what you want?'

Yes.

No.

Not if this is it. Not if you're going to regret it in the morning, I want to say.

'You said we shouldn't do this,' I say, trying to keep my voice from breaking. 'At Nuala's.'

She sighs heavily, her breath catching strands of my hair and she pulls my hand away. My lips tingle where she's kissed me. I can't believe she kissed me. Again. I force myself to focus on her next words. She lights a small orb in her hand and floats it to the side of the bed, the light just enough to see her by without having to guess at her expressions.

'I meant it at the time,' she says. 'I thought that was the right thing to do. The waiting, and the longing, had gone on for so much of my life I didn't know who I was without it. I didn't think trying to figure that out when our whole world is literally at stake was a good idea.'

'And now?'

'I don't want to wait anymore. Time is precious, even if we have more of it than the humans, it's so precious. Watching Lish and Lochlain has been'—she draws a breath—'I don't want to spend any more of mine fighting this.'

'Do you know she's not bonding with Kailoh?' I ask.

She nods. 'Riley said she was worried he'd feel pressured into not being General so he could be with her.'

'It's a shitty choice to have to make – your Court or your heart,' I say.

'But maybe it's not actually a choice,' Ciara says. 'Whether they are open about it or not, the love is there. No one can change that.'

I stare at her. I'm not normally this slow on the uptake, but this is the very last thing I expected from her today.

'And what will you want tomorrow?' I ask.

'You, Aeyva,' she says. 'I've wanted you for thousands of tomorrows, the next one will be no different. I don't know how many more tomorrows there will be for us and I refuse to not have this – you – while I can.'

It's my turn to kiss her then. However frail this is, however likely it is that she will change her mind, I need her now, too. I've always needed her and to have the opportunity for one night with her, to have her tell me she cares deeply for me, is more than I could have ever wished for.

She rolls me onto my back, her dark braid tickling my chest where it hangs over her shoulder as she leans down to kiss me. My shirt bunches under me where she pulls it up, and I arch into her so she can remove it.

'Oh,' she breathes as she feels nothing but skin underneath.

She dusts feather light kisses across my stomach, my insides tightening further the lower she goes. Trailing her mouth back up between my breasts she takes one in her right hand, massaging gently before finding my nipple. Releasing me, her fingers dip beneath the waistband, my skin burning in their wake. Rising to her knees next to me, Ciara removes my soft pants. Spreading my legs wide, she climbs between them and looks at me.

'You're flawless,' she says quietly.

She's right. Physically, my skin is almost completely unmarred. I'd thought once about marking myself in some way for every kill I made, something that showed on the outside the marks that were on the inside. But I couldn't bring myself to do it. Aside from Rory, my body is the only evidence of the daughter I was supposed to have. Her flawlessness is reflected in my own.

I laugh softly. 'Flawless is not actually a good descriptor for me, Kiki.'

'Maybe not,' she says between kisses, having found my mouth again. 'But it's not for anyone.'

Her tongue presses mine into silence. I let my hands move along her sides to remove her shirt and she wriggles free, removing her pants as well. And then she's over me in nothing but her simple, black lingerie. She sucks gently along my neck and I drag her face back to mine, greedily taking her mouth again, the taste of her setting fire to all rational thought. Her fingers stroke me gently over the fabric of my underwear, my hips pushing towards her on reflex. My blood pounds through my veins and I grind myself against her fingers that move rhythmically against me, my plain undergarments dampening with every stroke.

She moves them to the side, her mouth still capturing mine, and slips two fingers in deep. I press harder into the kiss, biting her lip hard enough for a moan to sound in her throat. Finding the clasp of her bra, I help the straps fall off her shoulders. Her fingers move within me as I take a breast in each hand. Her nipples are darker than mine and I lick and blow on them, smiling slightly at how they pucker and firm. Ciara starts to circle her thumb while her fingers massage me internally, and the last of my restraint buckles.

I reach my hand down to her, slightly frustrated that I can't see all of her from this position, but drunk on the sensation of her skin. She is beyond soft. And wet. The clear evidence of desire I find in the palm of my hand is almost enough to send me over the edge and I suck in a steadying breath. I cup my hand around her, just enough for my finger to run around her entrance and press the heel of my hand against her. She groans loudly and pushes against my hand. Her breath comes faster. At the same pace as her fingers.

I go first, my body gripping her, waves of ecstasy flooding through me. I could drown in this. But I find myself enough to keep my hand where it is. She grips my wrist and presses on me, harder, faster. Breathing into my neck. I press her higher up my body with my legs, lifting my knees until I can reach her with both hands and, with the one that's not cupping her, I slide a finger into her. Careful not to disrupt her sensation.

Her teeth find my neck, sending lightning between my legs.

'More.' Her voice is muffled. I stretch her gently with another two fingers.

'Oh,' she groans and quickens her grinding pace again. She tightens around my fingers as she finds her edge and leaps from it, kissing me hard as she rides it out. I pulse my fingers inside her, dragging out her pleasure.

She collapses on me, breathless. I wind my arms around her, running my fingers up and down her back until she shivers, little bumps covering her skin. She nestles in next to me as her breathing begins to return to normal and I carefully unwind her braid with one hand, letting the strands fall between my fingers.

Countless moments pass, but I know neither of us sleep.

'Do you want to talk about Lochlain?' I ask after some time.

She stills, the hand on my chest tensing. 'I don't know what to say about him.'

'Kailoh has contacts everywhere, we'll hear something.'

Her chest stops moving against mine as she holds her breath for a long moment.

'He's strong, Kiki.'

'If his heart wasn't breaking over Lish, I'd believe you – I would believe he could withstand anything. But without the knowledge that Lish is his pumping through his veins ...' She takes a shuddering breath that betrays all the tears she's not shedding. 'I'm terrified it won't be enough.'

I let Ciara drift off to sleep next to me as I mull over her words, staring at the ceiling. She's right – whether they tell the Court about it or not, Lish and Loch belong to each other. Whatever doubt Lish has cast on that for Loch, he knows he still belongs to her.

His Wolverton blood will still say that.

I now understand that's why the Custodian gave up the crown for Lochlain. He knew he needed a Wolverton but, with the Eternal Queen to give him everything she knew about Roisin and her tomb, he didn't need to wait for the Star.

CHAPTER THIRTY-NINE

LISH

My body vacillates between numbness and vomiting, not big enough to contain the emotions that fight for space in my chest. I force myself to walk slowly out of Aeyva's house and onto the deck, throwing myself down the stairs and gulping the crisp night air, the pain pushing me from the inside. Pain that feels like a wave crashing over me, pummelling my head and my face until I can't breathe.

I know the others need this rest, time to gather themselves. But every part of me is vibrating with the need to be moving again. I tried to help in Elenlea. I stopped myself from chasing him and made myself focus on the dead and dying in front of me. But I need him. I need him now. I can't wait for news from Kailoh. I just – I don't know how to find him.

The flame in my chest burns so hard it hurts, taking up all the space until I feel like I'm going to explode.

Lochlain's shadow drives me through the trees surrounding Aeyva's, my bare feet pounding the earth to escape. The stars look down on me blankly, as if the world didn't literally just fall apart, as if my heart wasn't just torn to shreds.

'Hey.'

I jump at Will's voice, his dark hairline glistening in the faint moonlight. He wipes an arm across his forehead.

'You didn't have to follow me. I'm fine.'

'Sure,' he says.

'It's gone,' I tell him after several minutes. 'The whole lot – Elenlea – is just ... gone. Everything we have been fighting for and'— a loud sob escapes me—'the person I was supposed to be fighting for has disappeared. And for what?' I ask. 'Nothing. The sapphire didn't do anything. It didn't put Elenlea back together, it didn't give me some great power to stop the death of the Mother or the Givings.' My body shudders as I drag in as much air as I can. 'It didn't even give me hope.'

I pace between the closely packed trees; even they whisper quietly in sorrow. The bark of the one closest is coarse as I slide down it and sit back in the dirt. Will crouches opposite me.

'I know you know not all of that is true,' he says. 'It hurts, but we still have hope, Lish.'

The gashes on my skin from the rubble of Elenlea remain, their dull ache fogging my senses. But not more than the shame that my injuries aren't worse when so many were lost.

'You know Elenlea is not all we are fighting for. Elenlea is not the whole of Airlie. Nor is it the human realm.' He reaches out and squeezes my knee. 'It would be good to save them from impending doom, too.'

I offer him a half-hearted smile and look around us, remembering a night long ago we sat in a different forest and talked about finding our people. At the time, I'd entertained the thought it could be Phoenix for me, not knowing both Will and I were on the direct path to finding the ones that were meant for us. And mine wasn't Phoenix.

'As for Lochlain,' Will continues. 'You can still fight for him.'

I look at him tentatively, afraid of what I might see in his face. 'What if he's—'

'We don't know that he is.'

I rest my head on my arms and listen to the sound of the night.

'He would have wanted you to continue this, Lish,' he says. 'But we'll find him. One way or the other, we will find him.' Will holds out a hand. 'Come back with me. The sapphire did give you a vision – an instruction – and directions on how to get there. That's our next step.'

I look at his still extended hand for a moment, his dark skin even richer in the moonlight. It's both soft and rough in mine when I take it and we pull against each other to stand. He doesn't let me go as we turn to walk back to Aeyva's place, gripping my fingers tightly as if he can transfer reassurance to me that way. His steady presence beside mine is a reminder that he is as much a part of me as Lochlain. I started this journey with him by my side. I'll finish it that way, too.

'He's it for me, Will.' A blue light sparkles above the trees, in solidarity or mockery is hard to tell, but I send my wish to it anyway.

He squeezes my hand harder.

'I know,' he says, and I silently thank him for not making promises he can't keep about finding him alive.

We walk in silence in the direction of Aeyva's, her villa the complete opposite of Lochlain's rustic cabin. Even the trees here close in with secrets, so different to the open green fields around Lochlain's. The air is cooling off quickly, far cooler than we ever experienced in Rhyton, and the hairs on my arms stand on end. The night is so dark I can barely see my bare, sore feet in the undergrowth. A memory of being with Lochlain in the wood as he led me towards Elenlea constricts my throat. The too-short time between my escape from the compound and who – what – I am now, burning my eyes.

A howl cuts through the thick, jet-coloured night and the blood stops in my veins.

'Did you hear that?' I whisper urgently.

Will frowns, his mouth falling open. A louder, closer, more desperate howl sounds but the voice is different. There are two.

'Fuck me,' Will breathes.

I spin back to look in the direction of the first howl. Only the rows of trees look back. Beyond them, everything else is smothered in night.

'Lish,' he says, 'we need to get help.'

Concern laces his words, concern at what I'm about to do. Something I would normally feel, but it bounces off the walls I have constructed around my own storm of emotions.

I wait for another howl, for any sound at all, but nothing comes. Until I take another step away from Aeyva's, towards the sounds, and twin howls cry into the night. Hope flares deep behind my ribs. The wolves aren't with me now, they haven't been since Elenlea. Maybe that's not because Elenlea is gone, but because they're still protecting one of the most precious parts of me.

'It's him. They want me to find him.'

'Lish ...' A warning sounds in his voice. I yank my hand away.

'I *know* this, Will. I need to go.'

I expect him to object and prepare myself to walk away from him.

'Lish,' he says sharply but I can't tear my eyes away from the trees. 'I'm not stopping you. But we need to do it sensibly.'

The practicality of his tone barely breaks its way through. But shoes, shoes would be good.

'I'll give you five minutes,' I say. 'And then I go without you.'

Not only does Will return with my black suit, boots, and weapons, but Rory, Ciara, and Aeyva. I leave the soft sleeping clothes I'd found in Aeyva's cupboard in a little pool at my feet and scramble into the thick, pliable fabric I've come to love like a second skin. I do things in this suit.

'Which way?' Rory asks, no doubt in his handsome face.

'Are you sure about this, Lish?' Aeyva asks, glancing at Ciara. I can see how desperately she wants to hope for herself but I think it's the risk of giving it falsely to Ciara that worries her.

'Yes,' I say, the sound of the howls echoing in my mind.

'Okay,' she says quietly. 'I'll stay here with the others – make sure they get some rest and be here in case Kailoh sends word of anything. Will?'

Will looks between Aeyva and me and I ready to take a step away, to leave him with Sofia where I know he belongs, too, and towards the howl I last heard.

'I'm going,' he says without missing a beat, stepping forward and taking my hand again. I squeeze it tight.

I haven't heard the wolves since Will left but I point in the direction of my best guess towards the closest howl. Rory jumps us through the trees and we all pause for a moment, waiting for another. When the sound comes, Rory pulls us in tight and we jump again. I've never travelled short distances with him, and the constant stop-start jolts my stomach and hurts my neck. At each stop, he looks to me as we listen for the howls that lead us, making sure we're hearing the same and agree on the direction. I can't see where the wolves are taking us and am unable to direct Rory to the final destination – if there is one. But Nuala showed me a connection between the wolves and the Wolvertons. One helped me heal Lochlain at the Challenge. They've been with me every moment since I went to Kailoh's as Queen until Lochlain disappeared.

I know beyond doubt that they are leading me to him.

Our breath puffs white before our faces as the night gets colder with every stop.

'Are we in Mercasia?' Ciara asks.

Rory looks around us and frowns. 'I haven't taken us through an entrance, but this is no part of Airlie I know. And it's too damn cold.'

I turn away from them, not caring where we are as long as it is the right direction.

'Come on,' I whisper to the night. 'Where are you?'

A soft crunch sounds to my left, and I whirl expecting to find a wolf. Instead, there's nothing.

'Please,' I beg. 'Let me find you.'

Ciara squeezes my arm, the sorrow in her face clearly apparent even with only the moon to see by. The blood drains away from my face.

I can't have been wrong.

It has to be him. Not just the wishes of a broken heart.

Follow the wolves, my mother used to say. *Please*, I beg her now. *Please don't let me be wrong*.

Scorching tears take a slow journey down my face and I don't have the energy to wipe them away, the only physical response I have left for him.

'Look at this.' Rory holds a small sphere of light over the snow I didn't notice on the ground. He looks at me and grins. 'They're prints, sweetheart. Wolves.'

'What?' Ciara's grip tightens on my arm and I pry her fingers off. 'Show me,' she says.

Rory and Ciara take the lead in following the prints in the snow, pointing out where a single set becomes two. Two sets of paws walking side by side across the white blanket. One set is bigger than the other, but they are each at least as big as my hand. I bend briefly to trace one with my fingers, their presence magnetic. Magical. Sinking deep into the snow, the clear weight of the animals reminds me how real they are.

The ground inclines beneath us, the only sounds the slightly laboured breathing from Will and me, and the soft crunching of our boots in the snow. Every part of Rory and Ciara is silent. They keep walking, each of them trying to move at a pace Will and I can keep up with. Their bodies trembling with anticipation, waiting for confirmation of some kind.

My heart fights the memory of this space, the not knowing if he lives. The knowledge I might not be that lucky twice pushes into my mind like a poison. But I won't allow it to take hold. Not now. Not when I've heard the howls that reverberated down my spine. Not when I follow clawed tracks in the snow. They lead me somewhere. They have to.

The distance between Ciara and the rest of us grows, as if she can't maintain the slower speed. Rory glances between her and Will and me constantly, as if torn between who we seek and who he guides through the snow in the dead of night. But there's no prickle against my skin, no blending of senses that is the signature of Lochlain being near.

Still, we walk in the silence, the shadows from the lights Rory and Ciara create flickering against the trees we pass. And I pray for one more howl.

If I wasn't watching Ciara when she froze, I might have almost mistaken her for a tree. Only the Calahi have the unnerving ability to be stiller than death. The snow flicks up behind her when she moves again, flying through the trees and out of sight, only glimpses of her light sphere showing where she's gone.

'Lish.' Rory holds his hand to me in quick demand. He already has hold of Will.

Rory charges us through the forest, chasing Ciara.

She's crouched in the snow when we catch up, a dark shape at her feet becoming clear as we approach cautiously. I let Rory go ahead and he circles the other side of the shadowed mound. Slowly, he takes the sphere of light and hovers it between he and Ciara.

Over a body, half buried in the snow.

And a wolf curled around his back.

Rory's eyes find mine and I don't notice the final steps I take to close the gap between the here and there. A ledge I have no choice but to go over.

Lochlain lies naked. Twisted on his side and covered in thick snow that's crusting over into ice. Dark rambling hair peeks out in a broken halo. It's the only part of him that appears intact. My stomach plummets into the cold abyss at my feet, dragging my mind with it.

I feel Will look at me and back to Rory.

'Is he ...' he trails off.

'Not yet.' Ciara's voice is hoarse and far away. With it comes relief and dread in equal measure.

Rory stands and gestures for me to come closer.

'We need to get him back,' he says, eyeing the wolf that hasn't moved but watches us closely.

I stare at Lochlain mutely, dropping slowly to my knees before him. His magnificent black and copper eyes are closed, ice in his dark lashes.

'There's no blood, Ror. Why is there no blood?' I ask as I take his hand and hold Lochlain's frozen bicep in the other.

The wolf stands and shakes itself free of snow, snowflakes flying into the air and onto my face. Its amber eyes glow as they meet mine and I stare at it. How many times will it help me save him?

I don't hear Rory's answer before we're whipped through the in-between, cradling Lochlain's limp and heavy form.

Dead weight.

They're the words that circle my mind in the blackness as we head back to Aeyva's villa. But Will said we still have hope. And now I have Lochlain.

Dead weight.

I can only hope we weren't too late.

CHAPTER FORTY

LISH

Rory lands us in the living room of Aeyva's secret house.

'Fuck.' Aeyva inhales sharply and drops to Lochlain, searching his neck for a pulse. 'We don't have a lot of time,' she says.

Will appears beside her, his boots wet from the snow and leaving dark footprints on the rug.

'We need as many blankets as you've got,' he says without looking at her.

Riley and Rory race away, returning less than a moment later with arm-fulls of blankets and bedspreads. Will lies one of the thickest over the black rug we stand on.

'Roll him here. Gently though, be careful with him,' he says as Rory and Ciara slowly shift Lochlain onto the blanket, his body still curled in a ball.

'Riles, we need a hot—'

'On it,' she says.

Their words swirl around me. I take in his face. The wolf on his chest. The arms that held me close so many times.

The thousands of open cuts on his skin.

Cheeks that flap open but don't bleed. The wounds on the wolf so deep I can see his ribs.

My own chest starts to heave.

'*Rein it in*, Lish,' Aeyva says, a bite to her words, but a warranted one. I blink at her.

Rein it in, I repeat to myself. Rein it in.

Act now, panic later.

'Get me Tiernan,' I say. The words spark movement in my limbs. 'Tiernan,' I say, 'the healer. Now.' Rory vanishes before my eyes.

Kneeling at Lochlain's now partially covered head, the room comes back to me. Will and Ciara continue wrapping him in the blankets. The sound of the water boiling and Riley opening and closing cupboards as she searches for things in the kitchen. Sofia's footsteps coming down the hall. Will telling her to keep Nico away.

The task before me is monumental. Impossible. But I've done impossible with Lochlain before. And this time I will have help I can talk to. As if reading my thoughts, Rory appears with Tiernan.

'Your Majesty,' Tiernan nods in my direction, dark eyes not missing a beat. 'Tell me,' he says. His expression gives nothing away as Will outlines Lochlain's injuries.

At Tiernan's instruction, I slide my hands carefully under the blankets and down Lochlain's chest, careful not to expose too much of his colder-than-ice skin. Pushing away the queasiness that rises in my throat at the sensation of his wet, open muscles beneath my palms, I look to the healer.

'Warmth first,' Tiernan says, as he takes Lochlain's feet in his hands.

Slowly, gently, I dive into myself and pull up the memory of healing magic I have used before. My sapphire magic leaping at my touch, my desperation to heal him reflected in the deepest parts of me. I soothe my magic and find the heat only, sending caressing waves over and through him. My palms heat slightly where they connect with his skin.

Methodically, and only after Tiernan tells me, I work my way down Lochlain's body. Healing the cuts and wounds, some more complex than others. I close my eyes and let the sapphire streams lead me as they seek out what's broken. Eventually, they meet Tiernan's magic and there's no more healing of wounds to be done.

The parts of Lochlain I can see look almost whole.

Almost.

Red marks show where the wounds have been, not the perfect skin that would normally appear after healing of this kind. He's a wolf bathed in scars.

I look up from his traumatised body and meet the gazes of the people around me. None of us speak as we turn our attention to Tiernan, whose hands still rest on Lochlain's body.

'I'm sorry,' Tiernan says.

I'm sorry.

Those words every being dreads to hear. Human or Calahi, they mean the same thing.

'He doesn't have enough magic of his own left to complete the process,' Tiernan says softly.

'No,' Ciara's voice breaks.

Riley moves to hold me from behind as I stand and move away from him. I shake her off.

He doesn't have enough magic to heal. Tiernan's face said the rest – without it he will slip away. I look down at his barely warm body and my mother's broken face flashes behind me. Then, I was like Nico, and I had no idea where to go or what to do. But today, I won't let Nico see someone die on the floor of the house he's in – a house he's supposed to be safe in. I can't do it to myself, either. This time, I won't be running away and never looking back. This time, I will do the saving I desperately wished someone would for her.

Gold flame burning, I draw on the sensation of how Rory travels, remembering how to move that way. Taking the obsidian magic that now also resides in me and calling it forth with a sharp visual of where I need to go.

Lochlain doesn't have enough magic – but I know where to get more.

My stomach twists as I throw up in the room beneath the obliterated throne room. A dark, airless place that hums with stolen life, protected by the thick white marble floor from the explosion. The hairs on my arms stand on end and I search. Search for the vials that contain the copper of Lochlain's magic.

They sing in my hands when I find them, more than I can count. How many Givings has he done?

A box of brass syringes sits on the floor, its timber lid partially off as if it's frequently opened. Grabbing one, I drop it in with the vials, and return to

Aeyva's with two timber crates, one in each hand. The others gape at me as they take in what I've managed to do.

'I have this,' I say to Tiernan.

His eyes bulge at the crates and wordlessly he looks back to me.

'It's his,' I say. 'How do we ... ?'

'I've never seen it done before,' he says, not dwelling on what I have and why. 'But ...'

Hope taps against my ribs.

'How do we use it?' I ask.

Tiernan blinks before clearing his throat.

'It - ah - it should be relatively simple,' he says, still staring at the syringe in his hand. 'Providing you're absolutely sure that magic is his.'

I look at the vials in the crates. There are no labels, nothing that marks them as Lochlain's. Except they were housed on a shelf that was separated from the others. Glowed slightly more brightly than the other copper vials I could see. And jolted in my palm when I took them.

'It's his,' I say.

Please don't let me be wrong, I beg.

Tiernan draws a long breath, closing his eyes briefly. Lips moving in words I can't hear. He lifts the brass contraption, and I pass him a vial of Lochlain's lifeblood.

'Talk to him,' Tiernan says, looking at me. 'I cannot be sure how this will go, there is supposed to be a kind of healing magic infused in these barbs here.'

He gestures to Lochlain's Calahi family. 'Hold him down.'

The dark fingers that press at Lochlain's neck are so soft and gentle I wonder if Lochlain can even feel them. His chest rising and falling so shallowly.

Tiernan looks at me one last time, and I look to Ciara, her face holding the same conviction I feel. Taking my nod as final confirmation, Tiernan pushes the sharp end of the needle against Lochlain's neck. His skin depresses slightly before giving way. The syringe hisses as Tiernan pulls the trigger and copper surges into Lochlain, snaking out under his skin where at least four barbs have extended from the needle itself.

The beating of my heart slows almost to a stop as we wait. The Calahi don't appear to breathe.

A roar splits the room.

Will, Riley and I scramble backwards, covering our ears.

Rory is flung aside, knocking Aeyva into the low table.

Only Ciara holds her ground at Lochlain's hip, pinning him to the floor as he writhes and fights against her. Tiernan presses his hand over the fresh, small wound at Lochlain's neck, eyes wide.

Lochlain's body stretches taut, his limbs twitching violently before slumping back to the floor, still as death.

Every pair of eyes moves to Tiernan. Waiting as he searches for a pulse and rests his hands on Lochlain's red ribboned chest to feel for breathing.

The collective inhale is audible as Lochlain's chest comes to life and draws gulps of air.

'Stay with him,' Rory says when we've moved Lochlain to a room in Aeyva's house.

I look at Rory's handsome face, the soft light of the bedroom spilling out and catching his cheek bones. The set of his jaw betrays the suite of emotions warring within him.

'Do you think he'll be okay?' I ask quietly.

More than anything I want to be with him. I want to touch him. To remind myself he lives. To be with him when he wakes. But after my mother, Benny, Hayes, saying goodbye to Will in the compound ... the look on Lochlain's face when I left him. I can't say another goodbye. And what if I see betrayal when he looks at me?

'I think he's in the best possible position to be okay now,' he says.

I look up at Rory, who fills most of the doorway, his shadow falling over me in the soft light. He tucks a strand of hair behind my ear.

'Don't look like that, sweetheart. There's a reason you were able to lead us to him,' he says quietly. 'And you know his heart is not that fickle – he won't hold the no-bonding or the leaving against you.' I wince as he says it out loud and he knocks under my chin with his fist gently. 'But for the love of all that is good, put him out of his misery and tell him you're not bonding with the King.'

Rory's smile lights up the room before he leaves and, for an instant, I understand what it is to be in his spotlight.

Lochlain's back is to me as I cross the room, watching his ribs rise and fall. I stand behind him, taking my time to absorb that he's alive. He's safe, and he's now warm. The usual heat radiating off him. No prickle caresses my skin, and the silence of his emotions is a vice that's hard to breathe around.

My fingers itch to run the planes between his shoulder and elbow, where his arm lies against his side, before dipping away to cross over his chest. Where the skin was once brown and smooth is now covered in red, partially healed, wounds. I tingle with the desire to relearn his shape and send myself into every one of those wounds and heal them. Bit by bit. To smooth out the hurt that's been inflicted on him. The torture he has endured.

Still, he breathes. I walk around the base of the bed and to the other side of the small room where I can take in his face. Underneath the slowly healing wounds, his colour is returning, the ice melted from his lashes. My stomach turns over itself looking at his cheeks, the memory of them gaping open and the cold, wet sensation along my palms.

I sink slowly onto the bed, trying not to disturb the mattress and wake him. Not knowing what else to do, I remove the boots Will had fetched for me and lie down on the bed. I close my eyes and listen to Lochlain's breathing, stifling an internal groan at the light and my inability to turn it off. There were switches in Ciara's house, she thought they were quaint; but I can't see any in this room. I put my arm over my eyes. The tiredness runs deep into my bones, so the light is unlikely to matter.

'Hi.'

I jump at the deep, soft sound of Lochlain's voice and roll over quickly to face him. His eyes are closed.

I stare at him, grappling for what to say.

A small smile dances on his lips, the wounds in his cheeks pulling. He grimaces slightly and drops the smile.

'I know you're there, Lish.'

His eyes remain closed, my name on his mouth as thrilling as it's always been.

'I can get—'

'No.'

He stretches a hand along the mattress towards me. Slowly, I take it in my mine, threading my fingers in his. He squeezes my hand and opens his black and copper eyes, the copper rings swirling.

'I don't want you to bond with Kailoh,' he says gravely.

My heart lurches.

'I want you,' he says. 'I want you to be mine. Properly mine.'

'What changed your view on the alliance?' I ask.

He takes a deep breath, his gaze never leaving my face.

'I saw my city brought to rubble and all I could think of was you. Even as they drained me of blood and left me for dead'—his chest expands slowly—'my mind was filled with how I'd failed you. How I didn't fight for you.'

Tears spill down my cheeks.

'I think,' he continues, 'it was the thought I hadn't done enough that kept me alive.' A ghost of a smile appears. 'Well, and you, of course. But the thought that I hadn't done right enough by you.' He pulls my hand gently and I shuffle forward on the bed to lie closer to him. 'I didn't want to die knowing I hadn't told you.'

'Lochlain,' I say, shame flooding my senses. 'I haven't been honest with you.'

His eyes flicker but he squeezes my hand tighter.

'It's fine,' he says. 'Whatever it is—'

'I'm not bonding with Kailoh, I never was.'

His face goes slack.

'What?' he asks. 'What about—' he stops, a growing understanding in his eyes.

'I'm going to save the Realm without being Kailoh's Queen.'

He stares at me. 'You found another way,' he says.

A smile creeps across my face despite my tears. I nod. Genuine fear mars his features, and he moves to sit up but decides against it. The white sheets scratching his skin as he moves.

'What did you promise?'

'Nothing,' I say. 'Kailoh and I ... we became friends.' His brows furrow and my hand begins to prickle where it meets his, just a fraction. 'He asked if I would bond with him and join our Courts and ... I refused.'

'But you're not dead.' He sounds genuinely confused. 'Nobody refuses the King.'

Somewhere, I know I should probably be a little worried about Lochlain's concerns about Kailoh. I don't doubt he has made brutal decisions in his time. But I believe he was real with me when I was in Mercasia, and he came to our aid in a big way in Elenlea. Is still coming to our aid. And it occurs to me that Kailoh is definitely one of the good ones. A Calahi willing to do anything for his Court, and his allies, without manipulating a return that benefits only himself.

'Not dead.' I smile. 'And with an alliance.'

He exhales loudly. 'You're pretty fucking incredible you know that?'

I laugh him off, seriousness coming back quickly.

'I'm sorry I lied to you,' I pull his hand and hold it against my chest. 'I never should have let you believe I was going to do that. Being General is so important to you, and I didn't want to make you feel you had to give that away because of what my life has turned out to be. But I shouldn't have made the choice without talking to you. I would never want to bond with anyone—' I break off, warmth washing through me as I realise what I've said.

But I don't want to take it back.

His injured chest deflates.

'Anyone?' he asks.

My flame burns with certainty.

'Anyone else,' I whisper.

He lets go of my hand and tucks his behind my head, applying enough pressure for me to know what he wants. I scoot closer again and he bends his face down to mine. His nose running the length of mine, our foreheads resting together. Our breath eddies in the space between us.

Winding my fingers into his hair, the only part of his body that doesn't look like it hurts, my tears slow.

'I'm sorry, too,' he whispers. 'You deserved more from me.'

'I deserve you, Lochlain,' I say. 'I just want you.'

He drags his fingers up my back. 'I love you, Lish *Wolverton*.'

My cheeks flush warmly again and I pull his hair gently. 'I should've known you'd find out about that.'

He chuckles softly, wincing at the pain it causes. He captures my mouth with his and I kiss him greedily. The force he returns my passion with firing life back into the kernel of hope I've been trying to protect. As he bites down on my bottom lip, drawing a gasp from my throat, I wonder if the wolves are protecting both of us for something more than just our happiness.

If the Queen and the General really are the pillars of Airlie Lochlain has talked about before, and if we will face our hardest test when we steal Roisin's magic.

I pull back from Lochlain's kiss and place my hand gently over his.

'You need to sleep,' I tell him.

'Only if you stay with me.' Slowly, he takes my hip in his hand and pulls me closer again. I move gently so I don't bump any of his wounds. As I let my body gently mould itself into his, I realise that the Court of Airlie might believe he should be able to protect without claim. But I want him to claim me.

Because I claim him.

'Always.'

CHAPTER FORTY-ONE

AEYVA

'Ciara!'

The pounding on the door jolts me from sleep. As a young one I would panic at being woken suddenly. I can still recall the shaky feeling that would swim down my torso and along my limbs. I look over to Ciara, her dark hair spilling across the pillow.

Daire's on the other side of the door when I open it, just enough for me to see him but not give him a view into the room as Ciara climbs from the bed.

'Let's see what you've got,' she says, tying her hair at the nape of her neck and ducking past me.

Rory and Riley are already in the living space when we congregate moments later, the humans looking particularly challenged to shake sleep. The only one absent is Nico and I'm pleased he isn't here to listen to his grown ones talk about war. For it is war now that we face – us, a blend of Calahi, both Airlean and Mercasian and some human rebels – against an army of altered humans.

'Scouts on the Rothani border report them moving north,' Daire says.

After our discussion with Kailoh yesterday, I think it's abundantly clear the Eternal Queen told the Custodian where to find Roisin's Resting Place. Which means the only thing we possibly know that he doesn't was the message about opening the tomb. But I think it's safe to assume the Eternal Queen shared with him how to take Roisin's power.

'They'll be slower than us,' I say, a growing urgency settling in my stomach as I watch Ciara pull Loch into a hard hug.

'Show off,' I mouth, and he grins.

Last night I wasn't sure he'd make it, but we don't do goodbyes. So I'd walked away and held Ciara through the too few hours of rest as we both prayed he'd make it through the night, that this morning we wouldn't be preparing him for a hasty burial before we saved the world without him.

The disbelief in Tiernan's expression is almost palpable. But then he, too, thought he was staying with us in case of that very real possibility. Lish moves to him, as Daire smooths a map on the low table between my couches, and takes his hands in hers. She bows her head low and he flushes deeply under his dark skin, bowing to her in return.

'It's good to have you back, mate,' Will says.

Loch grips his shoulder and pulls him into a forceful embrace. He murmurs something to Will that has his eyebrows raising before grinning slyly and slapping Loch's back.

'Blaire and David are leading the rebels here,' Ciara says, pointing at the map. 'Callie and Daire have trained there before and have a contact who can get us horses.'

'They didn't need guest status to bring the rebels?' Riley asks.

'No,' Rory says. 'The Commissioner was already an esteemed guest of the Realm through Airlie, so he can bring who he pleases. The compromised Guard members probably don't have it, but the magic in them would have gotten them through the shields, anyway.'

'Kailoh is going to head straight to Roisin's, along with the Royalists,' Ciara continues.

Loch looks at her. 'You're good at this.'

She shakes her head a little. and I can almost see the memory of Elenlea flashing behind her eyes. 'That's as far as we've planned,' she says. 'So, General, views?'

Loch crouches by the table, examining the map where we've marked the path, and I consider how good they both are at the roles they were destined for.

'Are there any wards or potential traps we need to be aware of in getting there?' Loch asks without looking up.

'No,' I say after a beat, realising I'm the best placed to answer that. 'No,' I repeat. 'The information on that part of the Realm is scarce – it's almost completely uninhabited. And we've never known to look for her Resting Place there.' I pause to delve a little deeper into the knowledge, like brushing away layers of sand to reveal something new or more detailed. 'I think it will be opening the tomb itself that will be the challenge. Everything we know about Roisin and the sisters confirms how powerful they were – but I don't know what that will mean for us on the way, or when we get there. But we should plan for the possibility our magic might be inhibited at some point, similarly to getting into the Palace.'

I don't know but, unfortunately, the Custodian might.

Daire points to a pile of black bags in the corner.

'There's gear in these,' he says, looking at all of us.

I nod in acknowledgment, grateful for the supplies. We all desperately need proper fighting clothes after we lost just about everything in Elenlea. I haven't even asked Ciara how she feels about her home. Later. It will have to be later. Daire begins selecting packs and throwing them at each of us, the solid weight thunking against Rory's chest as he catches his.

'I had to guess at your sizes but they should be pretty close. Callie's bringing another crate of weapons.'

Lish sends Tiernan back to Elenlea with the syringe she took from the throne room, a vial of her blood and instructions on how to open the cavity under the throne room floor. Part of me wondered if she would want to tell the citizens of Airlie herself that she'd found their magic and a way to give it back – a way to completely restore their strength and replenish the Mother. But she'd been adamant that Tiernan return immediately and start the process. We didn't need to talk about what happens if we fail because, in that case, there's no need for their magic anyway. The Calahi might as well have it back while they can.

If we succeed, Roisin's power will be released and the natural cycle will resume, meaning we won't have to Give anymore. Part of me wonders if we will ever know the Custodian's real motivation in taking our magic. Did he ever think it would help stop the world's hastening decline or was it always intended to build him a pliable army?

Half an hour later, while the moon is still in the sky, we're assembled on the deck ready to move. In addition to the clothes and weapons, Daire has organised Sentinels for Sofia and Nico. I watch Daire prepare himself.

When this is all over, assuming we have the opportunity to rebuild, I'm going to have to try and persuade him to switch Courts. He'd be good on Ciara's team.

I start as I realise, for the first time, I haven't considered myself a Sentinel.

The horses are restless when we arrive in the town Daire pointed out on the fading map. The stables are large and well-loved, memories of being forced to ride a feisty mare over and over – until I learned to stay on – racing to the forefront of my mind.

Lochlain and Lish lean against a timber fence side by side, their arms touching. She smiles gently at him before he leans down and kisses her on the mouth. Their easy affection warms me, despite what we need to face.

Ciara and I haven't touched each other since we left the villa. We certainly don't have the open affection Lochlain and Lish have. But it's no longer the unknown undercurrent that sits between Rory and Riley. The way she reached for me, and pressed her soft mouth against mine in the night, didn't sting of regret or goodbye. I look to her as she acquaints herself with one of the horses, a large bay gelding, and know I will die with one less regret if we don't come through this.

I drop back into the knowledge Nuala shared – what is now my knowledge – and my blood trembles slightly as I look for anything that would be helpful. The path to Roisin's Resting Place the sapphire showed rises up to meet me, floating to the surface, the sand falling away around it. For a moment it's all I can see, and I grip the timber post next to me to keep myself grounded, not lost in the shared memories from Nuala, the worn surface warm in my hand. This was the first test she gave me. Could I immerse myself without losing myself. But I've never been at risk of forgetting who I am and where I came from.

If the Custodian manages to get even a drop of Roisin's magic, he could do great and terrible things.

Nuala taught me, all of us, that Roisin was to be revered above all others. I didn't understand the risks of that magic being taken by another. The Guard are evidence enough that our magic cannot be consumed by them, not without bringing great destruction in the process. Certainly not by all of them, anyway.

Now I know, if Roisin's magic is taken by the Custodian and no longer sustaining the Mother, our world will be the price. That the destruction the humans have wrought will never be halted. That's what Nuala and Benny were so close to articulating; losing Roisin's power will only fast track our path to complete environmental destruction, and we'll have missed any opportunity to correct it.

The humming under my skin drops away and I find Ciara watching me. I wink at her but the muscles in her face only fractionally relax. Lish glances away when I notice her watching us, a smug little grin on her face.

'She'd be so happy to see you doing that,' Ciara says as she walks towards me with her horse.

Remembering Nuala passing all she knows to me pulls at my insides, the image trying to force its way in. I blink. Refocusing on Ciara.

'I'm proud of you,' she says.

I suck in a breath and stop myself from a backwards step. I stare at her.

'Proud,' she says again before placing a swift kiss on my cheek and walking away.

Behind her, Rory clasps his hands together and shakes them at the sky in a mock prayer. Smart ass. Riley smacks him on the shoulder, his grin turning predatory when he looks her way. I suppress the desire to laugh. I'll be able to get my own back, Rory and Riley is just a matter of timing.

The sound of hooves in the dust echoes around us and Loch hands me the reins to a broad chested palomino.

'Time to move,' he says.

We ride hard, the horses pouring with sweat as we push them on, trying to beat the Custodian to Roisin's Resting Place. The stallion I ride finally settled about half a day in after I'd frustrated him with my ability to stay seated as he skittered through the woods. Horses in the Realm are bred to be harder, tougher, than any found in the human world, but even the horses of the Realm need rest. No one has ever confirmed it, but I'm confident the horses bred here contain their own kind of magic. They have certainly been coveted by any human who has managed to stumble upon them. I've had to dispose of one or two who got too close to taking what wasn't theirs – the Society's jurisdiction not ending within the borders of the Realm.

The woods grow thicker around us as we travel deeper, continuing our path northeast. The vegetation around us grows so thick we're forced into single file, Daire in front, me second in line to give directions. Lochlain is a particularly skilled horse handler, and he brings up the rear. It also meant Will couldn't see the laughter Lochlain stifled watching him try to stay on his horse. That man was better designed to be in direct contact with the ground at all times.

The air shifts around me, waves in the sky like I'm suddenly submerged in water.

'Stop,' I say.

Daire responds immediately, his broad back straightening minutely. The muscles in his neck flex as he looks around us. The air continues to ripple but slows slightly. I listen to our surroundings but there are no sounds other than the animals and birds that inhabit these woods.

'Okay,' I say to Daire and he gently squeezes his roan mare onward with his heels.

The presence of magic grows as we move through the wood until it's so thick the horses bow their heads and lean into their shoulders, as if they pull us uphill, pushing through. But the path we cut is a gentle decline bursting with wildflowers. Small, furred animals I vaguely recall from my early days poke their little faces out from the undergrowth and the trees, darting away before I can really get a good look at them.

Daire's horse stops abruptly, refusing to go any further. I slide off my mount and move up beside Daire's, running my hand along her damp rump, and manoeuvre myself in front, catching a handful of scratches from the low hanging branches that stretch for my face.

There's nothing visible that would have stopped her, but I can sense what she does. A blockage telling us not to go on.

Nuala's voice sounds in the back of my mind. *Give yourself Aeyva, let yourself be seen. You know what you are now, so will she.*

Let myself be seen. What does that even mean?

The horses shift their weight restlessly behind me. Daire's roan nibbling impatiently at my shoulder.

Placing my palms out in front of me I attempt to let my guard down, let myself be seen. The world pulses under my hands, pressed against magic unseen, and shudders.

Who are you? It asks.

'My name is Aeyva ... Sentinel to the Queen of Airlie.' That was the last title that was at least somewhat formally given to me, in Nuala's living room.

That is your name and title, Aeyva. I asked who you are.

'I - I'm still working that out,' I whisper. But as the words come out I wonder if that's true.

Then let me see and I will decide.

The voice that is both everything and nothing disappears, leaving silence in my ears. Not even the soft sounds of the others behind me. I open my eyes to find myself in darkness. Darker than any place I've been before, it's—

A scream rips from my throat, my heart tearing through my skin.

Who are you, who are you, who, who. I think the voice implores me, pain making all coherent thought empty out.

Oh, it says, *oh. You are ... unexpected. The other one was ... expected. Uninteresting. After so long, the same old story plays itself out. But you, you are ... intriguing ... and welcome.*

My knees tremble. I try to draw on my training, all the nights I spent learning how to live through pain, to breathe through it. But the wounds I've suffered in old battles and carrying out my Societal duties are nothing compared to this. To having my soul separated from my body and held aloft for inspection.

You really didn't know before now, did you? You followed a path for self-flagellation but it's not who you are ... Aeyva. I can see what you want though. See her. See the destruction. And the resurrection. And, for that, I let you pass. For the hope of resurrection. For the futile hope of those who once loved this world. For those the world promptly forgot.

My knees bark as I hit the ground, landing sharply on an exposed root. Daire hauls me to my feet.

'Mother above, what happened?' he asks, gripping my elbow.

I run my hands over my chest. Intact.

'Something I do not care to repeat.' My words are breathless.

I turn awkwardly in the tight space that now seems lighter, easier to penetrate.

'Let's keep going,' I say as I stumble back to the snorting stallion and remount.

The wood thins out immediately, the air cooling around us and the horses breathing easier. The now dry blood on my face where my scratches have healed itches, and I scrub it away with the back of my hand.

The terrain changes under hoof, the horses finding their footing more readily as it levels out and becomes the soft grass of a meadow. Yellow flowers are scattered in the green blanket before it turns to white, and we shiver our way through until the temperature warms once more and leaves of all colours fall from the trees. As if we ride through the seasons of the Mother as we move towards the power that's trying to sustain her.

We ride in two rough groups now. Will's face moved from pale to irritated some time ago, and hasn't changed position since. I offer him what I hope is an encouraging smile and he grimaces back.

The stallion stumbles, the ground starting to give way, as we push ahead into a clearing and I leap off, sinking into the ground up to my ankles. The others aren't quite as far as me, still obscured by the trees, and I shoo my horse back to them. He looks at me almost sorrowfully before shaking his head and returning to the group, his steps sluggish in the clinging earth. I turn, slowly, and examine the woods around this small expanse of yellow-brown dirt.

There doesn't appear to be anyone else here but I still make my way back to the others and take the small cover of the trees.

'What do you think?' Lochlain asks.

'This is it,' I say, pointing to the middle of the bald space. 'The sapphire showed a cavern, it's underneath us.'

Lish and Will gape at me, genuine fear on their faces.

'There's no sign of Kailoh or the rest of our support,' Rory says, clearly having done a perimeter check.

Ciara's brow furrows slightly before she blinks and looks at the rest of us. 'They're close.'

Three howls shatter the quiet and Lish's eyes go wide.

'It's happening,' she says. 'He's here.'

My heart kicks in response. This is not what I was hoping for – the seven of us against an entire army. Seven of us, not all of us with magic, literally dropping into the darkness with no idea what we're about to face. But the look on Lish's face says it all. She trusts those wolves beyond any doubt. And I trust her.

This might be the last thing I ever do, but I will fight for my world.

The ground sags beneath us as we drag ourselves to the centre of the sandy bog. Our legs, knees and hips disappearing at different rates in the brown soil. Lish is almost completely submerged first and the panic on her face is palpable, Loch leaning down to whisper in her ear.

'Take a breath,' I say, 'and be ready to draw your weapons on the other side.'

Loch catches my eye as we quietly submerge in the sand, his trust unwavering that there is, in fact, another side.

CHAPTER FORTY-TWO

AEYVA

The stale air is the first thing I notice in the dark, dank cave. The second is that we're alone. I immediately find Ciara's gaze, already assessing the area and picking up the same things as me.

'Get a message to the others,' Loch says to Ciara, his clothes as dry as the rest of us despite what we passed through. 'He's inside the magic barrier Aeyva got us through. Tell them to prepare for an attack above.'

Briefly, I spare a thought for Blaire and the human Commissioner and hope they are up to this, but I have no choice but to leave them in the hands of Haryk who leads the Royalists – a combination of Royal Watch, Whispers, and other Airlie citizens – and the forces Kailoh is bringing.

Right now, despite what is about to unfold above us, we have an opportunity to get to the tomb and release whatever is inside.

The cave is both foreign and unsurprising. On the edge of an eternal spring, Roisin lies in a box. What remains of her. But I don't doubt that a considerable magic source is with her, she is rumoured to have been the most powerful Calahi to have ever lived. I also don't doubt that it's diminishing along with ours. Our generations have slowly diminished in power over time, that's always been known, and the firsts of us are revered. But during my lifetime this decline has increased in speed. Small signs at first and then the undeniable, tangible decline.

And then we had to start Giving, too.

A lightly sparkling expanse stretches before us, reflecting the night sky – but there's no sky to reflect. Deep blue flowers skirt the edge of the water, butterflies dancing on their petals.

Across the water, I can just make out a black slab. It's not like what we find in the Realm but is reminiscent of a concrete grave one might find in the human world. Just a raised concrete rectangle, nothing to mark it out as special.

Dipping my toe in the shallow water, I begin to walk across, pausing only to take Ciara's instructions. Ciara and Lish to come with me, the others to stand guard against the Custodian when he arrives. I have no doubt he will. The water doesn't change depth as the three of us make our way across, our boots splashing quietly. Lish's breathing evens out as we cross the middle and the water doesn't get any deeper.

Her hands shake fractionally at her sides, but her focus remains resolutely on the slab. Tomb. I like to think she's a different woman to the one I first met but it's just that her steely core is more visible now. Now, she's adjusted more to our world and the presence of magic, and who she is. In no small part thanks to Lochlain, of course, but the rest of us played a part as well, her human friends – family, as she calls them – included.

We're mere steps from the sand on the far side of the cave, several arm lengths from Roisin's tomb, and I glance back to the others circled around the place we dropped, prepared to defend it against the incoming army.

An unidentifiable unease starts to prickle at my neck as the water eddies around us.

'Move,' Lish says, pulling me to the far edge.

Beneath me, the ground shakes, throwing us into each other.

We stand shakily on the shore as a blinding white lightning flashes, the thunder that follows almost dropping me to my knees. As I look up, six figures land crouched before us. The mud and dust flying up around their knee-high boots with the impact of their entrance.

All the oxygen is sucked from my chest.

Wings.

They have white wings.

Large, blindingly bright, wings that graze the ground behind them.

'Oh – I – kneel,' I say hoarsely to the others, hoping I was both loud enough for them to hear but quiet enough for the winged Calahi not to notice. They draw to standing and wait. Motionless.

Either Lish and Ciara heard me, or they can feel the authority, the history, that radiates from these six individuals. They drop to the ground as it envelopes me in a hard, unyielding embrace.

The Sentinels of the First Queen.

The Sentinels that started it all.

The mystery of Roisin's magic that supposedly sent her mad has remained the most debated story of our history. While most debate the hows and whys of her madness, if it was even true; I've always wondered what her Sentinels' role was in this. What happened to the Sentinels who were never written about again?

It seems now I have the answer. Roisin never went mad, she was killed by the sisters. And her devoted Sentinels have guarded her body for countless lifetimes. It seems extraordinary that they have never been mentioned in our histories.

A small kernel of humble happiness burns in the back of my mind. Now I know, I will be able to share the knowledge with the Manorynxes that will come after me. Because there should be more than one. There is simply too much knowledge, and too much at stake if we lose it.

Assuming we make it out of here.

I keep my mouth shut and my head down. The power of these early Calahi far outstrips that of our current generations and I have no read on what to expect in this situation. Being obliterated doesn't take my fancy today. Not after the promise in Ciara's face when she'd kissed my cheek earlier.

Lish's fingers are pressed into the damp, dark sand and I focus on those while we wait.

'You may rise,' a voice that speaks of dreams and histories says. One that sounds eerily like the voice I encountered on our way here – that asked me who I am.

Gradually, I rise to my full height, taking in the First Sentinel closest to me. Laced white boots end at the knee giving way to deep blue tights moulded around corded thigh muscles. A broad, statuesque chest is covered in a mid-thigh length tunic that leaves the shoulders and arms exposed; gold and copper armoured shoulder plates strap cross-ways over the chest.

My gaze skips the face and lifts straight to the majestic white wings that tower over the shoulders.

Angel.

This is what humans refer to as an angel.

But as I find the face I should've looked at from the beginning, the dual ringed eyes clearly mark them as my ancestors.

'Finished?' asks the most handsome female I've ever seen.

Her obsidian skin is stretched flawlessly over high cheek bones, straight white teeth in a full mouth. Her pale hazel eyes ringed with turquoise flash not with irritation, but curiosity.

'Sorry,' I say, realising I have no idea how to address these historical figures. 'It ... has been some time since Calahi like yourselves have been present in the Realm.'

I glance briefly at the five others, trying to take them in, too. They all share the similar physical features of obvious strength and agility, and almost identical wings. If I had time to look for longer I imagine I would find small differences in each of the sets. But, if the legends are true, these First Sentinels were selected for being the best of the best from across the entire Realm. Their flaws will be few.

'And it has been some time since we have seen other Calahi,' she says, calling my attention back to her strong face. 'Are you really what we have become?'

The question saddens me, rather than offends. I knew from all the learning of history that we have changed much as the source of all magic slowly declined, but to see it in such stark comparison is jarring. How great we could have been if we'd understood how to keep a balance, how not to hide in the shadows, and taught the humans to value our shared world.

'Yes,' I say, 'we are what remains.'

I glance at Ciara and Lish, who are each staring with different expressions of awe. Although there is considerably less comprehension on Lish's face.

'We are some of the most powerful that remain.' My voice is quiet as I let my words drop.

The eyes of the other First Sentinels slide to me in disbelief, one cocks his head. The female in front of me exhales.

'That is a rather sorry state of affairs,' she notes in that voice that's both old and young. Wise and sorrowful. 'But we know Roisin's legacy has not been realised. Tell me you are here to release us.'

'We are,' Ciara says.

'Who did you bring?' the First Sentinel asks.

I hadn't thought about how to introduce Lish to those that still serve another Queen of Airlie. One who was Queen for the entire Realm, before it was split into the three Courts, and was certainly not half-human.

I glance again at Lish and Ciara, the latter nodding subtly. Lish looks wide-eyed at me, seeking guidance. I don't dare look backward to register what the others can see. But nor have I heard them splashing across the shallow lake. A sudden understanding reignites the apprehension in my mind.

'This,' I gesture to Lish, 'is the current, rightful, Queen of Airlie.' All First Sentinels assess Lish and her cheeks colour, even in the dim light of underground. 'Ciara Wolverton and myself are her Sentinels.'

One of the winged Calahi laughs. The female attempts to silence him with a look and he rolls his eyes.

'Rightful?' he says. His voice is deeper than the female's but has the same, almost hypnotic quality. 'Meaning she is not actually occupying the Throne?'

'Correct,' Lish says, her voice only slightly wobbly. 'The Throne is officially, for the moment, held by a Custodian.'

'And you call yourselves Sentinels.' She scoffs. 'You have a Wolverton though,' she says, sizing up Ciara. 'That is of some amount of relief – that the guardian's of Roisin's line haven't completely disappeared.'

'It's a complicated history,' Lish says, glancing at Ciara, 'and I imagine there are some things about the current state of the Court that you might find disappointing.'

My heart kicks at the limb she's gone out on. Telling these Calahi how badly we've failed may not be the best strategy.

'And you intend to correct the course?' the winged leader asks. I allow myself to exhale.

'I certainly intend to try,' Lish says. 'We all intend to try.' She gestures around the cave indicating Ciara and me and those behind us.

'And yet you have no crown,' she says.

The red haired one eases his neck to the side as if he's stretching the muscles. 'And that one,' he says, looking straight at me. 'Lied. She's not a Sentinel.'

My stomach lurches and I frantically look for a way to politely object, but the gaze of all six First Sentinels moves past us a moment before the sound reaches my ears – the telltale slide of sand and the immediate clashing of swords as forces drop through.

The quiet of the cavern is shattered by the screams and grunts of battle. A male First Sentinel, with raven hair and pale eyes, flicks his fingers and a shield is thrown up around us. Whether it includes us on purpose or not, I can't tell. We teeter on its edge.

Lish spins on the spot as she takes in the black uniforms of the Guard charging around the others, a swell of Royalists with them.

'Dammit,' Lish breathes.

Will takes a fist to the stomach and lashes out at the soldier, dropping him to his knees. Rory spins him by the shoulder and shoves him out onto the water. Pointing to us and shouting something I can't make out. Lochlain and Rory fight alongside Daire and Callie, but I quickly lose them in the sea of bodies as the Custodian's army and ours come together.

The Custodian himself remains seemingly absent.

'Are they with you?' the handsome female asks.

'Not all of them,' Ciara says.

'Can you help?' I ask the female First Sentinel.

She watches for a moment before lifting her gaze to the roof, to the same place we sank through from the other side.

Slowly, dramatically, the Custodian descends. Hands outstretched like a deity bestowing his grace on the world. Lochlain shifts to almost underneath him and throws one of the short-bladed knives he keeps at his chest. It bounces to the ground, and the Custodian grins down at him.

'Magic is wonderful, isn't it?' the Custodian says.

The Guard fan out under some unseen order and start to push our forces into the centre of the lake.

'Seize her,' the Custodian demands, pointing straight at Lish.

What could almost be exactly half of the Guard turn to face us where we stand, by Roisin's tomb, staring at Lish.

The Custodian doesn't bat an eyelid at the winged First Sentinels.

At Lish's side, Ciara and I blend our magic into a shield to protect her, and ourselves, from the oncoming Guard. The blank faced humans racing across the shallow lake, swords out – I note they're not carrying guns today.

The First Sentinels take two, coordinated, steps and place themselves between the three of us and the oncoming unit. Holding them short of the shore by an invisible barrier. Ciara and I hold our own shield as well. I suck in a small hope they might be about to help.

The Custodian walks behind the Guard, and they part for him as he makes his way to the front.

'Halt,' the lead female asks. 'These three claim to have come to release us, you shall not pass.'

The Custodian's face thunders. 'She lies.'

The First Sentinels watch him for a moment, and I let myself focus on the face that betrayed my whole Court, before they let him beyond their grip and he saunters towards us. The Custodian's gaze finds Lish and he points his jewel hilted sword at her.

'She is the reason Airlie has no Queen.'

The six Sentinels, still in unison, turn on their heels and face Lish, their faces stone. The red haired one looks at me and smirks, as if he's just caught us in a second lie.

Fuck.

CHAPTER FORTY-THREE

LISH

My whole body trembles.

'*She* executed our Queen,' says the one that killed her.

'No,' I say softly.

'No.' More loudly this time. 'You killed her,' I insist. 'I was there.'

'Exactly, your very presence killed her.'

I flinch.

Lochlain's restraint thins as it strums on my skin, his emotions having returned to being fully accessible to me. His shield remains around Will, the Royalists and the Guard held in an uneasy standoff as they watch to see how my interaction with the Custodian plays out. If he will get to the tomb before me.

His face is sincere as he looks at me and I realise he almost believes what he's saying. That killing the Queen, my mother, and taking her Throne was my fault, and not because he operates as though those in positions of authority should have more power than others.

But I only need to remember who had ready access to food and shelter in Rhyton to know that equation does not benefit the many. It benefits the one. In this case, the Custodian. And I have never been someone who can support that belief. Not when it was just Will and I fighting for each other in the orphanage, or when my entire Guard team was out on patrol, or pushing myself for the Team Leader role so I could represent them better.

And not now, when I have a blended team of Calahi and humans who all fight, and give, for the same thing, a team who fight for a world that thrives, in every corner. A world where the Mother isn't sacrificed for greed and the very thing that gives us life isn't sucked from our souls. A place where hope can build into life.

I startle when the iron grip of one of the winged creatures that fell from the sky finds my upper arm, realising I have stepped back into him. Stopping me from getting too close to Roisin's tomb.

I stare numbly at the hand holding me in a vice.

She was powerless to stop him when he cracked her skull, and left her to die on the hot, vinyl floor while her six-year old daughter watched. While I watched. The flashes of memory slam back into me, those from when I was a child overlaid with what I remember the day I listened to the Custodian's message in Ciara's house.

The one holding my arm flinches slightly and shares a meaningful look with the woman whose skin is the colour of midnight.

I look back to Will, the man I never would have found if I hadn't been shuffled to that orphanage. I focus on his chestnut-brown hair, bronze eyes, and kind mouth that I've grown up looking at; I remember the way his chin squared as we grew, how much harder it got to beat him at things, how mercilessly he teased and challenged me. But also how he's unfailingly supported me for almost my whole life, how he gave me a different sort of power. I clench my fists, my muscles tensing under the grip of the Sentinel.

The main winged female looks at the Custodian. 'If she cannot release us, are you suggesting you can?'

The Custodian nods. My gut swirls and I tug against the grip of the male holding me. But he's harder than stone.

'I have the means to release you,' he says solemnly.

The six uniformed ones exhale, their shoulder plates dipping a fraction.

'First, you must tell us why you wish to release us. Convince us of your motivation for Roisin's power. Tell us why you are strong enough to release it from its binds.' A golden male towers over the Custodian, his wings flared slightly to each side.

The smile on the Custodian's face doesn't falter.

'Of course,' he says inclining his head. 'I, Custodian and ruler of Airlie, have spent my life defending the Calahi of this Court, and the Realm, against threats both open and concealed. I desperately search for a solution to our declining magic, and this is a burden I am willing to bear to help us through these challenging times. To channel my magic, and Roisin's power, into mechanisms that will make us great again. We were great once, and so we will be again. I assure you of that.'

Ciara's face is livid, but she doesn't move against the large sword one of the winged ones has pointed directly at her.

The winged Calahi, I am now beginning to understand, must have been Roisin's Sentinels – or something like it. They bow their heads slightly in one motion, their wings pulling together above their spines.

Disbelief washes through my veins like ice. My gaze skips across the group around me, grappling to catch on to some other meaning here. They didn't just accept that, did they?

'You may begin to attempt the transfer,' the woman says. 'Do you have what you need?'

'No! Do you know what he has been doing to the Calahi?' I clutch at the Sentinel who has only just let me go, my arm aching. 'Have you seen what he's done to the very people he claims to want to save?'

Aeyva spins to the lead Sentinel.

Ciara draws her own sword, the sound echoing off the shallow water.

All six Sentinels fix their gaze on her as if they share a single mind.

Aeyva all but stops breathing.

'I asked if you have what you need?' the dark skinned one says, looking back to the Custodian.

For a moment, the contrast of such a beautiful being condemning us all to death is jarring, outside my scope of understanding. It is death she commits us to. The Custodian will never allow anyone here with me to live past today and he will continue to bleed the Calahi of Airlie dry. More humans will fall to him and then the world itself will fall. Nuala's vision will come to be – a world not only no longer supported by the slimmest access to Roisin's magic, a world in a hastening downward spiral, the magic meant to sustain it instead wielded as a weapon against it.

Because Kailoh is right, what is the power of creation if it's not also the power to destroy?

'I do,' he says, slipping a container of sorts from his short jacket.

Silently, a group of ten Guard flank him – five on each side.

My fingers shake visibly now, my knees going weak. Both from my own stress and Lochlain's overwhelming anger. His desperation to save his home, his own family.

The Custodian's steps towards Roisin's tomb are purposeful and confident.

I launch myself at him as he makes to pass me, screaming, but the air is knocked from my lungs as the stone arm of the golden Sentinel hooks around my stomach. He holds me to his hard, cold body again – a stone statue come to life. I kick against his shins and tear into his forearm with my nails, sweat beading on my forehead.

He doesn't move.

His breathing doesn't even change.

My skin prickles almost hard enough to bleed.

The Custodian puts the container on the top of the tomb as the winged Sentinels create a wall between him and us. I don't need to know their history to know they are more powerful than anyone in this room. A thought that's both awe-inspiring and fuels the anger in my chest. My small flame burning in protest that these powerful beings cannot see, cannot help – or won't.

A smile is on the Custodian's face when he turns back to the Guard nearest him.

'We do an honourable thing here today,' he says, loud enough for everyone in the Resting Place to hear him. 'Roisin's magic has been trapped here for too long – inhibiting our ability to regenerate in the face of so much loss, so much destruction by the human world that it started to drain our own.'

I pull in a slow breath, our views on that are not so misaligned – except I know the worlds are inextricably connected.

'Today, I will release Roisin from this ... purgatory. I will take her magic back to the centre of Airlie where we need it most. Where, in me, it will fuel our Realm back to its full strength.'

I glance back to the Royalists, those few I can see past the impossibly large chest of the Sentinel that still grips me like a cage. None of them seem to have a flicker of doubt on their faces.

'Today, the human world will give a small portion of what they've taken. To aid us in righting the balance for the Realm.'

'No. Don't do this.' I turn into the golden Sentinel, twisting in his arms and land blows to his gut with my fists. 'He's going to kill them. The whole world needs her power, not just him!' I scream my frustration.

The Custodian takes the final step back to the tomb. The place of the greatest power of the world. The magic *of* the world.

One of the Sentinels inclines his head at the Custodian, gesturing him to continue.

'I have the power of humans and Calahi combined,' he says to the concrete slab, as if he's addressing Roisin directly. 'And I have the blood of a Wolverton. One inextricably connected to Roisin's line.'

My heart sinks like a stone.

Is that what it will take? That it doesn't matter how twisted the joining of the human and Calahi lives are? Or that he will take what is pure, and good, and mine, to let us all rot?

The Custodian pours the contents of the container into the three indentations in the top of the tomb and the metallic scent of blood hits my nose.

This is why Lochlain was left for dead in the snow. The Custodian needed his blood – the blood of a wolf, my wolf – to give him access to Roisin.

The Custodian flicks his hand backwards and the throats of the ten Guard nearest him split open, blood trickling down their fronts. Slowly at first and then in a nauseating flow, almost synchronised, before they collapse to the ground.

He didn't even look at them as they fell.

I want to be sick. Rage thickens my throat.

Long sleeves fall away from the hands he stretches out and places flat on the tomb.

Nuala's vision flashes back to me. The stream the woman created. The wolves. The flower that died with her.

The room vibrates. Slowly at first and then my knees begin to shake. Silence fills my ears as the rest of the Guard and the Royalists remain in a standoff, every face now watching the Custodian, and it hits me. The Custodian is like me – he can draw her magic out like I can absorb others' as well. An ability I can only assume the sisters didn't have, and it makes him even more unpredictable. With access to all the magic of Airlie, is there anything his own magic doesn't know how to do?

A soft, blue light leeches out under his palms where they rest on the grey stone, quickly burning to white, illuminating the Custodian's arms and the red veins running through them that now flow blue. He lets out a roar as the light races into and through him, and the cavern is momentarily plunged into total darkness.

Roisin fell in that meadow, just like we're all going to fall here today.

'Lochlain!' I scream. 'I need you.' My voice is only a breath now. 'Stop him,' I say.

I can't see him, but the sound of metal screeching on metal begins again. Men and women gasp and groan as they drop in the dark sand to die, abandoned by the promise of a better life.

The winged Sentinel who grips me spins away from Roisin's tomb as the light returns, away from the Custodian, to the chaos erupting around us. My legs swing out with the force of his spin, my ribs compressed in the iron grip of his forearm.

Aeyva surges towards Riley where she battles a small circle of Guard, Aeyva's hand clutching fist-sized blades that whirl around her as she spins. Blood seeps into the water beneath them. More and more humans fall, but it's not just them. Blue and green clothes of the Royalists litter the ground as well.

Inside another circle, further across the lake, are Lochlain and Will. But I see what the Guard don't – their circle is thinning, attacked from the outside in as Rory, Callie, and Daire move in with the Royalists.

My energy starts to dip from fighting against the statue that holds me.

'Please stop,' I beg the golden one. 'He doesn't intend to do good.' I gasp, my lungs crushed. 'Those people didn't need to die. I wish you could see,' I say, picking up my struggle again. 'Let me go!'

'I see,' he says quietly, letting me slide to the ground and turning me around by the shoulders.

It takes an enormous amount of my resolve to watch the Custodian glowing with Roisin's magic. To look at the power radiating from him. The power I should have claimed. The power I would have used to help the Calahi of Airlie, the Realm, and the humans in the world. A power I should have had access to as Queen. But I didn't take the Throne, I stole the crown instead. Now I stand, a witness to the sealing of the fate of our worlds.

CHAPTER FORTY-FOUR

LISH

'Watch,' the Sentinel says quietly, letting me go. My heart stutters in response, trying to tell me something.

The flower that died with Roisin, it was blue.

The Sentinel twists me again, back towards the other side of the cavern, away from the tomb.

A soft light emanates from the centre of the lake, stretching out to the edges, lighting the flowers on the edge. Including those that have been trampled. The light chases the darkness up the walls like a sunrise.

Butterflies of every size and colour fill the room.

The air in my lungs catches and, for a long moment, a strange hope blazes in my chest.

Green grass grows outward from the water's edge, rocks turn from black to grey in the light.

Love sustained her. In turn, she sustained the world ... Kailoh's words bounce around my head.

Turquoise water now sits in the middle of the cavern, far deeper than what we crossed.

Familiarity pulls at me.

'Airlie is mine,' the Custodian's voice comes from behind me. 'The *Realm* is mine. She should have trusted me,' he says, almost sadly, and I know immediately he's talking about my mother. 'At first, she didn't think we could do it – take Roisin's power and rebuild our world. Didn't think we'd be able to find a way to bolster our resources by tapping into the human world, the very world that was killing us. Then she met your father.' His voice takes on a harder edge. 'And she didn't think we *should* do it.'

My stomach knots at the mention of the father I have never known.

'No. She wanted to let them *join* us.' He scoffs. 'Wanted to find a human to give their perspective into righting both worlds. Because suddenly my suggestions weren't good enough. Were too *dangerous* she'd said. I told her, then, I would do it with or without her,' he continues, 'that Airlie needed our strength, and here I am. She was always so desperate to do good, Catriona. Always wanted to give herself to make others happy, apart from Siosal of course.' He walks around the First Sentinels, towards me. 'But it made her so risk averse she hamstrung herself. We could have easily ruled and sustained the Realm between us, but, in the end, she wanted nothing more than Airlie. Just Airlie and her frail human. She forced my hand the day you were conceived.'

He reaches my side, closer than I have been to him since Lochlain's swearing in ceremony. I skim over his light brown skin, broad nose and dark hair that's softly going white, the power of Roisin thrumming in the air. My heart beats harder and the memories push at my chest. My gaze lands on Lochlain's blood that drips from his fingers and dries in a sticky mess on his palms.

Blood of a Wolverton that loves me. Me, a distant descendant of Roisin's line.

Roisin was the First Queen.

His face scrunches in disgust.

'I couldn't let an entire world fade away because you were born. Because the Queen of Airlie wanted you to have access to the human world as much as the Realm. That world is fucking *destroying* ours and I knew how to use them to fix mine. Something she should have done long before she died. But I knew she never would once you were born.'

I inhale the truth of his words. She gave everything to protect me, including giving up her responsibility to her people. To protect my innocence, she made a monumental sacrifice. Because she thought she had time to bring me back and find the Star together. Not because she was weak, as the Custodian is implying. But because she was strong. Because she believed in a better world.

'You're so like her. Wanting to be a Queen but unable to bring yourself to make any hard decisions. Choosing those so far beneath you as your ... companions. Choosing to try and save the humans, the exact reason the Calahi are suffering as we speak. How did you ever think you – a half-human bastard, shackled with a serving class Calahi – would truly rule a race as magnificent as mine? *Provide* for us?'

The man was her lover, the first Wolverton.

The hands that hold me release their pressure, blood racing back to the indents they've left in my tender shoulders and arms.

Love sustained her.

Find the Star.

Roisin was the First Queen.

The flower that died was blue.

I don't take my eyes from the Custodian's face as I step towards him. So close I can smell his breath, can see the faint lines around his eyes, how attractive he would have been if his soul wasn't rotting behind his eyes.

Behind him, the light starts to creep back down the walls and towards the edge of the lake that darkens to black once more. The light in the Custodian's chest begins to fade. My mind swirls with faded memories and conversations and sacrifices.

That misplaced hope in my chest begins to fade with the colours in the cavern. I know it's a reflection of what will happen if we don't have access to her magic. It's a reflection of what's already happening throughout the world. It's exactly what the sapphire showed us.

'I *will* rule this Court,' I say. 'Because they are not all like you. They are great and magnificent as they are. They are hurting now, yes – because of you.'

Pride ripples over my skin as Lochlain hears my words. But it's not only him – I haven't shut out Will and Riley.

'But I will restore them. I will restore *balance* without subjecting either world to the cruelty of the other. I will not take everything for myself. I will serve first and take second. I will do it with love, and I will do it while I save the fucking world.'

Butterflies start to drop from the sky and lie dead on the ground, their colours fading into blackness.

You must release them before all the butterflies fall.

A sunshine yellow, fading to grey, catches my eye and the memory of my crown of yellow wildflowers bursts forth. A memory I have treasured and tucked away for safekeeping.

Her magic is nature – the cornerstone – and it's been trapped here, in this tomb, when it should have been freed.

Released, the Sentinels said. They're being here is part of her magic, too, and needs to be let go.

Silence echoes.

'You're done here, *Alice*.' The Custodian glowers as he throws a fist to the sky.

The roof begins to fall, and hundreds of soldiers drop into the underground cavern, adding to the already brutal and bloody fight that's happening across the lake.

'INCOMING!' Lochlain's voice sounds from somewhere near me, the smell of blood quickly filling my senses.

Lochlain and Rory appear at my side. Rory spins and slams the blunt side of his axe into the temple of a soldier. It's not the blood seeping from her ear as she falls that captures my attention, but the uniform she wears. And the black veins that disappear into her shirt. She was once a Guard member, was once human. A human injected with magic that didn't belong to her.

Magic that should be given to the earth that's trying to sustain us. Because that's what we do for what we love – we give and it gives back. A cycle.

Looking up I realise they are not the only uniforms I can see. The entire cavern is a mess of black, blue, green and bright red. But our numbers are less than the Guard. Less than the humans who unwittingly destroy everything I am fighting for to make their lives better. Their numbers are small in comparison, but the Courts of Airlie and Mercasia are also here. My heart beats with a little more purpose. The Custodian thought he was dropping only his forces here, but he brought ours, too.

My hair whips around my face as Lochlain's shield slams into place around me.

'Where—' Rory starts.

I cut him off by pointing straight at Riley, where Callie has just about fought her way to, she and Will fighting in tandem.

'We need to go,' Lochlain says in my ear, breathless.

The Custodian laughs as he stands back with the First Sentinels and I think how much I'd like to run a blade through him. But when he's the one that holds all of Roisin's power, I don't dare.

'Feel free to run, Alice, there is no need for you here.' I know the use of my human name is intended to mock me – clearly, the Custodian doesn't know how proud I am of my heritage, how much I trust in the love my mother had for my father.

'No,' I say to Lochlain. 'I know what I have to do, I just have to find a way. I need more time ...' I glance around, how little time we have against this many is abundantly clear.

Lochlain looks about us, spinning on the spot. 'Ciara!' he yells when he sees her, her head jerking to find him.

She eyes Aeyva briefly before carving her way through the throngs, heads rolling if they get too close. She's breathing hard when she reaches us, and I feel ashamed of my steady breath. Of my unstained weapons.

Lochlain looks regretfully at her.

'We need you, Kiki,' he says. Her eyes flare.

She blows out a loud breath as she closes the space between us. Lochlain takes her elbow.

'There's no other way, Ciara. We won't make it out of here without you.' He looks around the cavern. 'We don't have enough numbers against the humans, we were never going to.'

The colour drains from Ciara's face in recognition of the truth in his statement. I glance at Lochlain, who remains looking at her. Imploring. Begging.

'He's got her power, Ciara,' he says quietly. 'We need to get our forces out before the Guard destroy them. We need'—he looks at me—'we need to give Lish time to try and fix it.'

'Whenever you're ready,' the golden Sentinel says. I jump at his proximity.

'Ready for what?' I ask, my heart beating as time contracts around me.

He looks at Ciara expectantly.

She looks wildly at the bloody scene unfolding on the other side of Lochlain's shield.

'I ...' The panic in her voice tears at my chest.

'What is it, Lochlain? What are you asking?' My words are hurried and stumble over each other as I try to understand, scanning the battle for Blaire and Phoenix.

Ciara turns black eyes on me, the hopelessness in them hurting my chest.

'Ciara, tell me,' I plead.

'Death.' Her gaze doesn't leave mine and I feel myself pulled into their endless depths. 'My *gift* is death. Destroying all barriers. I can't control it.'

I frown.

'That can't be true. I've seen you use it and it's never resulted in death.'

'Then you weren't looking in Elenlea – you haven't seen me with the stopper off.'

Aeyva launches herself from the shoulders of one soldier to plunge her short blade into the neck of another and I remember the feel of her magic. Of Rory's.

'Let me help,' I say, suddenly confident as the words leave me.

'What?' Lochlain asks, his eyes flashing. 'What if it takes you, too?'

Ciara protests next to me, but I don't hear her.

I look at the cavern around me, at the blue, green and scarlet clad warriors giving their all. The humans that fight in the corner where I can now see Blaire's form as she slices her way through the body of another person. I can do the same. However long they might have left, now that the Custodian has Roisin's power, I want them to have. They deserve to make the most of what we have left.

And I will do what my mother was going to. I will step into her shoes, not as Queen, but as the one who will give it all to do her best for the world.

Lochlain looks towards the Royalists fighting alongside Kailoh's forces, their numbers dwindling as the losses add up. The sounds of the battle around us screaming in our ears. He squeezes my hands as he looks back to me.

'You must go Lochlain, they need you,' I say urgently.

'No. They fight for—'

'*You*, Lochlain. They know you. They fight for you. You and Aeyva – all of you – you need to go to them. Help them, *lead* them. Don't let them die without knowing we were here. And get my family out. Please.'

'I can't say goodbye to you, Lish,' his voice cracks. 'You know I don't leave anyone behind, least of all you. I don't care what happens to the Realm. I will light the match myself and watch it burn if it means I have you.' He cups my face in his palm, my chest like a vice.

The warmth of his words washes over me, how easy it would be to say okay. And yet I cannot let him.

'I know,' I breathe at his chest, 'and that means more than you will ever know.' He looks warily at me as I meet his gaze. 'But, right now, there is no other choice but the Realm and Driarn. I am not worth more than those out there.'

'You are to me,' he whispers. For a moment the rest of the world ebbs away.

I stand on my toes and pull his head down to meet mine. The smell of smoke teases my nostrils, the sounds of the dying intensifying and forcing their way back in. There is no time to savour this, savour him.

'To have had you, Lochlain, is the greatest gift I could know. I will look for you on the Blue Pointed Star. I am yours. Always.'

The flower in the meadow was blue. Like the light that's sparkled in the sky more times than I can count.

His lips crush mine, the salt of the tears I can't hold back filling both our mouths. My heart thrums with a familiar pain as I push him away. I know what I need to do. My mother told me to follow the wolves. Benny told me they would guard me. And they have. I'm here. But never did any of them say I needed to take the magic of Roisin for myself.

'Go,' I say.

'See you on the Star,' he says, barely audible.

A solitary tear courses its way through the dust and mud on his face.

CHAPTER FORTY-FIVE

LISH

I watch him disappear into the fray, his shoulders slumped forward, my skin burning with each of our pain. After a few paces he straightens his spine and draws himself to full height. The first soldier who looks his way is almost sliced in half with the fury of his sword.

From a swarming mass of clashing bodies, I see Haryk run to Lochlain's side before I turn away. Back towards the Custodian and the winged Calahi as I grapple with what I need to do.

'So bittersweet these goodbyes,' the Custodian says, hands clasped behind his back. 'But what's your next move Alice? I have far greater resources than you. Your supporters will die here.'

I glare at him, conscious of Lochlain's emotions thinning from me as he moves further away and towards the Royalists.

The Custodian smiles softly. 'I'm pleased you're here, in the end. Wherever Catriona might be, I hope she can see I have succeeded where she could not. It brings me great comfort that you are witnessing it firsthand. I never wanted you to step foot in the Realm – certainly not in my Court. But I feel it's better this way. At least now you will see that I am right to have denied you.' He holds his palms up. 'With this power, the Calahi will endure. We will endure the human infestation and stamp you all out for the betterment of our world. I suppose I could thank you for one thing, though. Disposing of the Eternal Queen did leave me with one less problem – I would never have bowed to her, the same as I never will to you.'

He thrusts a hand towards me and I brace for impact, but none comes. A confused frown crosses his face as he looks at his hand and tries again.

Ciara grips my hand, her face grim, as she drops to a kneel in the sand, dragging me with her. The wet sand seeps moisture through the fabric of my pants as Ciara presses her forehead to mine.

'Take it and hold it,' she says quietly.

With every ounce of energy I have, I pull with my flame. Drowning myself with her magic. It's gold and hot. Burning lava down my throat, under my ribs, in my fingers. Ciara's fingernails bite into the back of my hand.

Flashes of General Siosal clutch at me and my flame stutters.

My eyes burn when I open them again. Ciara's pale but there's a resolution in her face that we can do this for all of us.

Aeyva is with us between blinks and looks questioningly at me. She starts to ask but, whatever my expressions says seems to be enough, and she doesn't voice the question.

'You can do this, Kiki,' she says. 'We can't have life without death. You are in control.' She backs away to face the Custodian, keeping him at bay.

'Tell me how, Ciara,' I say.

She stands again, pulling me with her once more.

'Close your eyes and visualise who goes and who stays. The image will waver, but you can never lose sight of who stays. Make sure you focus on who stays. That's what I—' she breaks off.

The palms of my hands burn, my fingers tingling as Ciara's magic begs to be let out. I can almost hear it calling to me, persuading me to let loose.

Ciara starts to say the names of who is here, who I need to remember.

Almost all the butterflies have fallen now, the flowers on the edges of the lake fading away. Like the rush of magic is being called back home.

The Custodian is shouting beside me, his rage useless without Roisin's magic coming at his command – as if it's faded with the life of the cavern. Aeyva's shield now takes the place of Lochlain's and mutes his voice slightly.

The sounds of the dying don't abate. A shiver runs down my spine at the thought of how I'm about to add to it. I can no longer think of those in the Guard as my colleagues. They are no longer human, not Calahi either. Now, they are my enemy.

They are my targets. Our targets.

Ciara's voice grows quieter, and I lean into the hum of her magic in my veins.

I let go.

Their faces carousel around my mind spinning faster and faster until they start to blur. I see the first line of black veined soldiers fall and then the heat of the wind burns my eyes and forces them closed.

Sand whips my face and stings my cheeks.

Screaming fills my ears.

I search for Ciara's chanting in the cacophony of the dead, dying and fleeing.

Her rhythm slows and I breathe in time with her. Digging my heels into the wet sand to pull back on the carousel of faces. *Slow them down, slow them down.*

I hold each face in my mind for the duration of a breath, focusing on the details I can see. Those I can recall. For those I can't see, like the Royalists and Kailoh's unit, I recall what I can and let my heart say the rest.

An eternity passes but slowly the deafening sounds soften into clarity before they begin to fade away.

It's done now. Open your eyes. Someone who is not Ciara says in my mind. Ice cold hands grip my arms over the bruises they created and shake me.

I peel my eyes open. The sand and grit having found their way through my squinted lids and tears trying to wash them out. Blinking, I look around.

The ground is littered with black uniformed soldiers. The bodies of those we lost now hidden underneath.

It's the quiet that makes my heart beat irregularly. The quiet of death. The death I have just caused, the scale of which is incomprehensible. A small number of Guard remain, and they look on, unblinking, at the armed forces around them. Forces that now include Blaire and Phoenix and Kailoh. The Commissioner pulls himself to standing next to Blaire, blood on his face and the look of a battle weary warrior underneath.

The golden Sentinel is beside me, his hands no longer touching me. The midnight skinned woman joins me on the other side. A strawberry blonde Sentinel whose face I don't remember helps Ciara to her feet, Aeyva with her. A tiny bead of relief registers.

I look around the cavern unseeing. Looking but not finding. Fingers flutter at my mouth and I realise, dimly, they belong to me.

'There,' says the golden one, pointing to the other side of the lake now choked with bodies.

A faint copper light emanates from the corner. A battered shield.

Lochlain's shield.

They run to us, at different speeds, swords out. And it's the Commissioner who immediately faces the Custodian, firing a great sense of pride in me. That, despite his appalling decisions, he's still here – fighting for all of us to correct the mistakes he's made.

'That was quite wasteful, Adelais – particularly for a Wolverton,' the Custodian says, lifting a brow at Ciara and showing no sign of concern that he wasn't able to attack me earlier. 'But there are more humans where they came from. Always more humans.'

I stalk towards him, not caring that my sword is dragging in the sand. Jamming it into the shield that he's somehow still holding on to, the magic gives but doesn't break. The Custodian's face flickers with uncertainty as he looks to where his shield weakens slightly around my blade.

'I know something you don't,' I say. 'It wasn't just Roisin's magic that gave her power. She was gifted by the Mother because she shared her love, and her gifts, and life itself.'

His gaze narrows.

'You have done nothing but take.' I circle his bubble now, wondering what it will look like when he realises he can't hold her power, just like the sisters couldn't, that it's already draining away from him. 'My mother – and who knows how many before that – the Airlean's magic, the freedom of the people in the Guard. And none of it because you loved anything other than the idea of power. You think you are the only one who could imagine a future for the Realm. You are as arrogant as the sisters.'

Aeyva smiles as I complete the circle. 'You can't have life without death,' she says and the winged First Sentinels raise their swords.

Inside the shield, the Custodian starts to shake.

'What's happening?' he asks, looking at the winged Calahi. 'I released you from this. I took her power – you're free.'

Kailoh joins our strange audience, his hair pulled free and hanging around his shoulders.

'I think what your *Queen* is saying,' he says, 'is that you can't hold, or use clearly, Roisin's power without love – for the Wolvertons, the Mother, and the world Roisin created. Protect without claim.'

'You know what happened to the sisters who tried the first time, I'm sure?' I ask, not daring to look at the winged Sentinels to see what they are making of this. They haven't moved against me, and I take that as a good sign. 'After they were cursed?'

Three wolves enter our space, the one with amber eyes taking a seat on my left.

'We killed them,' I say.

The lead winged Sentinel lifts her sword higher, as if she might take the Custodian's head off when his shield comes down.

'You are *not* the Queen of this Realm!' the Custodian shouts.

'I'm still going to save it.'

The Sentinels look at me and the moment stretches out between us. Part of me wonders if I can make this choice. If it makes me as cold as him when he took my mother. But, as I look at those around me, I know it's the right one.

I nod once.

As one, the winged Sentinels step forward to the Custodian's shield and pierce their swords through it, dissolving the faint crackle of magic.

Testing the weight of my own sword as I walk towards him, I think of my mother, of the vision Nuala's tracing showed me of her being crowned. I didn't see her face in that image, but I imagine her watching me now as I exact justice on the Calahi that took her life from her – and from me. The Calahi that plummeted Airlie into this chaos.

Surrounded by Roisin's Sentinels, I lift my sword and strike, slamming my blade into him. Blood burbles from his mouth as he stares at me, uncomprehending. Briefly he looks down to his chest where my blade took its mark. And then his head lolls back and I let his body slide off my sword and onto the sand.

A rush of something I can feel, more than see, races away from him and back towards Roisin's tomb. I try not to drop to the ground in relief. I can do this. I can find a way to free her magic without holding it myself.

A blinding light fills the cavern and fades away as quickly as it came, leaving spots of light in my vision. A sparkling blue mirage is left in its wake. The blood pounding in my head increases the pressure behind my eyes.

I think I see a star. A blue star.

CHAPTER FORTY-SIX

LISH

Roisin's tomb now glows blue, the light colouring the blades held by the Sentinels. The soft, blue light darkens to the deepest sapphire, menacing black shots of lightning at the edges. A loose set of chains flaps wildly on one side, in the wind that's emanating from what looks like a star hovering over the concrete. I squint. The other half of the Star is tethered to something inside the tomb.

The wolves howl in unison, the sound echoing around the chamber and sending a tingling sensation down my spine.

'Our Queen,' says the lead winged Sentinel as the six of them turn to the light and drop to one knee. They remain in the sand as the sparkling blue light takes on the shape of a person.

Roisin.

The Sentinel looks around until her gaze falls on me. 'Do you have what you need to release us?'

I swallow. 'I don't know,' I say truthfully. 'But everything I have, everything I am, and everything I love are in this cavern. So if we don't have what we need, I honestly don't know what more we can do.'

'Do you have the sapphire?'

A quick breath of relief escapes me as Rory, Aeyva and Ciara all step forward with the pieces they hold. Opening their hands, the lead Sentinel takes them one by one and shows them to Roisin.

'Hmmm,' she says softly. 'The Calahi of Airlie, support of the Manorynxes, and understanding of how to wield death. And I assume you have the pendant as well?'

I nod, too exhausted to pull it from my clothes.

'You've done well,' she says, kindly, but I note the tinge of sadness in her voice. 'What those pieces of the sapphire represent are the key for taking my power. Having those people in your life that embody those connections is even better. You, and your friends from the other world, give life to the last element – that human and Calahi alike need to fight for our existence.'

Someone breathes a heavy sigh behind me. In addition to the sadness, there's something else about what she's saying. A 'but' she hasn't voiced yet. And she didn't call the sapphire the Star.

Find the Star, Benny had said.

The flower was blue.

The sparkling light in the sky has always been blue.

I suck in a loud breath as I realise we have. He was just wrong about what the Star was. It's not the sapphire.

Roisin is the Star.

The winged Sentinels each draw air deeply into their lungs and square their shoulders. As if they ready themselves for something, but they tuck their swords away.

As I look between them, I realise they are preparing to stay. Roisin said the sapphire – the tying together of the things it represents, symbolised again by the people and Calahi behind me, would let me take her power. She didn't say it would release them.

The thinning layer of butterflies flies around the top of the cavern as if searching for a way out.

'What do you need us to do?' I ask.

The lead Sentinel slowly reaches out and drops the pieces of sapphire back into Rory's hand and I watch numbly. Have we done all this to fail? Or only partially succeed? If I take Roisin's power, does she mean I can hold it, or will I be cursed like the sisters? Or would she give it willingly, only to be trapped here herself?

'I … have hoped for a Manorynx to free me from my binds,' she says quietly. 'But it would take an exceptionally skilled one to do what needs to be done.'

Slowly, Aeyva steps up next to me, her sword held loosely in her hand. 'I can do it.'

One of the winged ones grins knowingly at Aeyva.

'You might not survive it,' Roisin says.

'But I might.'

I understand then what Aeyva's doing. She's claiming the power of the Manorynx – the role Nuala wanted her to take. But not because Nuala gave it to her. Because she fought for it, learned it, and is giving the best parts of herself to use that power and knowledge to serve her world. And, at the same time, I realise that's what I was trying to do when I said no to Kailoh. It wasn't just about Lochlain, or having the Calahi of Airlie want to fight for me, or even me fighting for myself. It was me not wanting to have to wait for permission from anyone to be Queen. Not my mother, not the Custodian, or Kailoh, or the Calahi of Airlie.

Just me.

I take Aeyva's hand as I look at her. She nods, she knows what to do.

'We are the Queen of Airlie, and her most skilled Manorynx,' I say. 'And we will release you.'

Aeyva drops my hand and holds her own out to the sides, a wind starting to whip through the cavern, sand spiralling towards the roof.

The wind roars now, my eyes stinging and hair tearing free from its braid.

Aeyva mutters to herself as she stands, head bowed, and points her palms directly at the side of the concrete slab.

An inky blackness rushes from her palms and up the side of the tomb, slamming into Roisin's side.

The cavern shudders and the blue light of Roisin flashes brightly, temporarily blinding me.

As my vision clears, five winged Calahi surround Aeyva, where she slumps on the chest of the auburn-haired Sentinel. Palms loosely held skyward, on her knees, blood streams from her nose.

'Aeyva,' I say quietly, stepping towards her.

Her head remains bowed. Thick red dripping on the knees of the Sentinel holding her.

'She is removing the rest of my binds,' Roisin says from somewhere. 'Force alone won't be rid of them. I believe you removed the first when you killed the sisters.' Her face lifts in a shadow of a snarl and I belatedly realise I probably should have bowed to her.

'You are the Queen, you do not bow,' she says. 'But you know what you need to do.'

'I do.' I think I do anyway. 'Your magic was never intended to be kept by one person,' I say. 'Arlo was additionally gifted by the wolves to be your protector because your own magic would diminish as you fed the world. Created the world.'

I blink and she stands before me, hair blowing on a phantom wind. Her slight fingers reach for my chest and the Wolverton Pendant appears in the palm of her hand. Her smile turns sad but her eyes, pure sapphire, sparkle when they find mine once more.

'Do you know this is the first time I am seeing this in person?' she says. 'You wearing it all this time tells me much I would have liked to know.' My flame warms at the tone in her voice. 'I watched its creation – from afar. The love and the power that was poured into it.' She closes her eyes for a moment. 'The love and power of the Wolvertons.'

I think of what connects Lochlain and me, the way my heart and my skin and my magic responds to him. The way he helped me remember how to heal. But I also think of Ciara. And how she trusted me with her own lethal magic. And how, not once, did she ask for the pendant that is as much hers as it is Lochlain's.

The chains that remain fixed to one side of Roisin, clasped at her wrist and ankle, slip free and she shines brighter. Aeyva falls to the ground, her lips covered in her own blood. Her chest doesn't move. I step to her, heart in my throat, but a Sentinel grips my arm and shakes his head.

'There is no time,' he says, looking at the still reducing butterflies as others continue to fall around us. 'Roisin is free now, but it will be fleeting. If you want what she has, you need to take it now.'

Roisin nods. 'I give it willingly. I am ready to go.' She looks around at her Sentinels, her eyes shining with tears. 'As are they.'

'Do I need to make a wish?' I ask, my mother's voice echoing in my head, the story she used to tell me about the Blue Pointed Star and its power to grant our deepest desires.

Roisin pauses.

'A wish,' she repeats slowly. 'That is ... reducing it. But I have watched from afar for a long time – you have seen me in the sky, I think – and I now know the ways both Calahi and humans have to condense these ideas, to package them up and make them into pieces of information to be examined and labelled.' The contact on my cheek when she cups my face is cool, and vibrating. Like light is shimmering on my skin. 'Call it a wish if you like, my young Queen, I can see you know in your heart it is far more than that. And you know what needs to be done – that is the most important piece.'

She removes the pendant from my neck and wraps the chain around both our hands. I watch numbly. *Aeyva*. I blink. Roisin reaches into my vest and withdraws the blade Lochlain placed there before we went to the Airlie Palace. A family heirloom, he'd said. Roisin smiles at it, feeling the engraving in the handle. The pads of her fingers run over the etching of the Star and the wolves, the just visible creek that runs around a meadow. I wonder how long it has been since she smiled before today.

'This I have seen before,' she says quietly.

I gasp as she draws the gold blade across each of our palms, the blood catching in the chain of the Wolverton Pendant.

'The pieces please,' Roisin says, holding her bloodied hand out to Rory.

In her hands, the sapphires fall together to create a single stone as they once did before. She considers it a moment before pressing it to her chest briefly and passing it to the Sentinel. As Roisin wraps our fingers around the Wolverton Pendant, the chain tying us gently together, the Sentinel drops the other pieces of sapphire into the three holes in the lid of the tomb.

'Now, Adelais,' she says.

I reach for Ciara's magic that now simmers under my skin and push it into my own barrier, dissolving any semblance of space between Roisin and me. Breathing deeply, a stream of rich sapphire pulls towards me.

'She loved you,' she says. 'I have seen so many of my line, and I remember them all.'

The Custodian and I, our magic is – was—

'There is no connection like you are imagining,' Roisin says quietly. 'He was not of my line. But your mother – I certainly remember how much she loved you. And your father. All she wanted was the right to follow her dreams. To give you a life where you could follow yours.' Her breathing is slowing now, and I keep drawing deep breaths. 'A life in which you could choose to step into your power and not have someone else's view of what that was supposed to be forced on you.'

My flame burns white hot.

'That's it,' she says, her words slurring now. 'More, Adelais, you need to take more.' I close my eyes and lower myself deep into my gut. And I pull.

'Wait—' I say with my eyes closed. 'My mother thought we'd meet again on the Star. I told Nico he'd find Sofia there ... but... you're the Star. What—'

'I am the Star,' she says. 'The Blue Pointed Star. Just because I am no longer bound does not mean I don't exist. You releasing me will allow me to simply *be*. I will be in the flowers and the butterflies and the wolves. I will be in the blue skies, and the dark ones. And I will hold a space for you all in those places, too. So yes, Adelais, you will still find your mother in the Blue Pointed Star because love, once held, never disappears. We send it places to give us life. To every tiny thing, we give hope.'

A small, yellow butterfly flutters across my vision, even with my eyes closed, and somehow I know it's her. Tears fall slowly, dropping from my cheeks where I feel its wings brushing my skin.

Sapphire bleeds to gold and still I pull.

When the strands that fill me turn red, I stop and open my eyes.

Roisin falls before me, two Sentinels waiting to gently lift her and carry her away.

You cannot have life without death, Aeyva had said when I took Ciara's magic for the first time. I swallow. Is that what Roisin means by 'releasing'?

'*You know what you need to do*,' Roisin's voice echoes in my head. I watch as they walk away. Into nothing. '*Thank you for releasing us, our Queen*,' she says.

I turn to Aeyva, still a crumpled pile in the sand. I move to her, my feet heavy like a dream, and grip the blade I have found in my hand once more. Slick with my blood – and Roisin's.

Roisin's magic sings in my veins and I'm not sure my feet touch the ground despite their weight. My head spins as I look at Aeyva's lifeless form and drop to my knees next to her. She's almost gone. I can feel the last shreds of her leaving her body. I grip her wrist as I open my mind, recalling Nuala's vision and what we need to avoid. I remember the flowers I brought to life over the burnt remains of Ciara's house, the life I helped bring back to the dying Calahi girl, to Lochlain, and the feel of Roisin and my mother who died to put me here.

The yellow butterfly with its gold tipped wings.

Roisin's power thrums through my veins, my gold flame burning hotter than it ever has before.

And I make my wish as I slam my blade into Aeyva's palm, and the earth on the other side.

I scream as I let go.

As I purge Roisin's magic from my body and into the ground, through Aeyva, Nuala's visions whip past me and my head pounds. But they are different this time. Changing. Destruction to reconstruction. Death, to the first shaky tendrils of life. The last thing I see is the single blue wildflower from the meadow, dead before Roisin's body, now glowing with yellow petals where once they were blue.

My throat is ripped bare and I give it all. Every last thread.

Aeyva's arm jerks in my grip, Roisin's magic of creation having flowed through her as well, and her voice swims around me.

'Come now,' she says. 'We're done here.'

CHAPTER FORTY-SEVEN

AEYVA

I watch the water disappear over my pale pink toes, their nails now a deep red, and along the floor of the shower. There is no blood to wash off today but it's hard to forget how much blood this shower has seen.

This villa, that was once my transition place, is now our only place. A communal share house for far too many people and Calahi as Airlie begins to rebuild its capital. I think of the hopeful faces of the Calahi of Airlie as Tiernan crowned Lish in the rubble of Elenlea, and a spark of hope for Airlie flares in my own chest. A spark that was reflected in the faces of the Calahi around me. Haryk had done what he did best – talk. And there were now few Calahi who didn't know what Lish had done the night our city fell and in the days after, that she didn't kill Queen Catriona. For any that needed more convincing, I gave him permission to use Nuala's package of messages we took to Kailoh.

Taking my position as Lish's Manorynx, in partnership with Ciara as her Sentinel, was a moment I'd wished Nuala could have seen. I've not wanted to share much of my successes with anyone. But, now that Keeva has taken leadership of the Society and formally released me from my oath, I can completely be both what I wanted, and what Nuala passed onto me.

And I think she would have been proud of that. I know she would have been – proud that I am finally living my life in the light, not a darkness of my own making.

Forcing my eyes away from the shower floor, I finish washing and disappear to the bedroom, conscious the others will all want to be clean and tidy for today, too.

Deciding what to wear was harder than normal. With dresses hard to source in Airlie – they were mostly made in Elenlea – I had to get assistance from Kailoh's Court. I'd wanted to look my best, without trying to overshadow the main attraction. Kailoh got wind of what was happening and insisted on helping dress everyone. No doubt we will all look spectacular.

Tiernan knocks gently on the open door.

'The others are ready.'

The others are outside when I find them, just below the deck between the house and the woods. It's a pretty spot with a beautiful, intimate outlook. They smile at me graciously as we wait and I smile back. The weather is colder today, more like the memories of my childhood than the slight warming we've had over the last few years, and little bumps dance on my skin.

I've left my hair down, the soft waves that cover my shaved sections and tattoos blowing in the breeze. I close my eyes into the sensation of fingers in my hair.

She's coming down the stairs when I open them again and I can't breathe.

A gold train trails behind her and I'm immediately thankful I went with black, the counter to the gold in her eyes. The softly shimmering fabric flares at her ankles and arches into her knees hugging its way up her thighs, over the curve of her hips and her narrow waist, before cupping her breasts. Full-length, sheer sleeves fall away from her shoulders.

I swallow thickly as her gaze finds mine, a soft smile on her lips.

Rory whistles under his breath and Riley laughs.

'Ready?' Tiernan asks me.

I nod, speechless.

Ciara takes my hands when she reaches me, and our friends and family gather around us.

'You alright?' she whispers, a faint flicker in her eyes.

I squeeze her hands and her magic sparks along mine, weaving between our fingers. 'If this is real, I am,' I say.

She smiles. 'It's real.'

The ceremony is a blur, I can't focus on the faces around me. Only hers. Only my Kiki's, her black and copper eyes never once leaving my face.

Her tears spill over as Tiernan announces the end of the ceremony, our magic dancing above us, and I pull her to me, wiping her tears gently before finding her mouth with mine. Kissing her in front of everyone was something I'd dreamed about once. The kissing part wasn't unusual for me to dream of, but the public proclamation she was mine was. And I'd loved it, even as it made me uncomfortable. Because this is as exposed as I can be – no secrets, no burning love I didn't think I deserved – just me with Calahi I'd do it all again for.

I break away before I lose the ability to think of nothing else but the feel of her mouth on mine, and smile broadly at Rory, who waits to take me in his arms.

'Congratulations, Aeyva, sweetheart,' he whispers against my ear, crushing me in an embrace. 'I'm so proud of you.' His voice is choked. 'You had me worried for a while, you know?'

I nod against him, my words gone. My throat starts to close over, and I swallow past the lump growing there.

'You deserve this,' he says. 'You deserve her.' He smiles. 'The Manorynx who can wield a sword, hey? You know you're going to inspire a whole new generation to be both Sentinels and our knowledge holders.'

'I think that's a good thing,' I say quietly. 'We need to remember what happened in that cavern, and everything that led to it. The damage a few power-hungry individuals can do. Sometimes, we can't hide from the pain.'

'Or the dangers of not understanding our impact on the world around us.'

I look over at Riley, who's talking animatedly with Will and Phoenix. She'd insisted she be part of the team we are putting together to find the Commissioner's family. None of us would have objected to doing it, but it still feels like the least we can do, given the risks he ultimately took for us. Bringing the human rebels to help us defeat the Custodian, even with his family at stake.

Rory draws back to look in the same direction and grins.

'Your turn soon, maybe?' I ask with a not-so-subtle raise of my brow.

'Don't even start,' he says, grinning.

Ciara lies panting from where I've been exploring her as we sprawl together on the bed. I listen to her breath resume its normal pace, content in the silence with her. Content with anything with her.

'You know, I never once thought I'd sleep with a Manorynx,' she says.

I laugh. 'I never considered Manorynxes even had sex lives,' I say.

She shifts underneath me, and I roll over her. Propping my weight on my elbows on either side of her body.

'Perhaps we should make the most of it, in case it runs out?' she asks, eyes wide and feigning innocence.

'Hmm ... you're probably right,' I say. I lower myself down her body and gently bite the inside of her knee. She smiles and, drawing her knees up, lets them fall open to the sides for me.

'Fuck, you're beautiful, Kiki.'

She laughs softly. 'You're also the only Manorynx I've known who swears.'

'It will be you swearing by the time I'm done.'

'Do your worst,' she says with a hungry grin.

I kneel between her shins and kiss and suck my way up each of her inner thighs, their muscles quivering beneath my mouth. I skirt around her most sensitive areas and trail my tongue in the grooves between her legs and her mound.

Her abdomen is soft under my lips, and I make my way to the underside of her luscious breasts, teasing them with my tongue before tugging her nipples between my teeth. She writhes against me, and I place a knee against her to give her something to grind against, her wetness finding my skin.

I groan. 'So beautiful,' I say against her neck.

Her earlobes are soft in my mouth, and I drag my teeth along them, grinning at the arched reflex of her back as I do. Moving to her face, I run my tongue along her lips and she opens her mouth for me. Grinding harder against my leg.

'Kiss me, Aeyva,' she begs.

'Of course,' I whisper, pulling my face away from hers.

She opens her eyes. 'What - oh.'

I kiss my way back over her chest, her nipples hard in my mouth, and kneel before her once more. Sliding my hands up the back of her thighs until I find her ass, I marvel at the incredible softness of her skin, the ache building in my centre insatiable. She lifts her hips slightly and I shift my hands underneath, a cheek in each, and I fulfil her request.

I kiss her soft and slow. So slowly, she pushes her hips against me, but I won't be hurried. I taste every crevice. Every soft and wet part of her. The core that begs me to finish her. Begs me to take her over the edge. Her moans are nearly my undoing, and I shift my own hand from her ass to between my legs where I massage gently in time with the rhythm of my mouth on her. Using the flat of my tongue to circle her, I take the hand that delivered my own pleasure and stretch her wide with my fingers.

Her hands are in my hair, pulling as she loses control and pushes her hips hard against me. I breathe deeply through my nose, inhaling her scent, never reducing the pressure of my tongue. My fingers find their way inside and she groans.

'Oh, Aeyva,' she murmurs. My fingers drag slowly in and out, finding the spots that make her toes curl.

Her hands shift from my hair and twist in the sheets suddenly as she bucks off the bed, my mouth following where she goes. Fingers moving instinctively.

'Oh - *fuck.*'

I grin against her as I kiss her through the experience. Slowly. Gently. Bringing her back to earth. Keeping my hands and mouth on her until she's more than spent and ready to move again.

She tugs at my hair gently when she's ready, words not forming yet, and I crawl up to finally kiss her mouth. The mouth of my bonded. My Soul Accord.

As I lie beside her, our limbs tangled, I close my eyes and send a wave of gratitude to Nuala. The Calahi who always knew I could do this – be deserving of Ciara – and a sword-wielding Manorynx.

CHAPTER FORTY-EIGHT

LISH

Lochlain's hands are warm on my skin as we dance in the increasing darkness with the others. Ciara and Aeyva are long gone. I can't comprehend the time they have spent waiting for each other; they have much to make up. The music is fast and joyful, and worms its way underneath my ribs as only Calahi music can. The group Kailoh sent as part of his gift to Aeyva and Ciara is incredible.

I throw my head back and laugh as Lochlain spins me around the grass dance floor, the brass lanterns bobbing in the night sky making me smile. I love those things.

'May I have this one?' a male voice cuts in.

The hum between Lochlain and me spikes. Not in jealousy, but gratitude. He moves to bow low, but Kailoh grips his shoulder and gently keeps him upright, pulling him into a tight embrace. Lochlain kisses me on the forehead after they separate and excuses himself.

Kailoh's dancing is just as I remembered – more graceful than anything I've experienced.

'Thank you, Kailoh,' I say, seeking out his handsome face. His auburn hair is tied loosely today, strands falling around his face. Perhaps he didn't feel the need to be so formal around friends.

'For which bit exactly?' he asks.

I smile. 'I do have a list somewhere, if you'd like to see it.'

He raises an eyebrow at me.

'Not joking,' I say. 'There was so much happening, I had to write it down afterward to help process it.' The sadness at how many were lost creeps back in, and I can feel my face shutter.

'Come now,' he says. 'None of that. Not tonight, when I understand congratulations are in order. The half-human Queen of Airlie showing us the true role of a Wolverton.' He winks at me. 'Even your Pendita is championing your relationship with the General after she saw you in Elenlea. Besides,' he continues, 'there is a very small group of folk that can say they saved the world. And you happen to be a principal member. With Roisin's power back in the earth, where it was always supposed to end up, it will find its rhythm again. The Calahi will be restored, and the human world will be far more livable. Stable. They will be able to prosper once more, they will just have to learn how.'

'For how long?' I stop dancing and Kailoh leads me to a bench seat that's appeared from nowhere. 'How long until either race, most likely the humans – let's be honest – gets too greedy once more. I don't suppose you've got any spare undead Queens floating around, do you?'

He laughs, a deep tinkling sound that draws a smile to my lips.

'No, no more of those unfortunately. There is only hard work ahead. And a huge decision.'

'What's that?'

'Do we make ourselves known to the human world, leverage the Commissioner, and work together to maintain the stabilisation of the environment? Or continue to try and do it under the surface?'

I consider this for a moment, something that's been on my mind as well.

'I think we need to work with them, somehow.'

Kailoh nods slowly. 'I think you might be right.'

'The how will be hard, though.'

'Agreed ... but I could always bend them to my will if I need to.'

I glance at him and there's no jesting on his face.

His mouth turns up in a sly grin. 'This magic of mine can do a great many things, Adelais. Being ... influential is just one of them.'

We watch our small group of family and friends dance on the grass for a moment and I find myself completely content in this space.

'Thank you,' I say again.

'What for this time?'

'For helping me. Helping, even though ...'

He pulls an inelegant face. 'I have an unfortunate affliction, you know. I seem to feel the need to wait for my Soul Accord. So, really, you did me a favour by turning down my premature offer.'

'Maybe I'll make that my next mission – Kailoh's match maker.'

He laughs. 'Better you than Aeyva, I suspect.'

Sofia, Will, and Nico dance with their hands linked before me. She'd been so strong when she saw Will again after we'd returned. Strong for Nico. Will had staggered towards her, gripping her to him as Nico leapt around the room. I knew, in that moment, she hadn't let him see the fear she'd felt while we'd been gone. That he didn't feel it vibrating beneath her skin, didn't see her knees give out as Will finally held her again, or hear her quiet sobs against his neck as she'd thanked him for keeping his promise to return.

I think back to General Siosal's compound when I'd said goodbye to him, a moment I'm not sure I will ever completely move on from. I'd told him to find his person. I smile to myself at the knowledge he found two. Kailoh pats my knee as he leaves me to summon Nico into a dance and my heart swells with the goodness in him.

The timber bench Kailoh conjured creaks slightly as Phoenix sits beside me, his eyes weary.

'How is she?' I ask.

'Tiernan's with her now,' he says. 'That one dance did her in though, I expect she'll sleep for days.'

My chest deflates. I hadn't realised Blaire was wounded in the cavern and I thank Tiernan, and the Blue Pointed Star, every moment that she didn't die on that battlefield.

'I'm so sorry, Phoenix, I ...' There's nothing I can say to convey how I feel about Blaire and the pain she's endured, about what it's doing to Phoenix. It was part of the reason only Will was with me last night.

He takes my hand and rests it in his lap.

'She'll be okay, in time. I won't let it be any other way.' His voice is tired. He's been sitting by her every night and most of each day, only taking a break when I insist I want to sit with her instead.

'I know,' I say, squeezing his hand. 'And Tiernan is incredible.'

Impatience and desire wash over me as Riley joins us. I fight the blush at her emotions and block her out; she's had enough wine for both of us.

'Seriously, what's up with Rory?' she asks. 'Is he just never going to ask me out?'

'Why is it up to him?' Phoenix asks.

'I'm not sure the Calahi really ask people out,' I say. 'He probably has no idea how to handle you.'

'Handle me?' she repeats, eyes wide. She breaks into a loud laugh. 'No, you're probably right.'

Rory moves across the grassy dance floor towards Lochlain.

Riley shoves her drink at me. 'Hold this.'

She intercepts Rory who glances at me over her shoulder briefly but I shrug, trying to swallow my smile.

'Here we go,' Phoenix says under his breath.

Rory's eyes move slowly back to her face, the fire in them clear from here. 'You alright?' he asks tentatively. He doesn't call her 'sweetheart'.

'Oh yes,' she says. 'Just wondering when you're going to kiss me already.' She shifts her weight to one foot and waits, arms crossed.

Rory blinks. 'Pardon?'

'You heard me.' The roll of her eyes is clear in her voice.

Rory glances around at the group and Phoenix and I belatedly pretend we are looking at each other.

'Do you want me to?' he asks quietly, sounding genuinely bewildered.

Riley says nothing. I imagine the answer is written all over her face. I take a sip from her drink and grin. Rory glances at me once more and I wink at him. A wicked smile growing on his face.

He smooths the hair out of her face and runs his fingers down her cheeks before cradling her head gently in both hands and pressing a soft, soft, kiss on her mouth. He pulls away before her hands reach his arms.

'Are you joking?' she breathes. 'Is that it?'

Phoenix chokes on his drink and Rory's eyes flash.

He narrows his gaze and pulls her so close her body is flush against his, taking her mouth passionately. Her knees go momentarily weak before she presses her body back against him just as hard and he stifles a groan, a hand finding the back of her head and disappearing in her hair.

I turn wide-eyed to Phoenix whose blush mirrors mine, and we collapse into giggles even as my heart soars for them.

'Walk with me?' Lochlain asks, holding out a hand once I've recovered myself.

I glance at Phoenix, who nods and offers Lochlain a tentative smile.

His fingers are warm in mine as we stroll through the cold wood, and I snuggle into him for warmth. Lochlain wraps a heavy arm around my shoulders and tucks me in tighter.

'I was hoping to make love to you under the stars,' he whispers. 'But I fear your chattering teeth might bite off my tongue.'

I smack his torso with my free hand, laughing.

'Maybe,' I say. 'Or maybe I'd bite something else instead.'

'That might get boring for you, a lifetime without my best feature.'

'Who says it's your best feature?'

I squeal as he tickles my ribs before scooping me up and carrying me back towards the house. Amber eyes blink at me from the trees as we walk away, and I send a silent prayer of gratitude to the wolves and their magic. For creating the Wolvertons and guarding me, and my heart, even when I'm unaware, for knowing the depths of my soul and keeping it intact, for saving Lochlain not once, but twice.

For leading me to Roisin and standing by me.

For giving me faith that the Blue Pointed Star really did exist. And still does.

As soon as he closes the bedroom door, shutting out the dimming sounds of the celebration of Aeyva and Ciara's bonding ceremony, my skin starts to shiver. The free-fall he sends me on, time and time again, reminds me I'm alive. Amongst all the death, we live.

Slowly, our clothes come off. Taking the time we now have to enjoy this moment. I push back to admire him. The visual feast he offers never gets old. I reach for him but he grips my wrist and holds it behind my back.

'Ladies first,' he says against my mouth, the words vibrating my lips.

He touches and teases my body from my neck to my toes, until I'm begging him to come to me. Moving behind me, he drags his thumb down my spine, the pressure making my back arch. He grips my ass and reaches through my legs to find my opening. I clench my legs together in an attempt to keep his hand there.

'Please,' I whisper. I try to turn to touch his chest, to feel his grooves beneath my hands but he presses his body against my back and crosses my arms over my chest so I can't reach him.

'No touching,' he says firmly.

His voice sends a shiver down my spine. His hands snake down my sides and up again to cup my breasts as he kisses the side of my neck. I drop my head back against him and sigh. I stand on my toes and press my ass into him.

He inhales sharply, pulling me to the floor. He kneels behind me, bending me at the waist and planting my hands on the floor. I tip my hips to meet him, and he grips me on either side with his broad hands guiding me back. And up.

My breath catches as he slides himself straight in, his hands moving me in the rhythm of his choice. A low growl sounds as he gets close and he pauses his thrusting for a moment, reaching around to touch me with his fingers. Being filled and stretched from the inside, as Lochlain pulses slightly within me, and his wet fingers spreading me wide, makes my muscles tighten and I feel his body react. His hips unable to stop moving against mine, gently moving himself in and out, in and out, until I think I will see stars.

'Lochlain,' I whisper.

The sound of his name on my mouth loosens his restraint and he slams into me, a moan now on my lips. He grips both hips once more and drives himself into me, hard and fast, and I can't stop myself calling out as I hurtle over the edge. He's not much quieter as he kicks inside me and I clutch him with my core, pushing my hips back to keep him deep.

When we're collapsed on the floor, breathing hard, I rest my head on his chest.

'I will never stop wanting that,' he says. 'Wanting you.'

I trace the lines of his wolf, knowing I will never be able to thank those wolves enough for returning him to me. Placing my hand flat on his chest, I savour the feel of its rhythm.

'It beats for you, you know,' he says. I smile against his warm skin.

I turn my hand over and assess the faint wound that heals up the inside of my forearm, my skin tingling where Lochlain's magic dances against my own. The Soul Accord ceremony was both nothing like I expected, and everything I wanted it to be.

'Mine too,' I say. I place my chin on his chest and look at him. 'It has room for others too, though.'

A slow smile spreads on his face. 'If you're talking about the rest of our friends and family, I get that – it's just one of the things I love about you. If it's the Court, that's also great. But if you're talking about creating our own family ...'

I take in his black and copper eyes, the vulnerability there.

'I would love a pet, Lochlain.'

I laugh before I can properly appreciate his perplexed response. He laughs heartily but briefly.

'I just realised we've never talked about it,' he says. 'Not more than that day I healed you in the compound anyway. I hope I haven't frightened you.'

A warmth grows in my chest and makes its way to my eyes.

'I would love nothing more than to try.'

Lochlain's mouth is soft and warm as he lifts my chin and kisses me deeply. A mouth that's both sinful and loving. And mine.

He sits up abruptly. 'I have something for you.'

I sit up and drag a blanket off the bed to cover myself while he collects a small, brown envelope. Tucking himself under the blanket, he watches my face.

'An Accord present for you.'

'Lochlain – I didn't—'

'I got what I wanted,' he says.

I open my mouth to object, but he points to the envelope.

Nervous anticipation skitters in my stomach as I carefully break the seal and slip out a thick piece of parchment. It's old and slightly discoloured around the edges, the corners frayed.

Turning it over gingerly I find a vibrant painting of a brown haired woman, laughing at a man who embraces her from behind and smiles against her ear. She wears a long gown of sapphire crushed velvet, her curls cascading over one shoulder. The man's face is dark tan compared to her alabaster, but her hair is darker by a shade. The eyes that look up at me from his face are green.

Eyes I saw this morning in the mirror.

Tears build in my throat.

A gold sash is tied below her bust, its ends trailing away over a roundness at her front. A roundness cradled by the man's hands at the bottom.

I gape at Lochlain, unable to stop the tears that now stream down my face.

'This is—'

'I had Kailoh help me find it.'

'I've never seen him before. They look – they're so happy.'

'As we are,' he says. 'As we will continue to be.' Lochlain kisses the tears from my cheeks.

I look back to the painting, to my mother and father, and I make a vow to not only right Airlie but to fulfil my dreams. To relentlessly pursue them in honour of the parents who gave everything to simply give me life. For Roison who should have had the life she longed for with her wolf – with Arlo. I will find the magic in every day, and deliver it to the people who don't have their own. Literally for the Calahi of Airlie, and figuratively for the human world.

Because that is my role, my power, and my responsibility. Because I choose it to be. I gently trace the crown of yellow wildflowers in her hair, tears blurring the image as my gold flame flickers with content in my chest, with the knowledge I don't need Roisin's magic. Because my own remembers it.

And for me, Adelais Catriona Millea Wolverton, I will create my own magic.

AMBER WOLF (DRIARN DUOLOGY, BOOK 1)

FRIEND. GUARD. ORPHAN.

Lish Taylor thinks she knows who she is.

But when her tactical team begins to investigate a series of abductions, the haunting questions she's carried since her mother's murder come flooding back. With the case growing increasingly suspicious, Lish leaves her climate-ravaged city to seek answers, even after she's ordered to stand down—only to be abducted herself.

Captured by the brutal General Siosal, Lish is determined to free not only herself, but also the General's other victims. With the enigmatic cell-guard, Lochlain, as her unexpected ally, Lish's escape catapults her into the hidden world of the Calahi, where magic pulses through the land. But, even with its incredible differences, Lish can't ignore that this world is also suffering.

The threads of her investigation soon draw Lish into a war for a dying kingdom. To survive – and reclaim her future – she must bring those she loves together and prove that healing a broken world begins with standing in your truth.

Amber Wolf is an adult, dystopian fantasy with forced proximity, found family, fated mates, climate themes and hidden worlds. If you love family secrets, slow burn open door romance and epic magic, this is for you.

BLUE POINTED STAR (DRIARN DUOLOGY, BOOK 2)

A new queen must save the Realm.
But those who would deny her the crown are strong.
Lish Taylor knows that she is the rightful Queen of Airlie. But, before she can officially claim the throne, she is accused of murdering the previous queen – her mother. Forced to retreat to a neighbouring court, the shadow of regicide at her heels, Lish's only chance to regain her throne, and prevent the collapse of both the Human and Calahi lands, is to reassemble the shattered pieces of the Blue Pointed Star.
Underground assassin, Aeyva Kaylneau, is one step closer to fulfilling her lifelong dream of becoming a Sentinel to the Queen. But Aeyva's past allegiances threaten to jeopardise everything she has worked for, and the secrets she keeps have the potential to not only push away the woman she loves, but bring the entire Court of Airlie to its knees.
As the Human and Calahi realms crumble around them, Lish and Aeyva must unite a network of allies across rival courts and the boundaries of magic, to expose a sinister conspiracy that imperils the very fabric of their worlds. As Queen and her Sentinel, they must show that the future belongs to those who fight for more than power.

Blue Pointed Star is the final book in the Driarn duology (sequel to Amber Wolf). Lovers of fated mates, slow burn open door romance, sapphic romance, found family and becoming who you were always meant to be will adore this thrilling conclusion.

When Secrets Beckon

Every secret has its price...

Rubilena Lanmiere can barely remember how it felt to live life for herself. Or what it feels like to live a life in the open. Raising her daughter in a world where it's dangerous to be noticed, her days are spent selling forbidden remedies in her grandfather's shop — and paying her brother Theo's debts in an underground fight den.

When their absent mother returns to gift Theo a mysterious medallion, Rubilena and Theo find themselves fleeing their home in Koamah, hunted by the entire Kingdom and its enemies. With the secrets of the medallion painting a deadly target on her brother's back, Rubilena is forced to seek help from a man who once broke her heart, and her trust.

In search of the mystical witches who can free Theo from the medallion's claim, the group find themselves wrapped inextricably in the tendrils of a prophecy. But as the fight for the ultimate knowledge intensifies, the weight of secrets already between them threatens to tear Rubilena and her allies apart.

And they can't be sure if the medallion is seeking to fulfil a deadly prophecy, or save them from the encroaching darkness...

*When Secrets Beckon is a standalone adult, dystopian fantasy with an epic second chance romance, siblings, clashes with royalty, prophecy, witches and a single mum FMC. If you love your fantasy with forced proximity, touch HIM and d*e, and open door romance, this one is for you.*

Traitors' Creed (Traitors Duology, Book 1)

Truth makes traitors out of even the most dutiful.

Zanteera Island has a secret: it has two prisons. Vana, the one the world knows and fears, and an unnamed compound lined with comforts.

Serving her National Duty at Vana's secret counterpart, Luka Brideoake doesn't question the unorthodox disciplinary system, or the VIP status of the criminals. But when the Warden offers her a prestigious new assignment in Parliament, she starts to see the prison and its inmates in an uncomfortable new light.

Then, her childhood best friend and his brother show up sentenced to Vana, and Luka is forced to go against every rule she's upheld to seek a dangerous new ally. All the while, the Warden's cryptic advice suggests a political web far bigger than Luka could have imagined.

As inmates start to die and the authorities move in, her path intersects with a man as enigmatic as he is powerful. But how much of the life Luka thought she wanted is she prepared to trade...for the truth?

Traitors' Creed is an adult urban fantasy with an epic slow burn romance. If you like your love interests cold to everyone but the FMC, with wings as sharp as blades (literally) and a touch of forced proximity and forbidden romance, this should be your next read. With political intrigue, high stakes and a found family that will sacrifice everything to save each other, you will love Traitors' Creed.

TRAITORS' PROMISE (TRAITORS DUOLOGY, BOOK 2)

Even the greatest escapes don't guarantee freedom.

With the gilded facade of Zanteera Island's prison smouldering in her wake, Luka Brideoake prepares to make her status as a traitor official. But nothing could have readied her for a summons to a second National Duty. This time, in the heart of Nuntainia's poisonous corruption: Parliament House.

Tasked by Quillian with finding the evidence needed to expose the political tyranny, and armed with an invitation printed with government ink, Luka has no option but to report for duty. Alone.

But as the net of her government's lies closes in, Luka risks returning to the island and the prison she didn't burn—Vana. This time, behind bars. With neither time nor magic on her side, Luka will discover just how much she can endure to reveal a truth that will unseat the highest powers.

Traitors' Promise is the final book in the Traitors duology. Full of an epic romance, open door spice, friends to die for, political intrigue, rebellion and high stakes, this is an adult urban fantasy not to miss.

FIND YOUR NEXT READ

All of Lauren's books can be found here, www.laurenparkerrhodes.co m/buy, or at all good bookshops and online platforms.

To stay up to date with all new releases (and inside stories...) subscribe here or at www.laurenparkerrhodes.com

Loved this book by Lauren Parker Rhodes?

I'd love you to leave a review wherever you purchased from or on Goodreads! Just a sentence or two, or even just a star rating, will go a long way to supporting this duology and it would mean the world to me.

After all, without readers, stories go unread and unheard.

Thank you! It's still very surreal that Lish's story has been completed in Blue Pointed Star and is now in your hands. I'm so appreciative of your reading time and energy, and I hope you loved the whole Amber Wolf world as much as I do.

To my husband, thank you for knowing that there are more than these two stories in my heart. And that I simply won't be me if I don't bring them to life, no matter how hard the process is. Your unyielding support means everything, and I feel more confident every day that you'll come around to my fantasy fiction obsession.

To my children, having dreams can be tricky in a world that's full of obligations and 'should dos'. You help remind me they are valid, and we need to turn down the noise to listen to our hearts. Already I can see you are learning much faster than me, and I can't wait to learn more from you.

To my Mum and Dad, I'm not sure more supportive parents could be found. Thank you for always picking me up, being interested in my wild stories and for all the midnight sense-checking on everything from blurbs to cover design! To my 'writing crew'. You're literally the best. My two critique partners, Amy Morse and Erin Ogilvie, have stuck with me through this duology even though we all live in different countries and their wisdom is incredible...as is their ability to read the same story several times and still provide wonderful insights! To my beta readers – Erin Thomson, Katherine Turner and Bronwyn Swasbrick – this story would not have been the same without you, thank you!

To my editors, Alexandra Dawning of Dawning Edits (www.dawningedits.com) and Danikka Taylor of Taylor Made Media (www.taylormademedia.online). My mind still boggles when I think about how much you each know and bring to the writing process. I have taken great learnings from both of you and I love how you push me to write better and better stories. To my 'writing crew'. You're literally the best.

Escaping to fantasy worlds is a specialty of Lauren's, either creating her own or reading other people's – providing there's a strong romance, Lauren is all in. Living in semi-rural Australia with her husband and two little wildlings, Lauren tries to teach her children of the wonders of nature. About the impact of all our tiny decisions and that, sometimes, it only takes one person to make a difference. When she's not living vicariously through her characters, or kid-wrangling, Lauren can be found at her second home, the coast; feeding her coffee and chocolate addiction; or trying to fit in a yoga class...even though Archie the labrador would much prefer a walk.

Instagram: @laurenparkerrhodes
www.laurenparkerrhodes.com